Born in the USA, RJ ASHBY moved to Australia in 1998. He has trained as an archaeologist, practiced law on both continents, become an environmental scientist, did a stint as a cleaner, worked as a zoo keeper and even worked for a time as a radio announcer. He now lives in north west Tasmania, where by day he masquerades as a High School English and History teacher. When he is not spending all night hunched over his computer, muttering and writing madly, he enjoys gardening, getting outdoors, and spending time with his two main sources of inspiration: wife, Helen, and daughter Laura. His works, both published and unpublished, include nine novels spanning the fantasy, science fiction and weird western genres. Much of RJ Ashby's writing is dedicated to bringing strong, independent and non-stereotypical female heroines to life. He considers the works of Wilbur Smith in particular to be inspirational, and is a mad fan of the gumshoe detective novels of Raymond Chandler and Dashiell Hammet.

THE ASSASSIN OF NARA

Also by R.J. ASHBY

The Airmen (Part 1: The Pirates of Aireon)

THE ASSASSIN OF NARA

R.J. ASHBY

T℻
Þ℻
Ticonderoga
publications

To Laura and Helen,
two butt-kicking ladies

The Assassin of Nara by R.J. Ashby

Published by Ticonderoga Publications

Designed and edited by Russell B. Farr
Typeset in Sabon and Usherwood

A Cataloging-in-Publications entry for this title is available from The National Library of Australia.

ISBN 978-1-921857-61-4 (limited hardcover)
978-1-921857-62-1 (trade hardcover)
978-1-921857-63-8 (trade paperback)
978-1-921857-64-5 (ebook)

Ticonderoga Publications
PO Box 29 Greenwood
Western Australia 6924

www.ticonderogapublications.com

10 9 8 7 6 5 4 3 2 1

ONE

"No man owns me!" Lydia tried desperately to make her child's voice deeper, more forceful as she yelled, but she was too angry to pull it off.

"Miss Lydia, open the door!" called Mrs Habden again from the ship's main passageway. Hands trembling in outrage, Lydia scrambled over the contents of her tiny cabin, searching for something to hurl at the thin wooden door. Her sparsely furnished quarters offered little in the way of projectiles.

As she fumbled about, near-blind in rage, she shouted, "No man owns me, Mrs Habden! I'll not bow and scrape like a slave!"

The thin timber wall quivered from the impact of Lydia's chamber pot. As she searched frantically for another missile, Lydia heard the deep purr of her father's voice, soft but clear over the many small noises of a wooden ship under sail on gentle seas. In her enraged mind she could see the smirk on his lips, mocking her as he spoke.

"Lydia, open the hatch." For years her father's commanding voice had resulted in instant obedience, but recently she had been slower to obey, even deigning to argue with him at times. She still loved and respected the man as no other, but found herself becoming angered when he treated her like a child or didn't allow her to make her own decisions. She even bridled when he teased her gently, or pointed out some flaw in the calculations kept in her own copy of the ship's log.

Next came the worried voice of the cow, Mrs Habden, meek now; in Lydia's mind crawling before the captain. "She's locked herself in, sir. I just tried to teach her to curtsey!" Lydia rejoiced at the despair in the woman's voice.

"Lydia, I'm sure Mrs Habden didn't mean to offend you." The smirk was still in his voice. Lydia tried a small metal cup's weight in her hand but found it too light to make a satisfying impact, so she flung it to the floor, and continued scanning the room for something heavier.

"I just told her that if she didn't learn a bit of grace, she'd never find a man to marry her," continued the ridiculous women in her nasal Talvonian accent.

"No man will ever own me!" Lydia shouted from behind the hatch, with a stamp of her foot.

In voice firm but also full of the good humour that counterbalanced his quiet strength, her father said quietly, "I pity the man who does!"

The wall shook from the impact of Lydia's water jug.

Outside, the captain smiled at Mrs Habden and gestured her away silently. He stood for a while, watching water seep from under the door to Lydia's cabin before shaking his head and following the narrow passageway to his own quarters. He knew Lydia would emerge eventually, when she got hungry or decided to come looking for another fight.

Lydia usually loved evening meals with her father. It was one of the rare times they had together, free of the constant demands on the captain. For as long as she could remember Lydia and her father had always shared their evening meal, even when they hosted guests in his richly furnished gallery at the caravel's stern. Lydia's favourite dinners were those with just the two of them for company, with her father's ancient, silent cabin boy serving their food, filling their glasses and clearing the table before their nightly game.

But the atmosphere of their private dinners had soured recently, maybe only in the slightest. Still they laughed less and paid more attention to their meals. Often during the silences that had begun to creep into their time together Lydia would look up from her plate and find her father watching her with eyes full of love, but also a faint hint of sadness. She always felt a hot flash of anger at being watched while she ate and would growl something at him, which only caused him to smile or shake his head and chuckle to himself. Even their games of fiest, the sacred and ancient battle of mind and wit, were less lively. She found herself moving the pieces across the three boards in a determined effort to defeat her father, a master of the game, rather than merely to prolong the match and the time that she had remaining before having to go to bed, as had always been her habit in the past.

During the days, Lydia undertook her lessons as usual, excelling as ever in whatever she was taught, but always underlying her attention to duty was a growing restlessness and simmering anger.

She did not know why she was restless, for she loved the ship and life aboard her, as well as the rough crew and her father's officers. Lydia did not understand the anger either, for in her calmer moments she would realise that everyone treated her with the utmost kindness and respect. Yet still it remained, deep in her heart, seething like a boiling cauldron. At times rage would threaten to consume her and Lydia's only respite was to climb high in the rigging to her favourite perch, atop the foremast where the ship below her vanished and she could imagine herself flying unaided above the water like the great albatross that would sometimes accompany her.

This had all started a few moons before as she approached the fourteenth anniversary of her birth and the ship was anchored in the port of Talvon, a land governed by the steady if brutal hands of the Six Lords, wizards who each ruled a different aspect of life from a top their cloud-cutting towers, soaring above the walled city of Parnith. It was said that they had ruled for nearly a thousand years; that they were deathless. Some said they were gods of wisdom, others, gods of wicked cruelty.

When the ship's business was done, just before they set sail for Danith, her father came back from the markets with arms full of bright bundles. Overcome with excitement, Lydia ripped the paper wrappings apart, littering the great cabin with shredded crepe paper and lengths of discarded ribbon. To her horror the parcels contained clothing of silk and fine linen, embroidered with flowers and graceful designs. To Lydia's eyes they were not unlike the clothes of the women who swarmed the docks when the ship first came to port, plying their carnal trade.

And worst of all, the captain had brought Mrs Habden with him. While Lydia shoved the clothes and hats and ribbons and petticoats out of the narrow window in her cabin, she was wishing that she could push that fat sea cow out of the porthole as well. Before committing this mutiny Lydia had waited until the caravel was safely at sea so that the clothes couldn't be recovered by a passing boat. *What is wrong with my clothes?* Lydia thought to herself as she flung bits of lace and embroidered linen out of the window. Her canvas pants and leather jerkin were like the sailors', worn soft from salt water and hard usage. Moad, the ancient dusky navigator from Sudeth, had embroidered her breeches with scenes of sea monsters and ships flung upon lee shores, hell birds swooping from cliffs above and plucking helpless sailors from the waves. Lydia felt they were far more fitting for a sailor than a petticoat.

Unknown to her, a small group of sailors had decided to fish for fresh tunny from the railing above her little cabin. The amused men made great sport of casting their lines among the floating clothes, hoisting them back aboard and speculating about the function of the various undergarments. When a bashfully grinning sailor rapped on her cabin door and bowed low, holding out a dripping bundle of finery before him, Lydia had almost slammed the door in his face.

But being made to wear the stifling and restrictive clothes of womanhood was nothing of an insult compared to being expected to bow in submission to gain the favour of some man. Of everything the idiotic she-pig had tried to teach Lydia since they departed from Parnith, that was the most outrageous.

Immediately upon taking up her post, Mrs Habden began teaching Lydia the manners of a *civilised* woman, as well as many other of the countless points of refinement that Lydia had missed during her life at sea. On the day Lydia locked herself in her cabin, the matron had just finished sharing in detail the reasons that young ladies should not sit with their knees agape. Failing to see the stormy look on her pupil's brow and the dark fire in her eyes, Mrs Habden had merrily embarked on the many occasions which called for an elegant curtsey. The result of this lesson had been Lydia barricading herself in her little cabin and the destruction of a bedpan and a pitcher. In the end, the girl had only been lured out by the smell of the evening meal, as predicted by her father.

Over a table laden with a feast of the finest morsels that the ports of the Western seas could produce, her father had declared, "Lydia, you need to learn a lady's manners." His voice, so strong and booming when he yelled orders at his crew, rumbled now with the soft, private tone he saved for his only child. But despite this gentle tone, Lydia's eyes flashed from across the table, their star-lights glowing like embers. *That infuriating smirk,* thought the girl as she clenched her fists under the table. Though she had been lured out of her cabin by food, she could grab a loaf of bread, run back and slam the door in his smug face. Seemingly not noticing her anger, the captain leaned back from the table as his stooped cabin boy removed his soup bowl and replaced it with a bowl of fiery Taja, the spiced meat stew from the islands off the eastern shore of Sudeth.

"Lydia, you are fifteen. You have spent your entire life among rogues, pirates, ruffians and cut-throats. You are approaching the age when you will become a woman." Before he could continue, Lydia interjected with a groan and a wave of a dismissive arm that nearly upset the bowl of Taja that the cabin boy was placing before her.

"But father, what do I need to be a woman for?"

The captain laughed at her response; his dark, forbidding eyes twinkling. She bridled even more at his kind-hearted merriment and was about to rush from the room and return to the fortress of her tiny cabin when he reached across the table and put his weather-beaten hand gently upon her arm.

"My dear, it is not enough to know how to swing from the rigging like a gibbon, fence with the Master of Arms, or to speak the languages of the world's ports. Like it or not, you are going to be a woman, and there's nothing you or I or anyone can do about it!"

"But Father, I will take over the ship from you, like we have planned. I will be her next captain. I don't need to be a woman to make a good deal in the markets. I don't need to be a woman to fight Sinjun Pirates or bribe Talvon's customs masters. The men won't take orders from a woman, they'll only whistle at me like they do those harlots on the docks and try to give me their pay to grunt and roll around with me in their hammocks." Lydia did not yet know what the sailors paid the dockside whores for, but she knew the disdain the men felt for the drab, bedraggled women after they had re-emerged from below the deck with the crew's hard-earned gold in their embroidered purses. She knew she had to avoid lowering herself to those depths in the unforgiving crew's esteem.

"Lydia, they will treat you as they do me if you are strong. Learning to be a woman is no different than learning to navigate through the Straits of Nambur, to speak Talvonese, or to fence with a Danithian sparring sword. All knowledge is a tool, and you must gain all that you may, so that you can use it when the need arises."

"But women are soft, Father! You are not soft." Lydia poked at the pieces of meat floating in the Taja sauce with her fork, disconsolately.

The captain's response was distant, sombre. "Your mother was a strong woman. She travelled the seas at my side and helped me run the ship, lead the men, and run my end of the family business."

"Father, she died, and you are still alive."

The captain chuckled affectionately, but with sadness in his rumbling laugh.

"We all die, Lydia, even the toughest of us." He raised a spoonful of the fiery meat to his beard-enshrouded mouth, and then saluted Lydia with his goblet of wine. "Now, you will do me the greatest honour, and make me the proudest father upon the seas if you will at least try to learn what Mrs Habden has to teach you, so that I have not wasted my money on her wages. Agreed?"

Lydia nodded, but she continued to frown into her bowl. That night she had beaten her father at fiest for the first time, though she remained convinced that he had let her win. The victory had brought her no pleasure.

Mrs Habden emerged from the closet that served as her private quarters late the following morning, ruffled but still determined. In fair weather, the journey from the small island of Talvon to the port of Danith would take only a fortnight, but five nights from Danith the northerly wind died, and the had ship lay becalmed for some weeks, stretching the voyage indefinitely and straining the crew's good temper. During this time, Lydia fulfilled her promise to the captain and proved to Mrs Habden that she could be an excellent student. During mornings under the matron's patient guidance Lydia mastered not only an elegant curtsey but also the order of cutlery used at the ceremonial table, how to sing a hymn properly and the steps of the Danithian Bride Dance. She even endured the greatest insult of all and learned how to place paint upon her face and wear stifling petticoats, though she did mutter dangerously under her breath when Mrs Habden tried to place a foot upon her back to tighten the laces of her bodice. But Lydia flatly refused to wear woman's clothes outside of her father's cabin, and would not even allow the ancient cabin boy or her friend Moad to enter when she was wearing a dress.

In the afternoons she shed her petticoats for the freedom of her richly embroidered duck pants and leather jerkin. From the men of the ship she continued her more practical lessons. Lydia learned the paths of the stars and their roles in the lives of mortals from Moad the navigator, the construction and maintenance of the ship from the carpenter, fencing, boxing and wrestling from Braide, the Master-at-Arms, and the arts of mathematics and bookkeeping from the Quartermaster. When the opportunity arose, she helped the healer with the endless sprains and bruises inherent in shipboard life. From the rest of the crew she learned stories, games and crude jokes, how to run across a yardarm, balanced on the thin beam above a plunging deck, and tales of a dozen lands. And from her father Lydia learned the languages and histories of the ancients, reading together from one of the many leather-bound tomes that lined the walls of his cabin. On some nights they would pour over charts and discuss the few ports that Lydia had not been to, how they were ruled and what could be bought or sold at each, or would work at complex navigational problems using the ship's charts.

Some weeks after leaving Parnith, having escaped the grip of calm seas their ship, the *Julia*, arrived at the port of Danith on the River Lythe and was moored under the shadows of the thin white towers of the City of Ships. The *Julia* disgorged the remains of her eastern treasures and the crew's purses grew heavy with merrily clinking gold coin. Relieved of duty, they vanished into the city of Danith, where they could be found wandering among its many white stone buildings or through the crowded bazaars and tree-lined streets where the goods of the world were traded, seeking to relieve themselves of their pay in the company of women and spirits.

The captain had the ship's figurehead, the unclad torso of a young woman, covered in gold leaf and the ship itself drawn from the water, her bottom scraped clean and the timber hull repainted in bright yellow and blue.

After the men had squandered their shares in the portside brothels and taverns they came dragging back to the ship, poor and eager to embark on the next journey. Often they came driven almost by force by angry spouses or mothers who preferred their men gainfully employed, and far off on upon distant seas.

While her father supervised the provisioning of the ship, Lydia found time to escape from her duties and wander the streets of Danith alone. The streets of her homeland were safe, even at night, and she had no need for accompaniment. While the ship was being overhauled, she and the captain lived with her uncle, a fabulously wealthy banker and merchant who owned one of the oldest houses of business in the city. There she stayed in a bedroom dedicated for her use whenever she was in port. The room was bigger than the whole sterncastle of the *Julia*, her father's quarters included. From the balcony Lydia could gaze upon the sun setting over the ocean, the sleepless port on the Lythe, and beyond the white stone walls of Danith to the fertile rolling plains of the surrounding countryside. Paddocks and groves made a patchwork across the landscape, known for producing the West's finest horses and richest olive oil.

Yet even in the elegant opulence of her uncle's palace Lydia found herself bored. During meals her thoughts often drifted to the open seas when the adult conversation turned to business, and her young cousins were throwing tidbits of food at each other while avoiding their mother's imperious gaze.

When the ship had been refitted, the crew re-enlisted and stores for the year-long journey to the Empire of Nara stowed, Lydia and her father went to visit her mother's grave. Lydia dressed in her finest silk frock, braided her black hair into a long plait and wore a broad hat with a black lace veil. She walked out of her father's cabin publicly dressed in a woman's clothing for the first time that day.

Mrs Habden had taught her how to brush her raven hair, so that it glistened like a fluted helmet upon her head, and also how to darken her tanned cheeks with the faintest touch of powder. Her eyes, so dark that they appeared black, were outlined with kohl, so that their twin depths appeared bottomless, and mysterious. One man even dared to whistle. She refused to look around and discover who the offender was. Head high and eyes rigidly forward, she crossed the freshly-sanded deck and went awkwardly down the gangplank to the waiting carriage, desperately trying not to turn her ankles as she teetered in her high-heeled boots. She spared not one glance for the gaping crewmen, or those saluting when she passed.

A coachman dressed in embroidered finery held out a hand for her at the vehicle's door, but Lydia ignored the man, hauled herself into the carriage and sank into the waiting seat with a gush of relief at not having plunged face first off the side of the gangplank, or toppled over a coil of rope on the *Julia*'s deck.

Shortly, the captain joined her. He was dressed in his richest suit of ceremonial finery and wearing a gold-hilted sword. He sat next to Lydia on the cushioned seat and solemnly took her gloved hand in his.

In silence they held hands while the carriage took them to the graveyard where the captain had erected a monument to his wife. While she had a memorial there, her remains had been given to the sea far to the south, near the Andaman Islands, where she died just as Lydia had come into life. Still hand-in-hand they left the carriage and walked to the arched entrance of the cemetery, a stone-walled expanse dotted with fine marble statues and monuments. Lydia was glad for the strength of the captain's grasp, for he steadied her across the uneven cobbles, when her boots threatened to cause her the ultimate disgrace.

The cemetery was nestled between a stately columned temple dedicated to the Goddess Drondia, Mother of the Hearth, the gardens of a large mansion, and backed by the city wall. Beside the ornate wrought-iron gate an ancient beggar crouched on the footpath. The man was dressed in the shabby white robes of a holy ascetic, an empty alms bowl on the ground before him. When Lydia neared the gate the beggar lifted his face to the towering height of her father, and she saw that he was blind, his eyes covered with a strip of dirty cloth. With one grimy, twisted hand the man pulled at the seam of the captain's cloak, while the other shook the bowl.

"Alms, Captain Estrella. I am a holy man, and will pray for the spirit of your wife, for only a small gift."

Lydia's father recoiled for a moment, apparently in shock at being recognised by the blind man, but recovered his composure quickly. Estrella was quite famous in Danith and Lydia assumed that the beggar had heard rumour of his approach. Lydia's father dug into his purse and dropped three gold sovereigns into the man's dish, a small fortune for a poor beggar.

"Say a good prayer, for she was an excellent woman."

"I will, Captain, I will." The beggar scooped the coins from the bowl, concealed them in a pouch under his dirty clothes and began to sing a prayer for the dead in an ancient, broken voice.

Inside the graveyard Lydia and her father weaved through the weathered, listing monuments until they came to the far corner, where they kneeled before the monument to her mother, a statue of a winged goddess, ascendant to heaven, and said their prayers in silence. Lydia placed a bouquet of Danithian bellflowers, her mother's favourite, at the feet of the statue. Around its neck Captain Estrella draped an ivory locket carved with Lydia's profile and hung from a slender golden chain. Lydia knew that the priestesses from the temple next door would collect the locket that same night and sell the gold to pay for their indulgences, but they would also say prayers for her mother, and their prayers would send the face of her daughter to the spirit world to warm the woman's dead heart.

They were turning to go, again hand-in-hand, when Lydia saw a single tear run down Captain Estrella's cheek, visible only for an instant before becoming lost in his beard. She had never seen her father cry, and Lydia felt unsteadiness at the sight, as if something fundamental in her life had shifted in its footings. So absorbed was Lydia in this sign of human frailty in the captain that she didn't see the blind man crouched at the gate of the cemetery until she stood upon his hand. The beggar howled in surprise and indignity. When he freed his fingers he grasped the hem of her dress in with a gnarled hand. She was paralysed by terror as the beggar held fast and pulled himself to his feet, nearly toppling her in the process. Twisted hands reached blindly in the air until one of them brushed against her cheek. Then he seized her with the speed of a night lion, clasping her face between his hands with such strength that she could not pull herself free. Despite her struggles he drew her face close. Something in the beggar's sightless gaze stilled Lydia's panic, and after her first flurry of resistance she found herself staring almost stupidly into the cotton-covered place where his eyes should have been. The beggar seemed to be peering back at her.

"I can't see you," the man muttered, almost under his breath. "You're *unseen*."

As she stood stunned, his fingertips explored Lydia's face, brushing lightly over her cheeks, her lips, and then reaching for her eyes. The pads were curiously soft like fine leather, and dry. The sensation of the man's fingers nearing her eyes shook Lydia from her trance and she cried out for her father, who stood at her side, equally bemused.

"Unseen, unseen! I can't see her, she's unseen!" The old man's voice grew louder, his toothless mouth working in curiosity when he wasn't speaking.

Lydia tore from the beggar's grasp as her father pushed the filthy man away, flinging him against the wall. Captain Estrella's other hand instinctively grasped the hilt of his broadsword.

"She can't be seen, she can't be seen! She's the one who can't be seen, come again!" ranted the old man, apparently heedless of the violence of his rebuff. His raving was starting to attract a crowd of passing Danithians. Heeedless, the beggar began giggling maniacally as Lydia fled to the waiting carriage, high leather boots splashing through puddles and slipping on wet cobblestones. Her father stood between the fleeing girl and the madman, glowering like a like a storm-enshrouded mountain, his hand still on his sword, an inch of bright steel showing now above the scabbard.

"What do you mean, assaulting the child like that?" he demanded in a thunderous voice. The crowd stepped back from the scene, aware of the danger presented by the captain's sheer size and legendary swordsmanship.

"She can't be seen my captain, she can't be seen! I can see you there, and where you're going, where you've been. The days seem long, my captain, before they become short, but short they will be, soon." After this, the man's voice started to croak in a macabre sing-song, repeating the word "Unseen" again and again. From the safety of the carriage, Lydia saw him slump into the vision trance that many ascetic beggars would feign to give authenticity to their pan-handling, or to escape from some misdemeanour in which they had been caught. The man slid down the rough stone wall of the graveyard, and his head lolled loosely upon his chest as if he were drunk, but his voice continued with renewed strength: less aged, more certain.

"Unseen! Unseen! Cursed are the ones who cannot be seen, for they are not of this land. Lost are they, to not be found, and hated ever by those who look. They are the night, the night, the night, and their hand spreads fear upon the seeing. Death is coming, and it cannot be seen!" With that, the withered beggar convulsed once and then seemed to shrink into himself and lose consciousness. After a moment, the man's toothless mouth fell open, and a thin line of drool escaped his dried lips and poured into his lap.

Lydia's father re-sheathed his sword and climbed into the carriage, his weight causing the vehicle to lean to the side as he resumed his seat next to Lydia.

"Bollocks," he grunted to himself as the carriage lurched to a start. He took Lydia's hand again, but remained silent and deep in thought during the trip back to the caravel.

TWO

The tip of Braide's sword flicked neatly past Lydia's parry and cut a short furrow into her cheek, just below the girl's right eye.

"That will remind you to keep your blade high and eyes upon your opponent," growled the Master-at-Arms, a marine retired for some years from the Talvon Navy. He grinned wolfishly as Lydia's hand darted to her face. When her defence dropped he swung his sword in a quick arc from the waist and slapped her hip with the flat of his blade. She howled in pained indignation and dropped a blood-dampened hand from the cut on her face. Lydia crouched low and then lunged at old man, thrusting her sword arrow-fast towards his navel. But the grey-bearded man easily stepped out of Lydia's line of attack and as her momentum carried her forward and off-balance his blade flashed again, this time stinging the girl across her buttocks.

"Bastard! I'll make you pay for that!" Lydia regained her balance with a cat-like agility rare in girls her age and turned on the grinning fencing master. She raised her sword before her and stalked closer to the man, who raised his own blade in defence, his eyes never leaving hers. He chuckled again.

"Your anger will be your undoing, girl." Lydia found his voice was infuriatingly effeminate and mocking, like those of all men of Talvon. *High-bred to the point of being a pansy*, she thought angrily. Carefully cultured tones clashed horribly with the grizzled veteran's scarred face.

The Master-at-Arms gave one last chuckle, and even as the sound escaped his lips he was on her like a great wave, the point of his sword inside her defence, her blade lifted from her grasp, flung in a shining arc through the tropical sunshine. Lydia's thin sword hit the deck point-first and imbedded itself into the thick timber, where it stood quivering for a moment before assuming the to and fro motion of the rolling ship.

Before she could retreat Braide made the final attack and finished the fight. The point of his blade cut through the haze of anger and frustration fogging Lydia's eyes and came to rest so lightly upon her throat that the razor tip pressed into her tender flesh without breaking the skin.

Seeing burning embers in her dark eyes, Braide bowed respectfully and sheathed his sword. "Enough, Lydia. The most important part of anger is to use it wisely, and to always remember to survive to fight again. Survive Lydia, always survive. And for the love of the Maker, be careful with that anger!" With a final bow, he turned to leave, his lesson concluded.

Lydia could feel the eyes of the crew on her. They had been watching the swordplay in fascinated silence. Their silence spoke tomes. She was convinced she could feel them appraising her weakness, making quiet note of her handy defeat by the old man. But above the humiliation of defeat, she felt the sting of the cut on her cheek and the rising welts on her hip and across her buttocks, the ultimate shame. She wondered how many times had she laughed with the man, begged him for stories of the wars, given him little presents painstakingly carved from bits of ivory on their trips home from Sudeth? Within her chest the increasingly familiar flood of boiling rage began to swell, spilling out of her pounding heart and filling her with electric anger. Moving as if in a dream, Lydia went to the row of belaying pins in their rack along sterncastle bulkhead. She pulled two free. The Master at Arms was about to descend the companionway to the waist and his back was to her. Lydia's rage-filled mind knew, as if by instinct, that she only had a moment in which to act.

The belaying pins were carved of dense oak and made excellent clubs. Reversing her grasp so that the heavy handles would strike the man, she let out a blood-curdling scream and hurled them one at a time at him. The startled Master at Arms was turning when the first pin caught him on the kneecap, collapsing his leg beneath him. As he sunk to the deck the second club crashed into his forehead, sending stars shooting through his vision. He fell backwards in a daze, and before he could regain his senses the girl was at his throat, the point of his own dirk held against his windpipe where it drew a dark bead of blood as it pierced his weathered skin.

"And you, old man, need to be careful who you piss off!" hissed Lydia, as if their last exchange of words had just ended. She watched with her dark eyes full of fire as the shock and fear in the old warrior's eyes became mingled with amusement, and finally new-found respect.

Lydia spoke of the fight with her father that night as the ship cleared the southern edge of the Arathean Sea.

"How did you know which knee to strike, Lydia?" he asked. "If you had chosen the wrong knee, the pin might not have taken him down, and you would have faced a superior opponent with no weapon in hand."

"Braide favours his left, Father. I think he must have an old wound to the right and when he turns he often uses his left, at least when the betrayal of the right would leave him in peril."

"I see. Well, be nice to old Braide, Lydia; he's the best fencing master I could find for you. Once he was the pride of the Talvon Navy. That sword of his has conquered many an enemy." His eyes sparkled with amusement again.

"He cut me father. What was I to do? And he told me to fight again, after all!"

"Yes, he did. I think perhaps it is time that you and Master Braide started using practice swords, rather than the real things." He shook his head and smiled despite the stern tone in his voice.

Earlier he had spoken to the aged veteran, who had limped into the captain's quarters while Lydia prepared for their nightly meal.

"Well Braide, your lessons are going well. She's pinked you today, I see. I'd prefer it though if she were to do it with her blade though, not yours. She needs to be tougher, faster." He poured the man a cup of wine, a courtesy unique to Braide among the entire crew and a sign of the regard in which old veteran was held. With the cup in his hand the captain gestured to the seat that Lydia would soon occupy. When the warrior had taken the seat Captain Estrella handed him the wine.

As Braide took a long drink he appeared to carefully consider his response. At last, Braide made his report.

"Captain, she is a mere slip of a girl. She is just fifteen, not yet even a young woman. And yet only through tricks and her lack of determination did I cut her today. She does not truly fight in our matches because she does not hate me, or fear me. On the other hand, I am an old hand and have fought my whole life, and when I attack her it is with all that I would dish out to my greatest foe.

She fights with one hand behind her back, such as it is, sir. But when she is putting her whole into the fight, it is anger that drives her, not cold determination. Anger can make one sloppy, as you know, but determination is the razor's edge on the blade. The child in her grows angry as it fades, but beneath that is the woman, who possesses the determination you ask about."

Braide often spoke in convoluted circles, and Estrella repeated his question, eager to know the fullness of Braide's conclusion. "Will she do against an enemy, Braide? I know she has a heart of steel, but will she do?" The captain had been his daughter's constant companion for her entire life, never further than a ship's length away for any great time, and yet he still harboured this great fear in his heart: that when it came time for Lydia to defend herself in a man's world, the steel she had in her heart would not carry through to her sword arm.

Braide took another gulp, and then wiped his lips on his sleeve. "Sir, I know you have fought many times, and the legends of your duels and victories over the Sinjun Pirates and in the Federation Wars are known throughout Danith, and even in Talvon. But with deep respect I must tell you that you are a sailor, a brave and battle-tried sailor, but a sailor nonetheless. Whereas I have spent my entire life killing men, teaching other men to kill, and leading soldiers into battle and death. What I have learned about other men is that their mettle is never known until it has been truly tested. So it is with your daughter. Who can tell until she has faced the blade's song for the first time?" The captain reflected on Braide's words for a long moment, his head bowed in thought. Then he nodded once and the conversation between the two men resumed, and turned to matters of the ship.

Braide had finished his wine and was rising to leave when Lydia knocked on the door. He rose stiffly from his seat and bowed low with a graceful sweep, surprising from such a large man.

"Miss Lydia, I fear I have creased your face." he said with a lopsided grin.

Lydia curtsied, and replied, "Master Braide, I fear I have dented your head." The veteran exploded into laughter, bowed to the captain and again to Lydia, and left the two alone.

THREE

Three months out from Danith, and after nearly a month trapped in the maddening calm of the windless doldrums, the *Julia* rounded the bottom of the forbidding lands of Sudeth, where a mysterious kingdom far from the coast ruled over vast and fabulously rich plains, jungles and deserts. A thousand sources of wealth were to be found in the Forbidden Lands of Sudeth: gold, ivory, gems, metals, spices, and slaves. Yet none who were not from the land of Sudeth itself had gone beyond the ports that dotted the long coastline. Rumours of the dark land abounded, of terrible monsters, of ghouls who rose from the grave and ate the flesh of those they captured, and of fire sorcerers, who conjured evil spirits with the blood of men. The dark-skinned people of Sudeth, even Lydia's friend Moad, refused to speak of their homelands, adding to the mystery that shrouded the kingdom.

At the great city of Calishwa, the southernmost port of the land, the ship took on fresh water, meat and a load of the tropical fruits and vegetables that would keep the dread scurvy at bay for the next leg of the journey to the great trading cities of the Far East. Calishwa, a city of rough-hewn stone and mud-brick buildings presided over a harbour of crystal clear blue water, the port host to sea-faring travellers from across the globe. The city itself was planted heavily with tall palm trees, which provided some shade against the fierce sun for the many colourful markets and narrow laneways, the plazas where camel merchants, slave dealers and spice traders all competed for sales in loud hawking voices. In Calishwa anything could be purchased, and could usually be found without too much trouble.

Lydia wandered the city with Moad while her father gathered news and gossip from the other captains in the portside taverns, or indulged the greed of the seemingly endless stream of corrupt harbour and customs officials that infested the busy docks.

They made a curious pair, the giant coal-black man from Sudeth, two paces in height and very broad, his head topped with the tight curls of his people, frosted grey with age, and the white girl at his side, tall for her age but not yet into womanhood, her tanned skin pale against the dusky hue of her companion. That she was dressed as a seaman only added to the incongruity. In the crowded markets they ignored the stares of westerners and Sudethians alike, bought sweets, stone carvings of strange and wonderful creatures, and a magical flute that would play random notes when first put to the lips, but nothing when it was blown into. They stored their many purchases in canvas bags slung over their shoulders.

After sampling a piece of bitter melon that Moad claimed was a delicacy among the desert peoples and spitting it out in disgust, much to the man's amusement, Lydia found herself drawn to a brightly coloured stall made of tapestries that displayed a row of long, curved knifes alongside beaten copper sheaths. They were of finely forged steel, with blades broad at the hilt that swept backwards and narrowed evenly to a needle point.

A merchant emerged from the depths of the stall when Lydia's eyes wandered over his wares. He was of one of the coastal tribes, skin more yellow than brown, flowing hair long and tied at the back. In heavily accented Danithian he greeted Lydia, and with a flourish he bowed and saluted Moad.

"May you forever reside in the light of the sun and grace of the Gods! I see your ladyship knows a quality blade when she sees one. These ones, my lady, will keep the young men at bay, like the dogs they are." With this, both he and Moad laughed. Lydia was slightly embarrassed, but she found her attention drawn to a short knife that hung in the darkened back of the stall.

"What blade is that, sir?" asked Lydia, pointing eagerly.

The merchant turned, disappeared into the depths of his stall and returned with a small scimitar, a scaled-down sword, curved in the fashion of Sudeth, likely designed for a young man.

Lydia shook her head. "No, not that one. The one that hangs from the tassels, in the back."

"You do not want that blade, madam. That blade is a karinga, a killing blade. It is bad magic, madam. Have a look at this scimitar; it has an emerald in its hilt." He held the weapon out to her hilt-first, so that the emerald sparkled in the sun, but she did not look away from the karinga.

"What is a karinga, Moad?" asked Lydia when she finally pried her eyes away from the knife, and was testing the weight of the scimitar disinterestedly. Her old friend did not meet her gaze, never taking his eyes from the blade hanging innocuously in the back of the stall. He made a small gesture with his hand, a charm that he used when afraid of bad magic.

"It is a killing blade, Miss Lydia. Small, but in the hand of one that hates, it will drink blood until it is full. Bad magic, Miss Lydia, made by the fire sorcerers."

"Poppycock, Moad. Let me see it, sir!" Again Moad gestured against the evil, and the knife merchant vanished into his stall, took the karinga from the silver tassels and held it out to her, hilt first. She drew the crescent blade from its copper sheath. The moment that it was first touched by the warmth of the sun the metal shone with a red fire, as if alight with burning oil. The ivory grip fitted perfectly into her palm, and the short blade was no longer than her father's outstretched hand. When she gripped the knife power seemed to surge into her arm, and for a moment Lydia thought she could hear the distant sound of drums beating and the hysterical chanting of a man conjuring evil spirits over a cauldron of boiling blood.

"The blade, it belongs to her," said the merchant quietly, more in wonder than in any effort to complete his sale. Lydia glanced up from the flawless steel in time to see him make a magical gesture like Moad had done before. Moad himself stood still beside her, watching with cautious eyes.

"Yes, the blade has chosen her," Moad responded, his voice sombre.

Lydia found the merchant was almost willing to part with the karinga, and she bought it for not much more than the price she would have paid for any of the other blades in the stall. The man took the silver tassels down from the roof of his stall, as if they too carried the taint of the fire sorcerer that had forged the blade, and wrapped them around the sheath. He said to Moad, as if in apology, or explanation, "The magic will not hurt her. It will only give bite to her anger."

"The gods tell us that the heart filled with hate is doomed to follow dark paths. I know the ways of the fire sorcerers." Moad spoke in a hushed voice still, as if afraid that the blade would overhear.

"Yes, sir, yes! But the blade has chosen her, sir." Lydia paid the man a palm-full of golden sovereigns for the karinga, but before she could take it, Moad reached out and took the blade from the merchant, putting it in the bag with the magic flute and carvings that hung from his shoulder. The merchant bowed as the pair left.

Having spent the whole of her money on the karinga, Lydia and Moad returned to the docks through the narrow, winding streets of Calishwa. At one point a small caravan of laden camels paraded across their path, and Moad stopped at her side as they watched the desert travellers pass. Lydia took his hand in hers and looked into the man's dark face.

"Why did you let me buy that blade, Moad?"

"It has chosen you." His eyes avoided hers.

"What do you mean, 'chosen me'?"

"The karinga is a fire spirit, Miss Lydia. It has been conjured for someone, and it has a destiny, like everything and everyone. It is a bad thing, but like all bad things, it can be turned to good. This karinga was made for you, though the man who forged it would not have known this. You could no more reject this blade than it could reject you. You are destined for each other."

"What do you mean I couldn't reject it?"

"Look in your bag, Miss." Lydia took her bag from her shoulder. The blade was at the top, above the sweets she had bought and a bolt of silk for Mrs Habden. She looked up at Moad in shock.

"But it was in your bag! You took it from me!"

"This is the way of the karinga. It is yours now."

She took the blade out, pulled it from its copper sheath, and was again overwhelmed with the sense of power it sent rushing though her. Red fire flickered over the blade. It was beautiful; more beautiful than anything she had ever owned.

"Moad, please don't tell the captain I bought it." She reluctantly put it back into her bag, burying it under paper-wrapped candies and the silk.

He shook his head. "No, he would not understand."

"But why did I have to pay for it, if it chose me?" The caravan had passed, and before them the narrow lane opened onto the harbour, where their ship was lying at anchor.

"Everyone has to pay for their destiny, Miss Lydia," responded Moad grimly.

Back in her father's cabin, she found the captain standing before the gallery windows that lined the stern, arms crossed behind him and face raised to the sea breeze wafting into the stuffy room. Her father would always start to yearn for the open sea, like a long-departed lover, after a stay in port. Without asking, Lydia knew that they would depart on the falling tide, early in the predawn hours of the following morning. He opened his eyes, arising from his reverie at the sound of Lydia's approach.

"Lydia, you're going to have dinner with me and the Grand Manseer of the city tonight. You will be able to test your new manners and clothes in public." Her protests about the clothing stopped when her father explained that the Grand Manseer had a colony of apes living in his garden that she could perhaps beg to see and even feed. In truth, this was a moment she had waited for over many years, for while she had been allowed to enter some of the great citadels with her father in the many ports they called upon, she had never been to an audience, let alone a feast with him, and she felt herself almost trembling with excitement.

With the matter settled he had said, "After all Lydia, you need to learn how to bribe corrupt officials too. It's as much a part of trading as keeping your ship off a lee shore in a gale, and much more dangerous."

Back in the privacy of Lydia's tiny cabin, Mrs Habden clucked and fussed over Lydia's dress, her hair and the subtle paint she applied to the reluctant girl's lips. Lydia scowled ferociously, but being dressed like some land-goer's doll was worth it if she was to get the chance to play with apes. Properly bribed with the bolt of Sudeth silk from the markets, Mrs Habden allowed Lydia to forgo her constricting bodice, and was happily braiding red ribbon into the girl's dark hair.

"Mrs Habden, have you ever hated anyone?" Lydia asked after a long silence, thinking of the knife merchant's mysterious conversation with Moad.

"No child, I never have. But when my husband and dear son died in the plague, I felt anger at the world. I thought I hated everything and everyone, especially Fate, for taking them and not me. But in the end I learned that I just hated myself for not knowing how to help them. As time went by I forgave myself. There was nothing I could do to save them and they would not have wanted me to die at their side. At least their memory lives with me and I can leave offerings at their graves when I am in Talvon." When the last bit of ribbon was braided into the long plait, Mrs Habden took a little silver mirror from the wall and held it out for Lydia to admire her handiwork.

Frowning petulantly, Lydia studied herself. "I look like a strumpet, Mrs Habden." Secretly though, Lydia admired herself. Her father would be proud to have a lovely young lady at his side, the envy of the other men at the banquet. She realised that Mrs Habden had seen a tiny smile flit across Lydia's lips and she quickly frowned and put the mirror back onto the hook in the wall.

"I look like a strumpet and I don't care what you say," she repeated petulantly, but there was no fire in her voice.

"No my dear, you look like a lady. Here—" she took a necklace and locket from her neck, one that she had seen Lydia secretly admire. "You will need something against your heart. This will be stunning with your dress." Lydia held the locket in her hand, pressed the tiny secret catch, and studied the miniature paintings inside. On one side, a man's face, on the other, a boy's. Mrs Habden took the necklace and hung it from Lydia's slender, muscular neck.

"There my sweet, while you wear that you will know my heart goes with you." The locket shone in the dim lamplight against Lydia's tanned skin.

"I'll take good care of it, Mrs Habden."

"I know you will my dear."

Lydia embraced the woman who had but a few months before been her mortal enemy and being fully dressed, asked her governess if she could have a few moments alone before leaving, to say a prayer for her mother. After clasping the girl to her bosom one last time Mrs Habden left, shutting the door behind her.

Alone, Lydia opened her sea chest, removed the tray that held her writing materials and some baubles, and from amidst her clothing took the karinga. She drew it from the copper sheath, admiring the red fire of the blade. Her dark eyes, dancing with the mystic flame, were reflected in the sheen of the blade's enchanted steel. "So beautiful, so very, very beautiful . . . " she muttered to herself. "I should hate to leave it behind, locked up here in the cabin, when it so wants to be with me."

There was a gentle knock on the door and her father's servant called out that their carriage was waiting at the dockside. Lydia stood frozen for a moment, gazing into her own eyes in the reflection of the karinga, and then only with great willpower returned it to its hiding place deep among the rest of the clothes the captain had purchased for her in Talvon. There between a white lace-bedecked frock and a fine linen petticoat the blade would wait for her, would be safe. She hurriedly replaced the upper tray of the chest, turned the key in the heavy lock and then placed it in her pocket. As her hand reached for the door handle, she paused, just for a moment, still not completely decided to leave the blade. It was so beautiful, so powerful, and it made her feel so strong. Maybe she could just hide it in the inner lining of her dress, hanging from the silver tassels. But no, she thought, her father would be very unhappy if he caught her carrying a knife. He had told her before that girls, ladies, shouldn't carry weapons to special occasions.

She was already in the carriage before her father joined her, having given last orders to the mates and Braide. The ship's lights were being lit as he climbed into the carriage, sitting across from her. In the dim light he studied his daughter, her silk dress, the red ribbon entwined in her long hair, the beauty of her dark, luminous eyes. They were the same as her mother's, coal black, with a strange light that danced within them. Sometimes he almost wondered if they would glow of their own accord in total darkness, by magic, but then he knew that he was only being romantic and silly, something a sea captain could scarcely afford. Nonetheless, he felt his heart flutter at the sight of his daughter, so nearly a young woman, seated across from him and awaiting his comment.

"I'm sorry, my love, but we can't let you play with the apes . . . " He shook his head in sorrow.

"But Father, I wore this blasted dress, and let Mrs Habden put paint on me, and play with my hair, and . . . You promised!" The lights in her eyes flared with petulance.

There was that smirk again, that mischief in his eyes. "No my love, you're far too ugly. The Grand Manseer might think one of his apes had escaped and was trying to steal food from his banquet!"

"Oh Father, really!" She pretended to pout, and he crossed carriage to sit next to her, putting an arm behind her and drawing her into his hard bulk.

"You're lovely, my dear, just lovely. Don't let Braide see you like that—he won't want to play swords with you anymore." He gave her a squeeze. "What's that under your dress, Lydia?"

She scrambled for an answer, and coming up with nothing suitable, replied, "A woman's got to have her secrets, Father." The captain shook with a booming laugh, and she laughed with him, though her hand secretly went to her side to investigate what he had felt.

The karinga. It had appeared under her dress, tied to her waist by the silver tassels.

The Grand Manseer's citadel stood on the side of a plateau overlooking the harbour. Hulking ballista and catapults lined the upper walls, capable of firing massive flaming darts or stones far into the night-shrouded waters, destroying any ship that sought to defy the will of the man who ruled the city in the name of his distant master, the King of Sudeth. The citadel itself was made of great stones, rough-hewn from the plateau and transported by thousands of slaves who had since vanished on the winds of the burgeoning trade in man cattle, or whose crushed bodies became part of the loose mortar that held the blocks together. The imposing stone walls loomed over their carriage. In size and strength the citadel rivalled many a fortress or castle in the more civilised northern lands, but it lacked the fine artistry of the buildings of other lands, appearing almost crude or brutish in places.

Ten heavily muscled dark warriors, taller even than Moad and wearing only lion-skin loincloths and belts of fell-serpent skin stood at attention before the gate. In their hands they carried the short, broad-bladed spears that were the favoured weapon of the mighty Sudethian army. The men strained to open the studded doors of the outer wall. As the carriage passed through the thick wall, Lydia discovered that a magnificent woodland was concealed within. Shadowy forms of many different trees loomed over the roadway, some cloaked with vines, others with long roots hanging from their branches like fleshy fingers, reaching for the soil, or covered in plate-sized luminescent flowers. Glowflies flitted amongst the undergrowth, and as the carriage passed one particularly large and ancient tree with branches reaching out like twisted arms Lydia was sure that she spied an ape, peering down from the shadowy heights. The Great Manseer, though a notoriously corrupt and at times cruel man, was a lover of all living things other than men, and in the many years that he had ruled over the city and harbour of Calishwa on behalf of the Great King he had transformed the barren inner court of his citadel into a jungle. In the depths of the forest howls of strange beasts could be heard, and as the carriage passed a peacock called with an ear-splitting alarm as some shadowy jungle creature scurried past its roost.

The carriageway was lined with squat pots of flaming oil that sent dancing shadows flickering through the dark trees. Between the pots, more Sudethian soldiers stood at attention, scimitars jutting from their belts and spears held before them. The road ran to a long, largely featureless building, several stories high and made also of rough-hewn stone blocks. The stern face of the building was pierced only by loops for firing arrows, a few small balconies, and a smaller pair of doors that were a match for the great gates through which the carriage had just passed.

Beyond those doors was the great hall of the citadel, to which Lydia and her father were admitted by a short, balding Sudethian man with a deep resonant voice. He called out "Lady Lydia" as she passed. Lydia marvelled at being referred to as a lady, but soon forgot the novelty of her new title when she found herself in a long, low room choked with scores of people, all dressed in the clothes of a different land and speaking in a bewildering array of languages, all seemingly at once. Lydia wondered if every sea-faring nation had sent an emissary to the banquet. She recognised the cultured and artificial tones of Talvon, a half-dozen dialects from the Far East, the musical fluting of the Andaman Islands, the nasal twang of several of the various Euralian lands, and many others. The captains, for each man at the banquet was the master of a ship moored at the docks below, or awaiting a berth in the clogged roads outside the harbour, were either gathered in groups, individually courting the small group of Sudethian nobles at the end of the hall, or talking quietly of serious matters in pairs or threes. Here and there members of a little group would glance over their shoulders with a conspiratorial air before returning to whatever secret plans they were discussing with their fellows. Powerfully built, elegant black women worked through the crowd, carrying pitchers of wine and beer from which flowed a generous stream of spirit. Some of the men, long at sea and not wanting to miss a chance at another man's grog, were visibly intoxicated. Others watched the women pass with ravenous eyes.

Captain Estrella took Lydia's hand and wound his way through the crowd, nodding, returning greetings and stopping to return embraces on several occasions. Lydia curtsied to the men as Mrs Habden had taught, and she was suddenly happy that her father and the governess had prevailed over her objections to this seemingly humiliating exercise. Lydia, unused to being dressed as a lady, was surprised to find the eyes of the men linger over her longer than she would have liked, and some looked at her hungrily. She returned their gazes steadily, firmly, so as to let them know that she was not to be cowed like some dockside wench. Inwardly she was glad of the looming presence of her father at her side and of the comforting weight of the karinga pressing against her flesh.

Finally, the captain and Lydia navigated their way through the labyrinth of men to the far end of the room where on a raised dais of stone sat a group of Sudethian men, gravely presiding over the mass of guests. They were dressed in richly coloured robes, fingers thick with gold rings encrusted with precious stones. Atop their heads were the colourful feathered plumes worn by Sudethian nobles. Lydia's father bowed deeply before them, removing his hat and brushing the floor in a graceful flourish. Standing a half pace behind, Lydia curtsied as low as she could, eyes turned to the floor.

The man in the middle was the Grand Manseer, an ancient with copper teeth set in a sharp, wizened face dominated by piercing, commanding eyes. Under his plumed headpiece the tight curls of his hair were snow white, and his fingers glittered with enough precious stones to buy and outfit a ship. Upon his shrunken chest he wore the heavy golden, ruby-clad chain of authority, a sign that he was the mouth of the King of Sudeth. His right hand rested upon a miniature broad-headed spear, with a shaft of fire-hardened wood. The spear had the tails of three lions dangling from below the blade.

Lydia knew that this was a very important man; the rank of all nobles in the Land of Sudeth was marked by the number of lion tails that hung from their spears. One tail denoted the mere favour of the King, the holder or a position of some importance in the kingdom, or an accomplished soldier, a tried and proven leader of men. Two were for the heroes of the realm, the favourites of the King, or for his newer, less important heirs, of which he was rumoured to have several thousand, all more or less slavishly devoted to the great man. Three, like those upon the spear clutched by the man on the throne above Lydia, meant that the noble had faced many enemies in battle as well as challenges in the more peaceful aspects of life in the service of the King and won great glory. Four tails were for the eldest and most important of the King's sons, his heirs and most trusted lieutenants, and only the gilt spear of the King was adorned with the tails of five lions. Lydia also knew that it was ancient Sudethian law that the tails tied to a man's spear must come from lions he slew himself, alone, with only the spear in his hand to aid him in overcoming the mighty cat.

At a small gesture from the ancient man the captain approached the Grand Manseer and bowed low, his forehead actually pressing against the black man's sandals. The Grand Manseer reached out a hand upon upon the captain's bared head. He spoke with surprising power for a man who would have seen more than seventy summers.

"Arise, Captain, you are welcome here. The Lion God, and the Gods that are my ancestors, smile upon you. Tell me, who is this lovely lady beside you?"

"My lord, this is my daughter, Lydia." Feeling the eyes of all those nobles upon her, Lydia's cheeks coloured and her gaze fell to the floor.

"Raise your eyes child, so that I might gaze into them." The old man's clear, direct gaze locked upon her and Lydia felt as if the man were examining her spirit with invisible hands. She felt her cheeks flush with embarrassment, but did not lower her eyes. For an eternal moment they looked into each other, and then the Grand Manseer chuckled to himself and smiled broadly.

"My captain, this is not a woman-child you have presented to me, but a lion of the desert. Her tail should be upon my spear, if I were more beloved of the King, though I would fear to do battle with her!" At this, the nobles and her father roared with laughter, and Lydia's cheeks burned even hotter. "Come, child, let your father take you to my Grand Sage Azursus. He is an old friend of your father's and not so demanding a companion as I. I am told that you desire the company of my apes, and if you are kind to him, Azursus might show them to you."

Lydia had heard her father speak of Azursus before, and remembered that the two had been on a journey many years ago, and had been friends ever since. Azursus was a dignified-looking man in his late fifties, powerfully built but given to the growing softness of middle-age. His spear had two lion-tails hung below the blade, and he wore the black robes of a Magi. He sat beside the Grand Manseer, and smiled as Captain Estrella repeated his ritual greeting before him.

In response to Captain Estrella's obeisance Azursus said, "Hail my old friend. Rise. May the Lion God and your Ancestor-Gods smile upon you, and may you live always in daylight." His voice was deeply resonant; each word was pronounced with elegant perfection. After receiving the captain's bow and Lydia's curtsy, the spellweaver stepped down from his throne, embraced Lydia's father firmly and looked Lydia over carefully.

"I saw you coming, my old friend, from a great distance, but this one," at this he bowed low to Lydia, "I did not foresee." He gave the girl a knowing smile. She peered up at him, the memory of the beggar's hands groping her face suddenly fresh in her memory. Her heart quickened, and she once again felt the presence of the karinga at her side, glad for its company. Why the man's words worried her so, she did not know.

"Lord Azursus, my old friend, The Great Manseer has requested a private audience with me. I am told that you could be persuaded to show Lydia the Great Manseer's troupe of apes, if she asked you with excellent manners."

"Is that so, Lady Lydia? Do you have an interest in apes? I fear to show them to you. Quickly might they grow jealous of a beauty such as yours, and carry you off to be their queen, in their tree-top kingdom."

Emboldened by the friendliness in the man's face and feeling rather silly at her initial fear, Lydia responded bravely. "That's what father told me, sir, except that he told me that I was so ugly that the Great Manseer might mistake me for an ape, and put me out amongst them, where they would make me their leader. But I would be very thankful if you showed them to me, Lord Azursus, and I will see if they think I am fit to be their queen myself." Both men laughed, and Azursus held out his hand to Lydia. She looked to her father, who nodded, and then allowed the Sudethian wizard to lead her out of the room by way of a small side passage that was concealed behind the skin of horse-like creature with black and white stripes.

The touch of his hand, hard and cool, soothed her nerves. But still she pondered his words, and heard the voice of the beggar in her memory, crying "Unseen!"

FOUR

Behind the doorway was a narrow stone hallway, lit only by torches at either end. Just beyond the hide covering, two men in black robes like that of Azursus were crouched, staring intently at the skin curtain that hid them from those gathered in the great hall. Before their feet were large books opened to partially-filled pages. As Lydia watched one man pointed to the book at his knees with his forefinger, then made a flicking gesture with the finger and his thumb. Letters formed as if written in fire on the page, and then faded to black ink. The man never took his eyes from the skin hanging before him. Lydia looked up in question at Azursus, who still held her hand gently.

Azursus raised his finger to his lips, and pursed them "Shhh . . . they are lesser Magi, men who serve me. They have the magic of far hearing. They listen to all that is said in the hall, and will tell us what we hear tonight. The Great Manseer has many allies, but he also has many enemies and his lordship likes to know what is on the minds of both friend and foe."

The hallway led to a small flight of stairs and then up to a patio overlooking the canopy of the jungle that surrounded the inner citadel. The humid air was rich with the scent of flowers, and the smell of dampness and decay coming from the leaf-litter on the ground below the spreading trees. From within his robes, as if by magic, Azursus produced a large apple.

"These fruit do not grow in this land, but the ape likes it best of all the world's foods. It is a lesson, I suppose; that which we long for the most is the hardest to get." He made a low, sustained whistle, and with moments the dark and hairy shape of an ape emerged from the dark canopy, swinging along a branch that reached out to within an arm's length of the patio. Azursus held the apple out for the ape, who took it in both hands, holding on to the thin branch with curling feet and greedily devoured the fruit. The smell of the apple's juice running down the ape's jaws coupled with his grunts of pleasure summoned more members of his clan. Soon the trees around the patio were full of hairy shapes, strangely human, yet also exciting and alien to Lydia. Their intelligent eyes glittered in the moonlight; they waited patiently for their share of the night's bounty, chattering quietly among themselves in an unfathomable language of low grunts and hoots.

"Look behind you child." On the patio, by the passage, a basket of the same large apples had appeared. The apes hooted softly when they saw it, and stirred in restless anticipation. Lydia took one of the apples, and held it out to the nearest ape, a small female with a baby clutched to her breast. The ape took the apple gently, their fingers touching, and then sat peacefully in the tree eating and gazing curiously at Lydia. The tiny eyes of her infant shone out from the hair of her chest as he too studied the strange, pale-skinned human.

As they handed apples out the basket seemed to refill itself, though Lydia never actually saw an apple appear. But whenever she returned to replenish her supply of fruit it was full.

"They are so patient, my lord. I thought they would be rude and demanding."

"These apes know that they are going to get what they want from us. If it were otherwise, they might howl, or even fling their dung." Lydia wrinkled her nose in disgust at this, but Azursus grinned. "It is better that they only fling dung at us, for our hunters fling arrows and poisoned darts at them. But they are like all living things; happy when appeased, but when feeling deprived or slighted, restive and even dangerous. So it is with men, especially so with men. We are the greediest of all things, don't you think?"

Though he was a stranger, Lydia felt safe with this man. *Maybe,* she thought to herself, *the karinga hidden beneath my dress makes me brave.* She knew from Mrs Habden that it was rude to ask forward questions, especially of those who are your superiors, but she felt a burning need to know the truth of what the man had said to her before, and after a moment of silence, she made up her mind to speak directly to Azursus.

"My lord, you said that you had not seen me coming. What did you mean? How did you see my father coming, and not me?"

Azursus took another apple from the basket and gently threw it to a young male who was too shy to approach within arm's reach.

The ape leaped from its branch, snared the apple with its feet, crammed it into his teeth in mid-air and caught the branch again with long fingers before he fell.

"Shy, that one, but one day he will find his courage and come to the forefront. So it is with men. It is funny, that we may learn so much of ourselves by studying the lowly ape." He threw another apple to the young male, who hooted in gratitude as it caught the fruit, again in mid-air. "There my children," he called, "that is all for tonight. If you eat more your stomachs will ache and you will be angry with me in the morning!" Behind them the basket vanished and two cushioned chairs appeared. Lydia did not see the man gesture to conjure the spirits that did his bidding, and realized that Azursus wove his magic by force of will alone, free from the hand motions, flaming powders and boiling cauldrons of lesser wizards.

"Come child, sit." He gestured to the chair by Lydia's side. She sat when he took the chair across from her, remembering that as a commoner she must not sit before a member of the nobility. For what seemed an eternity the wizard stared into the night-shrouded trees, lost in his thoughts. Then, just as Lydia was about to repeat her question, he responded. His voice was grave, but kind.

"This world, our world, is ruled by men, Lydia. Many claim that we but do the bidding of the Gods, but I have never witnessed the hand of any god in my affairs, or anyone else's for that matter. No, no . . . " he chuckled lowly to himself, "Humanity is its own master, for better or worse."

"But to say that we rule ourselves is not entirely the truth. You see, not all men are created equal. There are those who are born to serve, those who are born to lead, and those who are born to rule. And then there are the others. You can see this, even in your father's ship. Every man has his place, knows his place, is rewarded for doing his duty, punished for failure. Is this not so?"

"Yes, my lord, it is so. I shall learn the trades of each man on the ship, and then one day I will command the caravel, and my father will grow richer even from the earnings of my labour, safe in his country estate in Danith."

Azursus laughed deeply, perhaps amused by the picture of his swashbuckling friend dressed in the clothes of the Danithian landed gentry, growing fat on the labours of his peasants and discussing the breeding of hounds with his guests. "Yes, my child, you will make your father proud, I am sure. But while you may one day rise to rule your father's ship, it is not the same with the great kingdoms of men. To rule those kingdoms, you must be born to greatness. You see, as I said, all men are not created equal."

The magi pointed into the darkness, towards the courtyard where the carriages were parked. "What do you see, over there, my child?"

"I see only darkness, my lord."

"Yes, well, such as I expected. I see the darkness as well, but when I close my eyes, there is much more." At this, he closed his eyes, still facing the drive.

"What do you see now, my lord?" Lydia leaned forward in her seat, fascinated by the man who was intently staring into the night through shut eyes.

"I see the minds of the soldiers, standing along the way. In the trees, hidden, I see the spirits of the Grand Manseer's assassins, guarding against intrusion by stealth. And there, coming out of the doors now and into his awaiting carriage is the captain of that Talvonian barque that came to port this morning, helped, in truth carried, by his first mate. There, the coachmen hand the captain up into the carriage, and drop him upon the seat. They are not so respectful with him so deep in his cups, are they?" He chuckled for a moment, watching the scene that was far beyond Lydia's sight through his closed eyes. "Oh ho, what is this? Watch your back, Captain Lade; your first mate looks at you with envy, without respect. He might be taking your post at the point of a dirk before long!" Still smiling, he opened his eyes and returned his gaze to the amazed Lydia.

"See, child, so it is with the rulers of this world. We are men, like others. We bleed, we hunger, we love and we grieve, and we die under the blade like other men. But unlike other men, we can see into the hearts of those around us, see their purity or taint, feel their anger and hatred, and their feelings. Some, like me, can see over great distances. I saw your father's caravel a fortnight before it came, recognizing it well before it was within sight of the citadel. So it has always been with me. I recognized your father's mind, for we share the bond of friendship, forged in mutual danger and hardship. That bonds him to me, in a way, and so I can sense him at great distance. Others, I do not see their faces or their names, but I can see the evil in their hearts if they should hope to harm myself, or the king I serve. It is in this way the kings of the world rule, for they not only inherit their positions, but also the gift that raises them above their subjects."

"My lord, if the kings of the world can see into the hearts of men, then why do they need armies to protect themselves? Why do they fear the assassin's dagger, and use slaves to test their food for poison?" Lydia found the idea of men ruling the word in this manner inconceivable and repugnant.

Azursus nodded, apparently in appreciation of her question. "It is a dangerous thing to be a king, and while they may see in the hearts of men, there are many thousands of men around them, both good and fell, and it becomes very difficult to separate the wheat from the chaff, as the farmers say. Those with the sight often try to protect themselves by limiting the number of those who come close to them. Then they can scan each man, each woman, whom they allow close enough to strike a blow. Others, a few only, forego the trappings of ordained power and choose to use our gift from behind the scenes, allowing us to keep a hand in the running of things but also to live in slightly less fear than our masters."

"But Lord Azursus, you spoke of four types of men. Are there many like you, and who are the others? And am I of the lowest sort, for I cannot see anything but lights dancing in the darkness when I close my eyes?"

Azursus chuckled. "You are something different again. I will come to you in time, child. It is the wait before the sunrise that makes it brilliant, for any man may paint the dawn, but to watch it arise from black is to truly see it."

"Of the first class, those who rule, there are but few, very few. No more than a handful in any land, and none in some places, such as Haven or Yuntar, where the king and his family were killed in the Federation Wars. Some like me may see far. Others, such as The Great Manseer and the Great King, may see into those in their presence. But there are few of us, and the gift of sight is passed from father to first son, or rarely daughter, so that the number does not grow, but as the inevitable assassins find their marks against all odds, one by one we have fallen, until now there are not more than a hundred of us.

"But of the second class, there are many more. They are men who have souls linked to the Spirit World. Some may travel there and back, much as your father takes his ship from port to port.

Others have a book full of parlour tricks like boiling blood and flashing powders, each spell designed to conjure a different spirit for a different task. Some wander the world as holy men, having only a glimpse of the Sight that the rulers of the world possess, and seeing their gifts as the largesse of some god or goddess." Seeing the look upon Lydia's face as she again remembered the ancient beggar at her mother's grave, Azursus grimaced. "So you have met one of these men. Some are wise, and prophesy the future, which they may see in fragments, just as they see only parts of a man's heart, and not the perfect whole. Others are driven mad, rave and thrash about in the dust having 'visions' until they finally fall completely into stupor, or are confined in some hellish pit in a watch house or a charity hospital. Perhaps it was thus with the one you met. Finally, there are many wizards, lesser magi, spellweavers, warlocks and witches, and even the undead that have carried the gifts of the Spirit World to their grave with them. I once fought with a vampyre in the deserts of Nud who could conjure the sands to do her bidding, like so many slaves. Terrible was our battle, for not only did I have to overcome the evil magic that kept her from rotting and made her immortal, but also the sand genies and giants she flung against me, their arms hard like sandstone pillars, or soft and abrasive like the dust blown before the desert wind, able to eat the flesh from a man's bones.

To be born of this class is to be born apart from all other men, for the magic changes a man or woman, moulds them, sometimes twisting their shapes, or their essence, their spirit, or as some would call it, their soul. The pestilent fire sorcerers of the Inner Lands are of this caste; twisted by the evil of the spirits they are born bonded to."

Azursus cleared his throat and then continued. "The third type is mortal man, simple in his spirit and either noble or fell, as is his nature. So many times I envy the mere man, as weak as he can be, for he may choose his destiny, within limits, and he travels through life in blessed ignorance of so much that is happening around him. While he may be the pawn of other more powerful men he is never the pawn of a twisted spirit or preyed upon by the constant doubts that plague those whom read the hearts of others. Yes, it would be good to be a common, plain man."

"Am I a common woman then, Lord Azursus? I don't see into other people's minds or hearts."

"No, dear child, you are a most uncommon woman, for you are a fourth type, the most rare of all. You are not of the spirit world, not tied to dark realms or the pious and demanding spirits of good magic, and as you have said, you do not see into the hearts of others. But, my dear, when I close my eyes, I cannot see you."

"I thought you could see into the hearts of all?"

"No my dear, not all. Rarely, very, very rarely, one is born who cannot be seen. Yes, I can see you when my eyes are open, but when they are closed, and I use my inner sight, you are invisible to me."

"But why am I different?"

"I do not know, my dear. Perhaps it is your destiny. Perhaps you have some great duty to fulfil. Your gift could be like that karinga you hide under your dress . . . " He gave a quiet laugh when she recoiled. "Yes, I can see you little friend there. It is an evil thing, but then so much that is evil may be used for good in its own time. It has been made for a purpose and has sought you out for that purpose. Who can know what that is?"

"How will I know what my duty is to be, Lord Azursus?" Lydia found herself leaning forward, staring at the man in fascination. A gentle misting rain started to fall on them, though she did not feel the coolness upon her skin until Azursus removed his feathered cap and let the mist dampen his bald pate.

"No one knows their destiny, my child, no one, not even the most powerful magi. We are pawns in the grand game of Fate, played by unseen hands."

"My lord, you said you do not believe in gods, yet you speak of unseen hands." Lydia shook her head and leaned back, overcome by her confusion.

"Yes, yes, it is so, I do speak of them. But you must see, gods are the creations of men, stories created to tell children at bedtime. 'Go to sleep or the Sun God will burn your eyes out', or some such rot. The hand of Fate is something . . . well . . . bigger. Something we could never understand, never give a name to. To understand the puppet master that pulls our strings is very difficult, if we are only puppets, yes? Don't look so confused my dear, I am quite sure I don't understand it either!" He chuckled softly and returned the plumed cap to his head. Lydia leaned forward again and cupped her chin in her hands, peering at the wizard with renewed interest.

"But who am I, that I can't be seen? Is the same true of my father, my mother?"

"No child, I knew your mother, and she was a strong and brave woman, but she was but a commoner. So it is with your father. You, I suppose, are just lucky."

"Does this mean I cannot take over my father's ship?"

"I don't know. To be unseen can be a gift, but it can be a curse as well. We fear what we do not know. Tonight, if I had detected something in your spirit, revealed during our little chat, something dangerous, I was to have you slain. This was the command of my lord the Grand Manseer, and the order of the Great King, his master." At this Lydia shrank away, her hand instinctively starting to pull up the hem of her dress to free the karinga from its sheath.

"Hold fast, child, hold fast!" Azursus stood with his arms outstretched in a gesture of goodwill. Still alarmed, Lydia pulled her feet up onto her chair and drew the karinga from its sheath in a fluid movement. She leaned forward into a crouch, body bunched catlike and poised to spring. Azursus, who had held his spear of office through the interview, dropped his weapon now, and sank to his knees, a respectful smile upon his face.

"My, the good captain has spawned a she-lion, indeed. I have heard the story of your defeat of your father's Master at Arms, the famous Braide, and now I see that you do have the fire to do such a far-fetched thing. Put your blade away, my child. It does not lust for my blood, thankfully. See, I have dropped my spear, and my thoughts weave no spells about you."

Slowly, Lydia returned the blade to its sheath, lowered her dress, and took her seat. "See child, all is better. If I had wanted you dead, I would have slain you many times over before now, and at a greater distance, or if I may say, a safer distance! What my master feared is not in you, so do not let us speak of this again."

"But, Lord Azursus, what—"

He raised his hand in a gesture of finality. "No child, not again."

"What will become of me, Lord Azursus?"

"I do not know, child. You future is as dark to me as your face when I close my eyes. I know only that you are given a gift, and that must be for a reason. In a way, you are no freer to decide your fate then I was at your age, the son of magi, destined to be a magi. But come child, I insist, let us speak of more pleasant things, for all this is just the ramblings of a man too close to old age, and before your father calls for your return, I would like to hear of your journeys, and your impressions of my lord's apes."

Her comfort gradually returned after learning that her death had been considered and rejected by this man, an avowed friend of her father. As the misting rain passed over the harbour and the stars returned overhead, he asked many questions, and remarked with pleasure when she told him stories of the places that she had travelled. He particularly enjoyed the tale of how she had thrown her clothes from her cabin window, only to have them fished from the sea by amused sailors.

"Aw, thus it is, my child. We try to shed ourselves like so many garments, and yet Fate casts us back into our moulds time and again. She is a heartless bitch!"

Lydia cocked her head and asked, "You call Fate a lady. Why, my lord?" Azursus laughed deeply, and his eyes twinkled.

"Because, my dear child, no man fears anything more than a woman! The woman can be cold, hard and heartless, or warm and generous. When she smiles upon us, our days are full of sunshine and pleasure, but when she glowers, we run for shelter and duck our heads in fear of thunder. Yes, yes, Fate must surely be a woman. I believe this so well that I named my first daughter Fate, 'Nakwila' in our tongue. My eldest wife did not approve, and told me that the child would hate me when she became a woman for such a name. Imagine that, hating a person over a name. Well now she is to be married and will carry another man's name, and she can hate him for it!" They both laughed, and the ease of the new friendship between the powerful wizard and the young girl returned. The rest of the evening passed pleasantly, and they re-joined Lydia's father and the Grand Manseer in the banquet hall, where they feasted long into the night.

Back aboard the *Julia*, Lydia's father confirmed to the officers that they would be sailing in the morning. Lydia had kept close counsel on the return journey, and he had been engulfed in the many matters involved in the final preparations for a four-month sea voyage. When he had seen to the business of the ship and Lydia had changed into her sleeping gowns, folded her dress and ribbons and tucked them away into her chest, and hid the karinga back among the clothes she had worn, he knocked upon her door, and sat upon her hammock, watching her brush her hair out while she gazed in the silver mirror.

"Did you enjoy yourself tonight, Lydia?"

"Yes Father, very much so. The apes were very polite, and we fed them apples from a magical basket."

"Lord Azursus speaks highly of you. He tells me that he is sure that you are really a lion cub, stolen from the desert and turned by magic into a young lady."

"He said the same thing to me. He really was a nice man, for someone so powerful. It is hard to imagine him planning the deaths of others, and involved in deceit and plots."

"Well, Lydia, we all do what we are destined to do. I suppose Lord Azursus could be as dire an enemy as he is dear a friend."

"Do you always know who your enemy is, Father?" The captain thought for a moment, considering his answer.

"No, you do not. But I hope that over the years I have been wandering the oceans, and dealing with men of all shapes and sizes that I might have learned to smell a rat when I come across one. Some, such as Lord Azursus, I would trust with my life, or even that which is most precious to me, my beautiful daughter, Lydia, Queen of the Apes!"

She smiled at his small joke, and embraced him one last time before climbing into her hammock. But as the night passed, Lydia was plagued with a dream. She was being pursued in a great labyrinth by a host of ancient blind beggars who were cackling and drooling and yelling, "Unseen!", "Unseen!" with horrible toothless mouths. She would escape, only to find herself trapped in a dead-end passage, and the beggars would soon find her, reaching towards her face with outstretched hands and twisted claws for fingers. As they tore at her she would awaken soaked in sweat, heart pounding. Sleep would evade her for an eternity. When Lydia finally nodded off again she was back in the terrible maze.

FIVE

As the caravel left the middle latitudes and travelled northward once again the seas beneath her bow calmed. Every night thundering fronts would roll over the ship, swelling out of the east, bringing torrents of welcome fresh water coupled with the eternal risk of lightning strike. As if responding to the fears of the crew, disaster struck when they were but a month's travel from the port of Rimbu, in the land of Ngu, the first of the trading centres Captain Estrella planned to call upon. During the nightly storm one of the mighty bolts of lightning that usually leapt between the black clouds overhead plunged downwards instead, shattering the *Julia*'s main mast as the ship was pitched about on the raging sea.

Lydia awoke to a tremendous crash and the sensation of the ship quivering as if it were a living thing that had been mortally struck. She raced into the storm, only pausing to pull on soft leather boots for fear of fire or jagged shards of timber. On the main deck she was greeted with a scene of chaos. The driving rain was so thick that she struggled to breathe; it filled her mouth and nose, and howling wind nearly drove her off her feet. The ship listed as wind battered against her. Lydia caught a glimpse of the rain-shrouded forms of two men lifted by the tempest and flung into raging waters, where the remains of the mast and rigging that trailed alongside enshrouded them like the arms of a kraken and dragged them below to watery deaths.

Where the main mast had stood moments before, only a smoking stump remained. The rigging that had been attached to the mast was blowing free, striking men like living snakes or the maces of giants, threatening to pull down the two remaining masts. What was not flying loose was attached to the great mass of rope and wood trailing over the ship's railing, acting as a sea anchor and trying to pull her over. Lydia stood stunned for a moment, unsure where to start.

Then appearing as if by magic, her father was at her side, his voice a giant's, yelling orders and restoring order to a crew verging on total panic. Under his unwavering command men swarmed into the remaining masts and across the deck, armed with boarding axes hastily served out from the arms locker by Braide, assisted by Lydia. Ropes were severed, the remains of the shattered mast freed, allowing the ship to right herself as best she could in the tempest, and new ropes were sent up to replace those anchoring the lesser masts against the howling wind.

Lydia, not thinking of her small size, helped the crew pull ropes taut and then manned the bilge pumps with all who could be spared from the rigging. A jagged shard of the splintered mast had pierced a hatch cover and the rain and wave-wash had rushed into the lower portions of the ship, making her ride lower and respond too sluggishly to Moad's experienced hands for comfort. Nearly hypnotised by panic-stricken work and growing exhaustion, the crew failed to notice when the storm finally rolled off to the west, flickering menacingly in the distance as it raced towards the land of Sudeth. Their work continued unabated.

When the ship was freed from immediate danger the crewmen not on watch collapsed in exhaustion. Many did not return to the steamy crew quarters in the bowels of the ship, preferring to fall in sheltered nooks of the main deck. Lydia staggered back to her little cabin, fell upon her hammock and into the deepest sleep she had known since the encounter with the beggar at her mother's graveside.

In the morning she awoke after first light, far later than usual, and emerged upon the deck blinking and nursing the raw patches on her hands where she had worn through the skin while working the bilge pump. The ship, home for her entire life, seemed much smaller without the mainmast. The ship's carpenters had started cutting away the stump, preparing it for stepping a replacement, followed by binding the two pieces of timber together with rope, splints and iron spikes. Lydia knew that the ship carried a replacement for each of its masts in the hold, but she also knew that the process of replacing a mast, particularly the tall mainmast, was fraught with peril, especially on the high seas. The replacement would have to be recovered from the hold, where it lay buried beneath bales of trade goods, kegs of salted beef and pork and the barrels of water that were so vital to the ship's life. When the long timber span had been raised from the hold using the remaining masts as hoists, along with a great maze of supporting rope work, it would have to be shaped to match the joint in the stump and then carefully lowered until it sat in place. At any time a freak wave or gust of wind, a snapped rope or shattered block could send the mast through the floor of the ship and forty-six more mariners would quickly follow their two mates and the caravel to the bottom.

Before breakfast was served the men were gathered on the main deck and the captain addressed them as a mass, standing on a low dais made by two crates.

"Men, we have suffered a terrible blow in the night, but we have a ship with a heart of steel, just like her crew. We live on!" With this, a weak cheer went up among the men. When they quieted, he continued.

"As you know, we have given two of our own to the Deep, where they will have much good company. It is our fate to die at the end of a sword, or with our boots full of water. The wives and children of Holt and Marrick will receive their pay, and in addition, I will add a sailor's share from my own bounty." The cheer renewed, and Moad, standing next to Lydia, whispered to her, "See, your father wins the men with strength as well as compassion. Without one, the other would be powerless. Men will follow those they love with even more dedication if they believe their leader is looking out for welfare of his followers foremost. We are selfish beasts!" At this, he chuckled silently.

The captain continued: "Now, we are but a month from the port of Rimbu, in the land of Ngu. Like the rest of you, I yearn for dry land beneath my feet and the scent of cinnamon upon the air. So we can make our spare mast fast here on the open seas today, rushing to Rimbu, but then it will not be done properly, and we risk it falling through the deck, or failing in the next storm." The men exchanged worried glances, and a low murmur arose. The captain held his hands out to them, palms down, in a calming motion. "Now, now friends, let us not fear. There are islands to the north where we might find a safe anchorage, and step our mast in the calm of an island's lee. We'll make for the north, and in three fortnights we will be in Ngu, after the shortest of delays, safe and sound, and ready to start amassing our fortunes. There'll be a double tot of rum tonight, and by the end of the week you'll be eating fresh fish and sleeping on dry land!" At this the men, led by Braide, gave three cheers for their captain and dispersed, some to sleep for the first time since the shattering storm of the night before, others to their morning duties.

Five days later Lydia was peering through dense fog at first light, listening to the leadsman in the bow chanting the depth as the wounded ship limped closer to the unknown island. Lydia had seen the cluster of islands they were now amidst on her father's charts, tiny in the vast blue ocean and only vaguely described. They had been discovered recently by Danithian traders, and none had been explored thoroughly. The chart spread across the table in the great cabin said "Befogged islands, beware!" But the southernmost island, which the ship was approaching in the early dawn, had been described in the same flowing hand as: 'Having safe anchor to the south, though reefs leave but narrow passage to small bay.'

Sure to the description the island appeared in the predawn light as a high volcanic peak, jutting out of a featureless grey mass of fog. The island's position matched that of the land mass on the chart denoted as having 'safe harbour.'

They first spotted the place the evening before, and the captain had sent a ship's boat on the perilous journey through the maze of jagged coral heads and black volcanic stone to find a way for *Julia*. The boat returned after dark, reporting a small mountainous island, ringed with reefs but with a deep, sheltered harbour on the leeward side, perfect for anchoring a ship in calm waters and replacing a mast. They dropped buoy markers along the path they found through the coral, and at the slack of the low tide, during the darkest of the night, the captain personally travelled back through the maze to the island, fixing a cable to a tree upon the shore and then returning to the ship, fastening the cable to each of the buoys as he went. When done, Captain Estrella had created a well-marked path through to the shelter of the bay that could be followed in the densest fog.

As the ship edged through the carefully plotted course, her crew stood silently at stations along the rails, ready to react in an instant to orders from their tense captain, or to the screeching of wood rent by submarine coral. Beyond the chant of the leadsman, the only sounds were the slap of the tiny wavelets on the hull, and the splashing of the lead. The fog, closing in around them, seemed to draw sound into itself and devour it, like a hungry behemoth made of grey cotton.

They were only a short distance from the bay when out of the gloom the wreckage of a ship appeared, silently passing on the weatherside, drawing the eyes of every person upon the deck other than those of the captain, the helmsman and the leadsman. The water-blackened wood skeleton was torn apart and only the jagged remains of the bow could be seen, driven into a great crevice by a tempest. The stern must have been battered into driftwood, her crew swept into oblivion. The ship had been hurled high upon the rocks by a great wave, and so as it passed, the men felt it looming over them in the grey light, menacing and full of foreboding.

After a short but nervous time the *Julia* passed two great rock pinnacles, like fangs, on either side of the passage and then out of the perilous coral throat. Still afraid to make a sound and further silenced by the shroud of mist, the men remained at their stations until the captain called out orders to drop the anchors, and launch the boats, ready to receive the endless trade supplies, barrels of water and decaying meat that filled the hold and covered the spare masts. With the splash of anchors, the men seemed to come back to life. They gave a cheer to celebrate their deliverance from the narrow passageway and the dangerous waters beyond.

The first boat ready to be launched was Captain Estrella's personal gig, fit only for ten people, with eight plying the oars, one at the tiller and one in command at the bow. Lydia, seeing that her father had strapped his sword to his side and armed eight men with bows and cutlasses, composed herself to assault his certain refusal to her request to explore the island with him. The night before he had merely found a sound tree to lash the cable to, and had not examined the island further. Lydia loved the unknown beyond most things, and she was desperate to accompany the first party to shore. But the grave manner of her father's voice as he issued orders and the gravity of his dark eyes as he tried to bore through the mist quelled her. She asked just once. He laid his hand upon her head, and smiled down to her. "Lydia, my little pirate, I need you here to keep the men in line." She knew he would not waiver; it was in the iron of his voice, the metal that was always there when he was in command of a dangerous situation. He climbed down to the gig, where his bravest sailors rested upon their oars, and Braide sat with his arm upon the tiller, back arrow-straight.

She watched as the boat vanished into the murk, following the line to shore. When it was gone Lydia joined the cook and his mate, helping them drive the ship's dwindling herd of live animals into crates and boxes for storage during the unpacking, and soon became absorbed in her work. While it seemed to be only a short while, the morning meal had passed and the cook was preparing the midday repast when the watchman called "Gig ahoy!"

Within minutes, the gig navigated through the small crowd of craft now nestled up to the ship, waiting for the cargo that had begun to be stacked upon the deck. The captain sprung up the side, his leather pants and high black boots covered in mud, and his face scratched from pressing through dense brush. He strode to the first mate, spoke quietly to him for a moment and then turned to address the crew who paused in their work to await his news.

"Men, there's nought but a low shelf of rock for a beach, and that not fit for a camp. We'll be sleeping on the ship, and we'll be finishing our work quickly, for there are no topless sea-maidens in these waters, or friendly dockside lasses to give you all a bit of company and take your hard-earned gold. There's plenty of mosquitoes and brush on that island lads, and nothing else, so let's step to it, and get upon our way to richer ports!" When the crew returned to their labours, the captain called Lydia and Braide to his side.

"Braide, we've been short of fresh meat these last few weeks, and we could do with something to fight the scurvy. I want you to go back to the island, take Lydia with you; she's a sure shot with a bow and as quick as an ape in climbing trees. Take four men in the gig, and see what you can find. Stay within horn's call of the ship, and mind you don't get lost in this soup."

Lydia, heart racing with excitement, almost bowled Mrs Habden over as she rushed down the passageway to her cabin where her sword, bow and quiver were stored. The ruffled Mrs Habden started to cluck at the girl, but seeing the excitement on her and knowing that words would be wasted she just moved to one side of the passage and allowed Lydia to race past, smiling and shaking her head as Lydia called out for pardon over her shoulder as she disappeared into her cabin.

Lydia hurriedly gathered her supplies. She took her sword from its pegs on the bulkhead, her bow and quiver of arrows from their sling, and a small horn her father made her take with her on expeditions into the unknown. At the last minute she dug the karinga from its place of concealment in her chest and placed the cool copper sheath inside her leather jerkin, where it quickly warmed next to her skin. Taking it out again, she drew the blade, hoping to see the red fire, feel the power of it in her arm. But she was disappointed; for the first time since the market of Calishwa the karinga acted like any other blade, elegant and needle sharp, but of plain steel and horn. Puzzled, she stowed the blade back into her jacket and rushed up to the deck.

Lydia climbed down the ship's side to the gig, springing from the rocking side of the ship and landing perfectly balanced in the bow of the unstable craft. Four sailors, chosen for their skill in battle and stoutness of heart, were waiting. Soon Braide joined them, carrying his battle-scarred but immaculate cutlass, a heavy boarding axe in his belt, and an unstrung longbow across his shoulder. The Man-at-Arms settled into the stern and took the tiller as the gig pulled away from the ship.

"Now Miss Lydia, your father wants you to stay by my side, you hear?" Braide rarely spoke to her like a child, and it had a sobering effect.

"Yes, Mr Braide. What are you afraid of?"

Braide chuckled, and took his eyes off the looming shore to smile at her. "I'm not afraid of anything lass, other than a father's wrath if one hair on the head of his little girl is out of place when she comes back."

Lydia snorted in disgust. "I can take care of myself, Braide, and you can tell my father that too!" Though his eyes twinkled all the brighter, Braide forced the smile off his face, and gestured with his free hand to the front of the boat.

"There, Miss Lydia, you'll miss the first sighting of a new land if you're assaulting me with another belaying pin!"

Lydia turned in time to see a long, low shelf of rock loom out of the grey mist, not two boat lengths away. The gentle sea lapped at the base, which looked like a giant step leading down into the water. The earlier expedition had left a rope dangling from the side, so when the gig nosed closer to the shore two men scrambled up and waited as Braide and Lydia climbed up after them. The remaining pair lashed the gig to the rope, and followed.

The shelf was just big enough for the contents of the ship's hold, and then only because the ship was lightly laden with trade goods, and running low on food. Dense rainforest towered around the low, flat rock, silent and watchful. Lydia felt a slight chill, despite the intense tropical heat, as if there were eyes, many eyes, watching her from the depths of that dark wood. She felt for the reassurance of the karinga under her jacket, but with a shock she discovered that the blade had vanished. It could not have fallen from her, and she knew that the blade had betrayed her, had returned to its hiding spot against her wishes.

The crew stood on the wave-wetted stone shelf in a slight air of reluctance tainted with fear of the unknown until Braide clapped the man nearest to him across the shoulder and roared with laughter, "You great girl, it's just a bit of wood. You'd think there was a dragon in there, waiting to eat your charred remains, rather than a few apes and a tasty wild pig with my name on its hock. Haven't you ever been into the woods, laddie?"

With that, the men laughed, albeit nervously, and followed Braide and Lydia as they disappeared into the forest along an overgrown game trail. As soon as they left the stone shelf and entered the wood the heat closed in about them, even more oppressive. Clouds of mosquitoes swarmed about the party's heads, eagerly drawing blood from their unprotected necks and faces. The trail wandered for a while along the lower elevations of the island, and then split into many smaller tracks, wandering off in all directions. Braide stopped at the first split, took his water bottle from his pack and uncorked it. He took a small drink, and when he saw Lydia starting to gulp down her own water, he gently took the bottle from her.

"Nay, Miss Lydia, you might be wanting that later. Never drink it all, lass."

After a short rest, they continued along a trail that seemed to skirt the waterline until they came to a sandy clearing in the jungle where the ocean bit into the island and left a small, pleasant beach, ringed with coconut palms. The crew unslung their packs and started foraging in the brush for fallen coconuts. But amongst the shattered husks of the great nuts were many fresh droppings of wild pigs, and soon the men gave up on searching the ground. Braide pointed up to the top of the nearest palm, where a cluster of coconuts swayed gently in the breeze, and grinned at Lydia.

"Okay, Miss Lydia, the captain reckons you're half ape, so take your knife and climb up yonder tree, and get us some fresh nuts."

Lydia rested her sword carefully against a tree alongside her bow and quiver, and the little horn on the leather thong that her father insisted that she carry. Within a moment she was atop a narrow, fruit-laden tree, and as she cut the tough fibres holding the nuts the men below made sport of trying to catch them. Lydia had cut down at least a dozen, and was preparing to shimmy back down the trunk when the sea troll came upon them.

The monstrous mockery of a man emerged silently from the water, where it had been watching the small party since they had arrived at the clearing. It was as old as the reefs in the waters around the beach, and had lived in a grotto within sight of the little clearing for so long, dining upon the small fish, clams and mussels, and shark when it could catch it, that it too had become encrusted with coral and filaments of algae. The troll's leathery skin was the dark green of seaweed, rough and lumpy. Its head, vaguely like some distortion of a man's, was huge upon its short neck, and oversized dark eyes bulged from its skull as if pressed from behind. Jagged and uneven teeth jutted from a lipless mouth. The creature's massively muscled arms, each as long as a Lydia's entire body, ended in hands easily big enough to totally enfold and crush a man's head.

The men were all looking upwards at the girl as she started to back down the tree, and so when the troll enfolded the nearest crewman's head in its great hand and crushed his skull the others were unaware of his death struggles. The troll stood a moment, looking at the rest of the party, the still-twitching body dangling from its bloody hand, and then lifted the body over its head and hurled the corpse into the others with all of its might.

Flung to the ground and sprawling face first, the men rolled to their backs and pulled cutlasses from their belts while staggering to their feet, hampered all the while by the soft sand. Before they discovered the fearsome nature of their attacker, the troll grabbed the next about the waist, snapping his spine in a rock-crushing grasp and swinging him against the coconut tree Lydia was clinging to, nearly paralysed in terror.

The remaining three men backed away from the troll, who stood with the broken body of the second man dangling in one huge hand, leering with a crooked smile. The troll loved the meat of men and would dine well for many nights on this collection. It especially loved to remember the fear on their faces as it sat in its grotto beneath the cove, feeding upon their remains. Terror seasoned flesh delightfully and made the creature's wicked heart glow with warmth. And what fear it saw in the faces of these three!

Braide, cutlass in one hand and boarding axe in the other, fell back before the charging troll along with the others, but loyalty to his master and to the girl whom he had trained for so long stopped him from fleeing the clearing altogether. As the troll pulled up from its charge and leered at them, Braide regained his composure and planted his feet behind the other two men, who stared dumbly at the monster, their cutlasses held up disconsolately before them.

The troll roared. An ear-shattering bellow. A gust of hot air that stank of rotten fish engulfed them all.

"Lads, we'll have to spread out to kill this bloody troll," shouted Braide. "If we run, he'll chase us down one by one. Together, we can beat him. Scarson, you take left, try for his legs or his arms. Madderly, go right. I'll take the ugly bastard straight on."

The men spread out to flank the troll, who watched with monstrous amusement. From atop the tree, Lydia saw the troll's head swing from side to side and heard it mutter to itself as the men moved about it. She silently slid down the trunk, and landed in the soft sand with feline agility.

Scarson and Madderly stood just out of reach, crouched and ready to duck the troll's massive arms. Madderly was on the troll's right, where the body of his companion still twitched in the huge fist. The creature towered above them, their heads barely reaching its chest. In front of the monster, Braide wove his Talvonian cutlass and the boarding axe back and forth, trying to draw the creature's gaze and distract it. The four stood for what seemed an eternity, waiting for the perfect moment to strike. Finally, from deep inside its barrel chest, the troll started making a horrible wheezing noise. A long, purple tongue snaked out of its mouth in a hideous imitation of licking its lips.

Braide let forth a tremendous roar. He flung his boarding axe straight at the troll's head. The weapon buried itself deep into the thick hide of the troll's forehead, bursting one of the monster's leering eyes. Scarson and Madderly both lunged when the troll clawed at the axe, Scarson sweeping low with his blade, aiming for the tendons along the back of the troll's ankle. The cutlass hit the mark, but Scarson misjudged the toughness of the troll's leathery hide, and he failed to cut deep enough to cripple the creature. Madderly, unmanned by the sight of his friend's body dangling from the troll's fist, swung blindly and missed his target altogether. His blade sunk into the dangling body of his dead friend, still clasped tight in the troll's hand, and stuck fast.

The troll pulled the axe from its forehead with a roar that blasted Braide and Lydia, who had edged up behind the warrior. Gushing black blood from its forehead, the troll swung the body of the dead crewman in a wide arc, hitting Scarson and flinging him far across the clearing. He slammed into a coconut tree with a bone-crunching snap. Madderly, completely unnerved now and weapon-less, turned and fled to the jungle path, but the troll flung Braide's gore-covered axe at the man's back: the heavy axe sunk deep between his shoulders with a meaty thud.

The troll turned to face Braide and the purple snake tongue flicked again, sampling its own blood. Braide sensed Lydia behind him and backed slowly away from the troll, his cutlass before him but one hand held back and to the side as if to shelter the girl.

Without turning, the Talvonian barked, "Lydia, run! I'll hold him here. Take your horn, and run!"

The troll dropped the crushed body, and started to lumber deliberately towards the remaining pair of humans who were backing away slowly. Lydia nearly tripped over her weapons, still resting against the palm tree where she had left them. She could have shot out the one remaining, leering eye, allowing them to flee into the jungle and back to the safety of the ship. But leaving a bow strung in the humidity of the tropics meant that the gut bowstring would stretch and become useless within a short time, and therefore she would have to bend the thick laminated wood bow and re-string it before it could be used. With the troll bearing down on them Lydia had no time for that. She pulled her small sword from its sheath and stood at Braide's side.

"Lydia, no! You must flee!"

"I'm not running; it will hunt me and kill me anyhow, if we don't kill it."

A horrible wheezing started again in the depths of the troll's chest, and Lydia realized that it was laughing. The rows of jagged, broken teeth gaped at them as the creature smiled, its tongue still licking at the dark blood flowing from its wound.

"Run little girl, run. I will crush the old man and run you down. You can help me eat the old man; nasty, tasty old man." The troll's voice was as deep as the oceans, as powerful as the tides.

"Its hide is too thick, Lydia. You must thrust, not slash. Use the point, not the blade!" Braide gave his pupil one last lesson before he unleashed an arrow-fast thrust at the sagging belly of the troll, blade first punching hard into the skin before it cut into the troll's belly. The creature howled and swatted Braide aside, even as he tried to drop below the giant fist. Lydia had no time to see what happened to her teacher. The monstrous creature was upon her.

First the troll lunged, reaching out with both hands and trying to grasp the pretty little morsel. It might keep her alive, for she was both pleasing to the eye as well as to the stomach, at least until it had eaten the rest. But she ducked so quickly that its hands completely missed her head and Lydia's blade slashed from beside him and bit into his flank, though not deeply.

"Not with the blade, girl," the troll's awful mocking laugh wheezed again. "With the tip!"

The troll turned, this time swinging a fist at her with the same careless gesture that had flung Braide from the fray. She ducked the blow and again her blade stung it, biting deeply into the troll's thigh, the tip glancing off thick bone. She pulled her sword from the wound and tried to ignore the rancid black blood that spattered her face. The troll roared again, and struck her in the chest with his balled fist.

Lydia saw the blow coming and could not avoid it entirely, but she flung herself backwards even as the troll's horny fist crashed into her. She heard her breath pounded from her chest in a mighty gush and experienced the sickening sensation of floating through the air, almost as if suspended, before hitting the sand and sliding backwards to a stop. She struggled with consciousness as the troll loomed over her, its horrible grinning face, slit nostrils and snaking purple tongue coming in and out of focus. It was reaching for her, a bloody hand descending in slow motion for her head. She could see the many scars and rents in the ancient flesh of its palm and the mingled blood and hair of its victims under ragged black fingernails. The sight of those nails galvanized her to action. Lydia felt the hilt of her sword still in her outflung hand and with all of her failing strength slashed at the leering face. Powered by the superhuman strength of pure terror, her slender sword bit deeply into the ropy muscles along the side of the troll's short neck. The troll recoiled in agony, clasping its hand to the wound in an effort to staunch the flow of blood streaming down the broad chest.

Lydia drove herself onto her feet, fighting desperately to regain her breath as the troll staggered back to the waterline. She thought the lumbering creature was leaving, and was about to look for Braide when she saw the troll stoop and lift the trunk of a palm tree that was lying at the water's edge. Trolls are difficult to kill, and when angry they will ignore even mortal injury until they have gained vengeance. Though gravely hurt, this troll was not yet slain. The trunk was as thick as the smaller masts of her father's ship, and as tall as Lydia. Turning, the troll advanced. Feeling the weight of her injured chest pulling her back to the ground and head still reeling from the loss of breath, Lydia raised her sword in a futile defence. The troll was going to crush her with that trunk. She knew with a certainty that there was no way she was going to survive this next onslaught. He was no longer smiling or laughing. His one remaining bulging eye gleamed with cold malice even as blood drained from its destroyed partner.

The troll raised the branch over its head. Lydia wondered if she had enough strength to duck to the side if he swung the trunk forward and tried to crush her with a hammer-blow, or to fling herself backwards if he feinted and swung the trunk in a wide arc.

She knew she didn't.

Instead Lydia backed slowly away, towards the forest. Then her boot caught on something in the sand. She stumbled backwards and fell, sprawled across Madderly's body. The handle of the axe buried between his shoulders dug into her back. The troll's crushing blow that would have stove in her head swooped harmlessly in an arc just inches above her. Before the troll could recover to swing again, an arrow, appearing as if by magic, buried itself deep into its side, driving into its lung. The troll roared in agony, frothy black blood escaping its maw, and reeled backwards.

Lydia sprang to her feet and thrust upwards, desperately, at the troll's remaining eye, the tip of her sword slicing through the tough membrane and burying itself into the bone at the back. He flung his head in agony, and Lydia's sword, still buried, was torn from her hand. The troll probed its wound with thick fingers, roared again. Arms wide, the monster lunged forward, blindly hoping to catch the girl. Under the troll's outstretched arms, Lydia saw Braide, across the clearing, leaning against a palm tree. He was fumbling with her bow, trying to notch another arrow. The troll nearly caught her before she could leap from its grasp. It must have heard her land in the soft sand. It turned towards her and lunged again. This time, she dove under his outstretched arms, rolling in the sand like Braide had taught her and recovering her stance behind the monster. To her side was the fallen body of Madderly. The troll rushed blindly in her direction as she ducked to the body and wrenched the axe from his back. Then the troll was upon her, and though it failed to snare her with its flailing arms it did strike Lydia a glancing blow, once again driving the breath from her. Falling to her knees and gasping, Lydia started to spiral into blackness as the troll's groping hands came closer. The troll had also sunk to its knees; the sand beneath him grew black with his flowing blood. Lydia saw the horrible hands come closer, but remained paralysed despite the screaming voice in her head that told her to *strike, strike, strike*. The searing pain in her chest and the growing blackness before her eyes stayed her arm as if by a vast weight. Reality faded.

An outstretched hand came down upon her leg, just brushing her knee, and the monster grinned, gathering for one last lunge. The touch awoke Lydia from her stupor. She lashed out frantically with the boarding axe, clutched in both hands, severing three of the fingers on the hand that had just found her. The creature rose on its knees and howled in agony, clasping its injured hand to its side, flailing with the other fist. Marshalling the last of her strength, Lydia leapt to her feet, swung the axe at the troll's throat. The heavy blade sliced through the creature's windpipe and bit into bone.

Lydia's last sensation as she slipped into unconsciousness was the overwhelming stench of the troll's blood as it gushed from the horrible creature's wounds and spurted over her in a gory fountain.

Sometime later, Lydia burst into consciousness, mind screaming to flee, to get help from her father, from Moad, from anyone. She tried to leap out of her sandy bed, but collapsed back, wracked in agony that radiated from broken ribs, a dozen bruises and cuts. Her gorge rose, and she rolled to the side just in time to avoid vomiting into her own mouth. When her gut was empty and the pain in her chest was replaced by an ice-hot splitting sensation in her skull, Lydia struggled to her feet and looked woozily about the little clearing. The sand was littered with the bodies of her fallen companions, crushed beyond recognition, cruelly used as clubs and then discarded. Slumped against a palm tree was Braide, Lydia's bow lying by his side, an unused arrow dangling from insensate fingers. And just by her was the huge mound of the troll, flat upon its back, hands clutching a great wound in its throat. Black blood still dribbled from the arrow-wound in the troll's side, and sheeted from the slashes in its neck and throat. Iridescent flies the size of Lydia's thumb were gathering in the dark fluid. Braide's boarding axe lay by the troll's side, surrounded by monstrous severed fingers as thick as sausages, with obscene black nails.

Lydia staggered past the troll to Braide. The old warrior's face was a deep grey, but there was life in his wasted body. He looked much older than his years, and frail. His normally bright eyes had sunk deep into his skull, but flickered when Lydia touched his shoulder. He smiled weakly at Lydia who, terrified that her mentor had died, wrapped her arms around him and began to sob softly. Braide gasped, his body swept by agony renewed by the girl's frantic embrace.

"Braide, you killed the troll. You saved me! I thought you were dead!" Lydia's tears streamed down her face, and fell upon his forehead.

Braide's voice was weak, distant. "No, child, it was not I. You slew the troll; I only wounded him. Never have seen a single man slay a troll, and yet you did it alone."

"But you shot him with my bow . . . " She was cut off by his battered hand, pressing her lips shut.

"It was you that slew the troll!" His voice rattled in his throat, and he coughed once, recoiling in pain as his body shuddered.

"But Braide, what will my father say? You are supposed to protect me, and instead I have had to save you!" She wiped tears from her eyes, and tried to laugh at her joke. Braide's chuckle was interrupted by another racking cough, and his lips turned wet with the blood that was filling his mouth.

She tugged at him. "You have to get up, we have to get back to the ship and get you help." She tried to lift his arm, to help the large man to his feet, but Braide only groaned and was stricken with a new bout of coughing.

"I am slain, Lydia. You must leave me. Find your horn and call for your father." Lydia started to recoil, suddenly seeing the extent of his injuries, the blood running from his lips, the unnatural twist to his leg, and the labour of his breathing. He reached and pulled her close to his face so that she could hear the words that he could only just manage to whisper. His grip, suddenly returned to iron, caught her in a vice as he whispered in a wheezing rattle.

"Lydia . . . you must always remember . . . strike not in anger . . . only in need. It is how you slew the troll, not with anger . . . with need." He was seized with a fresh spasm of coughing, dark blood welling now from his lips as he fought to remain alive. With a great effort, he spoke a final time.

"Tell your . . . father . . . I saw your mettle. Tell him . . . I saw . . . " Though his grip did not relax from her arm, Lydia saw Braide's spirit pass from his body as she looked deep into his eyes, and knew that her guardian was dead. Numb, Lydia rose from Braide's side, found her way across the clearing to where her horn lay in the sand next to a fallen coconut and mustered the strength to blow a long note. The agony of cracked ribs washed over her as she blew, and she dropped to her knees afterwards, retching drily in the sand. Then she crawled to where Braide's body lay, and Lydia lay her head upon his muscular, silent chest before passing back into oblivion.

SIX

"Lydia . . . " A man's voice sliced through the void, through darkness dominated by thirst. Her body felt as if it had been drained of all moisture under the desert sun, dried like leather, and she dared not open her eyes, less the pain in her skull explode outwards and kill her.

"Lydia . . . " The voice was familiar. Deep and worried, sounding like safety, like comfort. She struggled to answer but her tongue was withered and would not respond.

A hand held hers, a strong warm hand pressing firmly. Lydia felt her body enfolded in the embrace of a hammock, swaying with the motion of a ship at sea, rocked on a gentle swell.

She was so very, very thirsty. In the darkness, she tried to say as much, but could not know if she actually spoke, or just begged for a drink silently.

A strong hand cupped the back of her head and raised her lips. Cool water ran over her lips. She gulped ravenously. The trickle was withdrawn before she could get more than a mouthful.

"Lydia, you must go gently. You have been asleep for a long time, and you must not drink too fast."

Gradually she defeated the blackness and struggled to open her eyes, each lid weighted as if by lead. The world about her was unfocussed. Her head pounded and the effort of breathing made broken ribs scream in protest. Yet she persisted in fighting her way to consciousness, and was greeted by the face of her father, floating about her in the half-light of his own cabin. He looked old, older than she knew him to be, older even than Braide. His eyes were ringed in black, and pale face drawn in worry.

Memories came flooding back into Lydia's mind in a torrent. She sat upright in sudden terror, the name of Braide resounding in her mind. "Father . . . Braide . . . he's gone."

"I know, Lydia. Now lie back." He gently pressed the girl back into her hammock. "Braide died bravely, a warrior to the end. He will be among his ancestors in the next life, and they will be proud."

"He died for me . . . trying to save me," she sobbed. The heaving of her chest renewed the agony of her wounds.

"Lay still, my darling. He died protecting you, for he loved you like the child he never had. What happened?"

"He slew the troll, Father."

"Did he? He was a mighty warrior then." The captain smiled, as if Lydia had told him a silly story, like she used to make up in younger, happier times.

"He said, before he died . . . he said to tell you that he saw my mettle. What did he mean?"

The captain pressed his hand upon his daughter's forehead. His palm felt cool against her skin. Lydia's body was beginning to sweat. Beads of perspiration joined to make rivulets and tickled her unpleasantly as they ran downwards, and dampened the rough canvas beneath her.

Captain Estrella's smile faded, so slightly that it would have been imperceptible to any but Lydia, and his eyes grew solemn. "Quiet now Lydia, and rest," he purred. "You're far from well."

Lydia lay deathly still all through the arduous task of stepping the new mast, awakening only in the evening of the *Julia*'s departure from the fog-shrouded island. After a brief rally she sunk again, this time into the ravages of fever. Her body fought not only to knit broken bones and bruises inflicted by the terrible hands of the troll but also to quell disease carried to it upon the tiny wings of mosquitoes, drinking of Lydia's blood and injecting poison with needles even as she fought her battle on the beach. Day and night, Mrs Habden nursed her ward under the supervision of the ship's healer and Captain Estrella. They mopped the girl's fevered brow, damped her lips and held her wasting body fast when nightmares threatened to fling her from the hammock. Lydia, ensnared in a half-living world of phantasms and spectral terrors, felt their ministrations only as if from a great distance. She was often pursued by the blind beggar, through a crumbling graveyard. He pursued her through the forest of stones, wailing, "Unseen . . . unseen." When he cornered her, which he always did, his fingers groped her face and pressed against her eyes; gouging, digging.

It was not until a week from Rimbu that Lydia was able to pull on her duck trousers and leather jacket and climb up to the quarterdeck where Moad stood on his night watch at the ship's wheel. The trip from her cabin was so familiar that she normally did not think of the steep steps up to the deck, the bulkheads she passed through, or the low roof-beams to duck. This time, every step was as if through a new landscape. Each stair was a terrible task, requiring all of her strength, and when she bent low beneath beams it was a struggle to right herself rather than sink to the deck and surrender.

When at last the journey of some two dozen steps was done she found the big man looming in the dark, invisible but palpable, like a warm blanket, enfolding her with his presence. They sat in companionable silence for a while before Moad spoke, voice soft but deep, like distant thunder.

"Look upon the starboard. It is your namesake, Lydia, the Evening Star, rising upon the horizon. We sail towards it, even as other stars set behind us. Thus is the way of life. We sail upon the waters while the heavens spin around us. Stars rise and set as we go, but always they fall from the horizon." Though he spoke of nothing, Lydia knew it was an invitation to speak her worries.

"It was terrible, Moad. It was going to eat us. It told me it would make me watch—" She couldn't continue.

"Yes child, it was terrible. Evil, fell things are trolls. They grow ancient and their hearts twist until they know nothing but hatred and hunger."

"I tried to take the karinga with me, but it vanished. I thought it had left me. On the boat I found that it had vanished from my belt, but when I awoke it was hidden again, in my chest."

"Perhaps it was not time for the karinga. It is for him that you hate most."

"What could I hate more than that horrible troll, Moad?"

"There are many evil things in the world, Miss Lydia, some monstrous, and some human. It is the humans that are the worst of evil, for they are not born to be evil, but seek it out, like a moth to the ship's lantern."

Lydia pondered his words in silence, and steadily felt herself slipping into unconsciousness again. At some time she felt Moad put his cloak over her, but she did not fully awaken from her doze until the sun rose, and she found the ship's crew tip-toeing around her as they went about their daily duties.

The busy port of Rimbu was an explosion of colour, erupting from dark, ancient jungle. Every building in the town, from the bamboo huts high above the port at the edge of the forest to the great stone warehouses on the waterfront was painted in what appeared to Lydia to be a different colour. The effect was dazzling, and the flocks of parrots in the skies overhead seemed to be nothing more than an extension of the riot of colour below. Other than the stone docks and storehouses most of the port was made of bamboo logs, lashed together in intricate and amazing designs. Some buildings were no more than platforms with thatched roofs over them, sides open to whatever fresh air that would come from the ocean. Others were of several stories with windows from which the sing-song voices of the Rimbuan people drifted. Along the waterfront, roads were paved with cobblestones, often the ballast of ships from the west. As the town rose up the slopes of the island, streets became a chaotic maze of lanes and passages, and cobblestones gave way to bright red clay and knee-deep mud.

The Rimbuan people who swarmed in a large collection of small boats around the caravel as the ship eased toward the docks were small and delicately built. The women were graceful and had tremendous smiles. The men, though compact, were finely muscled. They were a happy people, content to swarm over the coastal seas day after day, taking colourful reef fish in their nets and returning to their colourful town at night. But despite their pleasant nature and broad smiles the people of Rimbu were notorious pirates. Many of the larger fishing craft Lydia saw as they slid into the harbour showed the recent signs of repair. New planks of freshly hewn wood had been used to patch holes from ballista, massive crossbows mounted on the western trading ships; white stripes on grey, weathered ships.

Over the entire harbour hung the scent of cinnamon, that most valuable of spices, the promise of profit to all who traded in the precious bark.

Lydia had been to Rimbu many times before. Her father knew that well-placed generosity could grant immunity to the ravages of the local pirates. As soon as the ship was made fast to the docks he leapt ashore with a small chest under his arm. With Moad and Lydia at his side he summoned three groups of Rimbuan men who were huddled in the shade of one of the great stone warehouses, reclining against the side of sedan chairs. They hefted the chairs and then lowered them at the feet of Lydia and her companions. Lydia climbed onto the sweat-stained cushions and gripped the edges of the chair. The upcoming journey would be as unsteady as climbing the rigging of a storm-raked ship.

Swaying over the heads of all they passed, the captain and his companions were carried to an audience with the Lord of Rimbu, a powerful merchant who had declared himself ruler of the land some years ago after slaying the previous lord. Both men were vassals of the distant Emperor of Nara, a vast empire across the sea to the north that held most of the eastern lands under its sway.

Lydia knew that many of the pirate ships that terrorised the waters around Ngu were personally loyal to the Lord of Rimbu. It was not a closely guarded secret.

The Lord ruled over the city and its island host from a massive fortress built in the middle of the colourful town. It stood alone, for in the custom of the east no other structure was allowed to be erected within bowshot of the walls. The citadel was painted a brilliant blue, the colour of royalty in Rimbu, and the featureless bamboo outer wall reached as high as a ship's mizzenmast. Guards peered over the wall at the crowds passing below.

Lydia and her companions descended from their chairs when they were placed before large double doors of bamboo trunks bound in iron. The doors were open and led into an inner courtyard where another building of several stories could be glimpsed, with many windows and balconies peering from under a thatched roof. The inner building was of bright yellow. In the passage through the outer wall a line of slender Rimbuan guards stood at attention, grim-faced men clad in long shirts of mail over black pantaloons and gambesons, carrying beaten iron spears. Moad and Lydia stayed at a distance from the men as the captain walked to the line of soldiers and halted before them. He called out in a clear, strong voice.

"I, Markus Estrella, captain of the caravel *Julia* of Danith, come to beg the audience of his Imminence, the forever-living and all-seeing Lord of Rimbu!"

The guards before the open gate did not respond to the captain's hail, and for a moment Lydia thought that her father would have to repeat his call. The captain remained patient, and soon a small, wizened man, dressed as the guards but with a large headdress of long, bright feathers emerged from behind the gate. He was stooped under his mail coat, and yet the man still managed to impart an air of dignity as the guards parted for him. Lydia's father knelt in the tropical mud as the man approached.

With a frog's croak the Rimbuan said, "The Lord of Rimbu hears your supplication, Captain Markus Estrella, and bids you enter." Without further greeting, he turned and led the small party into the inner building, where they entered a long, low hallway, lined on both sides by warriors, and at the further end, a gathering of nobles, the richest merchants of the town, and the Lord's closest advisors. The air was stifling, and stank with the twin scents of hot bodies and cloying incense.

The Lord himself sat upon a vast throne, too large for the squat room, and peered down upon his subjects, looking rather like a grossly-fat toad. The bird-like figure of a Rimbuan man was lost in his distended body. He wore the same black pantaloons as his guards, but his great belly sagged over them, and he was bedecked with bright gold chains, studded with gems. Rubies like pigeon eggs hung from his earlobes, which stretched under the weight of the stones. As Lydia's party crossed the audience chamber and approached, the Lord of Rimbu's tiny eyes glittered as they lit upon the chest carried by Lydia's father. The crowd gathered in the hall parted for them, and when they stood before the man's throne Lydia's father and the others bowed low on a matt of fresh-cut grasses laid for that purpose. The Lord beckoned them forward with a bangle-adorned arm.

"Come, Captain Estrella. No need for formalities here. You and I are old partners, are we not? Come, come and show me what you have brought me." The Lord of Rimbu's voice did not match his form; it was strong and clear, and he spoke in only slightly-accented Danithian.

Lydia's father bowed again, and stooped as he came forward to kneel at the foot of the over-sized throne. He placed the little chest at the feet of the Lord, and with his head still bowed, flipped the lid open. Lydia could feel the press of the other nobles gathering behind her, straining to see what treasure from Danith the captain had brought to pay for the forbearance of the dreaded pirates. Inside the box was a series of small bottles, each with a name written in mystical symbols. The Lord clapped his hands, and a servant appeared from behind the throne, lifted the box to him, so that he could paw the contents excitedly.

The Lord of Rimbu was known far and wide to be a lover of the black arts, a mixer of potions that could prolong life or cause agonizing death. When he had examined the contents he gestured for the servant to carry the box away, and clapped his hands twice, the golden bangles rattling merrily.

"Excellent, my friend, excellent. You know me well!" The box contained the reagents for many spells, none of which a conjurer could easily get in the east. Lydia had gone with the captain to the magic markets in Talvon, where, with the assistance of a trusted apothecary, they had chosen these vials carefully. She felt a surge of contentment that the gift she had helped put together had been met with favour.

"Now come, Captain, sit at my feet and tell me of your plans. I do not know the fair lady who comes with you: present her to me." Lydia made her curtsey as Captain Estella introduced her, and joined her father at the Lord of Rimbu's feet, listening intently to their discussion of plans and the advice the ruler shared with him. While she knew the Lord of Rimbu was merciless and suffered from insatiable greed, he also seemed to be genuinely fond of her father; his eyes sparkled as the captain told of the distant ports they had visited, and he whistled with amazement at the story of the defeated troll, though Lydia's father only hinted at her involvement.

"Foul creatures, sea trolls. They should be driven from those islands. Perhaps one day I will leave this throne, and return to the sea to deal with them. They are bad for business!" At this he laughed, bangles tinkling merrily and great stomach quivering.

The twinkle in the man's eyes died whenever a noble man or servant would approach. He quickly became cold, haughty and dismissive; the archetypical merchant-king. But when the intruder was gone, the man would return eagerly to his conversation with Lydia's father. More than once Lydia she saw him turn wistful at the mention of some distant port or the description of a particularly complex or daring act of seamanship.

The heat in the audience hall was oppressive and Lydia, still recovering from her illness and wounds, was starting to flutter at the edge of faintness when a particularly dignified nobleman approached the throne, and after bowing low before the feet of the Lord, handed his master a small note. The Lord of Rimbu frowned deeply as he read the note and then waved the nobleman away.

With a deep sigh, he drew the conversation with the captain to an end. "My good captain, the duties of command call. I enjoy our chats, captain. Your tales remind me of the fresh sea breeze upon my face, the smell of salt spray and tar. I do miss the sea, my friend. But now, come closer so that I may speak to you in private, away from the chattering monkeys of my court, of matters of great concern."

During the whole conversation, Lydia's father knelt at the Lord's feet. Now the large man bent forward with some effort and whispered urgently into his upturned ear. The captain's eyes grew serious and his lips taut as the Lord concluded his speech. He then withdrew and bowed low before the man, in the Rimbuan ritual of departure.

"Go my friend, upon your way," replied the Lord of Rimbu. "I know that you have only come for the cinnamon stored in my warehouses. You'll not get any special deal from me." The Lord of Rimbu laughed as the captain bowed again. "Now, Captain, send your little one here to speak to me before you leave." Lydia looked up in amazement, for the Lord of Rimbu had all but ignored her throughout the interview. She curtsied low and then climbed up to the throne where her father had kneeled before. Again, the large man bent down, and he leaned close to Lydia's ear.

"Now make sure you obey your father, child, for he is a wise man, and knows his way through uncharted dangers. He knows a friend from an enemy, and that is perhaps the greatest pearl of wisdom. You have his spirit, but you have more as well, my dear. You are a warrior, are you not, child? No man's slave, eh? And not easily seen, eh?" The fat man chuckled, and patted her on the head. Lydia stood motionless in stunned silence, wondering how the man who had appeared to pay her so little attention had in fact seen so much in her, or not, for that matter.

"Now my dear, go and join your father and remember always that I am your friend." With this he dismissed Lydia and she rejoined her father, who was waiting at a distance with Moad at his flank. The three paid their last respects to the man on the throne, and walked backwards from the hall so that they did not turn their backs upon the Lord of Rimbu, a sure sign of disrespect in the land of Ngu.

From amid the gathered courtiers and merchants, a man watched Lydia and her companions intently as they left. He was not Rimbuan, but he was of the east, taller than those around him, more solidly built, and his dark eyes were protected from the tropical sun at the sides with folds of skin. Had Lydia seen the man she would have recognised him as being of the Empire of Nara. But he was lost in the sea of faces, and they passed within an arm's length of him without noticing his intent gaze, which followed Lydia until the hall's doors closed behind her. When they had departed, the man turned and left from a small side door.

That night, unnoticed by any, including the officious Harbour Master who collected the Leaving Tax for his master, a small, swift boat separated itself from the mass of shipping in the port and silently set sail, racing northwards before a freshening breeze, carried as if upon the wings of Fate herself towards the distant Empire.

Four days before the northerly wind and the small ship slid into the natural harbour of a tiny jungle-clothed island, one of thousands in the waters at the edge of the Empire of Nara. Three of the dingy, crowded flat-bottomed craft favoured by the traders and pirates of the region were already at rest in the quiet water, waiting for the tall Naran man.

SEVEN

The captain summoned the officers and Lydia to his cabin for a sumptuous dinner as the island of Ngu vanished beneath the horizon. Agoris, the captain's ancient servant, had spent a large sum at the markets of Rimbu and the captain's larder was overflowing with such fresh meats, vegetables and delicacies as the men had not known for many months. When they had eaten the table was cleared and the captain had a glass of the heady Ngu ale laid before each, and a half-draught for Lydia. The amber ale had been stored in wet sacks hung from the mainmast spar and was refreshingly cool in the stifling tropical heat. Lydia sipped at hers. The amber stuff made her head spin pleasantly, though it tasted rather stronger than she preferred.

Shortly, the men's talk quieted as the effect of good food and ale combined with the heat. When the festive nature of the meal was at last ended, the captain stood and spoke about what Lydia knew had been privately troubling him since his audience with the Lord of Rimbu.

"Men, it is not just for your fine company that I called you here tonight. I have had troubling news from the Lord of Rimbu. He tells me that we are sailing into dangerous waters. In the last few years since we have been here unrest has grown in the Empire of Nara. While the Emperor still rules, his generals fight amongst themselves, and factions have arisen in his armies. There is much intrigue in the Imperial court, and the knives of the assassins have been busy at their bloody work." Some murmuring started around the table, and the captain raised his hand.

"Nara has been ruled by the Emperor and his ancestors for many years, and the Five Kingdoms have been joined as one Empire for at least five hundred years. While I could conceive of civil war in this land, the Empire has weathered the tides and typhoons of five hundred years and even in times of trouble, trade must continue.

But, as many of you will deal with those ashore, traders, officials, we must all remember that we cannot become involved in these matters. Politics, my friends, are bad for business, unless you are a swordsmith!" At this the crew chuckled heartily. Captain Estrella let them have their mirth before continuing. "Just remember, we are here for spices, for the black timbers of the east, and for silks. We're not here for any trouble. The Lord of Rimbu has told me that the Emperor's eldest son, and most trusted general, Hso Tuan Zhe, is the most powerful of those who would squabble, and as the rightful heir and favoured son of the Emperor he stays loyal to the throne. Thus it is unlikely that open warfare would break out, for none are brave enough to openly oppose Lord Zhe. I have met him once. He is a great man; far-sighted, cunning and dangerous, but committed to order and the prosperity of his lands. He is the greatest warrior of the land. Some claim the entire world. So, I am certain there is little to worry about, and I'm sure with some precaution we can turn our profit with no trouble at all." At this, the captain unrolled a large chart on the table, plunged into discussions of the ports they would visit, and what they wished to purchase or sell in each. The meeting carried well into the night and the heat mingled with a third cup of Rimbu ale made Lydia pleasantly drowsy, so that when at last the men departed to their cabins or duties, Lydia's father had to gently shake her awake.

A week later, almost within sight of the next stop of their journey, they turned eastward to avoid a large eastern craft which took the same heading as the *Julia* when both ships' mastheads were high enough above the horizon to identify each other. Captain Estrella climbed to the masthead himself and peered over the distance at the pursuing ship, and his face was grim when he returned to the deck. "Pirates, almost certainly," was all he said to the small group who waited for him at the foot of the mast. Though by then the hull of the pursuing ship was just above the horizon, the captain ordered the deck cleared, the squat ballista at the prow and stern strung and giant darts tipped with iron spear-heads brought up from their store in the hold. Then he spent the rest of the day on the deck, frequently adjusting the set of the sails or making small alterations to the heading of the ship so that she would travel as fast as she was able before the variable tropical winds. For a while the eastern ship gained steadily on the *Julia*, so that by the beginning of dusk her shape could be clearly made out, as well as the black flag of the pirate flying from her masts. But then the wind changed to favour the *Julia*, and by the time that Lydia's star was rising on the horizon the distant ship's sails were again just visible on the horizon.

As night fell the captain ordered the ship to turn northward to the island of Jaru, their next intended destination. He explained to Lydia that even though the night was clear and a full moon was rising on the horizon, he hoped that the pirate would miss their turn and think that the *Julia* would continue to flee upon the eastward winds, rather than taking the slower tack northwards to Jaru. Towards midnight the lookout reported the sails were no longer on the horizon. The captain had the crew turn in, leaving only the night watch to guide them northward, though with careful instructions to maintain a constant watch for the strange ship. He went to his great cabin for a quick meal, and returned to the deck in a short time. He found Lydia at her position against the binnacle, enjoying her peculiar, silent friendship with Moad, who was at the helm, feeling his way along the fickle winds with a mastery born of many years at sea.

"Come, child," he said. "Race me to the mast head." With that he sprang into the rigging, and began pulling himself along the night-shrouded lines with the speed of a much younger man. He had made sport of racing up the rigging with Lydia for as long she had been able to leave the deck with any degree of safety. Despite her recent illness, Lydia won the race by a good margin, and was sitting perched upon the cross-arm and peering intently to the south when her father pulled himself into the tops at her side. He had long ago discovered the almost unnatural sharpness of his daughter's eyes and often relied upon her when long vision was required.

"Can you see the ship, Lydia?"

"I don't think so, Father. There's a squall far to the horizon, and the ship could be under the darkness cast by the clouds, but I do not see it."

"You remember what to do if we are attacked?" They shared the same conversation every time the ship came into peril. Before she had been born and her mother had passed, her father had had a secret compartment in the hold, normally used for smuggling goods past greedy customs officials, refitted to hold his daughter and any other women who might be on the ship. Pirates were not kind to women captives, even those whom they sought to ransom.

"Father, I hate that stinking hole! I'm old enough to fight! I killed that troll all by myself after it broke Braide . . . " At this, her father started laughing. He knew that she was going to use her victory against him soon enough, even if she hadn't admitted to him that she had killed the troll, and not Braide.

"I thought you said Braide slew the troll, Lydia." In the darkness he saw her shade look away, obviously realising her gaff.

"Well, he did put an arrow into its lung, but I was the one who cut its throat. I'm old enough to help Father—I'm as good a shot with a bow as any on board, and you know how hard I worked with Braide at the sword. Let me fight!"

"I promise Lydia, soon. But for now, you are still weak from your battle and the fever. No, I will have no argument. You will keep Mrs Habden company in the hold if we have trouble."

Lydia was about to try one more half-hearted attempt to sway her father when she caught a glimpse of something out on the sea, the briefest flicker upon the north western horizon.

"Father, out there—another sail. I'm sure I saw it!" He peered past her pointing finger, scowling as he tried in vain to pierce the darkness.

"Could you see anything else, Lydia?"

"No father, just a sail. I'm sure it was, just on the horizon. It's too far north to be the pirate ship though."

"Yes, well, there are many ships upon these seas, so close to the waters of the Empire of Nara. Not all of them are pirates. I'll return to the deck and speak with Moad. You stay here, and see if the sail grows closer."

By the time he returned a few minutes later, Lydia reported she had seen the sail several times more, and from the faintest speck upon the night horizon, reflecting the bright moonlight over the gentle waters it had grown larger, so that she could begin to make out the distinctive shape of an eastern ship's sails.

Estrella listened to her report with increasing grimness weighing his heart. When she was done he called down a new heading to Moad. Within moments the ship heeled slightly as she veered to the northeast. Gradually, the distant sails slipped below the horizon, and then at the approach of midnight, Lydia reported that they had vanished.

Despite her protests Lydia was sent below to get some rest before the morning meal. Though exhausted from the excitement of the day, she found she could not sleep. Lydia took the karinga from its hiding place and drew the blade, feeling the now-familiar rush of power tingling up her arm. Red fire danced hungrily along the curved blade, as if in anticipation. She fell asleep at last, her face and the rest of the cabin bathed in the light of the magic knife still grasped in her hand.

Shortly before first light a crewman knocked on the door, reporting there was a new ship to the west and that the captain called for her. Lydia, who had fallen asleep in her clothes, stowed the karinga hurriedly in her chest and ran to her father's side. He stood at the rail, peering through the pre-dawn murk at a ship looming out of the fog, within bow shot. A huge lantern hung from the ship's bow, and shed light upon the colours of the Empire of Nara, flying from the foremast.

"Who are they, Father?"

His voice was taut. "They fly the colours of the Empire, Lydia, and I think they are a warship. They came upon us in a fogbank, the only fogbank upon this accursed sea. If they are what they appear, then the pirates who were pursuing us will never dare close with the *Julia* while we are in her company. But I wonder if she is a warship—from the filth that streaks her sides and the untidiness of her crew, I'd say there's a good chance she's a pirate, dressed as a warship. I've paid my dues to the Lord of Rimbu, and he controls the pirates in these waters, so I'm sure we will be allowed to pass. Nonetheless, I want you to wait in your cabin, with Mrs Habden. At the first sign of trouble, you are to flee to the hiding spot." Sensing her imminent protest, Lydia's father cut her off with a slashing-motion of his right hand. "This is not the time to argue, Lydia. I need you where I don't have to worry about you, and you need to look after Mrs Habden."

Lydia turned to the gangway, but before she went below caught glimpses of three ships closing on the *Julia* from the other points of the compass. Two were the wide, flat-bottomed ships of the eastern islanders, square-angled and blocky, each with massive keel-boards lowered from their sides and lashed into place by twisted hempen ropes as thick as her waist. In the growing light she could see that one was the first ship that had followed them, driven now by black sails that were all but invisible upon night seas. It was joined by another ship of large size, coming from the direction of the second ship they had encountered during the night, also flying black sails. The fourth was a small, dark vessel that slipped quickly through the water, a far more elegant design than the pirate ships, perhaps a private yacht, or the ship of an imperial messenger. The smaller ship curved off, staying well clear of any ensuing conflict, apparently preferring to stay within sight and watch, but out of bowshot.

Lydia's shout of alarm was joined by the voices of half of the crew upon the deck, and Lydia's father took the horn he wore at his side and blew three short blasts upon it, warning what of the crew that was still emerging from below decks of the danger. Braide's mate hurriedly unlocked the arms chest and stood by, ready to hand out boarding axes, quivers and cutlasses. He looked to the captain for orders as the men swarmed to the arms chest, but Lydia's father shook his head at the man and called out, over the din of panic. "Arm no man, Jeeb. Not until I tell you otherwise. But stand ready." Jeeb knuckled his brow, and brandished his own axe menacingly, keeping the rest of the crew at bay as they swarmed about him, eyes wide with terror.

The warship, in the meanwhile, had drifted closer to the *Julia*, and her captain hailed in heavily accented Danithian, through cupped hands.

"Greetings captain. I am Captain Dheree of His Imperial Majesty's Ship *Dso*. Lower sail and raise no arm!"

Lydia stood in the stairwell, while her father raised his own cupped hands to reply. Before he could respond, a dozen arrows flew from the rigging of the warship and plunged into his body, piercing his chest and upper legs. His crew stood transfixed as Captain Estrella staggered backwards and then sank to his knees. Before Lydia could respond, she felt the tremendous strength of Moad's hands upon her shoulders, lifting her bodily and carrying her down the companionway. She struggled fiercely against the giant Sudethian but her strength was no match for his. He propelled her down the passageway to the door of the hold. Mrs Habden was waiting there, still in her nightclothes, and she took Lydia into her arms, perhaps instinctively knowing that the girl was in peril. Lydia struggled to get free, desperate to run to her cabin, to draw the karinga from its chest and to throw herself upon the body of Captain Dheree, raking his face with the blade. The two adults were too strong for Lydia. They bundled her into the hold and then the secret compartment behind a false bulkhead.

Lydia still fought to escape Mrs Habden's embrace as Moad tried to seal the entrance. She lashed at the man with her feet even as she writhed in Mrs Habden's fleshy arms, thinking only to get to the karinga and feel it suck the life from the pirate captain. So blinded was she with rage that she did not see Moad draw back his fist. He struck her with a single blow upon the chin, whipping her head back and felling the frantic girl instantly.

Lydia awoke to near silence. Buried deep in the ship's bowels she could hear the normal creaking of a timber ship rocked by the sea, but there were no sounds of battle coming from above, no men's shouts, no thumping of ballista firing their great bolts or massed crews of the enemy. Her face radiated fire where Moad had struck her, and though she understood the reason for his blow she still felt hot anger towards the quiet Sudethian who had been her friend for all her life. In the darkness she could hear the sighing breath of Mrs Habden, and then she realised that the woman she had hated so recently was clutching her almost painfully, and rocking her gently. Her soft body was wracked with sobs from time to time, which Lydia felt her fight to control.

And then, there in the blackness was the scene again, fresh in her mind. Arrows streaking out of the near-blackness, meaty thuds as they plunged into her father's body. His jerking as each one found its mark. The thump of his body falling to the deck.

She had not seen his face before he died. She had not heard his voice. She had not been able to tell him that she loved him. She was not sure when she had last told him that she loved him—her mind frantically raced back over the days, weeks, months, desperately seeking the time that she had said those words to the man that had given her so much, who had not seemed to need to hear them from her. She could not recall a single time, though she was sure she had said it. Her mind slipped into hysteria, and she frantically started clawing for freedom from Mrs Habden's embrace, to rush on to deck to where he would still be laying, to tell him before he was gone.

"Be still child, we must hide until night and try to steal a boat—stay . . . !" Mrs Habden's whisper was frantic. Lost to madness and anger, Lydia struck out at the woman, thrusting her elbow into her chin and sending her head crashing into the bulkhead. Stunned by the blow, Mrs Habden relaxed her grasp and Lydia burst from the compartment and raced through the hold, past bales of trade goods, barrels of water and food stores, thick-walled jars of cinnamon from Rimbu, to the doorway that led to the main passageway. The ship seemed deserted, and she ran up a narrow flight of stairs to her cabin, shutting the door after her and driving home the bolt. Lydia flung open her chest, digging frantically through her clothes for the karinga, remembering only the words "hatred" and "killing blade." She emptied the contents, flinging the ladies' clothes from Talvon, her trinkets and her winter cloak about the cabin in her desperate search. The magical blade was gone.

She looked about the room wildly, eyes coming to rest on the long, thin Danithian sparring sword she had wielded so often in mock battle with Braide. The blade felt like an extension of her arm as she drew it. The steel gleamed in the dim light of the below-decks as if by its own magic. Gripping her weapon, Lydia fled the cabin, trampling her possessions underfoot, raced to the gangway and burst into the sunlight. Blinded by the mid-day light she held her blade before her as her eyes adjusted to the sudden glare.

At her feet, in a haphazard row, lay the bodies of her father's crew. They made a carpet between the forecastle and the quarterdeck. Her eyes swept over the corpses, finding the huge black form of Moad, a fierce grimace of battle frozen on his face, and there, at the end was her father's body. The thin arrows bristling from him seemed almost toy-like.

The deck ran red with blood and Lydia had to fight back a wave of nausea at the overwhelming, hot-iron stench of it. She saw the blood pooling against the rim of the hatchway from which she had just come. It was covering her bare feet; warm, almost hot.

Rising from her blood-soaked feet, her eyes swept the deck as she realized that she was surrounded by men, mostly dressed in rags. They stood silently, some grinning, others looking at her hungrily, or with cold hatred. She searched for the one who would be Captain Dheree, thinking that she would instantly know the man who had caused her father's death. But no man stood out from the crowd of filthy, rag-clad pirates. They started to close in around her.

She was about to throw herself onto the mass of men, blade thrusting wildly in an effort to kill as many as she could before they pulled her down when Mrs Habden exploded onto the deck. With speed unbelievable in such a large woman she stepped in front of the girl and raised a hand before her, barring the leering mob from her ward. In her other hand she gripped a bloody boarding axe.

The men laughed and jeered at the site of the woman, still in her night clothes, wielding a heavy axe. One pirate, large for a man of the east, with a bald pate and a skull tattooed over his face, stepped forward and reached out to take the axe. With the ferocity of a mother bear protecting her cub, Mrs Habden buried the head in the man's skull, splitting it nearly into two.

Too powerful a stroke, said some deep voice within Lydia's mind, a voice that stayed calm, despite her rage and panic. *You'll lose your axe.*

As Mrs Habden struggled to pull the weapon from the slumping man's body the other pirates swarmed over her like a mass of ants, dragging the axe from her. They hauled the kicking, screaming woman towards the stern, where her struggles continued until she was struck from behind with the pommel of a cutlass and fell to the deck. The pirates closed in around her like ravenous sharks.

Lydia flung herself forward as they swarmed Mrs Habden, thrusting wildly into the mass with her thin blade, driving the men who stood before her back. Her blade sank indiscriminately into the bodies surrounding Mrs Habden, jabbing almost as if possessed with a spirit as malicious as the karinga. Coldly, despite her emotion, Lydia aimed for heart and throat, eye and liver, killing strokes each. Pirates babbling with fear tumbled away from the bloody needle-tip of her sword, clawing at each other in their terror. Lydia ducked the swinging club of one who stood his ground, and thrust her blade into his gut. As she plucked the blade free something crashed into the back of her head. A flash of white followed by a red mist that blotted out the light. She felt herself land hard on her knees, only half-aware that she knelt as her father had before his death. Her sword fell from her lifeless fingers and the clatter of the blade on the deck reached her through the whirling red mist. Then the padded club crashed into her dazed skull again, sending her to the deck. A pair of black boots loomed into her fading vision, and a face filled her narrowing consciousness as she slipped away. A rugged, hawk-nosed face. Hands pressed the swelling at the back of her head, probing the extent of her injury. Lydia tried to spit in the leering man's eye, or lash at him with the crown of her head, smashing his nose. But she could do nothing. The face smiled.

She fought to keep aware long enough to remember that face, just long enough to remember.

Lydia awoke spluttering, mouth and nose full of seawater. When she tried to kick at the man who loomed over her bindings bit into her ankles and hands. She was trussed tightly and dumped haphazardly in a chair. As she swayed and nearly fell to the deck, her head threatened to split asunder from the pain of the blows that felled her.

The pirate vanished from her quavering vision, replaced by the solemn face of the man she had seen just after being clubbed down, the man she knew to be Captain Dheree. He was leaning back in her father's chair, black boots on the table where Lydia and her father had dined and played fiest so often. The pirate was drinking from her father's cup and around his feet were the remains of a rich meal. The smell of food rich in oriental spices made Lydia's stomach heave. Seeing she was awake, the man spoke in his heavily accented, intelligent voice, words dripping with sarcasm and evil intent.

"Good, the little lady wakes up. I'm glad to see you are not hurt too badly, my dear. It would be a pity to bruise such a valuable little fruit too deeply."

The slumping body of her father, the lifeless face of Moad, the struggling form of Mrs Habden being borne away by the mass of filthy pirates, all appeared before her eyes even as she struggled to focus her failing vision on the man at the table above her.

"You're going to make me a pretty profit at the man-cattle markets of Nara. I'm sure we can find some rich man who will pay well for your pretty pale skin, and when they hear what a tiger you are, well . . . " the leering pirate chuckled deeply before he continued, and pulled at his greasy moustache thoughtfully. "They'll pay . . . .they'll pay. A girl of your years who can slay four pirates is a tempting dish indeed, for a man who likes a spicy wench."

Lydia struggled to respond, and fought back the tears of loss and hot rage that threatened to well out of the agony in her chest. Finding herself unable to speak without giving voice to her emotion, she clenched her lips shut, choosing to remain silent rather than give the gloating man any satisfaction. But she did not turn her gaze from the smiling pirate, refusing to be cowed. Behind her back, her nails dug into the flesh of her palms. Fresh pain fed her anger all the more.

Captain Dheree sat contemplating the girl in silence while he smoked a pipe of pungent gavesh, seemingly not noticing the hatred she knew flashed in her eyes. When his bowl was empty he knocked the ashes out on her father's carpet and had two putrid men carry Lydia to a looted store room. They dumped her on the deck and one of the pirates squatted above her and started to grope her body with filth-blackened fingers. The other pirate stood in the doorway, leering and passing small comments in their language. As the man's hands rose to her chest, Lydia arched forward and bit his wrist, feeling her teeth sink through dirty flesh. She clung to the man's arm as fiercely as a terrier would to a rat, letting all of her hatred and anger flow into this one act of revenge, however small it might be. The man roared in pain, and as Lydia clung to his wrist and tried not to gag at the blood filling her mouth, he grabbed her head with his free hand and pushed it into the deck with strength borne of agony. The impact jarred her so badly that Lydia's mouth fell open as she gasped. The other hooted in laughter as the wounded man grasped his bleeding wrist and drove a bare foot into Lydia's undefended stomach, driving the wind from her and making the room go grey. The wounded pirate backed away from the girl, and before he left, he smiled down at her.

"You make good fun. Big man pay fun; big pay, big fun!" He then spat upon her face. His spittle was hot and foul-smelling on her forehead, pooling in her eye socket. Cradling his bleeding wrist, he followed his laughing mate down the passageway after they bolted the door. Lydia, left in total darkness, struggled to her knees as the tears and vomit she had struggled against erupted at last, both overwhelming her at once.

EIGHT

Apparently worried about their prize losing value, the pirates brought Lydia water and food. She rejected all but the smallest drinks of foul water. Once, the man with the bitten wrist came and brought her food, glaring at her with flaming hatred. Lydia saw with satisfaction that his hand and forearm was swollen, and the flesh around the bite was turning septic. Soon the man would lose his arm, and then most likely, his life. She saw him fighting the urge to kick at her grinning face. Instead, he spat on her again, and smiled.

"You stink, shit piss. Man no pay for you. We feed you to shark." He bolted the door, and then returned with three other pirates, each bearing a bucket of sea water, which they upended over her. The saltwater burnt like flaming oil on her wrists and ankles, where her skin had been torn by coarse ropes. Lydia struggled to loosen her bindings, but after hours she found that as her blood soaked the fibres, they grew tighter, and at last she gave up.

Sometime later Lydia fell into delirium. In the dark of the storeroom, her vision began to dance with spectres of the dead. A beautiful young woman, the mother she didn't know, was there, standing by the side of her father, the arrows still sticking out of his chest. Grimly, Moad stood behind, and Mrs Habden, eyes full of tears. Then there was a shaking of the floor, a heaving of the deck, and Lydia struggled in terror as the troll approached, groping for her while its sightless eyes bled. Finally, she felt strong hands on her shoulder, shaking her, and there was Braide, his face before hers, his high, cultured voice urging her to stay alive, to fight again. He was shaking her even as she opened her eyes and blinked in the dim light that flooded the storeroom. Captain Dheree was shaking her shoulder, firmly but not roughly.

"You must eat, or you will die."

Lydia struggled to free herself from the grip of her delirium.

"You eat, or I give you to the crew." He pushed a plate of thin gruel towards her face. When she did not rise from the floor, he gestured to the men who gathered in the passageway to lift the girl, and hold her head up. He took a spoonful of the gruel, gripped her jaw and forced her mouth open. The gruel was almost sickly sweet; against her will, Lydia swallowed. The pirate captain smiled, and nodded his head.

"Good. You live, you bring a good price, I'll not give you to the crew. Maybe some rich merchant buy you and make you his daughter." At this, cold, horrible all-embracing anger threatened to overwhelm the girl. Not missing the play of emotion on her face, the captain chuckled. "Yes, girl, you get strong quick. There is much anger in you, it make you strong." He rose from his knees and handed the spoon and plate to the man who stood at his side. Captain Dheree said something quickly in their language, and made an exaggerated biting motion, and the men all broke into laughter. As the captain left the room, the man with the plate squatted above the girl, keeping well out of her reach.

After several days, when Lydia's strength had begun to recover, she heard a great commotion on the deck. The flap of bare feet on the planks overhead and the shouts of Captain Dheree and his officers came through the thick timbers of the storeroom, awakening her from a light sleep. She started to sit up, but slumped again when her bindings bit into raw flesh. More gingerly Lydia eased herself into a sitting position against the bulkhead and put an ear to the rough wood, just as the ship resounded with a thudding impact. Lydia recognized the sound of the impact of a heavy ballista bolt, shot from a nearby ship. The giant, squat crossbow would have fired an iron-tipped, barbed arrow as thick as her leg, which had pierced the side of the ship. The tail of the bolt was connected to a cable, which could be wound in, drawing *Julia* to her attacker. As she listened, four more impacts shook the ship, and Lydia knew that the pirates were bound firmly to their attackers, whoever they might be.

The pirates' shouts of anger, outrage and fear change to yells of pain as Lydia heard the hail-like thumping of arrows raining upon the deck. Soon, the patter of arrows was replaced with the noise of hand-to-hand combat, the crash of bodies as they fell, and the screams of officers rallying their men for a last push. Lydia heard the scrabbling of those who fled the pitched battle on the deck like rats before a flood, seeking shelter in the many dark corners the ship below the main deck.

The ship had been taken again.

With a metallic rasp, the bolt to her cell was drawn, and the door cautiously opened. Three men in the uniform of sailors of the Nara Imperial Navy pointed crossbows into the gloom, covering the huddled figure in the corner as their officer carefully entered the room. With the tip of his sheathed sword, the officer gently prodded the figure, until Lydia looked up at him with glaring eyes. The officer gestured to his men, who lowered their crossbows and helped the girl to her feet. With his dirk, the officer slit Lydia's bindings. When the men released her, Lydia found herself unable to stand, and the officer caught her as she tumbled to the deck. He lifted her in his arms, the cold metal of his breastplate hard against her still-tender chest, and carried her into the blinding sunlight that flooded the deck.

Lydia was brought before the officer who had assumed control of the ship. He was a young man, not yet thirty, but his dark, eastern face and fold-covered eyes showed the weathering that comes from many years at sea. He bowed in salute as Lydia was placed on the deck before him. From his uniform, Lydia saw that he was a lower officer in the Imperial Navy. He spoke to her in the language of Nara, which she only haltingly understood, and when she did not respond, he called for and gestured to a wizened man who was kneeling over a sailor lying on the deck, clutching a bloody stomach wound. The elder man washed his hands in a bucket and came over, bowing first to the officer and then to Lydia. The officer spoke rapidly, and the elder man listened intelligently, and then turned to Lydia.

"Do you speak Danithian, child?"

"Yes sir, I am from Danith."

"My name is Patha. I am the healer of His Imperial Majesty's Ship *Dawn Sun*. I am speaking for Lieutenant Hassun, who does not speak your tongue. The Lieutenant wishes to know what your name is, and how you came to be on this ship."

"My name is Lydia Estrella, daughter of Captain Markus Estrella, captain of this ship. We were surprised by pirates who disguised their ship to look like an imperial frigate, and they killed the crew. They were taking me to be sold . . . " The healer held up his hand to pause her story, and translated for the Lieutenant, who nodded his head, and spoke in return.

"The Lieutenant says that you are now under the protection of Lord Zhe, son of His Glorious Majesty the Emperor of Nara, and Commander of the Imperial Fleet. I am to see to your wounds while we speak." A sailor brought a barrel over for Lydia to sit upon, and the Lieutenant turned to his men, issuing a rapid string of orders that saw the bodies of the pirates on the deck thrown overboard to the ravening pack of sharks that surrounded the ships, drawn by the blood that still ran from the decks into the warm ocean in little rivulets. Lydia saw that there were only a few dead, and that Dheree was not among them. The healer returned to where he had been tending the sailor, now dead, and gathered a small iron-bound box from the deck. He came back to where Lydia sat, kneeling before her and examining her ankles and wrists. From his box he took a small jar of nacreous yellow ointment, which he smeared upon her wounds. The ointment immediately began to sting. When she tried to pull away the aged man held Lydia fast with surprising strength. His head still bowed over her wrists, the man spoke to Lydia in his gentle voice.

"Did your captain not pay the Lord of Rimbu his tithe?"

"Yes sir, he did. And the Lord pretended to be Father's friend, even."

"I have heard that he grows greedy beyond all control. Soon, an assassin will be sent to him, if he does not regain his senses."

"I'll kill the bloated pig myself, when I get off this ship . . . " The vehemence in her voice, the sudden strength in the voice of this young girl seemed to take the old man aback, and he looked up to her face for a moment, seeing the cold steel in her eyes.

"Anger is a demon, my child, who lives in the soul and devours the inner light. With hatred, there is no joy." He bent back to work; his words falling on deaf ears. Lydia's eyes were riveted on a black-booted Captain Dheree, who was being escorted up the gangway by a detail of armed sailors. Their eyes met, and the pirate captain, now in chains, leered at Lydia, gave her an evil-natured wink. They were not more than twenty paces apart when the sailors pushed the pirate to his knees on the deck to await his audience with the Lieutenant. The man still smiled at Lydia, who felt dark rage take her senses, blotting out the many noises of the ship, clouding out the scenes of gore and the Naran crew washing the blood from the deck with buckets of sea water, until her whole consciousness was focussed on the squatting man. Her hands clenched into fists, though she sat still as the healer anointed the last places where rope had bitten into her. The healer was returning the jar to his box when the pirate captain pursed his lips and blew an obscene kiss to Lydia.

In an instant, she sprung to the top the barrel she had been sitting on and tensed to spring. The karinga appeared in her fist, burning with red fire, conjured by her consuming hatred. Not even aware of what she did, Lydia crouched animal-like and then leapt over the head of the healer, who looked up in time to see the girl's feet push off from the barrel, sending it rolling down the deck. As he turned she hit the deck in a roll, tumbling to her feet and leaping upon the pirate captain who fell backwards as he tried to get away from the glowing red blade. She fell upon the man with knees gathered under her, so that when she hit his chest he was driven to the deck beneath her, the breath driven from his chest. His lips still held his mocking smile, defiant now, but his eyes were full of terror. Lydia felt the surging power of the karinga, heart ignited in black passion, ears ringing with the chanting of a fire sorcerer fallen into the insane litany of the spirit trance, the beating of drums, and the sound of her blood rushing through her veins. She lifted the blade in both hands over her head and drove the needle point down towards a point exactly between the man's terrified eyes. He heaved himself in terror, and managed to shift the girl perched on his chest so that the blade drove not through his forehead but into his shoulder, where it sliced effortlessly through bone and sinew up to the hilt and pinned him to the deck.

In her hands, the karinga seemed to throb, and she could feel it drawing the life from the man. Red fire played over the man's chest, and up her arm. Where it touched her it burnt, but the pain was mingled with the greatest pleasure the girl had ever known. She stared into the man's eyes, seeing terror overwhelm his last vestiges of bravado, the dawning realisation that the blade in his shoulder was drinking his life, like he would drink a glass of cold sherbet on a boiling day. Lydia revelled in the man's understanding that after a life of violence and deprivation, his end was coming now at the hands of a child. The burning hatred in her spread from her heart to her chest and her limbs, like the warmth of a tot of rum, but infinitely more intoxicating, and she heard herself laughing as she pulled the pulsing, drinking knife from the man's chest and raised it to slash his throat. As her hand fell, one of the stunned sailors who had been watching leapt upon her, knocking Lydia from the man's chest and onto the deck. She kicked him off as Dheree lashed out with bound feet, trying to push away from her, across the blood-slicked deck. Still laughing, Lydia crouched to spring upon the pirate for the last time. Already in her mind's eye she saw the point of the karinga sink through the terrified man's neck and pin him to the mast that he'd backed up against. Before she could spring, men fell upon her from all directions, and Lydia was pressed to the deck despite her struggles and blows. She tried to plunge the karinga into the chest of the man who pressed her arm down, but the blade had vanished when she was tackled this second time, and with it went the superhuman strength and the joyous hatred that had filled her.

Gradually the weight of the men and the heaviness of grief bore her down, and her rage abated.

When Lydia's struggles came to an end, the men who smothered her rose. Each held an arm or leg, so that she was powerless to act. The pirate captain's face had flushed grey, and he collapsed to the deck, lying against the mast. The barking voice of the Lieutenant rang out in Naran, and the men hoisted Lydia to her feet, still holding her fast. The officer stood before her, yelling angrily in words that she couldn't understand. He turned, gestured for two of his men to take the feebly stirring pirate below decks. He turned to follow.

The healer, clutching his box, translated the Lieutenant's tirade. "The Lieutenant says that you are wrong to try and punish this man yourself. This is not the way of Nara, but the way of the Western barbarians. This man will be taken to trial before Lord Zhe, and will be punished for his crimes. It is for Lord Zhe to dispense justice, and no other. To take the pleasure of lawgiving from the Lord is to take his right as the emissary of the Glorious Imperial Majesty, which is the greatest joy a man may have. The Lieutenant says that you are to stay in the cabin at the aft of the ship, and not to return to the deck, upon pain of death." With this, the healer turned and followed the departed group below decks, where Lydia knew he would struggle for most of the night to save the life of the man Lydia and the karinga had so nearly taken.

Imprisoned in her father's cabin, Lydia was trapped in a storm of memories and regrets. For three more days she was given good food and fresh water, and otherwise left to the ghosts that haunted the room with its sweeping windows. Often she stood as her father had, at the open window, feeling the sea breeze on her face and letting the fresh, salty air burn her throat as she drank it in. Then she would lie upon her father's hammock, enfolded in the smell of the man, and she would try to cry, but she found that she had no tears left for any of them, for the people who had been the central pillars of her entire life.

In her time alone in the cabin, she thought also of the life she knew that she was losing. *Julia* had become a prize of the Naran navy, along with the wealth of its cargo. It was the ship she was to command, named after her mother. This did not trouble her as deeply as she might have thought. Watching the wake vanish over the horizon, Lydia knew for the first time that though she would always love the sea, her life was going to lead her in a different direction.

The karinga reappeared after her confinement, slipping itself mystically into her belt. She felt a moment's anger towards the magical blade that had vanished when she needed it so desperately, but when she pulled it from her belt and went to throw it from the gallery windows she found herself unable to part from the wicked thing, from the feeling of power it sent coursing through her arm. She spent hours holding the knife, seeing the faces of her lost friends and family in the red fire dancing along the naked blade. Then, as quickly as it had returned to her, the blade vanished from her grasp while she slept, leaving her completely alone with her memories. Awakening to find herself abandoned by the magical blade, Lydia wept at last, for hours. In her anguish, she wondered if the blade had felt betrayed when she had failed to drive it into Captain Dheree with a killing blow.

Three days passed before the lookout atop the masthead cried out at the first sighting of land, and in two more days the caravel slipped into the harbour of Masanda, a coastal city upon the mainland of the Empire of Nara, mooring alongside the frigate that had recaptured the ship from Captain Dheree. The Lieutenant respectfully knocked at the cabin door as the ship came to rest, and when Lydia opened the door he entered, accompanied by the healer. Lydia curtsied before the man, eager to gain his favour in order to learn what was to become of her. The officer bowed in response and the healer spoke for him.

"The Lieutenant has come to tell you that you have been ordered to the Great School at Marchit, the imperial capital. You have been sponsored by the Lord Zhe, who is your father now, and you will learn what the monks will teach you, that you may be of service to Lord Zhe. It is a great honour, especially for a person of the west."

"What if I don't want to go to the school? I want to go to Danith, to have a monument built for my father."

The healer's response was flat, devoid of sympathy. "The Lieutenant says you are no longer of Danith. You are of Nara now. What you wish is of no matter."

NINE

Lydia had never been to the imperial capital, as it was some days travel from the ocean, and rarely visited by seafaring merchantmen. The walled city of Marchit was built upon a plateau, the only high place presiding over vast plains that stretched for many days travel in all directions. As the carriage in which she had ridden for more days than she could recall bumped across the stone-paved road, Lydia leaned out of the window and watched the city rise up out of the surrounding fields and villages. Two ramps led to the plateau's top, which at the base of the walls was already higher even than the reach of the greatest longbow. These ramps rose to openings in the wall that were taller than ten men standing on each other's shoulders. The entrance that Lydia found herself taken through would allow seven wagons to pass at once, without the risk of colliding. As Lydia's carriage pulled to the top of the ramp and sped through the entrance, she saw that the two gates, made of huge planks of wood and bound in iron bands thicker than her body, were flung wide open. At either side, against the base of the flanking towers, two cages held the hulking bodies of five stone trolls. Her escort, the healer from Lieutenant Hassan's ship, told her that they had been captured in the far off mountains and brought to Marchit to open and close the gates at the Emperor's command. The trolls stared out of their cage listlessly, and as she watched, one spat a partially chewed human leg out of its gaping maw. Lydia had heard rumours that the Emperor fed his gate trolls the worst criminals his vast lands produced, as both a punishment to the wrongdoer and a reward to these bestial slaves.

Inside the gates was a city as large as it was mysterious. The entrance opened to a great plaza, many hundreds of strides on a side, where rough-clad peasants were gathered in a vast market, selling their wares to artisans, soldiers and bureaucrats of the city, clad in fine silks and snowy linen.

At Lydia's side, the healer spoke as the carriage and its escort of mounted warriors pushed through dense crowds. "During state holidays, the Emperor has the market cleared. There are seats along the edges, built into the walls. The whole city, noble and slave, comes here to watch ball games, horse and foot races and contests of arms. The Emperor, in celebration of his hundredth birthday, ordered a battle between two divisions of his army here. Two thousand men fought until there were no survivors among the losers, and as a prize the victors were granted their own body weights in gold." Lydia shivered at the thought of men being killed for the entertainment of others, but then she also knew that this practice was common enough in Euralia, let alone the east. Still, it was barbaric, and she hated it.

Surrounding this plaza was a city made of finely-dressed yellow stone buildings, topped in thatched or black-tiled roofs. A broad avenue ran the length of the plateau, from one gate to another, and this was lined with all the trees that were found in the vast empire, many hundreds of years old and twisted with age, others growing large enough to form a green tunnel through which the carriage sped.

Lydia came to ignore the healer's chatter as she glimpsed many other wonders fleetingly and the carriage bumped through the enormous city. At Marchit's centre, the hub from which all streets ran, was another plaza, nearly as large as the first, surrounding the towering citadel of the Emperor of Nara. This rose well over even the highest building in Marchit, with sheer walls made of buttery yellow stone. From the centre of the citadel rose the Great Tower, said to be the highest anywhere, from atop which the Emperor ruled his domain. Lydia doubted that even the stoutest ballista could send a bolt to those heights. Far overhead, circling like vast crows, swooping in and out of passing clouds, flew the citadel's guardians, the Empire's finest knights. Lydia had read that they were mounted on dragon-like wyvern, and that they flew in constant watchfulness. From the carriage window, Lydia fancied she could hear the distant cries of the flying reptiles, drifting down from far overhead.

To her relief the carriage did not enter the ominous, gaping jaws of the citadel but rather skirted around the sheer walls and turned down a side avenue, pulling to a halt before a large, many-storied building that overlooked the plaza. The building was made of vast blocks of the same yellow stone as the rest of the city, smooth as fine glass, and girt by pillars twice as thick as a caravel's mainmast. Small windows lined the walls, some open, others barred to the dust and noise of the street, and a featureless double door stood closed at the head a short, elegant stair, in the building's very middle.

The healer climbed from the carriage and motioned for her to follow. In the three fortnights that they had travelled together, the man had been polite to Lydia, but he had never shown her overt kindness, even when he tended her wounds. Now, he gave her his hand as she descended from the carriage, and he quickly brushed the dust from the black uniform he had donned before leaving the inn they had stayed at the night before, straightened his sword belt and his fur-lined helmet, and with an outstretched hand directed Lydia to the door at the head of the stairs, following her as she climbed.

The centre of each of the double doors was adorned with a metal wolf's head knocker, holding a ring in its clenched jaws. The servant raised one of these and let it drop against the door with a resounding thud. The door opened almost instantly and a small, bald man, well past his prime, wearing only a black robe and sandals. The servant spoke to the man quickly and then turned and left Lydia standing alone with the old man on the doorstep.

"You have come a long way, child." The man, who spoke in accented Danithian, studied her as he spoke. She was sure that the priest, for he was dressed as the priests of the empire, was more than just a holy man. He had a regal air, and a voice heavy with authority.

"You speak Danithian, sir," she replied, not knowing what else to say.

"Yes child, I have travelled to that far land many times in my quest for knowledge, and to all the other great kingdoms of the west. But though I have spoken to you in this tongue, I shall never do so again after today, as it is no longer yours, but the language of a foreign people. As you have been told, you are a child of Nara now. I wish only to tell you that this is your home, and that you will reside here at the pleasure of Lord Zhe and his exulted father, The Most Glorious Emperor. When you step over this threshold, you shall be reborn, a servant of the Empire's greatest men."

"But I am a free woman! I am a Danithian, and no man's servant."

The man chuckled merrily, and laid his hand upon the girl's shoulder. "Come my dear, let me show you to your new home. No one is free in this land; we are all the servants of the Emperor." With this, he led Lydia into the building that would be her home for the next years of her life.

Lydia longed to fling the man's hand from her shoulder, but she had nowhere else to go, and so she let him draw her in.

The depths of the school were as impressive as the facade. The hallways, chambers and galleries were all of the same yellow stone as the outside, lined with small columns, and almost unnaturally quiet, for the men and women who lived within the school were dedicated to their studies, and rarely were heard to laugh, jest or sing.

In fact, there was a teacher for almost any interest to be found somewhere in the building. The school was the storeroom for the collected learning of the world's largest empire, and no greater repository of knowledge was to be found. Medicine and the healing arts, magic, alchemy, the nature of plant and beast, philosophy, statesmanship, history and the ways of the Gods could all be learned behind those doors. Poets and story-tellers developed their craft there, as did the sons of the great trading houses who were also destined to follow their fathers in the pursuit of business. In the central library, a thousand scribes spent their days recording the knowledge that poured into the school, adding to the millions of scrolls and heavy tomes that already lined the walls of so many rooms within the wolf-headed doors.

Lydia caught the merest glimpse of a hundred wonders as she followed the aged priest through the maze of galleries and corridors. Many times they passed groups of students clad in white robes and hoods. All bowed respectfully to her guide. Other times they would pass small groups of monks, apparently the only teachers in the school. As they walked, the priest explained the school to Lydia.

"This school has served the Emperor for many hundreds of years, and has grown rich with knowledge. Each area of learning has its own college; its own rooms, dormitories, dining hall, chapels and classrooms. We have thirty-seven colleges here, some with a thousand or more students. When a child comes to us, they are tested by the elders, and sent to where they are best suited. Most come to us very young, before their eighth birthday, so you see my dear, you are quite old to be starting, though we are told you are not without gift in your area of natural skill."

"My father trained me to be a merchant, like him, the captain of a trading ship."

"Yes child, you have learned much, but that is not your destiny. If you look into your heart, you will know that you are drawn to a different fate."

"Am I not to be tested , to determine what is right for me?"

Again the man chuckled, "You have already been tested, my child, and your path is clear."

"What am I to learn, then?" Despite herself, Lydia felt herself fill with curiosity.

"You are going to join the oldest school of all, the College of Black Art."

"Am I to be a sorcerer then?"

"No child, blacker than that. You are to be trained as an assassin."

TEN

The College of Black Art was located at in the furthest depths at the back of the school, in an area strictly forbidden to outsiders. While the students there wore the same clothing as the others, they were treated with far more respect by their mentors, and seen as the most important in the school.

Like their students, the monks who taught at the college had been gathered from throughout the lands of Nara, recruited for their excellence in skill and dedication to their arts, and initiated into a secret order that sought to develop a state of perfection in just one area of the adept's life. They took no pleasure in the company of lovers, or fermented drink, or in the bowl of a gavesh pipe; they shed their earthly desires upon entry to the school, and became the living embodiment of their craft.

For the first month Lydia had a small cell to herself, furnished only with a thin, hard bedroll, a single blanket and a bowl for bathing water. She shared meals with the other students in a long gallery, seated in silent rows at great stone tables. During the days she wandered from classroom to classroom, trying desperately to learn the strange language that surrounded her. By the fifth day, she was starting to know the names for basic items, the necessary rooms, the names of students and teachers. At the end of two weeks she was able to converse in a basic manner, greeting other students and teachers, responding to questions about her welfare, asking for a second helping of dinner.

At the end of her first month, Lydia was summoned from her cell after the evening meal and led to a small chapel she had not previously entered. The room was austere; a small featureless alter to the Naran God of Death dominated one wall, accompanied only by a single brazier in the centre of the room giving both light and heat. Sitting cross-legged and staring into the fire before him with unseeing eyes was an ageless monk. He was completely hairless, his skin was weathered and he bore a fine nest of wrinkles about his eyes. When the monk raised his eyes to Lydia's, she somehow knew they were ancient, deeply wise and vastly experienced. For the years that she knew the man, she never felt that she could guess his age. The servant who had escorted Lydia left silently, and the seated monk gestured for Lydia to sit across the brazier from him. She sat in a position like his, and waited. When he spoke, he did so slowly, choosing his words carefully so that the Danithian girl could understand him.

"You have learned well over the last two fortnights. I am told you will speak as one of us soon." Lydia, hearing no question in his voice, merely nodded. She felt strangely oppressed by the man.

"It is time for you to begin your lessons. You will learn the ways to serve the Lord Zhe and the Emperor. When you have learned all that you need to know, you will leave this school, and serve your masters' bidding."

"There is sadness in your heart, and anger. While I cannot see into your soul as I can the others, it is written clearly upon your face. You will forget these things, and find joy in the service of your masters, as we all have."

"You will now be given a room with another student, who will help you learn the ways of the school, and you will join in her classes tomorrow. I am Master Nhil, Dean of this college, and the foremost of My Lord the Emperor's assassins. When you next see me, it will during a test, to determine if you shall pass to the next stage of your studies. All who enter this college are tested, and only those who pass leave these halls."

"What if I fail?" Still intimidated by the man, Lydia's voice quavered slightly. Upon hearing the fear in her voice, she clenched her fist in anger; Lydia was coming to despise any sign of weakness in herself.

"There is no failure here. You pass, or you die. That is all." With that, Master Nhil's eyes seemed to glaze over, and he returned his stare to the fire. Lydia realised that during the entire interview, the man had never blinked and that his eyes had never left hers.

Summoned as if by magic, the servant who had fetched Lydia from the dining hall now led her to a small cell in the long hallway that was one of the common dormitories for the college. Scores of doorways opened from the columned-lined passage, each covered with a thick black curtain which, if pulled aside, would reveal an identical room.

The cell was dark except for the glow of a single candle, placed in the centre of the floor. Lydia could see the walls only dimly in the meagre light, barely a pace away in any direction. Shadows danced on the yellow stone as the candle guttered in the draft from the open doorway. The servant left, drawing the curtain behind him. Alone, Lydia felt watched. She stood silently in the dim circle of light, try to catch the smallest sound from the dark corners, and feeling slightly ridiculous at her unfounded fear. The room was not much bigger than her cabin on her father's caravel, and she knew that if there was anyone else in there she would have seen their silhouette when she entered. Still, there was that feeling of unseen eyes.

She heard a tiny giggle, barely smothered, from the furthest corner. Lydia stepped back from the light, towards the curtain and doorway. There was a slight breeze, and in the next moment Lydia was enfolded in the arms of a girl, who held her firmly but playfully from behind. The girl tickled Lydia's ear with her breath, and then whispered, "I am Shandala, the Shadow Dancer. I am told that I am going to be your roommate." Heart racing, Lydia didn't know if she should twist about, grasping the girl's thin wrist and turning the hold against her, or drive backwards with her head, hammering the girl's nose, or if she should allow the girl to hold her. Before she could decide Shandala was gone, vanished into the darkness and giggling once more from the far side of the room. As hard as she peered, Lydia couldn't see the girl, though she could see all of the corners and walls clearly as her eyes adjusted to the dim light. In a moment, the giggling stopped, and Lydia felt the soft breeze against her cheek once again. This time, she waited for the briefest moment, and then took a step back, running into the girl who stood again behind her. Without turning, Lydia found the arm of the girl, leaned forward and using the leverage of her body as Braide had taught her, threw the girl over her shoulder. She fell onto her back on the mat at Lydia's feet. She started to shake, and for a moment Lydia was afraid that the girl was hurt. She reached down to help the girl to her feet, and when the girl took her outstretched hand and pulled herself up, Lydia found she was laughing. Lydia performed her best curtsey, and said in broken Naran, "Greetings, Shandala Shadow Dancer, I am Lydia, Shadow Bouncer, and your new roommate."

In the morning, Lydia officially joined her first class. As an outsider wandering the hallways and galleries of the vast school she had witnessed many different types of lessons. While students in the other areas of the school attended sessions in large groups, those at the College of Black Art were small, with never more than a handful of pupils. The monk-teachers were all experts in some aspect of killing by stealth. Among the many who taught there, there were a few that Lydia came to know well. Master Han specialised in the long blade, especially the katana, a gently curved, light and razor-sharp blade forged in the east, known to be among the finest blades. Master Zongo was an expert in the small blade. The blowgun, crossbow, long and short bow were the provinces of Master Chunshen, a man from the steppes that formed the empire's far western reaches. He could fire an arrow with deadly accuracy while hanging under an unsaddled horse at full gallop, or while tumbling from a high wall. Mistress Amalin possessed the secrets of all the poisons of the world, their cures if any, and the small magic of potions, salves and dusts. All forms of unarmed combat were the art of Master Dahang, a wizened man well past sixty, yet still as limber as a young sapling and capable of driving his bare fingertip through an oak plank. And the most mysterious, revered and feared teacher of them all was Master Zumo, who possessed the secrets of the high magic that some assassins would use in their dark dealings. His was the ability to see into the hearts and minds of his enemy and the power to enter their consciousness, spread fear or bleak hopelessness, so that his opponent would drop his defence and stand stupefied, placidly awaiting the killing blade.

Before the first of dawn's rays warmed the yellow stone exterior of the school the girls arose from their sleeping mats, washed their faces and took a light meal in their silent row in the mess hall. Shandala then led Lydia to a large room, filled with sunlight filtering through an opening in the roof. The walls of the chamber were lined with swords, axes, spears and pole arms of every conceivable form, all arranged neatly in racks. Lydia vaguely recognised that the weapons were in groups according to their place of origin. Even present were the stone-tipped weapons of the lesser peoples.

Lydia and Shandala sat on the bare floor, and soon they were joined by four other students who appeared to be their age, though Lydia had some difficulty in knowing how old many of the Naran people were. They were boys, not much bigger than Lydia in height, but already wrapped in sinewy muscle. The six sat in a line, awaiting their lesson, white robes gathered around them and their white hoods drawn over their heads. They sat with such silence that Lydia thought the others might have slipped back into sleep, but when she secretly peered around she found that the lips of the boy next to her were moving in a noiseless chant, repeating some mantra in silent meditation.

Master Han appeared shortly. He was tall for a Naran, agile, like so many Naran people, and sombre. He entered the room silently, walked around the line of students with almost feminine, cat-like grace, and then stood in front of his disciples. He looked from face to face, and then raised his finger to Lydia. Unsure of what the Master wished, she started to ask, but Shandala pushed her to her feet, and whispered, "You are chosen to fight. You must take a weapon to use."

When she faced the Master, the man made a quick, short bow, and then shrugged off his black robes, revealing a well-developed body, bound by muscles as tight as twisted rope but not so large as to create a slowing bulk. Small, thin scars, some from the points of knives, others long and clean, left by the sweeping blade of a sword, criss-crossed his bare torso. At his waist was a sword tucked into a sash, which he drew. It was the gently curving blade of the east, a katana, with a triangular point and long grip, suited for use in two hands. He gave Lydia a tight-lipped, grim smile and gestured to the racks of weapons.

Lydia chose a Danithian sparring sword for herself, a light, elegant thrusting weapon with a thin blade that would not tire the arm, flexible enough to bend in half and still spring back to form, and long enough to keep an opponent at a distance. She also removed the bulky robes she had been given, leaving only her undergarments, feeling the crisp morning air on her bare skin. Lydia returned to the centre of the room, where the other five students had moved to sit along the side, leaving only Master Han waiting for her, sword held in both hands above his head, body in a tense crouch, ready to spring forth in lightning attack and defence. Lydia unsheathed her sword, tested its balance, held the blade before her in the classic Danithian hanging guard, and nodded her head to indicate readiness.

The man stood completely still for a moment, and then was upon her. Seeing the beginnings of his attack she thrust with her sword, hoping to keep him at bay with the classic "fence" of Danithian sparring, an invisible wall created by the tip of her sword, at her fully extended lunge. To pass this wall was to invite the sword to thrust into the body with lethal effect. Lydia knew that the man's katana was a shorter blade, made less for thrusting and more for sweeping, and that if she could keep him at a distance she might prevail. However, while technically perfect, Lydia's attack failed to take into account Master Han's nearly inhuman speed: he merely stepped aside as the tip of Lydia's blade passed his chest and then moved inside her zone of defence to a distance where his slashing weapon would prevail over Lydia's sparring sword before she could strike again. He swung his blade in long, fluid chopping sweeps, creating an impenetrable wall of lashing steel, and through this defence he would loose lightning attacks, powerful sweeping swings that Lydia's thin blade was unable to effectively parry, leaving her to duck and fall back before his attacks. But as fast as she fell away the fencing master advanced, never letting his opponent gain the distance she needed to thrust effectively with her own blade. Unable to mount her own offense, Lydia knew that the man was just toying with her, testing her defences before he struck home. Several times the blade nearly cut into her: only by twisting and one time leaping clear of the blade did she avoid injury.

The man tested her every defence, and when apparently satisfied that she had been pressed to the utmost, he withdrew to the far side of the room, where he assumed a defensive position, his blade held to the side and low. Lydia approached the man slowly, on the balls of her feet, wondering how best to penetrate past the man's almost unseeable blade. Knowing that she could not match the man in strength, she elected to try a feigning move, striking for the man's right shoulder, and then sweeping under him with a tip cut to his ankle, a daring move, as the sparring sword was thin and not ideally suited to cutting attacks. Both blows were brushed casually aside, so Lydia retreated again, regathered herself, and tried a series of arrow-like thrusts to the man's chest, testing his defences with the speed of her strikes, knowing that each jab, if it found home, would not slay them man, but would weaken him. This was the classic attack for a sparring sword, where its long, thin and light blade would prove its greatest worth. Again, the man thwarted her, though she did lightly penetrate his side, the tip of her blade creasing the man's skin and freeing a small welling of blood.

Unable to gain a winning blow, Lydia withdrew again, circling the man in contemplation. He smiled grimly, not openly mocking her, but with a definite air of condescension. As she turned in her pace she launched her final attack, first feinting with a low sweep, ducking below his responding swing, rolling under his blade and then springing to her feet on his other side, her blade sweeping towards his undefended flank. She had recovered from her roll facing away from the man, leaving her undefended in a last-ditch effort to take advantage of his recovery from his sweeping stroke. Her blade found nothing but empty air where the man should have been, must have been, and at that moment she saw his blade arcing towards her undefended body from an impossible quarter; the thought that the man must have vanished and reappeared to move so quickly came to her as the blade bit deeply into her belly, turning from cold steel into white flame as it sliced into her, exploding every nerve ending in her body in agony far worse than any she had ever known.

The blade left her body as quickly as it entered, returning to steel as it came free. Lydia collapsed to the floor, muscles in spasm and nerves on fire, hands clutching her stomach, groping for the wound that she knew would spill her intestines from her body. As the torturous pain receded, Lydia found that the blade had left her uncut, causing no damage other than the pain. Feeling shamed, she wiped the tears from her eyes and rose to her feet, still holding the sparring sword loosely in her hand. Master Han gestured to the row of observing students and Lydia resumed her seat next to Shandala, still quivering from the agonising mystical bite of the Master's blade.

"Now students," said Han levelly. "Let us examine the new one's attack, and see if we may discover the fifty-seven mistakes she made in defence, and the seventy-three in attack. Who can tell me the first mistake she made?"

Over the following days Lydia was tested by all of her teachers, and she gradually felt her former sense of competence in warlike-skills eroding. Of all the disciplines, Lydia did the best at swordplay and the small blades, moderately well at archery and unarmed combat, and she showed little aptitude for the mixing and use of poisons, and the assassin's black magic. there, ears into hearing where there was no sound. At the end of two weeks, Lydia found herself with a schedule of sorts. Her days were full of sword training and archery.

She had extensive lessons in the many ways of unarmed combat and the use of the almost endless range of small, bladed weapons, both hand-held and thrown. She continued her studies in poisons and black magic, but only to the extent that she learned how they were used, and how to defend from their powers, detect them from afar, and avoid their effects if possible. And like all students, she learned the other crafts of assassination. Stealth, concealment, opening of locks, climbing with ropes, spikes or bare fingers, disguise. Torture and sabotage.

Lessons stretched from the first light of dawn until well into the night. When she was finished, Lydia had little energy for socialising. Nonetheless, she found herself drawn to the frolicsome and light-hearted Shandala. The girl was her age, and was also the daughter of a wealthy merchant, though her father's wares were plied upon the long caravan routes that stretched across the lands of Nara, and not upon the oceans. Shandala had come to the school on her eighth birthday, and in seven years, she had not left its confines. She told Lydia that when the students reached sixteen they would be allowed to venture forth into the city of Marchit, and in some cases even further afield, so that they could learn how to assimilate into the outside world; until that time their entire world was to consist of the Art of Death. She eagerly awaited her first venture outside the school, after so many years of confinement.

Shandala studied the black art of shadow magic, bending the darkness to her will, concealing herself within it like a child in its mother's skirts, travelling unseen wherever shadows were deep enough. In addition, she was learning to master the small, thin blades that assassins from Euralia preferred. Needle-pointed knives and short swords were her passion; she had learned to find the smallest chink in a suit of armour and drive her blade into a vital artery or organ with a single quick thrust. Shandala was even learning to send a blade no broader than her little finger through the thickest armour without blunting the weapon or weakening the blow.

Though her previous training was not as intensive or painful as that endured by her classmates, Lydia quickly came to surpass her peers in many ways, especially in handling of swords, and in the many arts of unarmed combat. Within months she was crossing swords with students two or even three years her senior, besting even these opponents in most matches. Only Master Han and the eldest students could reliably outmatch Lydia with a sword.

She came to prefer the katana over the sparring and longer swords of her home land. It was shorter than the long swords, broadswords and two-handed great swords that the knights of Talvon or Danith would use, and while those weapons could be used with great efficiency in the open, a short katana was superior in cramped conditions. Katana could be honed to a razor-edge, and though the swords were not designed to fight the heavily armoured, their blades were sturdy. Lydia, though practical experience, found them to be the deadliest weapon in the small rooms where combat was taught in the Great School. Still, she practiced with other weapons as well, in particular the Euralian broadsword, a thicker blade than the katana, straight and tapering to a broader point but with two edges, rather than one. Behind her back, the other students quietly mocked the foreign girl for using this weapon, seen as crude by eastern swordsmen, but Lydia had seen its full potential in the hands of Braide and her father, when they had sparred upon the deck of the *Julia* to the amusement of the crew. While the katana could cut on one edge, the broadsword could cut on two, and this effectively more than doubled the weapon's potential uses in an unconfined area. Also, the broadsword's blade could be gripped in one hand while the other remained on the hilt, effectively turning the whole weapon turned into a short spear of sorts, which could punch through light armours and poorly-made mail.

Lydia came to learn the language and customs of Nara well. Shandala was an excellent tutor in these. But Lydia had shared the company of men her entire life, and she had little experience with women of any sort, let alone a girl her own age. At first, Lydia found it difficult to understand the girl's motivations and interests. But as time passed, they became close friends, often sharing secret jokes and whispering well into the night, when the younger monks would patrol the quiet hallways, harshly demanding silence and sleep from the students. Shandala had developed a crush on an older student, a boy whom she would not name to Lydia, but for whom she endlessly pined. She even attempted to recruit Lydia into assisting her in a poorly-planned scheme to sneak to the boy's room in the late night, so that she could profess her love for him and pursue its consummation. Lydia humoured the girl by listening, but she also knew that to be caught unsupervised in private with a student of the opposite sex was absolutely forbidden, and violations were dealt with through draconian punishment. When Shandala began to make firmer plans to see the boy, Lydia quickly distanced herself from any action that would violate the school's strict rules.

Lydia had problems of her own, but Shandala would never have guessed of their existence. For Shandala, their whispered late-night conversations and secret sharing was a bit of rebellious fun to be had with her exotic and stormy friend. For Lydia they were something far different. When Shandala finally fell asleep, often with a small smile upon her lips, Lydia would lie on her mat, stiff, staring at the invisible ceiling: waiting. And she was never made to wait long.

First there was the image of her father, slumping to the deck, bristling with arrows, back to Lydia, eyes hidden from her in his last moments. The line of bodies upon the deck. Then Mrs Habden, wielding the heavy boarding axe, comical in a horrible way. Not only could Lydia see the scene clearly before her eyes, she could hear the woman's bellows, her own screams of terror and rage as the pirate horde dragged the struggling woman to a death without dignity. Lydia could feel the blow from Moad. Her fingers would reach behind her head, feeling where the lump had been, where the she had been struck and denied the death at her father's side that she so longed for. And finally there was the bloated, cheerful, deceitful face of the Lord of Rimbu. Night after night she looked into his fat-enfolded eyes, and she would fall into a fantasy of death, killing him a different way every time. Always there was the karinga, hacking at the man's grinning face or slitting open his vast swollen gut, spilling his intestines before his shocked eyes. The rush of power, the memory of the joy she felt as it drank Captain Dheree's life intermingled with the roaring flames of her hatred. Lydia would awake burning with rage and anger, taught muscles aching but still twitching with murderous desire. Her hand would long for the hilt of the karinga, and she could still feel it pulsing in her grip for long after it had vanished, along with the rest of her dreams.

Taking a weapon into her hand in the morning sword training session was like dancing with those fantasies; it made her dreams melt into waking. The Lord of Rimbu's face, freed from her tortured nights, would replace her opponent's visage, driving her into a cold fighting madness. Summoned by the chant of ringing steel, Lydia would slip into an all-seeing, all-hearing trance during which reason gave to instinct and swordsmanship and her soul was consumed with unrelenting, pitiless bloodlust. In defeating her opponents living, she defeated that evil visage that haunted her, if only for a moment.

Whether her blades cut too deeply and she spilled too much blood on the sandy floors of the practice rooms began to matter little to her.

Indeed, as the months passed it became increasingly difficult for Lydia to resist driving her blade home into the bodies of her practice partners, and the other students began fear her, for they could sense the anger seething below the surface of her calm face, see it burning in her large, dark eyes. And yet they could find no way in which to use this anger to unbalance the westerner. She would smile inwardly when her blade bit into an unprotected shoulder or flank, for just an instant, before she regained herself. The effect was unnerving.

Lydia had never before taken pleasure in causing pain to others, and had only acted in violence to defend herself, with the exception of her wounding of Braide with the oak clubs, an act for which she still felt deeply hidden shame. But as she vanquished each opponent on the sparring floor, Lydia felt the pain in her heart turn to cold hatred, steely determination, providing relief from the hot agony of sorrow. Her mastery of arms became a form of narcotic, allowing her to drive the painful memories from her mind, and daily punish the wrong-doers that had unhinged her life.

But by the time evening came, Lydia would have spent much of the anger that welled out from her dreams and flooded her day. The small part of her heart that was still a young girl's longed for Shandala's whispers, for her one chance to grasp normalcy before the night terrors began again and the burning anger rekindled.

After two seasons, and the nearly forgotten fifteenth day of her birth, Lydia had surpassed most of the students who studied under Master Han, so that almost every day when she sparred, it was with the Master himself, for even the eldest of his pupils bore the scars of her blade. The Master watched his star student develop with a combination of enthusiasm and concern. He understood the fervour behind her relentless pursuit of excellence, and in his regular meeting with Lord Zhe's messenger, Master Han confidently stated that Lydia would far surpass the Lord's expectations. But Han also confessed that he was still concerned that Lydia only learned to kill so that she could exact vengeance upon one man, rather than with the more acceptable, and controllable motives of loyalty or ambition, or even for the love of the act itself.

After an evening session during which he had nearly been unstrung by the girl's katana, Master Han went to the chamber of Master Nhil, and the two elder assassins discussed her long into the night. When Master Han returned to his austere cell Shandala was just slipping into sleep and Lydia was awaiting her night of remembrance and anger. The Master hung his sword, the magical blade that would turn to mystical fire as it struck, from its pegs on the wall. He sat at a small writing table where he composed a letter to Lord Zhe personally, a man he had served with slavish devotion for his entire life.

ELEVEN

Several weeks later Master Han appeared for his morning session with Lydia's class, trailing an unknown man. He had called all of those students of the long blade to his practice room where they sat in three silent rows, awaiting their master. Lydia, as one of the younger intermediate students, sat in the middle row, behind the young men and women who were closer to graduation.

The new man was not a monk. He wore his hair unshaven, in a long plait, and his clothes were the expensive silk gowns of a nobleman. Though his hair was touched with silver, his eyes were youthful. He was taller than any Naran that Lydia had seen, and moved with the regal elegance and power of a male lion in his prime, secure in the knowledge of his ultimate supremacy. Afterwards, Lydia heard it said that he was considered devastatingly handsome by the girls. He wore a katana in his belt, with a glittering ruby set in its pommel, the size of a hen's egg.

The man drew his sheathed sword from his belt and sat upon a low cushion across from the rows of waiting students while Master Han stood slightly behind him, in a sure sign of deference. Master Han gave a short bow and addressed the students.

"This man is one of the greatest swordsmen in the service of his most Glorious Magnificence, the Emperor of Nara. His blade has vanquished more enemies of the Empire than any ten of you could ever hope to slay. He has been sent here today to test the best of you, to make sure that when your emperor calls upon your services you are not found lacking in skill or loyalty. You will find that his sword is not like mine—if it bites you, it will draw your blood. And my lord is not a man to feel pity for the weak." With this, Master Han clapped his hands, signifying the start of the formal lesson, and the stranger rose to his feet, unsheathing his sword in a fluid gesture and placing the scabbard to the side. He paced the length of the room, studying the first row of students, the eldest, with an arrogance that made many of the pupils hunger for the chance to prove themselves to this peacock. He strode to the end of the line and bowed before Damio, the eldest and most lethal of the senior students. Damio sprung to his feet, bowed gracefully before the stranger, and took two katana from the wall.

Damio was one of the rare swordsmen who possessed the ability to use two blades at once, with equal effectiveness. His speed and skill was near inhuman, and he was easily capable of defeating the most advanced students in the school. Even Lydia struggled to defeat the boy, and she had taken many cuts and punctures to the healer as a result of her sessions with him. She also despised Damio; he was aware of his superiority and took great pride in demonstrating his prowess, often inflicting serious and unnecessary wounds on his opponents and laughing at their pain. In the two seasons Lydia had attended the school, Damio had slain two of his classmates. But it was the boy's posturing and malicious manner outside of the sparring ring that Lydia most abhorred; she had quickly come to realise that death in combat was just one of the many results of failure at the school, and she could forgive the boy the lives he had taken in the ring. But being a bully was a far different and inferior act to proving oneself in combat, and it was a despicable sign of weakness in her eyes. Damio was a terrible bully.

To compound Lydia's hatred, only the night before Shandala had finally revealed that he was the boy she had become enamoured with, in a hushed, fervent whisper. He had shown no interest in Shandala whatsoever, at least that Lydia had seen, and the silliness of Shandala's plans had started to truly vex Lydia. Thus it was with some satisfaction that she watched the two opponents face each other, weapons drawn, eyes locked in a struggle to divine their opponent's intentions before the first move was made.

The contest was over so quickly that Master Han had little to discuss with the class afterwards. Damio waited for the stranger's first thrust, parrying with his left hand blade, and swung his right hand katana in a lethal arc towards the stranger's unprotected left arm. The man simply bent away from the blade and let the razor tip pass within a hand's span of his chest. He followed his lean backwards, balancing on one bent leg and bringing his other foot crashing up into Damio's groin. Briefly stunned by the pain of the blow, Damio staggered backwards, raising his dual blades in defence as he struggled to regain his composure, even as the man nimbly sprung to his feet. Resuming an aggressive stance, one sword held over his head and the other across his middle, Damio approached his opponent a second time, more carefully, seeking to entice the man into another attack so that Damio could again try to parry with one blade and strike with the other. The newcomer circled for a moment, walking almost casually, with the slightest smile on his lips, eyes full of fire and mirth. Then in a flash the stranger exploded into attack; from the furthest reach of his katana his blade swept outwards in a shimmering arc, so fast that Damio had only begun to raise his left sword in defence as razor-sharp tip of the man's blade drove towards his throat. Damio continued to raise his sword for a moment after the blade's tip passed, and then started to stagger backwards, a stupefied look on his haughty face. He stumbled and a red crease formed across his neck where the blade had cleanly passed through the flesh without touching bone. A blow that would invariably kill, without leaving the slaying weapon embedded in bone. A perfect strike.

As Damio fell to his knees, dropping his swords and fumbled to close the wound to his throat with desperate hands, the man strode over to where he had dropped his scabbard, retrieved it, wiped his blade clean on Damio's slumping shoulders, and then sheathed his weapon with a metallic click. The stranger turned then to face the students and spoke in a quiet voice of great strength, clear above the dying rattles of the student at his feet.

"I am Lord Zhe, the eldest son of the Emperor, heir to the throne of Nara, and lord of this school. This—" with the point of his foot he rolled the faintly struggling body of Damio onto his stomach, before continuing, "would-be assassin was to leave this school at the next new moon. He had accepted his first assignment already, an assignment that was to test his loyalty to the man he thought his master. That man, a general of my father's army, would slay a man known to be dear to me. What this . . . " again Lord Zhe jabbed his foot into the now-lifeless body, "failed to understand is that *I* am his master, and no one else, other than the Emperor."

The students, stunned to see their best so quickly dispatched, all nodded in unison, eyes full of awe and fear.

"Now, who is Lydia?" Lydia felt her heart stop at Lord Zhe's query. An icy sweat broke upon her brow, and her bowels turned liquid. She rose, eyes to the floor, desperately trying to discern what transgression she might be punished for, but finding nothing.

Seeing the look on her stricken face, Lord Zhe gave a short laugh. "Do not fear, my child, I know of no one dear to me that you have tried to kill, other than Master Han. I wish to speak with you. Come." With that, he turned and strode from the room, never turning to see if his ward followed, apparently knowing that this command, like all of his orders, was being instantly obeyed. As she hurried after Lord Zhe, she heard Master Han begin the rest of his lesson: "Now, class, what we can learn from that is that you should never be too sure of yourself."

The trembling girl followed the broad shoulders of Lord Zhe to a small cloister, open to the sky, and elegantly gardened in the formal and controlled style of the east. There was a dwarf orange tree in the garden. When it had been in blossom the heavenly scent had filled the corridors and classrooms nearby. Now it was hung with fruit, strictly forbidden to the students.

Lord Zhe again pulled his sword from his belt and laid it upon a bench of the same yellow stone as the school was built. He strode to the tree and pulled two oranges from the lower branches. Lydia stood a few paces away, stiffy upright but eyes upon the ground, unsure how to conduct herself around the famous and powerful man. He sat upon the bench, next to his sword, put the oranges down and placed the sword across his lap, making room for Lydia to sit. When she did not move, he patted the seat and said, "Come child, do not be afraid. What have you done to fear me?"

Lydia sat, hands upon her lap and gaze still cast downwards while Lord Zhe took a small knife from his pants and deftly peeled both oranges. He handed one to Lydia and kept the other, pulling it apart and eating it in silence, segment by segment. Lydia, afraid of the cane strokes she would receive for eating the forbidden fruit, but more afraid of offending the leonine man beside her, hesitantly started to eat.

Lord Zhe finished his orange, and patiently waited for Lydia to finish hers, though she did start to swallow larger and larger mouthfuls of the delicate fruit when she became aware the man was waiting for her to finish before speaking. When the last juicy segment was gone the man turned in his seat, facing Lydia, and looked at her intently.

"Did it upset you, watching me dispatch that traitor?" Lord Zhe's eyes were even darker than Lydia's, quick and intelligent, and utterly unfathomable. He gazed into her. She felt as if he was seeing into her mind, straight into her soul, and unlocking all the secrets therein.

"No, my lord. He was . . . unpleasant. But—" Lord Zhe smiled, not unkindly, as Lydia faltered. She felt slightly emboldened.

"But what, child? Speak your mind with me, always. It is both my command and my pleasure."

"I was just surprised, my Lord, at the speed of it."

"Justice is often swift, my child, and often brutal. Tell me, why do you think I have sponsored you at this school?"

"I do not know my lord. I have often wondered why a man as great as you would bother himself with me."

"It is because we both seek the same thing, Lydia. What do you think that is?"

Lydia strove for an answer. Her mind raced over all the possibilities, but she could find nothing suitable. But then the words came to her, remembered from many lessons.

"To . . . serve the Emperor, my lord." At this, Lord Zhe laughed deeply, and patted the girl paternally on the knee.

"You've learned the lessons of the school well, my child. But that is not the right answer, for there is something we both desire, even more than the pleasure of serving my great father. And you know what it is that we seek. It is what tortures you, drives you."

"*Revenge!*" The word that so dominated her life of late slipped from her lips before she even knew what she was saying, in a ghastly, spectral whisper. She looked quickly to the face of the man beside her, afraid that he would feel betrayed that her greatest desire did not involve service to the land of Nara. The man was still smiling, gently, and Lydia felt the pressure of his hand increase upon her knee. Where she would have been alarmed at this touch from another man, Lord Zhe's intimacy reminded Lydia of her father's firm but gentle manner.

"Yes, child, that is one word for it. But I have another word, a better one. The word you are seeking is Justice, not Revenge. Revenge is just an unthinking response to a perceived wrong. There is no restoration of balance, no betterment of Life, no rightness in Revenge. It is nothing more than a brute response to a brute act. But Justice . . . well, that is something different. For, to mete Justice, you must yourself be Just. Whereas Revenge seeks only to injure one as you have been injured, Justice seeks to punish and repair the damage an act of evil does to the entire world. Justice is a far nobler goal than mere Revenge, don't you agree?" Lydia nodded, automatically.

"Though I am the second man of the Empire, and as the heir to the throne I command the imperial courts and armies in my father's name, I often find myself unable to act against those who would disrupt the order of things. Politics can be terrible shackles, and often I am forced to turn a blind eye upon grave wrongs in order to maintain the peace of the realm. But, wrongs unpunished multiply like rats, and would soon overwhelm us. Thus, I must be able to strike at wrong-doers, unseen, but still strong, still in the name of Justice. I need you, your skill, your dedication and your pure heart at my side, to win the Justice that I cannot in the courts. You are to be my hand in these matters, Lydia. I would trust few others as I trust you. Do you see?"

For a reason she didn't understand, Lydia had started to silently weep. This man's wisdom, his kind but firm sense of fairness was too close to her father's, still looming so large upon her memory. Through the veil of tears, Lydia nodded.

"That is why I have had you saved from those pirates; for yes, I did know of you upon that ship, of your plight, and I sent the frigate to recapture your father's ship. I had you sent here to learn, so that when you are a woman you can go forth and gain your own Justice for the wrong that was done to you. Do you understand?"

"Yes, my lord. Thank you." Her voice sounded weak, irresolute through her sobs, and she placed her hand upon Lord Zhe's, clinging to the small hint of her father's solidity and strength that she sensed in the man.

"Lydia, I have brought you a gift. It is something dear to me, and I entrust it to you, for though we have only just met, I know we will become great friends. He took his hand from her knee, and placed his sword in her lap. For a moment, Lydia thought he wished for her to hold the blade while he produced some trinket, but when he sat still, awaiting her response, she realised that he had given her his katana.

"My lord, sir, I don't know what to say. It is so beautiful; how can I accept it?" Her fingertips ran over the smooth lacquered scabbard, over the grip adorned with its large, blood red ruby.

"You can accept it because you will use it to slay our enemies, my dear. Those people who would do wrong to us, to the righteous." She nodded, her eyes again full of tears.

"Yes, my lord, I will. Thank you, my lord."

"Now, Lydia, I have come here today for two reasons. The first is to deal with that traitor, Damio. You now hold the blade that despatched that dog, and many, many others like him. The second is because Master Han has written to me, saying that day by day you grow more strained, more worn, and that while you become more deadly which each lesson, he fears that you will soon collapse, or that your fervour will lead you into a fatal mistake."

"My lord, I am—" He cut off her objection with a raised hand.

"No, no child, do not object. I know of your nightly struggles, of your dreams of revenge. This is not the way to overcome those who would prevent you from winning Justice for yourself, for your father. You must sleep, and soundly, for in a few moons you will face your first test. If you fail in this, the next time I see you will be at your graveside. Tonight, after the evening meal, you are to go to the chamber of Mistress Amalin, who has prepared a vial for you. Three drops upon the tongue, and you will dream only of happiness and contentment. The magic of the vial to bring you joy in your sleep is greater even than the power of your hatred, thought it seems boundless."

When she had secured her new sword in the cell she shared with Shandala, Lydia returned to her lessons, well aware of the curious stares of the other students as they went about the day's activities. During the evening meal, sitting beside the unusually sullen Shandala, Lydia was absorbed in her own thoughts. Why had Lord Zhe chosen her? How did he know about her?

Shandala was lost in her own thoughts. The two often kicked each other under the table in silent rebellion against the strict rules of the hall that forbade interaction between students while food was upon the tables, but a rift had formed between the two friends. Shandala would not even meet Lydia's eyes. Lydia was so immersed in her own concerns that she dismissed the other girl's distance, and never connected it to Damio's death.

After dinner, Lydia sought Mistress Amalin in her chamber. The elderly woman responded hastily to Lydia's subdued hail, drawing the curtain aside and inviting the girl to enter. Lydia knew that she had been a source of some frustration to Mistress Amalin, for she possessed almost no interest in or capacity for magic, other than learning how to avoid its effects. On her part, Mistress Amalin sensed a great resident power in Lydia, something buried deep within the girl, and unlike anything she had encountered before. What she saw in the girl was not like the raw power of those destined to become Magi, or even the more subtle forces of those who could learn to use their mystic abilities to kill or heal with the help of potions, salves and dusts. Deep within the girl was something mysterious, powerful, and brooding. Despite her own vast lore and deadly skills, Mistress Amalin was afraid of Lydia.

She bade the girl sit on a small cushion, facing the brazier in the centre of her chamber. The elderly woman took a vial from a table against the wall and handed it down to Lydia. She then sank to the floor next to the girl, occupying the same position Lord Zhe had so many hours before.

"Lydia, the whole school has been gossiping about your meeting with Lord Zhe. The students are all curious about the nature of your time with Lord Zhe, and many think you may have had a hand in the death of Damio . . . " Mistress Amalin quickly placed her hand on the girl's shoulder when the student rose in shock. Emotion played across her face, something Amalin was unused to in her pupils.

"But Madame, I had nothing to do with it!"

"Yes, Lydia, I know this. We, the teachers, know this. But despite his . . . shortcomings . . . Damio was well-liked by many in the school who admired his skill. He was a fine swordsman, the best we have seen here for many years, but his pride was his foible, and it cost him his life. To think he could act against the wishes of Lord Zhe, even indirectly," she shook her head in wonder, "this was folly indeed. Nonetheless, I have been asked by Master Nhil and the others to warn you that when you next practice with the small blade or the bow, your opponent may not be seeking to withhold their blow."

It was obvious from the interplay of emotions on the girl's face that Lydia, who had shown a sort of growing elation throughout the day after her meeting with Lord Zhe, felt herself plummet into the familiar depths of fear. Mistress Amalin patted the back of her head with an ancient hand and clucked in sympathy and mild approbation.

"Now child, you are here to learn to kill. And no one here who wears the white robes has as much potential as you. I am sure you will do just fine. Just remember, your life is dedicated to the intricate plot, the hidden knife, the silent blow, and we, the teachers, would not be serving the best interests of the school if we were to interfere. The strongest must survive. We cannot help you. Now, you place three drops of that philtre upon your tongue, and never mind the bitter taste. It will hold the night terrors at bay, but leave you aware enough to defend yourself should you be beset during your sleep."

When Lydia returned to her cell she found Shandala already on her mat, facing the wall. Thinking her roommate and friend was asleep, Lydia silently stripped off her white robes, bathed quickly and was about to place the first of the three drops on her tongue when she heard Shandala roll over. The girl's face was soaked with tears.

"He was so . . . beautiful. Why did you betray him? He never did anything to you!"

"I didn't betray him, Shandala. Why would I have done that? He was nothing to me." Lydia's dismissal came out sterner than she had intended.

"That's not what everyone is saying. They say you betrayed him to curry favour with Lord Zhe, to make up for being so . . . different to us."

"It's not true! I didn't even know Damio, other than from sword training."

"That's not what they are saying . . . you've got your reward, hanging on the wall there. You can say what you want, but we know the truth." Shandala turned again to the wall, and lay quietly sobbing to herself. Lydia felt a flush of emotions, but overwhelming them all was disgust at being the subject of petty gossip and conjecture, and her friend's mulish crush on someone as unworthy as Damio.

Lydia ignored Shandala's tears as her mind raced across the faces and names of the students who obviously loved or at least liked Damio enough to seek revenge for his death. The list was not long, but then Lydia had quickly learned that the people of Nara do not demonstrate affection or loyalty in the open and public way of the west, and she often had difficulty in determining who was loyal to whom in the student body. As an outsider, consumed with her own demons and driven by an unquenchable thirst for revenge, Lydia had been too involved in her own affairs to pay much attention to the social networks of the school anyhow. She would have to mistrust everyone, starting with the girl who shared her room, and her life for the last half year. The girl who could disappear in and emerge from shadows like a ghost and drive her needle-like blade through a victim's heart, without warning or sound.

Lydia placed three bitter drops of Mistress Amalin's potion on her tongue, took Lord Zhe's katana from the wall and placed it beside of her mat and lay with her hand upon the hilt, the egg-sized ruby reassuringly pressed against her. Her mind kept leaping from possible assassin to possible assassin, until sleep finally overtook her. She lay in a death-like state, but with her mind never truly abandoning its vigil, and her ears never ceasing their endless groping search for a cautious footstep in the night. Though her consciousness, cradled by the magic of Mistress Amalin's potion, drifted off into happy dreams of her childhood, and of the wondrous places she had witnessed in her travels, her right hand never left the hilt of her sword, and in her left she clutched the vial of sleeping potion, so that no unseen assassin could taint the contents.

TWELVE

The following morning, preparations began for the school's annual examinations. Much had been said about this event to Lydia, often in hushed whispers. Over the last weeks, as the event approached, the school became even quieter, students spending far more time and energy at their studies. Prior to her meeting with Lord Zhe, Lydia paid little attention to talk of the trials, as she had been grappling with the ghosts of her past, and now, with the possibility of deadly enemies lurking among those with whom she had grown so familiar, she continued to think of the examinations as some abstract, theoretical exercise. Lydia arose to find that Shandala had already left at some point during the night. Lydia performed her morning toilet, donned white robes and set out in the few moments she had left before the morning's routine started. In her mind were hopes of finding her friend and convincing Shandala of her innocence in yesterday's killing. She came across the girl in a practice court, sparring with another girl their age, Arsanda, a student of the small blade and the long, braided leather whip. Shandala had just deflected a thrust to her face from Arsanda's long, thin knife, and had brought one of her thin blades into a killing position, thus ending the match as Lydia entered the room. The two opponents bowed to each other, and then parted. Shandala brushed past Lydia, pretending to not even see her roommate. Lydia began to reach out to her friend, to hold her by the shoulder, but there was something in the girl's carriage, the stiff way that she walked past and carried her blades unsheathed that caused Lydia to withdraw her hand. Instead of calling out to Shandala, Lydia, heart awash in conflicting emotion, watched the girl stalk from the room.

At the morning meal, Shandala was still silent, remote, and Lydia began to feel the first renewed stirrings of the anger she had experienced the previous night. It was ridiculous, childish of the girl to suspect her, and Lydia felt herself tiring of the girl's cold shoulder.

Shandala and her opponent from the morning were not the only students who were practicing their deadly studies with extra vigour. For the students in the other colleges of the great school, failure of an examination meant immediate expulsion from the school. Students in the College of Black Arts faced examination by combat, very real combat, and the losers left the school for their graves, not the ignominy of expulsion. As the fortnight progressed Lydia found herself without a partner for practice, so she sought the company of Master Han, who obliged the girl by sending her into writhing agony time after time with his mystic sword, dispatching her with steely silence that somehow spoke of disdain.

At the end of the fortnight the students were summoned into a great hall. The gallery was lit with blazing torches and braziers the size of wagon wheels, so that the yellow stone walls were cast red from the glow of fire. In the room, seated in the familiar pose upon the floor were the instructors, monks of death. Master Nhil, sitting slightly before the others, was in the centre, as appropriate for his position as the Dean of the College. He sat in contemplation as the students filed in, assembling in four long rows facing their elders. When the last, youngest of the students, not much beyond eight years of age, entered, he looked up, clapped his hands to initiate the formal session, and spoke in a strong, clear voice.

"Students, the time has come. For those of you who have never undertaken the Examination, it is this ritual that allows us to ensure that those who graduate the school are indeed the finest in the land at the arts we have all come here to study. Today, you will each face an opponent, one of your own rank, in combat. You may use every skill, every trick you have learned to prevail. When the match begins, there are no rules. In the end, only one may leave the room of examination. Tomorrow, those who survive will be given the name of another student, whom you shall slay, or be slain by, before the end of the day. On the third day, you will have passed the Examination, or perished. This is the way of the school, and it has been so for as long as this College has been convened. Go now to your cells; spend your time in contemplation of your trial, and await your summons."

In their tiny cell, Shandala and Lydia sat silently, trying to appear as if they were ignoring each other, when in fact they were straining every sense other than sight to determine the others' condition. Lydia's thoughts raced. Inwardly she asked, *Will it be she that I'll fight? She truly wishes me dead, and that will give her an advantage. Is she afraid? Does she sense my fear?*

After an eternity of waiting the curtain to their cell was drawn. One of the younger monks stood grimly in the doorway.

"Lydia, follow me. It is time."

As she rose, took Lord Zhe's sword from its pegs on the wall and started to follow the monk down the corridor, Lydia heard Shandala whisper, loud enough to be clearly heard by her roommate, but strangled with anger and hatred. "Justice will be done!"

Lydia was led to a room used for lessons, a square chamber, twelve paces on a side. The centre of the low ceiling was open to the midday sun, which filled the room with a warm glow. Sitting in a row at the far side of the room was Master Han, Master Nhil, and another figure, robed and hooded so that his face was hidden from view, appearing only as a black void in the opening of the scarlet cowl. He was large and broad of shoulder, and Lydia found herself hoping with an anxious heart that it was her master, come to see his protégé prevail.

Along one wall was a table upon which were laid rows of deadly weapons, bottles of poisons and magical essences, and various pieces of armour. Lydia strode to the table, handling several of the weapons before choosing a long, thick-bladed dagger to complement her katana, as well as four light but razor-sharp throwing knives. She tested the balance of these blades and rejected two of them as being slightly too heavy in the blade. Finished, she arranged her weapons in her belt. She briefly considered armour, particularly neck protection or a hardened leather chest guard, but in the end rejected the idea of protective gear. Lydia knew all too well that the bulk and restriction of movement caused by the heavy protective equipment could give a real advantage to a quick unarmoured opponent trained in the ways of assassination.

Leaving the table, she stood before her two instructors and the hooded figure, bowed deeply, then waited to discover the identity of her opponent. Lydia kept her eyes fixed upon the wall above the others' heads, struggling to keep her heart still and her thoughts from racing to panic. She hoped that her fear was not noticeable to those whom she knew were watching her.

Shortly another student entered, went to the table, and gathered weapons. It was a boy, nearly a year older than Lydia, named Myandar. Lydia did not know him well; he was a withdrawn and sullen student who spent much time with Master Nhil, studying the areas of black magic most useful to the assassin. Lydia felt a weakness in her bowels; it was magic that she understood the least, and thus feared the most. She knew she could defeat any opponent her age with a bladed weapon, and that she would be able to cross the distance of the small room and dispatch even the fastest archer before they could knock an arrow, draw their bow and fire. But magic was different; it was wildly unpredictable.

The boy had gathered three long, tapered daggers from the table, taking two in his right hand and one in his left. He came to stand next to Lydia, and both students bowed to their elders. Master Nhil clapped his hands, and the three spectators rose, moving to far edge of the room before resuming their cross-legged position on the floor. Lydia and Myandar, knowing this was the signal to begin, assumed their starting positions. Lydia took a place near the centre of the room, knowing that she needed to close with her opponent to bring her katana into effective play. Before she could move to strike, Myandar backed away, deftly flicking the three daggers he carried into the air and juggled them. When all three blades were in constant motion, he dropped one hand to his side, and raised the other to his forehead. Rather than falling to the floor, the daggers rose and floated around the boy's head. Lydia, fearing his next move, took one hand from her katana's hilt and drew the dagger from her belt, holding both the thick knife and her katana in loose readiness.

She did not have to wait for long. The boy smiled at her and with a gesture from his free hand sent one of the daggers streaking towards Lydia's chest. The blade flew point first, thrust by invisible force as quickly as an arrow. Lydia swept her katana across her torso and caught the blade just before it plunged home. Myandar's dagger spun to the side and clattered to the floor, but after a moment rose, and plunged towards Lydia's flank. This time, she caught the blade in a parry with her dagger, and then fell backwards and to the side just in time to avoid the second of the boy's blades as it streaked for her stomach.

For what seemed to be an eternity, Lydia stood her ground in the centre of the room, bathed in the warm midday sunlight that streamed through the opening in the ceiling, fighting against the unseen hand of the boy sorcerer who directed his onslaught from the safety of the room's periphery. As her fight progressed, Lydia learned that the two blades would not come at her in unison, but rather one at a time, and so learned that Myandar was incapable of directing two attacks at once. Dodging a blade that sought to slash her throat and leaping a wide swinging blow to her heel, Lydia stole a glance at the boy who still stood at the edge of the room, his brow furrowed in concentration, one hand to his forehead and the other orchestrating the blades. His face has red, and he was lightly sweating from the mental exertion his attacks must demand. The last dagger floated about his head like a deadly steel butterfly. As her attention returned to the silent blades that circled her, seeking an opening, she saw the third blade race from its position by the boy's right ear in a silver streak, thrusting straight for her forehead. Lydia caught the blade with her katana and sent it spinning across the room, but was unable to keep track of three blades at once, and as the third dagger spun away the first deeply scored her left arm. Lydia felt cold steel cutting through her, sliding cleanly through flesh, but well before the pain of the wound hit her, she was struck with the sudden realisation that she could easily lose this match, and her life, to the boy in the corner. She felt a flush of anger, and weaved in time to send the second blade shooting past her right ear, an instant before it would have buried itself into her neck.

Unable to think of another defence, Lydia drew in a deep breath and released an ear-splitting scream, her high voice lending such a pitch to the sound that it nearly caused pain to those in the room. She dropped her katana and dove to the floor, rolling in the direction of Myandar, hoping that the sudden noise would have shaken her opponent's concentration enough that he would fail to have his daggers following her. At the end of her roll, not more than three paces from Myandar, she sprung to her feet and sent her own dagger spinning into the boy's chest. He fell back against the wall, eyes suddenly wide and full of fear, gravely injured but still concentrating on guiding his deadly missiles, though with a shaking hand. Lydia was nearly flung to the floor at his feet when one of his blades struck her from behind, lancing into her left shoulder, the point driving though the front of her chest. Ignoring the instant agony of the wound, she pulled the throwing knives from her belt, holding them in an almost senseless left hand and throwing them one after the other into the boy's chest with her right. His hands dropped as he slumped to the floor, and Lydia heard the two remaining daggers fall. One, streaking from behind towards her spine fell to the ground between her feet and slid into the space between the two students. Lydia stooped, took the blade in her right hand, and cleanly slashed Myandar's throat. Then, suddenly weighed by the fatigue of blood loss and the shock of her injuries, Lydia staggered back to the centre of the room and bowed before the three spectators, who had watched the battle with impassive interest. Lord Nhil rose to his feet, returned the girl's bow, and clapped his hands. Five servants raced into the room, one to guide Lydia to the healer's room, and the others to remove the crumpled form of Myandar and prepare the body for its return to the boy's family, rich money lenders from the city of Nambo, far to the north.

Lydia wavered in the sunlight, hot blood pumping from her back and chest, slick where it flowed in a sheet from the wound in her arm. The room spun, and her vision began to recede into a deep tunnel when she felt the servant's hands upon her, holding her up, drawing her away. She was too near death to rejoice in surviving.

In the chamber that served as quarters for the school's healer, Lydia was laid upon a mat alongside a score of her classmates, some superficially cut or bruised, but others gravely wounded, burnt by magical fires, pierced by an arrow or crossbow's bolt, or slashed deeply. One of the healer's assistants, a student from the College of Healing, removed the knife that still jutted from Lydia's back, mopped blood from the punctures and bandaged the clotting wounds. When the young man moved to the next casualty, Lydia lay back upon the mat, and waited for the healer, an elderly man with a long, thin white beard that reached to his belt line and kindly, glittering eyes that always seemed amused, even when his patient was passing into the next life.

She had grown duller and more lightheaded from the pain of her wounds and loss of the blood that soaked through her bandages when the healer leaned over her, gently pulling the dressings from her shoulder, fingering the slash to her arm and whistling quietly to himself as he probed the hole in her chest.

"I hope the other person looks worse than you, Lydia."

She said nothing, and the man shook his head, knowing that the girl's shock could overwhelm her, or at least leave her unprepared for the test that would occur tomorrow, the test of stealth and strategy, far more deadly than that day's open, face-to-face conflict. He rose, bustled off to his storeroom, and returned to the nearly insensate girl, carrying a small glass jar containing a deep purple, slimy substance. He knelt over Lydia, gently squeezing her uninjured shoulder to recall her to consciousness.

"Tomorrow you'll have to fight again, but tonight you'll rest. If you are to have enough strength to survive tomorrow's test, I'll have to use this on you. It is the Devil's Cure, made of a dozen deadly poisons mixed in perfect proportion, each lending its evil to create a life-saving mixture." He pulled an oiled calf-skin glove on his hand and unstoppered the jar. The smell was vile. Both the healer and Lydia struggled to swallow their rising gorges as hints of rotten flesh, burning hair and brimstone filled the air about them. He sunk his fingers into the jar and pulled them out, coated in the foul slime, which he quickly slathered over Lydia's injuries, even pressing the purple medicine into the punctures in her chest. Where the medicine touched it burned as if it were made of fire. Lydia's body arched off the mat in a pain-induced spasm, and she was flung back into full consciousness as much by the sound of her own ear-splitting screams as the flaming agony of her shoulder.

The healer pressed her down and called for the assistant to help as Lydia tried to tear at her wounds with bare fingers. The two men held her until the pain started to fade to a point where it was only just bearable. The old man chuckled to himself as the girl's body relaxed beneath his hands.

"Now, now Lydia, at least you will live to fight another day." As he moved to the next patient tears streamed down the girl's face, and she prayed silently for unconsciousness that would not come.

Throughout the day bodies were brought into the healer's quarters, some living, some passing, and many already gone. Few received the painful ointment that had pulled Lydia back from the brink, and from the attentive assistant she learned that the medicine was rare, powerful, expensive, and only used for the most grave of wounds, to save the most worthy of patients. The ointment varied in its effect on her injuries; at times it was merely uncomfortably hot and otherwise caused numbness, but then the heat would grow until Lydia feared that it had turned to acid and was searing into her healthy flesh. At these times the pain became so intense that she tried to see if her shoulder was actually burning. But the powerful poisons worked in concert as the healer had described, and by evening Lydia's injuries had closed, leaving only thin red seams where gaping wounds had been and a persistent numbness and angry swelling in her shoulder.

Shortly before the evening meal, Lydia was visited by the man in the red robes who had observed her battle. She was struggling with a renewed bout of burning in her shoulder, her body held rigidly to resist writhing in agony and eyes clamped shut, fighting a flood of tears. The man walked directly into the room, concealed face passing briefly over the patients stretched upon the mats until he found Lydia. Her eyes opened as the man approached; she could not see his face, but she recognized his gait, his imperious stride. For a moment, her tortured heart leaped in excitement. It was her father, she was sure of it.

Feverishly, Lydia struggled to rise from her mat, to embrace the man that she knew must be dead, but her pain was too great and she fell back in renewed agony. The man knelt at her side and placed a hand upon her forehead. It was cool, smooth, almost soft skinned, but with iron strength underlying, a hand unused to labour other than that of wielding a sword, but of great power. The man spoke to her in Naran, and gently pressed her back to the mat.

"Lydia, it is I, Lord Zhe. I came today to witness your examination. I had to know if you were all that I had been told." Lydia, who had known in her inner heart that it was impossible for her father to live, nonetheless gained some relief in her mentor's presence. *How like my father he is . . .* she thought to herself. Aloud, she managed to croak a barely audible, "Were you pleased, my lord?"

"Yes, my dear, I was. You will be a powerful woman, soon. I am told that the boy you defeated was one of the deadliest in the school, and that with the death of Damio and he, there will be no one to match you with in next year's examination. Perhaps you shall have to fight two." The man chuckled quietly to himself with an air of deep satisfaction, giving Lydia, not for the first time, the impression of a regal lion.

"I am glad then, my lord," Lydia whispered, feeling her strength fading. Lord Zhe barked a quick order, and the healer rushed over with a bowl of cool water and a soft cloth. Lord Zhe dipped the cloth into the water and mopped the girl's head gently. The cool liquid on her forehead seemed to cut through Lydia's agony, quelling the fire in her shoulder.

"Tell me Lydia, before I go, was that the first man you've slain?"

"No, my lord, I have slain others, just pirates, when they . . . they—"

"Yes girl . . . " the man interrupted, seeing the pain of the memories added to her physical torment, "I forget."

"He was the first . . . in a duel."

"How did you feel? When you found out who you were matched with, did you feel fear?"

Lydia closed her eyes and reflected for a moment. She had felt terror, true, but not at the prospect of a contest of arms. It was something else. She pondered this for a moment, and then responded.

"It was the magic that I was afraid of, my lord, not knowing how he was going to strike."

"Did you overcome the fear?"

"I suppose I forgot it when I was wounded. I became angry, and . . . worried . . . but I forgot about the fear. Then I knew I had to kill him, and his magic was just like any other weapon."

"Yes, this is true. Magic is like any other weapon, only as deadly as the wielder, and always capable of being overcome. Do you believe me?" Lord Zhe looked deeply into the girl's eyes, studying her response.

"Yes, my lord."

"Now, I have prattled too long, my child, and I can see you are weak. Tonight you will be carried to your chamber, and you will sleep soundly with the medicine I have ordered for you. In the morning you will arise with nearly your full strength, ready to face the day's challenge."

"The other students . . . I am told they plot against me, my Lord. I'm not sure I can face them like this." Lydia despised herself for admitting weakness to this powerful man who was so like her father, but she also understood that he had made an investment in her, and felt some responsibility to him for his efforts. Also, deep within her there was a little girl who needed a guardian to comfort her, to tell her that the plots of her enemies would come to nothing.

"Don't worry Lydia. It is strictly forbidden to act against another before the start of the second day. By then, you will be strong again. The Devil's Cure works quickly."

"Sir, I have a question . . . "

"Yes?"

"Do you know who I will be facing? It's not that I want to know, it's just that . . . I didn't know if you picked my opponents."

"No Lydia, I have not picked your opponents. The College of Black Arts is enshrouded with tradition, and one of the oldest and most rigid of all rules is that none may act for the benefit of a student."

"Yes sir, I just wasn't sure."

"That is not to say I am without my influence." Lord Zhe dabbed the cloth across her brow one last time, and then gestured for the attentive assistant, who took the bowl. "You see, I cannot act to ease the difficulty you face, but I have spoken to Master Nhil and made sure that you faced the deadliest challenges possible." The calmness of this statement, made with a slight smile, belied the alarm it sent through the girl.

"But why—" She was interrupted by his raised hand.

"You are destined for greatness, Lydia. You are destined to burn across the heavens like a comet, and to shake the foundations of kingdoms, and empires." He smiled almost to himself at this. "If you are to fulfil your destiny, you must be stronger than any. Do you understand?"

She nodded feebly. "Yes, my lord, I do."

"Good, my child, good." He took the ruby-handled sword from her side and placed it across her chest, where she clutched it. "You have not shamed this blade, Lydia. You have acted righteously, and prevailed, just as I have always done."

"Lord Zhe, I have one more question . . . "

The powerful man had risen to his feet, and rather than crouching back down at her side, he merely leaned over.

"Yes, what is it?"

Lydia raised herself onto her elbows to ask the question that she had been pondering since their last meeting. "I am greatly honoured by your care, and your visits, but I wonder why a man as important as you would bother with my progress in school, even if I am to be so powerful. Why not send your servants to watch me?"

He laughed at this. "Well, you might be more important than you think. But anyhow, I would never trust a servant with a question of arms, for no man knows combat as well as I. And why do I come, rather than rely on the reports of Master Han and Nhil? Well, you should know the answer to that!"

"But I don't, my lord."

"It's because I can only see you when I'm in your company, and not from the comfort of my palace. You should know that, surely Lord Azursus told you as much on his porch. Or were you too preoccupied with his apes to listen?"

Lydia sunk to her back with the revelation that Lord Zhe knew of her, about her, so long ago. *How could he know of the conversation I had many months ago, on the other side of the world?* As if reading her mind, which she knew he could not, he responded to her unspoken question in a quiet but strong voice.

"I have watched you for a long time, child, as have others. There are others, you know this, who see great distances, into the hearts of men, into the dark places of their hearts. And while we cannot see you ourselves, we employ spies, traitors, assassins to do our bidding for us, to act as our eyes and ears. That is why you are here, under my care, and the care of the Emperor. We know of you, and many of us fear you. This is the best place for you, where your talents and your . . . ability . . . can be moulded into a power for Good. For Justice."

A horrible thought blazed across her mind, and she unconsciously tightened her grip on the blade lying upon her chest.

"Did you know of the attack on my father's ship before it happened?"

Lord Zhe grew very grave. He straightened himself, and looked down upon her in his regal manner, but not without sympathy. "Yes Lydia, I did. I sent the frigate to intercept your father's ship, to warn you and to bring both of you to me so that you and he could decide on the best path for your life, with my council, and the council of the Emperor. But someone, surely the Lord of Rimbu, acting on behalf of an unknown other perhaps, reached your father's ship before my frigate. My ship retook you as soon as it caught the pirates."

"They told me that I was going to be sold as a pleasure slave."

"Would you have believed them otherwise? Anyhow, the pirates were just mercenaries, and surely unaware of those who sought you and their plans for you. They have been dealt with by my own hand for their role. And you, Lydia, have been a pawn in a vast game of Fiest, unaware of the powerful but unseen hands that have moved you about the game board."

The young assistant healer helped Lydia return to her cell that evening. She leaned upon his arm, still unsteady on her feet, her arm numb and shoulder burning from the putrid medicine. After he handed her down to her sleeping mat, the young man turned to Shandala, who had been sitting meditatively, watching her injured roommate's struggles.

"Master Mallum has ordered that you assist Lydia with any necessities that she may require during the evening. He has instructed me to tell you to remember that this is your duty as a student of the College." Shandala smiled sweetly to the man and leaned over to pull the blanket up around Lydia's prostrate form.

"Don't worry. I'll take good care of her."

Finally able to succumb to her fatigue, Lydia nonetheless fought against her slide into sleep. She had been too fatigued to remove her robes and was mortified at the idea of being helped out of them by the young healer's assistant. She found the vial from Mistress Amalin in a hidden pocket where she had carried it throughout the day, and placed the drops upon her tongue. She grasped the hilt of her katana tightly and hoped that she would be able to maintain the semi-conscious vigil that all assassins learned, that state which allowed enough sleep to vanquish fatigue, but also enough awareness to perceiving the many threats they would face in their lives.

Still hanging on to the edge of sleep, Lydia managed to whisper, "I am glad you survived your examination, Shandala."

The girl snorted grimly and replied, "You will see, Justice will be done. You won't be so smug then."

Lydia shook her head and let the vial's magic work on her.

THIRTEEN

At the usual hour, well before the first light of dawn, the surviving students were summoned. They gathered in the great hall, half as many as the day before. Most bore wounds: nicks, little punctures or bruises. Others had heads bandaged, limbs splinted or in slings, and a few were even borne on litters by servants. The examination had proven cruel to all, those who passed the first day as well as the losers. But there was to be no relief from the relentless process for the gravely wounded; to survive the test was to survive both days, not just the first.

As predicted, Lydia was stiff, and her wounds ached dully, but before reporting to the assembly hall she took her katana from the wall, and when the silent Shandala had left, swung the blade in a series of warm-up moves, testing her battered muscles and sinews, letting herself flow from one guard to the next. Finding her body reasonably responsive, Lydia worked herself for as long as she could, until she was in danger of running late. As the last gong rang out she slid her sword into her sash and hurried to the hall, but not before pausing to drink deeply from the water jar in her room, forcing tepid fluid into her gut until she felt as if it might burst. On the second day of testing she knew that she could not trust anything to eat or drink.

Again, Master Nhil addressed the students from his place before the solemn line of the school's monks. As Lydia hurried into the room she saw that his impassive face was lit by the flame of two roaring braziers, each as wide as a large shield, but not large enough to dispel the bitter, early-morning cold into which the students' breathe steamed, forming a mist about their heads. Master Nhil clapped his hands as Lydia sank into her designated place.

"Today is the last of the examination. Each of you have survived the trial of combat. This day is the test of strategy, stealth, planning and foresight. This is the test of what you shall become, for we are to excel not just at arms, but also in the use our minds and hearts. Who better to test ourselves against, than those who are our equals?"

"Each of us, your instructors, have sat where you are today, many times in fact, and have survived. Some of you will survive until next year. As many will fail. This is the way of the assassin. We take life without hesitation, and shed life as quickly." Many heads along the silent line of instructors nodded gravely in agreement. The firelight shone on the bald pates of the men.

"You are to return to your cells when dismissed. Upon your sleeping mats is an envelope. This envelope has been sealed by me personally, and the wax upon the seal cannot be broken by any other than that whom the letter is addressed. You will open your envelope, read what is therein and then spend an hour in contemplation in your cell, without action. Any who acts before the gong for the morning meal will forfeit their life and their honour as a student of this school and a servant of the Emperor. Mistress Shandala, what is the penalty for failing to maintain the honour of the school?" Upon hearing her name, the girl at Lydia's side sprang to her feet and responded in a loud, clear voice.

"To lose honour is to lose one's life to the slow blade, and the Emperor shall have the lands and holdings of all those of the fallen one's family, within two generations, and their lives at his pleasure." She resumed her seat when Master Nhil nodded.

"We are not barbarians like so many of those around us. Even in Death there are rules. It is what makes us Masters of the Black Art, rather than mere killers. Is this not so?"

As one, the students responded, "Yes, Master Nhil."

"Then, let this day end, as all other days end, at midnight, and thus all plans must come to pass by that hour. When you return to your cells reflect carefully, plan and consider. There will be those of you who will receive a name in your envelope, and others who shall have nothing. Those with nothing written shall be the target of another's schemes. Beyond this, there are no rules, other than you must do as you would do on any other day. All classes shall meet, all meals be attended, and all shall face the same danger as the others."

"You are now dismissed. Go, and show that you are honourable." The students rose, collected weapons from long tables that had been arranged around the room, and left.

Lydia, who had been seated closer to the entrance to the hall than Shandala, arrived back at their cell first. There were neatly folded envelopes on both mats, each inscribed with a name in Master Nhil's flowing script. She paused briefly, tempted for a moment to try and read the name on Shandala's note through the thick paper, but like the others, she feared discovery and dishonour and so quickly dismissed any idea of cheating. Instead she took up her own note, turning so that it could not be read over her shoulder, and broke open the red wax seal on the back. When the wax crumbled, she felt a tingling wave sweep from her head to her feet, and the curious sensation that she was being studied by some distant observer. The feeling passed as she opened the note and found nothing inside. In the instant that Lydia realised what this meant, the note started to smoulder in one corner. Startled, she dropped the folded paper, which burst into flame and was completely consumed before it reached the floor, not even leaving ashes upon the gleaming yellow stone.

So I am to be a victim she thought to herself as Shandala came into the room and scooped up her note, breaking the seal without hesitation, the faintest smile crossing her lips as she read what was on the paper. When her note had been consumed by the powerful magic of Master Nhil, she turned to face Lydia and sank to the floor, sitting in a meditative, cross-legged position, so still that even her breath was undetectable in the tiny room. Lydia stared at her former friend's face, wondering if it had been her name on Shandala's note. Unable to tell anything from the girl's expressionless face, Lydia also sank to the floor and spent an hour rapidly reviewing the possible attacks she would face during the day.

Lydia had expected the hour to be tortuous, but she found that she was able to sit quietly and sink into a state of deep meditation, as she had been taught by the monks, and allow her mind to run over the list of possible opponents she would face during the day. She considered what attacks they would be likely to employ in what places and at what times. Most importantly she pondered how she could know if a student was the one sent to kill her. She reasoned that the person had to be someone she would most likely see throughout the day, someone of her age or older, and formidable, based on the previous day's discussion with Lord Zhe. Half of the students she would have faced were dead, therefore Lydia reasoned that there must be one hundred and twenty opponents remaining. She knew most and had learned of the weapons of choice employed by those who were close to her equal, which would only be a handful. In the end, Lydia narrowed the identity of her potential killer to a dozen names and faces. Among them was her roommate and former friend, Shandala the Shadow Dancer. Lydia remembered the small smile that had played upon Shandala's lips when she read the name secreted in Master Nhil's note. *Was it mine,* she asked herself, once more.

The gong in the dining hall resonated, calling the students to the morning meal. Lydia and Shandala arose as one, both with weapons in hand. Lydia held the ruby-handled katana loosely. In the small of her back, under her broad belt, a heavy dagger balanced for throwing was concealed. She did not expect Shandala to attack in the bright room, if she was to be Lydia's opponent. Her most effective strike was from the shelter of shadow where she could use her powers to the utmost. Shandala herself, obviously aware that Lydia would suspect her, held two long, slender-bladed daggers, each longer than her forearm; light, elegant weapons perfectly balanced for slashing, thrusting or even throwing. The hilts of her knives flared out to cover her hand, and then turned upwards in the direction of the blade, ending in points themselves. A deft flick of her wrist in a parry and Shandala could lock a larger blade in the hilt of one knife, immobilizing the blade while striking home with the other. Though short and light, they were fearsome weapons in the hands of an expert such as Shandala.

The girls locked eyes for a moment, trying to read each other's intentions. But there was nothing to read; they had been too well-trained to betray themselves with a look of fear or anticipation. Lydia lowered her blade slightly and backed to the wall of the cell furthest from the doorway. She bowed and allowed Shandala to slip from the room safely. Lydia herself approached the doorway, lifted her katana, and used the polished blade as a mirror, scanning the hallway for danger. Students were emerging from the cells that lined both sides of the hall, some with weapons at the ready, and all with cat-like caution, ready to pounce at the slightest hint of danger. Lydia could see no immediate danger in the scattered crowd, though she realised that when the attack came it would be lightning fast and from an unseen quarter. She sheathed her sword, checked the accessibility of the knife tucked in her belt and left the room.

She had only just left the safety of the doorway when Lydia felt a wave of danger pass over her. Lydia had felt this premonition of danger with increasing regularity over the last few months; it was not quite prescience, but close enough that she had questioned Master Han about it, and whether it was supernatural. He had only smiled and replied that she was becoming a true master of arms, and that was a magic unto itself.

She spun in the busy hallway to face an attack that would certainly come from the rear, and just as she turned an arrow streaked past her face. She drew her knife, knowing that in the time she had reached her opponent with her katana a second arrow would find its mark. *Endo*, she thought to herself, *master of the short bow. He can hit a coin flipped into the air from thirty paces. He should have hit me.* Rather than presenting a target, Lydia drew her katana in her free hand and stood at the ready just inside the doorway where she could not be shot from down the hallway. A moment passed; students who had dived into empty cells were returning to the hallway. Those who had fallen to the floor or crouched to make a smaller target rose to their feet, cautiously, but with obvious relief. Endo strode past the doorway, unaware of Lydia's aggressive crouch. She leaned out to see him drop his bow at his feet and draw a long, thin knife across the throat of a figure slumped on the floor, an arrow jutting from her back. Lydia sheathed her katana and walked past as Endo rose from the corpse, face filled with relief at his early victory.

"Good hunting, Endo," murmured one of his friends as they passed on the way to the hall.

During the morning meal the students all sat apart, and no one but Endo ate. Upon the tables cups of water stood untouched. The poisoners, and there were many of them, were going to have to be creative in their art. Uneaten food was removed by servants, and the students rose to leave. At Lydia's side, Shandala sat tensed, weapons tucked into her belt but hands never far from the two hilts. They rose at the same time and Lydia hazarded to speak to the girl.

"Shandala, I hope that you have good fortune today." Shandala sneered but said nothing as she turned and left. The two girls shared most of their lessons during the day, as did many of the others on Lydia's list. If Lydia's name was on her note, she would have ample opportunities to exact vengeance and complete her duty as a student of the College. And Lydia discovered something else at that moment. Shandala was not to be a victim, for if she were, she could not have known that Lydia was not her opponent, and thus would not have turned her back on her so quickly.

Unwilling to come too close to others, the students left the dining hall alone, making a slow procession to their first lessons. Not far from Lydia, one girl reached out almost casually as she passed behind a boy who was still at his seat, watching the person sitting across from him intently. She touched his neck with her extended index finger. Lydia saw the metal tip of the finger, the thin needle that jutted from the metal, the drop of clear liquid that clung to the tip as it pierced the boy's neck. He turned, looked into the girl's eyes and then collapsed into a heap at her feet. Despite herself, Lydia felt her skin crawl as the girl calmly kneeled beside her victim, feeling for the movement of blood within the lifeless body, and then returned the tiny thimble with its deadly needle to a pouch hidden in her robe.

The day passed as a montage of seemingly endless scenes of violence. At times Lydia found herself battling a creeping sense of ennui as her attacker failed to reveal him or herself time and again when she was vulnerable. In order to draw the person out, Lydia intentionally appeared to drop her guard throughout the day, hoping that her would-be assassin would strike in a time and place of her choosing, yet as the day progressed she was left unassailed. She witnessed many deaths, and with each one felt less shock and revulsion. The victims were not the only ones to fall; many assassins lost their lives to a well-executed defence.

Despite her growing familiarity with it, Lydia still found herself quailed by the use of killing magic. During the midday meal, an older student had thrown a pinch of cinnamon in the air, chanted five quick words, and before anyone could determine who his target was the young wizard's hands became encircled with crackling blue electricity. As students fled in swarms from the boy, struggling against each other, he called the name of his opponent in a ghastly, inhuman voice and stretched his hands out towards his target, turning the palms downward so that the lightning fell to the floor like electric water. There it streaked in a jagged line along the yellow stone towards the victim. The other student fled as the bolts sought him out. Before he could take five steps twin tendrils of light arced from the floor up his feet and across his body, which became enmeshed in a web of electricity. The room filled with the smell of scorched flesh even as the boy's rigid body fell to the floor, his head and heels touching the ground while his back arched upwards towards the ceiling. A spasm-wracked moan escaped from his lips. When the lightning dissipated it left only a smoking, blackened corpse in its wake, surrounded by gaping onlookers. Two more were slain as they viewed the spectacle.

When the spell had started, Lydia had been well away from the apprentice sorcerer, but knowing that killing magic could travel great distances, she had drawn her throwing blade in preparation to strike at the boy before he could his turn his magic upon her, if that was his intention. She knew that the charred victim could have knocked down his attacker with a quickly hurled knife or axe, and maybe even with a sword thrown in a last-ditch effort before the magic reached him. The fallen boy had been slain by his own fear, by his own lack of immediate resolve. Despite her fear of it, Lydia knew that this was the weakness of most magic; it was slow, relying on gestures, chants, commands, ingredients being mixed at the right time and in the right proportion. While the conjurer was distracted with his chants and gestures he could be slain by the quick blade or arrow. Nonetheless, she remained haunted by the memory of the arching body of the electrocuted boy.

By the evening meal Lydia still had not been assailed. The pressure of the day and the endless anticipation of death threatened to overwhelm her caution and weigh her down with a sense of torpor as attack after attack occurred around her; she seemed to float above the fear she knew her subconscious was feeling, as if seeing the events of the day in a dream; a terrible, blood-filled dream. But as the night approached, the calm that first seemed to Lydia to be a result of her own self-control grew into unease, and finally fear. When she followed the others into the dining hall Lydia found herself wishing that the moment of attack would come so that she could end the uncertainty of the day. The survivors were laughing by then; some were eating, while their peers, the few who remain untested, were all showing signs of great distress.

Calm, Lydia, she told herself. *An assassin, a smart assassin, one that Lord Zhe would want me to be matched against, would wait for the right moment, using time to weaken my resolve. Don't give in!* She felt her fists clench as she took her seat beside Shandala, who was laughing with another girl at some mutual joke.

By the end of the meal, she came to the conclusion that Shandala was to be her opponent, and that she was waiting for the shadows of the evening to attack, when she was most powerful, and Lydia, worn thin by the stress of the day, would be at her weakest. Between the midday and evening meals the two girls had gone separate ways, Lydia to her archery practice and Shandala to work with Master Nhil, where she would have been mastering her ability to cloak herself in shadow. There were still four others on her list of likely assassins that had not been struck down or survived an attack, but Lydia was becoming more and more convinced that her roommate would be the one. After all, Lord Zhe had warned that her opponent would be deadly, and who would be more deadly than someone who knew their victim intimately, and hated them as Shandala seemed to hate her since the death of Damio?

To make the tension worse, the two girls had sat at their assigned seats, next to each other, through the entire evening meal. When she finished laughing, Shandala ate her meal enthusiastically, a knowing smile upon her lips. It was like a declaration of open hostilities.

Lydia, sitting very still, keeping her eyes rigidly forward but straining every exhausted sense, thought to herself, *she's not afraid of poison. She's either faced her challenge, and lived, or she is to be my killer. She must be the one!*

Adding to her suspicion, one of the boys on her unwritten list of opponents slew his would-be assassin in a katana duel during the meal. There were now only three on the list. Maiso, a master of unarmed combat and magic powders, potions and poison. Older than her, but still close in age. Lydia saw the young man across the room, eating calmly. *Has he acted already? Has he used some exotic paste on someone else in the room, someone who is going to die when they touched some small personal item, coated carefully in a thin smear of contact poison? Has he thrown a magic dust into a doomed face, and is he now just sitting so quiet and still to hide the fact that he has already struck, waiting for his attack to work its evil on the doomed victim's body? Am I his victim, and am I already killed? Did he poison me in some way I could not know throughout the day?* She did not feel poisoned, but that did little to alleviate her fears.

Then there Darjin, a fencer of great skill, though not quite as quick and deadly as Lydia. *Unlikely*, she thought to herself. He sat near to Maiso, looking about furtively.

Arsanda, Shandala's new friend and sparring partner. Mistress of the small blade, knives and razor-edged throwing disks. Proficient with a whip, which she could use to entangle the arms or hands of an opponent, draw their feet from under them, or cut into the flesh like a sword. *Good, but not as good as Shandala, and not as good as I*, thought Lydia, *and therefore unlikely*. It had been with Arsanda that Shandala had been laughing when Lydia entered the dining hall, however, which kept her on the list of the suspicious.

This left Shandala. *The obvious choice.*

The evening meal ended and the time for retiring to the cells was fast approaching. Servants came to clear the remains of the meal, and there was a crash and clatter when one of the old men who brought their food and took their dishes dropped his heavy tray just behind Lydia. She jumped in alarm, turned about and then suddenly realised that Shandala, who had been sitting beside her, had vanished. Under the table, she caught a darker shadow within a shadow; it flowed away, into the deeper murk. Lydia leapt upon the table, away from the darkness, scattering metal plates, cups, dishes and students around her. In a flash her katana was out as she groped around the room with every sense, awaiting attack, trying to detect the piercing blade before it leapt from the shadows and plunged into her heart.

What shadows are there? Lydia quickly reappraised the room, for she had been mentally considering every possible location for the assault since she had concluded that Shandala was her opponent. The hall was square, forty paces at least on a side, with five rows of stone tables, each table holding forty students. Along the outside were columns set against the walls, each casting a dark place. On the walls large racks of candles gave light, joined by a glow from large oil lamps that hung from the ceiling by thin chains tied to brackets beside the columns. These shone over the table tops and stone benches, but beneath them lurked many more shadows than Lydia could keep track of. It was a perfect killing ground for the Shadow Dancer.

To overcome Shandala, Lydia needed to cast as much light around the room as possible. She was most worried about the shadows cast by the tables, which provided a safe harbour throughout the centre of the hall, a thousand places from which her opponent could strike. She could avoid the shadows cast by the columns along the walls by staying in the centre of the room, but she could not avoid the rows of tables. Her table, the table she was standing upon, was in the middle, for at the age of sixteen she was in the middle ages of students at the school. She would have to cross the hall to get to the door, leaping from table to table, a span at least as wide as a man was tall before she could reach the doorway. To use the floor was certain death, for Shandala would instantly strike out from the darkness beneath the tables. But fleeing to the hallway was no better; the corridor was also lined with columns and was narrower and less-well lit than the dining hall.

Students stood in small groups around the outside of the room, watching her with great curiosity, for Lydia's skill was well-known. She could not know if it was a semiconscious reaction to a look of surprise on one of their faces that warned her, or if it was her growing combat sense, but she looked over her shoulder just in time to discover that from behind her and to the side three small metal disks were streaking towards her, thrown by Shandala's friend. *Arsanda! It is Arsanda, not Shandala!* Lydia leapt to the side, spinning away from the deadly missiles. She recovered from her spin in mid-air and landed in a crouch on the side of the table, ready to drop between the stone tabletops and use their cover to get close enough to Arsanda to strike effectively with her throwing dagger. She found the girl, opposite the door, watching Lydia while climbing slowly onto the table in front of her. As their eyes met Arsanda took the whip from a thong on her belt and unfurled it. A slow smile spread across her face.

Lydia was too far to use her throwing knife effectively, and as an expert in the use of such weapons Arsanda would be ready for that attack. Lydia prepared to drop to the floor, into the shelter provided by the tables when a ball, not bigger than a small apple, landed before her and exploded into a cloud of green, shimmering dust. Lydia, already crouched on the table's edge, launched herself backwards onto the next table, holding her breath as she passed through the cloud. She had seen such magic before and knew that the shimmering green dust would enter her chest upon her breath and turn to fire inside her lungs, causing her a long, painful and certain death. It must have come from Maiso, who had been watching Lydia from the side of the room from the front of a group of younger students.

Lydia landed on the next table on all fours, dropped to her stomach and slid across the tabletop and onto the floor between the last two tables. A quick dive and roll under the last table and she would be in the sanctuary of the hallway, where she could face her two opponents in closer, more easily defended quarters. Arsanda's whip cracked just over her head as Lydia dropped. She landed just in time to see Maiso's feet leave the floor as he climbed onto a table top. With her throwing dagger in hand Lydia looked for Arsanda's feet, but she was still on her table top. They were going to hunt her from above.

From out of the darkness under the last table before the door came an arm wielding a needle-sharp knife. It reached out and the tip came to rest against the throbbing vein in Lydia's throat, stinging icily as the thin blade began to slide into her flesh. Before Lydia could roll backwards away from the blade and into her opponent she felt the point of a second blade pressing into her back. She braced herself for the killing strokes, feeling almost nothing but exhaustion and a sense of surrender. She was trapped between two blades, both razor-sharp and poised to instantly kill.

"You betrayed me," Shandala hissed in Lydia's ear. "You betrayed Damio. You're nothing but a western whore, with no family, no honour." Raising her voice, she called to her accomplices, "I've got her!"

From above Maiso called, "Bring her up, so I can kill her." He was the type of student who had been attracted to the school through his love of killing rather than any sense of honour, duty or desire for power. His statement confirmed at last that it was he who had drawn Lydia's name. Shandala jabbed the knife into Lydia's back, the tip cutting through Lydia's black robe and pushing just into her skin.

"Get up . . . slowly," she hissed. "You might be Maiso's to kill, but I would cherish the feel of my knife slipping into your throat." Lydia rose to her feet, still holding her katana but pinned between the two blades. Maiso and Arsanda were both facing her, not more than ten paces away, at the ends of the next table. Maiso was smiling with a maddened, intoxicated grin. Arsanda looked nervous, and Lydia noticed that she was standing on the balls of her feet, ready to strike or flee. *Arsanda. Why is she attacking me?* Lydia wondered, despite her predicament.

Maiso made sense as her opponent. He could break a man's neck or cave in his chest with a single blow, and he was a master of the killing magic that Lydia feared so much. Shandala also made sense. Maiso, knowing of her animosity, must have recruited the

Shadow Dancer. But Arsanda had no real friendship with Shandala or Maiso that Lydia knew of. She would not help the others out of a sense of loyalty or generosity. So Lydia wondered why she was attacking her with the others.

In that instant, Lydia's mind cleared and she hatched a desperate plan as a wild guess entered her thoughts.

"Arsanda, you must tell the truth," she blurted. The girl with the whip started at Lydia's voice.

Behind her, Shandala growled "Shut up," into Lydia's ear, and drove the blade in Lydia's back further in. As she fought the instinct to struggle, which would have led to a slit throat, Lydia's mind raced.

"Tell her, Arsanda. Tell her about you and Damio!" Through the thin metal blades that connected their bodies, Lydia could feel Shandala stiffen. Lydia sensed that her desperate plan just might work. Hope blossomed in her heart.

Arsanda looked over Lydia's shoulder at Shandala with horror on her face. She took a step back. Lydia had fallen upon the truth, that Arsanda and Damio had been secret lovers, defying the strictest rules of the school with hidden trysts in time stolen from the hectic schedules both students maintained. *That is why she joins Maiso against me*, declared Lydia silently, triumphantly. Shandala saw the desperate shock of discovery on Arsanda's face. The next moment, Lydia knew, was the most important that she had ever faced, and it must be executed with exact timing and unwavering confidence.

Lydia continued to play her hand. "That was what Lord Zhe wanted to see me about. He was furious that the rules of the school were being broken. He knew, he *knew*, before he spoke to me, about Arsanda and Damio, for Arsanda is with child, and has tried to hide it! He wanted to know if there were others with Damio, if the rutting had involved others. I told him nothing. But he knows about you, Arsanda!" With that, the look of fear and shock that overwhelmed Arsanda's face was washed away by a wave of pure hatred, twisting her pretty, somewhat delicate features into a demonic mask. Her lips drew back as she growled through clenched teeth.

"Liar," she spat. Arsanda lashed out with her whip, the leather lash curling around Lydia's chest, causing her to cringe in agony, but also wrapping around her and slashing into the arm that held the knife to Lydia's throat. In an instant, Shandala was gone, vanished into the shadows under the table, leaving Lydia only slightly wounded, but still in possession of her katana. Maiso, whose laughter had been growing throughout the entire exchange, stood over her, but he made no move as he watched her. Lydia sensed that in his madness, he was waiting for the outcome of the three-way battle he had incited, and would attack any who lived.

In the instant after Shandala released her hold on Lydia and vanished the lash returned, stinging Lydia across the face. Arsanda was striking out of anger, not thinking about disabling her opponent, otherwise she would have tried to entangle Lydia's legs or sword arm, or aimed the tasseled tip at her eyes. The lash across her face stung like fire, and galvanised Lydia into action. She leaped backwards and up into the air, onto the table behind her, katana held before her, and then sprung backwards again, flipping and landing on her feet near the doorway to the dining hall, back nearly to the wall, but facing her opponents. Apparently fearing her opponent was going to flee, Arsanda dropped her whip and drew two more of the razor-edged throwing disks from leather pouches on her belt. She flung them, but Lydia was prepared and swatted the disks aside with her katana, sending them skittering across the floor into a small group of students who leapt out of their path. In her recovery from the deflecting sweep, Lydia slashed upwards over her head at the chain that ran from the anchor point on the column behind her to the great oil-filled lantern suspended over the centre of the room.

With an audible snap the chain parted and rattled through an iron loop in the ceiling as the lantern it held plunged to the floor. The glass and metal vessel crashed to the ground, split, and spilled oil across the floor. In the next instant, the burning wick ignited the spreading liquid and the room was transformed into a raging inferno. Flames shot up between the tables, sending both Maiso and Arsanda leaping to the middle of the table they both stood on.

The Shadow Dancer was lurking under the table nearest to where the lantern had fallen. Oil splashed on her robes, and fire quickly followed. Lydia saw her rolling away from the spreading blaze, desperately trying to quell the flames engulfing her body. Shandala screamed in a high, eerie voice as her skin scorched, and then she was into shadow, and vanished.

As the fire approached Lydia she advanced once more into the room, towards her opponents, and leapt back atop the first table. Maiso, unable to bring his skill in wrestling or his deadly fists into action, pulled a ball from the pouch hanging from his belt and threw it at Lydia's feet as Arsanda sent another three razor-edged disks streaking for her. The ball exploded with a tremendous flash and a bang that would have left Lydia stunned had she been caught in its blast. Lydia had seen her opponents' attacks before they released their weapons, and she had leapt high above the missiles, flipped again in the air and landed on the next table, closer to the pair. She had no sooner recovered her feet than Arsanda's whip curled around her thighs, holding them fast. Arsanda tried to pull Lydia from her feet and into the fire roaring up behind her, but she was not strong enough. She leaned backwards, pulling Lydia with the weight of her entire body. Lydia struck at the whip with her sword, severing it cleanly. The sudden release of tension sent Arsanda tumbling backwards, and she stumbled into Maiso, who was saying the words of an incantation and preparing to hurl a fresh paper ball at Lydia. Maiso pushed her away, and the younger girl slid off the side of the table, and fell into the burning oil.

Ignoring the girl's shrieks, Lydia kicked the severed end of whip from her feet and leapt to the same table as Maiso. Lydia sensed that the boy, a few years older than her, must know that his magic, limited to balls and powders that he threw and to poisons for food, drink and blades, would be useless against her at such close range. His spell was still half-woven, and he had no time to finish. She had twice proven herself too fast at dodging his missiles and still had her throwing dagger, tucked back into her belt, which he would not be able to avoid with ease. His best option was to close with the girl and her katana, to use his hands and feet as lethal weapons. He could easily crush a grown man's chest with a single well-placed blow, and he had once broken the neck of a bull with one windmilling kick. He had also mastered a dozen ways to get a weapon from an armed opponent. He wore armoured bracers that stretched from his palms to his elbows, which would turn even Lord Zhe's keen blade, allowing him to parry her blows and strike himself with as much effectiveness as if he were armed.

She saw him throw the half-finished paper ball into the fire that surrounded him, and knew he'd come for her with empty hands. She approached, easing along the table with small, gliding steps, blade held before her. They locked eyes, both waiting for the other to strike first, trying to read the intentions locked inside their opponent's inscrutable face.

She wanted to kill him, more than anything. And the idea thrilled her.

Though he was still giggling madly, Maiso faltered when his gaze flitted from Lydia's large dark eyes, alight with the flames that surrounded them, to her mouth. Lydia realised she too was smiling. But not with a taunting smile contrived to unnerve a weaker opponent or the mad grimace of bloodlust that he was wearing. She felt her lips gently upturned, and knew the surge of joy she felt as she closed with her opponent was displayed on her full, western lips.

Lydia saw that Maiso was realising that he had seriously underestimated his opponent. She'd dispatched his two flunkies, and now she was coming for him.

Starting to show the beginnings of true fear, Maiso dropped to the table surface and tried to take Lydia's feet from under her with a wide-sweeping kick. The girl leapt and easily avoided his first strike, landing cat-like in her same ready position, the look unchanged upon her face. He sprang to his feet, ducking a swinging blow from her katana and punched for her nose with a vicious, fast jab. Lydia dodged, but he caught her in the stomach with a glancing blow from an off-balanced kick. She recoiled slightly, retreated a pace, and raised her sword again.

I'm going to kill you, she said silently, feeling the smile on her lips grow as she edged further back, pulling him into pursuit. He ran at her, launching himself into a flying kick aimed squarely at her gut. Lydia fell to her knees before his foot struck. Her free hand crashed upwards into his groin as his kicked passed over her head. Maiso fell on top of Lydia and bellowed, enraged and stunned by roaring pain.

Lydia kicked him away, and picked herself up. He staggered backwards, and she followed him, sword held high.

She struck. He tried to get inside her swing, catch her wrist and break it. But Lydia had foreseen his intentions, and instead of snaring her, he caught the edge of her blade. The gently-curved steel with the wavy line along its length sliced cleanly through his hand through his metal glove, leaving only a thumb on the bloody stump.

Maiso had been trained too well to drop his attack, even with such a brutal wound. He lashed out with his foot, snapping her face around.

Bleeding now from the nose and mouth, Lydia shook off the pain of the blow, dodged another, and slashed deep into Maiso's body, pulling the katana back towards herself as it slid through the flesh between arm and waist, feeling it cut through bone and muscle, and lastly deep into his body cavity.

She drew her blade out of Maiso's body with as much fluidity as she had cut him, and then cut the top of his head off when he fell to his knees. His skull spun off, leaving a dark trail edged with chunks of gore across the table top as he fell backwards and pumped blood out of his wounds.

He smiled, even in death.

Finding nothing other than oil upon the stone of the floor to consume, the fire had retreated into a few small pools that half-heartedly flickered. Lydia crouched and surveyed the room. On the floor between the table she was on and the next was the charred body of Arsanda, blackened but not fully consumed. She carefully dropped to the hot floor beside her, and drove the point of her sword into the girl's neck. Arsanda gave a choked, gurgling cry, and then died. Of Shandala there was no sign. Though there were many shadows in the room, Lydia had seen her roommate rolling away from the fire, robes scorching, skin reddening. The Shadow Dancer would have fled, unable to continue the fight. Still, she did not trust the darkness beneath the tables. Using their tops as giant stepping stones Lydia crossed the room and then leapt down from the last table, giving the hall one last scan before squatting and searching under the tables. There was nothing to see, other than Arsanda's smoking corpse.

She turned to leave, but found the doorway blocked by students and even some teachers who had been watching the battle, and now followed her with wide, staring eyes. She ignored them as the crowd parted silently, forming a wide path to the hallway.

Staying to the centre of the corridors, away from darkened doorways and the shadows cast by the numerous columns of yellow stone, Lydia went to directly to the cell she shared with Shandala. The curtain was drawn across the doorway, and when she flung it open with the tip of her katana Lydia saw that the room was dark. Even if it had not been for the smell of oil, burnt cloth and flesh Lydia would have known that Shandala the Shadow Dancer was hiding in the darkness, enfolded in the shades that she gathered about her like a cloak.

Shandala was in the far corner, for she had gasped when Lydia threw aside the curtain. She was gravely hurt; her breath rasped in her scorched throat, but even wounded she could move, silently, invisibly, from shadow to shadow. Lydia entered the cell, merging with the gloom.

"Why didn't you tell me about Arsanda?" Shandala's voice, a bare whisper, wracked with pain.

"It was all a bluff, Shandala. I made it up. I just got lucky." There was a moment of silence, while the enormity of it sank into Shandala's pain-weakened mind.

"You . . . bluffed? You lied?" Her voice, which had moved from Lydia's left to a pace or more in front of Lydia, was full of doubt, indecision.

"What did you expect?" replied Lydia flatly. "Did you think I'd just let you kill me over some pathetic little romance?" Lydia's voice held no trace of sympathy.

"You lied!" Shandala hissed in renewed anger and hatred in the darkness. At the same time Lydia swung her katana double-handed in a low arc to her left, the same side from which Shandala had held the blade to her throat just before, her body twisting so that the blade swept far behind her. The katana caught the girl under the right arm, which was raised over Shandala's head, poised to drive her blade into Lydia's back. The razor-sharp steel bit deeply into Shandala's chest, cutting under her ribcage until it came to rest against her spine. Shandala fell to her knees, the katana still buried in her abdomen, and her mouth gaped open as blood gushed out and joined the flood pouring from her chest. Lydia put her foot upon the girl's chest, pulled the blade free. In the half light from the open doorway, Lydia watched as Shandala's silhouette slumped forward and finally sagged to the floor.

With the total detachment of a butcher at work Lydia casually traced a bloody line across Shandala's throat with the tip of her sword as she cut the girl's throat from ear to ear, leaving a gaping wound that was impossible to survive, even with the aid of a healer's magic.

I am an assassin, at last, she declared to herself, triumphantly.

FOURTEEN

Lydia took new interest in her studies. Already an attentive student, her instructors found that after her victories in the examinations she approached challenges with fresh enthusiasm. In combat her movements became more fluid, more instinctive and less mechanical as she allowed herself to merge mind and body into one lethal machine. Lydia sought out new weapons, adapting them to her distinctive style of combat, breaking traditional rules of their use, the methods that had been developed over centuries by countless masters, always with lethal effectiveness. Lydia was fast becoming a true master of the black arts of assassination.

Her opponents on the sparring floor tried to hide their reluctance to oppose Lydia, but it was becoming increasingly obvious that her skills were far surpassing even the lesser of the monks, master assassins themselves. Within months of her victory, training with Master Han and other instructors came to completely dominate her exercises at last, a trend started before the examinations. More than once she drew a thin line of blood across her opponents, even the most skilled instructors, and she relished each of these little signs of progress.

Other students treated Lydia with distant respect. The fear and trauma of their recent examinations was fresh in their minds, leaving many students subdued, while others tried to cover their angst with joviality. All watched as Lydia returned to her studies, apparently unmoved by the battle she had waged against not one, but three opponents, one of whom had been her closest friend. They studied her with a growing appreciation for the girl's inner strength and resolution.

Hidden beneath each smile, behind each cloud of contentment that accompanied a new accomplishment, Lydia concealed her true motivation. She felt as if she had awoken from the fog that had enshrouded her since her father's death, and even before. Feeling as if she had come to accept the truth about herself after years of painful denial, she started each day by saying to herself, *I am going to become the world's greatest assassin.* And when she had completed her training, reached the pinnacle of her powers, she knew she was going to kill the Lord of Rimbu and everyone who stood at his side. From Lord Zhe she had learned that this act would not be merely revenge. She was going to become the hand of Justice. She cherished this knowledge in the secret depths of the night, using it to warm her heart which otherwise threatened to grow cold and remote.

Three weeks after the examination Lydia was summoned to the small cloister garden during the midday meal. She found Lord Zhe sitting on the bench under the tree, thoughtfully peeling an orange with the same knife he had used the last time they had sat together. He gestured to the empty place next him. Lydia bowed and then sat beside the heir to the Empire of Nara. Lord Zhe finished stripping the thick skin from the orange, and pulled the fruit apart with his powerful yet nimble fingers. He handed half to Lydia.

"I see you have recovered well from your wounds. And Master Han tells me that you put my sword to excellent use during the examination."

"Yes, my lord, thank you. It is an exceptional weapon."

Lord Zhe nodded. "I'm told that you are sparring almost exclusively with Master Han now."

"Yes my lord, though he often bests me."

"Well, you must learn from your failures. Master Han's practice sword hurts worse than fire. But you have tasted the real pain of steel and learned that the pain of his weapon is nothing more than training for the real bite of a blade wielded in anger. Is this not so?" Lydia nodded.

"Tell me then, how do you sleep at nights now?" Lydia's vial from Mistress Amalin had run dry two nights before but she had not been able to find the time to call upon the elderly assassin. Without the magic philtre to ease her into repose Lydia had lain stiff on her bedroll on the night after she had consumed the last of the bitter fluid, waiting for the parade of horrors that had nightly visited her before Master Zhe's intervention. But the images did not come. The anger that had plagued her was but a distant memory, and she had fallen asleep peacefully in the quiet of her room. Lydia was reluctant to take the drops if she did not need them, afraid that they might blunt her awareness during the night, but she knew that she should obey her master, regardless of instinct. Her failure to do as much shamed her deeply.

"Well, my lord, thank you."

"Yes, I thought as much. Are you still taking the medicine I ordered for you?"

"No, my lord, I am sorry. Two nights ago I used the last of it and I have been unable to call upon Mistress Amalin since." She was worried that the great man beside her, a man whose orders were never disobeyed, would be angered at her failure to continue the treatment he had ordered.

"Did you not worry that you were disobeying my orders for your treatment?" he asked, echoing her concern.

"Yes my lord, but I have not had the dreams since I stopped taking the medicine."

"Yes, well—" he paused as he ate the last of his orange. "You did right to think for yourself, but in the future, you must always follow the orders of your superiors, without question."

"Yes, my lord, I will." Lydia's answer was nearly automatic, unthinking. She had argued with her father, with Mrs Habden, Braide, and even Moad when she felt they were in the wrong, or when she had been feeling contrary; but since the loss of her former life at the hands of pirates, the rebelliousness she had felt as a child had surrendered to anger, dedication to her studies, and now, most recently, her passion for the achievement of perfection as an assassin, for Justice, for the power to kill. Rebellion seemed far less important to her than before.

"I was impressed to hear that you overcame the magical powers of three opponents in the examination. As I told you, magic is no more than a weapon, only as powerful as the one who commands it."

"Yes, my lord." Lydia was still ashamed at her failure to replenish her sleeping draught, and her voice was solemn.

"Now, I've come to say goodbye. I've been ordered abroad in command of his Most Glorious Imperial Majesty's fleet, to quell an uprising among the Sinjun Pirate Lords. I shall be away for some time. I trust that you will continue your studies with your current vigour." Lydia felt a sharp pang of regret at the news of the lord's departure. He had become a distant link to her former self, a man not unlike her father: hard and demanding but also generous and fair, and in his imperious manner warm, even nurturing. She had started to feel a deep fondness for him, added to the respect and gratitude she had always regarded him with.

Lord Zhe smiled when he saw the look of sadness upon the girl's face. "Now Lydia, soon you will be coming with me on such a mission, or even going in my stead. But in the meanwhile you must prove yourself up to the tasks before you. Perhaps I will be able to send you a note from time to time with my dispatches. Would you like that?" Lydia nodded sharply, suddenly feeling very lonely indeed, and struggling against tears. Inwardly, she was amazed at the strength of her feelings for the man.

"Well then I shall send you a note, once a moon, upon my oath as heir to the throne of Nara. You shall be my good luck charm!" The man rose to leave, quickly straightening his sword in his belt and throwing his travelling cloak over his shoulder. Lydia saw that his new sword was plainer than the blade he had given to her. Instead of the ruby in the hilt the sword ended in a steel ball, etched with a map of the globe, and clutched in an eagle's talon. He saw the direction of her eye and drew the sword, holding it up for her to see. The hilt was of dull grey metal but the blade glittered with a green fire, not unlike the red glow of the karinga. Despite herself Lydia gasped at the beauty of the blade.

"It is a special blade, an ancient and mystic weapon passed from father to son in my family for over a thousand years. When my grandfather took the throne of Nara from the pretender who sat upon it he also took the dog's head with this blade. Ancient metal grows weak, brittle, but this blade only grows more powerful as it ages." He struck the bench with the sword, an almost gentle, casual chopping blow. The glowing blade sliced through the hard stone cleanly, cutting it cleanly in half.

"When my father saw that I had passed my sword on to another he bestowed this upon me. It is the greatest gift I have ever received; proof of the Emperor's faith and his love."

"It is beautiful, my lord." The green fire of the blade danced in Lydia's large eyes.

"Yes, well, it will have much work in time to come, and it will have to work hard to match the glory I have won with the blade that now hangs beside your bedroll. But as we speak the fleet is preparing to leave and I must depart."

He sheathed his sword. "Remember Lydia, work hard, learn well, and you may become the hand of Justice. Never forget!"

Lydia fought the urge to embrace the regal man who had been so kind to her, and bowed instead. He bowed slightly in response and turned to leave. She watched him stride from the garden, his long pace and rolling muscles reminding her again of a lion's. Her father had been a bigger man, more powerfully built, but Lord Zhe emanated a power that seemed to make him tower over all those around him.

The war between Lord Zhe, Admiral of the Imperial Fleet and heir to the throne of Nara, and the pirate hordes from the five vast archipelagos that formed the region known as Sinjun, lasted far beyond anyone's expectations. The Imperial Fleet could easily crush any seaborne enemy in the east and was second only to the mighty navy of Talvon, far away to the west. But that was in pitched battle. The Sinjun pirates, organised into a federation of thousands of captains, each calling a different small island in the archipelago home, refused to engage in open battle that would result in sure defeat at the hands of the superior Naran forces. The pirates instead opted to fight in small groups, ducking and dodging the Naran Navy in a series of running engagements over a vast area of open water and uncharted islands. Faced with a highly fragmented opponent, Lord Zhe was forced to split his armada into small squadrons who then chased the furtive pirates or sought and destroyed their home bases and unprotected families.

In return for this merciless destruction the pirates pounced on isolated ships and small squadrons, supply ships and lightly armed transports, snapping up victims when they could and inflicting terrible punishment upon those so unfortunate as to fall into their hands, burning officers with their ships, keel-hauling or quartering the crew that would not join them.

Despite the tremendous work of organising, coordinating and managing his many hundreds of ships, Lord Zhe faithfully found time to write small notes to his protégé. They would arrive by messenger every moon, and Lydia found herself spending what little free time she had dreaming of his adventures on the high seas, or commanding forces in a siege of a fortified pirate base. She longed for the day that she would be free from the school, for the chance to join in the glory of war in service of the Emperor of Nara and her master.

Two more examinations passed, each becoming less worrisome for Lydia, and she grew taller than her instructors, and the few students of her age who survived. Lydia's body began to change into a woman's as she reached eighteen years. With age Lydia fought to control the tempestuous passions of a young lady, finding relief from her swinging emotions and sudden rages in swordplay and dreams of battle.

She had been assigned a horse, a fine-boned, small-headed creature that was agile on its feet and highly intelligent. His name was Amaranth, and he grew quickly to love his mistress, learning to respond to her commands even before she had issued them, so that the girl and the steed became as one on the practice field. Riding bareback and clinging to Amaranth's sides with her vice-like legs, Lydia could cleanly sever a thick bamboo post with Lord Zhe's sword, or send an arrow through a loop smaller than her fist that had been flung into the air, both while riding at full gallop.

She learned more of the small magic and herbal lore that would heal wounds, and how to relieve pain with a gentle pressure from her fingertips, though she still did not excel in these studies. She was sent out into the wilderness, taken in a closed carriage for many days until she reached a distant mountain range, where she was left with nothing but a knife for a month, during which time the snows fell deep and she learned to appreciate the taste of raw meat. Her lessons in infiltration, sabotage and acrobatics continued unabated as well.

In her last two years at the school, scholars from other areas were brought to her dwindling classes where they shared their knowledge of History, the many lands of the world, and a vast array of animals, plants and even fell monsters. She learned something of the religions of other peoples, much of which she remembered from her time on her father's ship, and many of the myths and legends that had been collected by the scholars of the Great School over a millennium.

For the first time in three years, Lydia left the rambling, imposing school unescorted and wandered among the commoners and nobles of Marchit. At first she was completely unsure of how to function outside of the rigid confines of the college, but quickly became more comfortable both in the company of strangers and in the slender black pants and the richly embroidered red tunic worn by girls of her age. While the clothes felt tight and restrictive at first compared to the robes to which she had grown accustomed, Lydia came to be at ease in the strange garb. But while she was dressed as other

Naran girls she knew that her height and light skin still set her apart from the throngs of the great marketplace. Many eyes followed her as she wandered the streets, eyes that were often not friendly. She knew that when the time to act as the hand of her master came she would not be able to mix freely among the commoners of Nara, as her colleagues could, and she couldn't rely upon the anonymity that a Naran could expect in a city full of his fellows. She would have to disguise herself somehow.

From Master Zeno, an ancient, bright-eyed, cheerful scholar with a thin beard that reached below his knees, Lydia learned the names, positions and the mannerisms of the enemies of Nara. She learned of the many pirate lords, rebellious vassals, rogue monks and even some of the lesser of the Emperor's own relatives who would disrupt the empire, rob her ruler of his wealth or act against his power. Lydia worked with the ancient man long into the night, for he was tireless and never seemed to sleep, discussing the many real and suspected plots hatched by these men and women, veiled plans within plans. Lydia learned more of the labyrinthine mind of the strategist, how to apply their own tortuous skills against them in her own work as an assassin of those who would plot against her masters. With Master Zeno she developed plans, both short and long-reaching, strategies to get close to potential victims, and strategies to escape after she had struck her blow.

When she had spent some months in the man's tutelage, Master Zeno gave Lydia a name in a little envelope, and she was given two weeks to steal something from his person, for the master knew that if she could steal something personal from the nobleman she could also strike him dead.

The man was a general in the army, surrounded at all times by underlings, envoys and fellow officers. Lydia had scrambled to gather a disguise. Dressed as a soldier, she infiltrated his barracks as a recruit. Ten days later she escaped from the barracks, carrying the general's severed plait inside her jacket. Master Zeno was delighted at the prize she presented to him, and declared it the finest he had seen. While the outraged general's bodyguards searched the city for the imposter who had drugged their water and defiled the body of their master, Lydia had spent the day working with lance, sword and bow from the back of Amaranth, a smug grin on her face.

And still the letters came, some short, a few words only, and others long, flowing and descriptive. All were in the same elegant script, handwritten by her master. She preserved them carefully in a tight bundle in her cell, and re-read each one dozens of times.

In the nineteenth year of her life Lydia was summoned to Master Nhil's chambers. Masters Nhil and Han were awaiting her, sitting in their contemplative manner, side by side, facing the door. She entered the room, sank to the floor silently and waited.

After a further moment of contemplation Master Nhil began. "Lydia, you have reached the end of your time among us. During the last five years you have come to be our best swordsman, and you show great promise in many other areas. You must also remember though that while you have bested all those you have met in battle here at the school, there are many in the world who will be as strong as you, or even stronger. You must never lose your sense of humility, for it is with blind pride that we hide our weakness from ourselves. If you cannot match swords with an opponent, stab him in the back, for the hidden knife kills as surely as the open blade." At this, Lydia nodded.

"Master Han has kept Lord Zhe apprised of your progress, and the lord will accept you into his service. It is the greatest of honours to be accepted directly into the service of one as important as Lord Zhe. But then you know this, do you not?" Again Lydia nodded.

"Well then there is nothing left beyond this." Master Nhil handed Lydia a sealed letter addressed to her in Lord Zhe's flowing script and sealed with blood red wax. "You may open it tonight when you have left the school. You are to collect your possessions and then report to Master Han at his chamber." At this the sword master nodded once, sharply. "He will conduct you from the school. There is also this." Nhil reached into his cloak and withdrew a small leather bag that clinked merrily as he handed it to Lydia.

"What is this, Master Nhil?"

"You came to us with nothing, Lydia, but we could not send you from us with nothing. Unlike our other students, you have no family to buy you the things you will need to live on the outside. Lord Zhe has asked for us to advance your first month's wage."

Lydia bowed her head again in gratitude. "Thank you, Lord Nhil. I shall use what you have taught me with honour."

But the ancient assassin said nothing, and his eyes seemed as distant as the mountains that rose beyond the horizon. After a moment Lydia rose and left.

Lydia gathered her meagre possessions and looked for the last time around the cell that had been her home for the last five years. Bare now, she was struck by the smallness of the room; it was not much bigger than the closet that had served as her cabin on her father's caravel so many years before. She did not know where she would be living that night, but she thought she'd prefer a room with some space and perhaps a window, even though it presented a risk to security.

Taking her bundle with her, Lydia drew the curtain across the doorway to her cell for the last time and reported to Master Han's chamber. The master was waiting and after a bow by way of greeting led her through the maze-like hallways of the school and out through the wolf-doors into the blazing Naran sun. Walking side by side but in silence the two crossed the central plaza under the Emperor's tower that reached to the clouds, circled by the ever-vigilant guard of knights astride their wyverns, through the crowds of ambassadors from a hundred different cities and minor Naran nobles who gathered at the gates of the citadel, waiting in some instances for months for an audience with the Emperor's many representatives.

When they had crossed the plaza the pair followed a tree-lined avenue to a small courtyard that adjoined the plaza where the markets were held. Huge stone trolls squatted in their cages, awaiting fresh criminals to sate their lust for human flesh. The courtyard was shaded from the summer sun by dense, spreading trees and bounded on three sides by buildings of three or four stories with open balconies on each floor and small shops tucked into their ground levels. From a cafe the smell of fragrant Naran food wafted across the plaza, causing Lydia's stomach to grumble resentfully. Master Han led her to a doorway in one of the buildings, between a flower-dealer and a spice merchant's shop, and then climbed the narrow staircase that was just beyond the door to the building's servant's quarters. The silent monk ascended four flights of stone stairs, passing three landings, before he reached a single door at the top of the stair. Without knocking he lifted the latch and entered.

Lydia followed, immediately enwrapped by a cool breeze that flowed through the single large room inside, coming from an open balcony. The balcony doors were drawn to the side so that the room, more than twice the size of her father's stateroom, seemed to extend out into the sunshine, where tubs of fragrant flowers were bathed in the bright sunlight. The room itself was furnished in simple elegance with a large and soft-looking sleeping mat upon the floor surrounded by sheer silk curtains that had been drawn back, and a tiled bath in one corner. Against the plaster walls was a large, ornately painted wardrobe, a small dressing table with a polished mirror, a carved wood dressing screen hiding a larger, full-length mirror and a small writing desk with an elegant chair. To these had been added a range of colourful mats and cushions arranged around the room for seating. The entire floor, made of finely polished and waxed timber, was dominated by a large and intricate silk rug with whirling colours and patterns that seemed to come to life and dance before Lydia's eyes.

She turned to the monk at her side. "Whose place is this, Master Han?"

"It is yours, Lydia."

"But it's so rich," she stammered.

"You are a servant of Lord Zhe now Lydia. Of all men in the Empire, he is the second richest, second most powerful, and the second most feared. To be in the service of such a man has great rewards. But never forget, Lydia, that to be in the Lord's service means doing his will in all things."

"Yes, Master Han. I will not forget."

"Well, then, there is nothing left for me here. Before I leave, allow me to thank you for many, many wounds, and more than a few lessons in humility!" The man smiled broadly at her, and extended his hand to her, in the Danithian fashion. She clasped his forearm in the salute of her homeland, and then bowed as her teacher left. Though his lips had smiled, his eyes had remained cold and distant, as always.

Enticing fragrances from the cafe below wafted through the room on the gentle summer breeze and mingled with the sound of a minstrel playing his flute for the pleasure of those who ate a late midday meal under the shade of the trees. Lydia was sorely torn between the desire to explore her new room, to test the softness of her bedding, the cushions upon the floor, summon hot water from the servants on the ground floor for a bath, and her desire for the food, music and the cool shade of the plaza below. But there was her duty to do first, in the form of the letter from Lord Zhe.

Lydia laid the sealed note on her desk, quickly unpacked her few toiletries and garments and placed the large bundle of letters from Lord Zhe into a deep drawer in the writing desk. Behind the dressing screen she took off her white robes and dressed in the black pants and embroidered red tunic popular among the women of Nara and then studied herself in the polished silver mirror hanging on the wall.

During her time in Nara, Lydia had come to see her long western features, her nose and full lips as vulgar. In her adopted homeland the subtle, round-faced and thin-lipped women possessed smaller, more delicate features that set the standards of beauty. The swell of her breasts, not large by the standards of Danithian or a Talvonian woman was nonetheless too great for the Naran eye, and her long, muscular legs too ropy for their tastes.

But it had not bothered Lydia to be seen as ugly for so many years; the part of her that cared about what others thought of her appearance had waned as Lydia's pride in her skills grew, and she had grown to be dominated by the desire to master the assassin's skills and use them to destroy those who had taken her life from her. She only saw her appearance as something to be altered in order to get closer to her victims.

Lydia crossed to the writing desk where she had placed the letter from Lord Zhe, addressed in his flowing script. She broke the red seal and unfolded the letter with fingers trembling slightly in anticipation.

To Lydia, Servant of Lord Zhe
From Lord Zhe, at Sea,
the 15th day of the Month of the Rooster,
Year 2137

Lydia,

The time has come for you to enter the service of his Imperial Majesty. There is a man of Marchit, Lord Darran, who has done grave ill to the Empire. By day he swears his loyalty to the Empire and speaks on behalf of the Emperor to the traders who call upon the capital, but at night he directs bandits upon the plains to the richest caravans, taking of the spoils but not sharing of the danger. Kill him, but leave no trace of yourself or my involvement. That I have ordered Lord Darran's death is to be unknown to any but you.

By the end of the Month of the Crow punish his disobedience.

Lord Zhe

As with all of Lord Zhe's confidential letters the note consumed itself in mystic flame when she had finished reading it, leaving nothing more than powdery ash where it fell to the floor.

The end of the Month of the Crow was only a fortnight away. Lydia forgot the temptations of her new freedom and took up her katana, pacing from side to side of her room, holding the sheathed blade in her hands as her mind ordered itself in preparation for her upcoming mission.

My first real kill, she said to herself, rejoicing.

FIFTEEN

Lydia found her contact in the murky light of a smoke-filled tavern, deep in Marchit's poorest district. His name had been given to Lydia by Master Zeno at the school, who had told his eager student that the man was a tremendous source of knowledge with a great memory and a sharp ear for gossip, which he gathered like a spider from his shop and favourite tavern. Most importantly, he was loyal to Lord Zhe, and could be trusted as far as anyone could be.

But despite Master Zeno's promises that the contact was reliable and utterly confidential, Lydia did not trust anyone with her true identity. It would be too easy to link Lord Zhe to a young, exotic woman living in Marchit. Earlier, Lydia had gone to an obscure tailor's shop down one of the back alleys of the city where she had ordered a set of travelling clothes made in the Danithian style. She took her clothes to her room and washed them in her tub with a caustic mixture that made the grey and black cloth appear weathered and aged. To this she added the high, thick leather boots worn by overland travellers and a tattered cloak purchased from a rag dealer.

Sitting at her dressing table, Lydia pulled her long black hair back severely and into a thick club which she bound with a small length of black cord in a fashion popular among Danithian youth when she was last in her former home. She then took a tight-fitting girdle from her wardrobe, pulling it tight across her chest, until her breasts would disappear under the loose shirt she had purchased. Over this she donned the worn black shirt and grey pants, a battered leather sword belt and the travelling boots, and then examined her work in the silver mirror. The effect was acceptable; she appeared like a young Danithian man, somewhat weather-beaten, perhaps a bit effeminate. She took a non-descript broadsword from her wardrobe, hung the scabbard from her belt and left.

The contact was middle-aged, heavily built for a Naran, and unclean. He needed to shave and his lank hair was greasy. His clothes, once fine and certainly expensive, were now dishevelled and grimy. As the young Danithian man approached he raised his eyes from the table, took the pipe from between his lips and smiled, revealing two rows of perfectly white, sparkling teeth. He half rose from the seat as the youth silently slipped into the empty seat across from him. The man had fat-enfolded eyes that darted nervously around the room as the Danithian youth settled himself.

"What can Rasun, merchant of fine silks and man of honour do for you, my young lord?" The man waved his hand with an indulgent flourish as he described himself.

"I am looking for information. I am told that you will give it to me." Lydia dropped her voice, and to her ear it was convincingly like a young man's.

Rasun leaned back, contemplating the quiet young man across from him. Lydia could see the disgust clearly written in his porcine eyes.

"I have much information, my young lord, all about silks. What would you like to know? Are you looking for a bolt of finery for some young lady back in the west? Or young man, perhaps . . . ?" added Rasun caustically.

Lydia leaned forward and spoke in a conspiratorial voice. "That's not the sort of information I seek. We have a common friend who tells me that you know more than any man about the comings and goings of the people of Marchit."

Rasun spread his hands in a gesture of futility and smiled broadly. "I am not responsible for what others say of me, and in this, your sources are mistaken. Now my elegant young friend, you should leave before you get into trouble."

Lydia leaned closer to the man, her voice barely above a whisper, but still audible above the wailing flute music and conversations of the tavern's patrons. "Master Zeno will be displeased if I gain nothing from you!" she hissed.

Without showing any recognition of the name or the statement, Rasun whispered, "In the alley, to the rear." He never dropped the foolish grin from his face or his air of civil disrespect, and as Lydia rose from the table and turned to leave he called out, "Maybe you should go elsewhere to buy silks for your pretty young boyfriends, lad!" The other patrons nearby roared with laughter as Lydia stalked from the room, playing her part in the man's charade perfectly.

After the cramped, stifling room the cool night air was bracing. The meeting place was in a deserted, filth-clogged laneway that started just up from the tavern and meandered between sagging tenements and the backs of shops. The cobblestones ran with sewage, and Lydia had to pick her way around numerous pools of indescribable filth as she found her way to the rear of the tavern. Through the back door she could hear music and raucous laughter, but the alleyway was deserted. She concealed herself in the blackness of a doorway.

Within a short time Rasun emerged from the tavern's door. He staggered a bit as he called out a last farewell to someone inside, but when he pulled the rough wood door shut behind him and could no longer be seen from inside he straightened and looked purposefully around the alley.

"Psssst . . . boy," he whispered. When there was no response Rasun swore softly, and then called out in a louder voice.

"Hey you western fairy, where the fuck are you?" When there was still no response he swore even more crudely than before and began to walk down the alley in the direction from which Lydia had come. In the gloom he kicked a broken jar, stubbed his toe and cursed again beneath his breath. Trusting at last that he was alone, Lydia still followed him as he picked his way down the alley, carefully avoiding piles of excrement and other filth as she went. When Rasun had gone a dozen steps but showed no signs of setting up an ambush or waiting for compatriots to join him, Lydia cleared her throat. Startled, he spun and faced her.

"Well my fine young friend, I've not seen you before. You know what it is to use Master Zeno's name wrongfully, without his knowledge?"

"Yes, I do. I know his ways well. I am sure that you will speak to him of the Danithian youth before you give me what I ask."

Lydia was nothing more than a dark place in the shadows of the alley, and Rasun shivered when he saw that the Danithian youth had crept close enough to kill him without his knowledge. This was not lost on Lydia.

He shrugged his shoulders. "Fine, then. How can I help you?"

"I seek knowledge of Lord Darran, a minor servant of the Emperor."

"I see. A man of substance. He is the distant cousin of Lord Zhe, and due to his royal blood, he serves the Empire as a noble, an emissary for the Emperor. What else do you wish to know?"

"Tell me everything you know of him." In the dark, the dishevelled man grunted to himself. Lydia suspected that he was considering whether he should check on the young man's credentials, but the very act of using Master Zeno's name said that the Danithian was an assassin trained in the Great School. Apparently, Rasun decided to trust the young man.

"So, his dealings with the bandits are to come to an end? So be it. Some small graft is the benefit of every noble in the service of the Emperor, but like so many others, Lord Darran grows too greedy, too grasping. I am told that the last caravan his silent partners raided held goods that belonged to Lord Zhe's chamberlain."

As the night passed the man told Lydia everything he knew of Lord Darran. He was married, had four children, three whom lived in the small compound he owned in the wealthiest district of the city, one who was in service to the Emperor as a soldier. He led a lavish, wasteful existence, and his wife, a rough and uncultured woman, was known to be brash and crude. Darran himself kept the company of courtesans, but especially preferred the company of young men. Rasun even knew the names of the man's servants, who were all stealing from their master. He was guarded by four mercenaries, well-paid and experienced veterans, protected wherever he went, for he had made many enemies in his double dealings. In addition to the mercenaries, wandering the gardens of his small compound were Naran fighting dogs, trained to tear intruders apart. The waist-high beasts had been bred over a thousand years for their size, ferocity and loyalty, and particularly for their long fangs and powerful, vice-like jaws. They wore jackets of hardened leather, which could turn an arrow or a glancing blow from a sword.

Lydia nodded at each of these details and then asked many questions about the man's appearance, his habits and his haunts. When she had gained an extensive picture of her intended victim she quickly thanked the man and then turned to leave the alley. Rasun called quietly after her, "Wait! What is your name?"

Lydia paused for a moment at the end of the alleyway, barely visible in the early morning light. "My name is . . . Damio." She turned and vanished into the laneway.

SIXTEEN

Two nights later, and four before the end of the Month of the Crow, Lord Darran was lounging in his private chambers, stretched upon a divan in his favourite red silk kimono. He was watching a slender figure bathing behind an opaque screen. The young man, not much more than a boy really, was his latest fancy, a fresh pleasure for the Lord's insatiable lust. Darran lifted a gilt cup to his lips, taking a deep drink of expensive wine. A little rivulet of red ran down his chin, and he wiped it with an embroidered sleeve. Darran's eyes, burning with desire, never left his lover's silhouette. The cool night breeze that wandered through the room from the balcony did little to quench the heat with which he burned.

A flock of pigeons took flight from the roof above the balcony, their noisy flight disturbing the quiet summer evening's stillness. From the road below came the sound of drunken soldiers, but they were distant.

The middle-aged man heaved his body from the divan and lifted his cup to his lips for the dregs, licking at the last drops of the exotic vintage. He dropped the cup to the floor and reached for the tie that bound his robe, starting towards the screen, for the slender body behind the screen. Sensing the looming presence of his wealthy patron, the young man started to softly sing to himself, an old Naran song about lovers.

As Lord Darran reached for the screen a figure clad from head to toe in tight black dropped silently onto the balcony outside his chamber from the roof above, landing in a crouch just outside the doors. Consumed with his lust, Darran failed to notice the tall, slender figure rise and reach for the ruby-encrusted hilt of a katana. Darran heard the faintest metallic rasp, but before he could turn the assassin's blade arced out, biting deep into his neck. Darran's head was nearly severed, and it flopped forward against his chest in a gout of gushing blood as his body slumped backwards, falling with a solid thud upon the floor.

Hearing the thump, the bathing man rose, called out to his lover. When there was no response he sank back into the hot water of the bath and resumed his song, sliding down into the water, luxuriating in the scented heat, knowing that the bloated old lecher was watching him. The young man was enjoying his brief power over the older man, and began to sing louder until he saw something creeping across the floor, from just around the edge of the screen. He rose in the water, giving a scream of alarm when he realised that he was watching a pool of blood spreading across the stone floor.

The mercenaries had been banished to the hallway, as always when Lord Darran was entertaining with his young men. Hearing the man's screech they burst into the room, crossbows held high and sweeping for a target. The body of their employer was splayed across the floor, blood spurting from his wound and sending tentacles like an obscene red octopus across the tiled floor. Careful to avoid the spreading pool, the men searched the room thoroughly while their captain pulled the soap-covered man from the bath and pushed him violently.

"Where is he? Tell me, fairy!" The young man, overwhelmed with shock and fear for a moment, stared sullenly at the warrior, at the crossbow bolt aimed at his gut, but recovered quickly.

"I never saw him. Why didn't *you* see him?" He pushed the crossbow away, grabbed a robe from a peg on the wall and crossed to the body of the fallen Lord. He crouched at the side of man; his feet nearly touching the blood, and gazed into what had moments before been the face of a powerful and wealthy nobleman. He wondered how he would get paid for his services now that Lord Darran was dead.

Finding the room empty, the bodyguards rushed to the balcony. There was nothing but pots of flowers and darkness to be found there. Leaning over the stone railing, the men looked down the sheer, featureless side of the building, down two floors to a paved area surrounded by a high hedge of flowering shrubs. As they leaned over, a large black shape separated itself from the greater blackness of the hedge and stalked across the pavement. One of the lord's dogs, unaware of the chaos above, was wandering the grounds in its eternal nightly vigil. The dog looked up at the men's faces high overhead and gave a half-hearted bark.

There was no other escape than across the flat roof. The building was surrounded on all sides by a high-walled garden and stood too far from the windows of adjacent buildings for any assassin to leap to safety from the porch.

"You three, come here!" beckoned the captain, and he climbed up on the cupped hands of his underlings, who lifted him to the roof.

Crossbow at the ready, the man peered over the edge, seeing nothing in the light of his upraised torch. He dropped his crossbow over the small parapet and pulled himself up. The roof was empty save for a nest of fledgling pigeons. He angrily kicked the nest into the darkness below, and then saw something hanging from the opposite side of the parapet. He ran across and found a small grapnel, painted black and connected to a thin but strong rope that stretched into the night, making a slender bridge to the adjoining building. The captain drew a knife from his belt and severed the rope, hoping that the assassin was still suspended well above the ground, somewhere in the darkness, and that he would be dropped into the gardens below where the dogs would rip him apart. The rope, unweighted, fell gently, startling one of the fierce dogs, who immediately started barking upwards into the night. The other dogs raced to join their companion.

The mercenary returned to the other side of the building and dropped to the balcony, where he was greeted by the high-pitched keening wail of Darran's wife, who had just burst into her husband's private chamber to discover a young man kneeling over the body of her husband, struggling to pull a thick golden ring from the dead man's fat finger. The three other mercenaries stood by, grinning in amusement, as the blood-spattered pair fought.

Lydia fled the vacant room at the other end of the thin rope, still wearing the black garb of an assassin. She crossed to the far side of the dark building, a trading house that had been deserted for the night, and then set another small grapnel into a window sill and dropped a line to the street two floors below. She slid down to the street, looked about her to see if she had been spotted, and then ran into the night well before any of the mercenaries emerged from Lord Darran's gates to summon the Night Watch. When she had fled some distance, Lydia ducked into an alley, quickly pulled her black outer clothes off, folded them into a small bundle and hid them under a pile of rubbish. She emerged dressed again as a young Danithian man in weathered travelling clothes. By her unsteady gait she was clearly somewhat inebriated and just emerging from relieving herself, or himself, in the dark alleyway.

She crossed the resting city on foot, frequently doubling back to catch anyone who might be following her. During one of these sweeps, she unhooked her girdle, leaving it loose under her shirt, pulled the black ribbon from her clubbed hair, shaking the tresses free, and reversed her grey shirt, which was lined inside with rich red silk, embroidered in the popular style of Marchit. Dressed again as a woman she returned to the small courtyard by the great plaza. She paused for a moment before going up the narrow stairs to her room. There was some sort of commotion coming from the gates, the sounds of celebratory horns echoing in the night and shouts of joy coming from the guard. Wishing to be away from any eyewitnesses who could tie her to the assassination of Lord Darran she spent no more than a moment at the foot of the stairs trying to ascertain the cause for the celebration. But she could determine nothing, and so sped up the three flights to her room, unlocked the heavy door and entered the darkness within. From across the great plaza, sky rockets streaked into the heavens over the gates, bursting into huge fiery blossoms and drawing the few remaining sleepers of the city onto their porches and balconies.

A man was standing on her balcony, hands upon the rail, watching the fireworks. He was somehow familiar to her, large for a Naran man and broad shouldered. She cautiously snuck to the open doorway, drawn katana before her. Sensing her approach the man turned to face Lydia, folding his arms across his chest and grinning broadly.

"Now then, Lydia, where have you been this evening?"

The assassin sunk to her knees, bowing low. "Lord Zhe, you've returned," she gasped.

SEVENTEEN

"My lord, I did not know you were returning!"

Lord Zhe gestured for Lydia to rise. She realised that she was nearly as tall as he. In the coloured light of the fireworks Lydia saw that his hair had become more frosted with grey and his eyes were sunken from worry and exhaustion, and surrounded by a maze of fine wrinkles.

"Our war with the Sinjun Pirates is at an end for the moment. I am sure that in my time on the throne, some other admiral will have to be dispatched to deal with their impunity. That is why the Guard of the Gate are celebrating with this show." He gestured to the fireworks. "I have returned ahead of my commanders, upon the back of a wyvern, so that I could give the news of the peace treaty with the pirates to the Emperor before the celebration of the Last Day of the Month of The Crow. The Emperor will wish to speak of the victory when he addresses the nobles."

The last day of the Month of The Crow was the longest day of the summer and considered to be the last day of the year in the Empire of Nara. During the holiday even the poorest Naran citizen joined in the celebration of the passage of another year of the Emperor's rule. The Emperor himself would address the many thousands of nobles and dignitaries who would gather in the great square of his citadel, speaking from a high balcony in the tower itself. For the many that would be unable to hear the Emperor's words a great scroll was slung below the balcony, as wide as twenty men are tall. The elegantly lettered transcript was unfurled when the Emperor's speech was finished.

Lord Zhe stood back from his protégé, examining her with a critical eye. She felt slightly uncomfortable as his eyes wandered over her, and then suddenly became alarmed that this man, who reminded her so much of her father, would be interested in her as a man would be interested in a young woman. Lord Zhe clapped his hands softly with pleasure, and smiled.

"You have grown into a woman in the time I have been away. I should be proud to have any of my daughters grow into a woman of your grace and beauty!" Lydia had never thought of Lord Zhe as a man with a family, and she must have looked surprised, for he chuckled and added, "Yes, Lydia, I have daughters, and sons as well, and more wives than I can afford. I am a man, after all!"

"Yes, my lord." She joined in his laughter, feeling somehow deeply relieved.

"So, have you completed the task I set for you?"

"Yes my lord, I have just returned."

"Excellent, Lydia. He was a corrupt, degenerate man; a blot on our nobility and our honour. You have done well. And you could not be suspected?"

"No, my lord."

"Well, very well. Now sit and tell me of the end of your schooling, and I will tell you of the battles of the war, if you would like to be one of the first people of Marchit to know the story." He gestured to one of the cushions on the balcony, taking another for himself. "I have many, many tasks in the coming day, but I am not tired at the moment. The rockets are lovely, so let us spend this small time together before the morning light comes and my duties take me away."

They sat upon the cushions watching the fireworks of celebration illuminate the city around them. In turns they spoke of their lives until far across the wide plains surrounding Marchit the first light of morning appeared as a rosy glow on the eastern horizon. Lord Zhe paused for a moment, staring into the pre-dawn gloom where the last rocket had just burst, and then rose.

"I must go, my dear. I must prepare myself for a day of formalities. Thank you for our chat. It has been nice to see you again."

"My lord, I am the one who should thank you. I do not know how to thank you for . . . " Lydia found it difficult to find words adequate to summarise the generosity the man had shown her; "For everything!"

"You have repaid me tonight in a small way. By ridding the empire of that foul parasite, Darran, you have acted as the hand of Justice. For me, that is a rich payment indeed." Taking a small silver tube that hung from his neck by a light chain and placing it to his lips, Lord Zhe made a shrill whistle. Within seconds a great black shape, larger than the balcony, descended from the pale morning sky, and with it came a strong wind that threatened to knock Lydia from her feet. In silence eerie for such large beast, the wyvern landed upon the balcony, tucking its wings to its body, for otherwise it could not have fit upon the landing space. Lydia had never seen one of the fabulous creatures from such a short distance. It appeared to be a dragon, or at least it had the reptilian head and long, sinuous neck of a dragon, with the same glowing red eyes and dagger-teeth jutting from its closed mouth. But the feet on the stone of the balcony were those of a great eagle, ending in talons as thick as Lydia's forearm, and tipped in bright steel which would allow the wyvern to rip through metal armour. Unlike a dragon, the wyvern only had two legs. But like a dragon, it had a long, whip-like tail, ridged with bony spikes and ending in a great club, as large as a big man's head. The entire animal was covered with black scales, except for its face and upper neck, which were covered only with a thick grey hide. The wyvern was saddled, and crouched down at the approach of Lord Zhe, who sprang lightly onto the beast's back. With a final, short wave, Lord Zhe pressed his heels gently into his steed's sides and the winged creature crouched low before leaping into the air, spreading its wings at the apex of its leap and soaring off into the pale morning sky with a great rush of wind.

The following year was unlike any Lydia had known before. Other than the seven missions she completed for Lord Zhe, she found herself free to wander the streets and laneways of Marchit, one of the largest cities in the world, and certainly one of the wealthiest. There were hidden gardens to be discovered at the end of rambling alleys, dark and smoky taverns where merchants from all corners of the Empire gathered to gossip and relax when their caravans had been secured, and large, open plazas shaded by flowering trees and home to artists, poets and musicians, all industriously creating works of intrigue and beauty. Lydia was a particular fan of the wyvern races held every two months in the great central plaza, when the Imperial Guard would race their winged steeds around a course of large pylons erected around the sides of the open space, all desperately vying for the honour of victory. Sometimes the massive winged creatures even collided with each other and crashed to the ground in a lethal tangle, killing or maiming both beast and rider.

Lydia also discovered the less well-known quarters of the city where poisons could be purchased, where small magicians were available for hire to place a curse upon an enemy, and all of the other illicit goods and services citizens of the great city could desire were for sale. There, Lydia found the shadowy places where she could purchase the tools and services necessary to her trade without question from blank-faced shopkeepers. Disguises. Information. Hollow needles that could be fitted into the end of a cane, capable of injecting poison or acid. Ropes, grapnels, collapsing ladders. And naturally, weapons of every description.

After each assassination, Lydia would return to her apartment over the small plaza, surprised at the ease of the mission she had just completed. She was unsure if she was trained to a point that the standard defences employed by the corrupt officials, traitors and civilian bandits that she slew on behalf of Lord Zhe were simply insufficient to stop her, or if her natural skills were such that she was unchallenged by hired mercenaries, trained dogs or big cats, and trapped doorways. But for whatever reason, she found killing the wicked men and women a simple matter, once her meticulous preparations had been completed.

Lydia saw little of Lord Zhe during the year she lived above the small courtyard. He was rarely in the city as his many duties often called him to the far sides of the empire. When he was, Lord Zhe was usually involved in some ceremony, a meeting of state, or closeted with his father the Emperor, discussing the many perils and challenges that faced the empire.

The balmy summer nights like those of her first kill gave way to bitter winter winds that swept across the plains and over the plateau upon which Marchit stood, which in turn became mild spring breezes that warmed further into the balmy summer days where the air hung still and humid, heralding the end of the year.

Lydia began to find herself restless at times, suffering a sense disappointment when she wandered into a distant corner of the city only to find that she had explored the area previously, or annoyance when she was engaged in conversation with a man in one of the many taverns and the chat turned into a familiar, dull litany. The great city, once so exotic, threatened to become ordinary to Lydia, and she found herself yearning for a change, or a challenge.

A few weeks before the end of the year Lydia leaned against the edge of her high balcony, long hair drifting in the warm summer night breeze, replaying the events of the evening during which she had dispatched her eighth assignment, a man who had plotted directly against Lord Zhe. She had slipped through an open skylight into the man's bed chamber, slid down a slender silken rope like a spider, crossed a floor covered with near-invisible trip wires, and crept to the bed where he slept in the company of his wife. After pausing for the briefest of moments to ensure the man was her intended target she had killed him with a long, thin knife driven into the back of his neck, just under the base of his skull, without even waking the woman who slept at his side. Lydia pulled herself back up the rope, drawing it up after her, leapt to the next roof and made good her escape without ever raising an alarm. The man's death would not be noticed until his wife awoke in the morning, soaked in his blood.

While Lydia considered the ways in which she had improved since her first mission, where she escaped only just ahead of four heavily-armed guards, an unbidden thought came to her.

I am becoming bored.

None of her missions had been a true challenge. She had not crossed swords with any enemy; she had not faced an aware, prepared opponent, or even the real likelihood of failure. Her first mission had been exciting; the planning, preparing the disguise, her route of entry and exit, and the act itself had been like a great adventure, full of risk and with a noble purpose. But this last killing had been . . . she thought for a moment . . . *well . . . boring.* For years she had dreamt of becoming an instrument of Justice, and while she found satisfaction in her work, she found the long weeks between her missions left her too much free time, and she longed for something she could not name. Lydia was dispatching enemies of the state and good order, but she longed to see the fat-encrusted eyes of the Lord of Rimbu as she drove her acid-covered dagger into his guts. She longed for her own justice, to be free of the yellow-stoned city, and to travel in lands where the people did not see her as a foreigner to be suspected and shunned.

That night, as Lydia lay upon her mat trying to capture a short sleep before the sun rose, a figure appeared in her room, part ghost, part memory. The shape walked to the edge of the bed mat and looked down upon Lydia. Lydia awoke to the sensation of being watched, and when her eyes opened she saw the man staring down at her, face devoid of all emotion, except for a burning flicker deep in his eyes. She fancied that it was the flame of anticipation. The man was her father. He stood over her until the first light of dawn entered through the open balcony doors and then was gone. Lydia had lain upon her bed, transfixed, paralysed by those burning eyes. For the rest of her life she didn't know if she was visited by the ghost of her murdered father, a manifestation of her own deeper feelings, or perhaps had merely fallen into a light sleep during which her drifting mind had manufactured the entire visit. Regardless of the source, the vision left her even more restless and she spent the morning pacing her chamber, katana in hand.

As if in response to her feeling of ennui a messenger from Lord Zhe came to her that morning, bearing a sealed note. The man left without a word when he had completed his delivery. Lydia opened the paper at her writing desk, breaking the blood red seal with the tip of the long knife that she kept in her belt.

To Lydia, Servant of Lord Zhe
From Lord Zhe, at his Most Glorious Imperial Majesty's
Palace, Marchit,
the 20th day of the Month of The Pig,
Year 2138.

Lydia,

Four men are meeting in twenty days' time, in a tavern on the road between Marchit and Zaran, on the border between Nara and Movenda. The tavern is The Heavenly Cloud in the village of Stowe. The men are Lords Sera and Mentha of Marchit, Ambassador Arhjet from the land of Movenda and Cilliac, servant and emissary of the Lord of Rimbu.

You are to kill all of the men at the meeting and leave them as a sign of my displeasure. Bring me the head of Cilliac. He is the eldest of the four.

I have been pleased by your service this year. Our actions have removed eight enemies of the Empire. Complete this mission and we shall discuss the death of the Lord of Rimbu, an enemy to us both.

Lord Zhe

Her heart lurched as she read the welcome words. *Does he read what is written upon my heart?* she asked herself, not for the first time.

Stowe, she knew, was a small village tucked into the foothills at the base of the most frequented pass in the high mountain range that separated Nara and the Kingdom of Movenda, to the south and west of the empire, a vast natural rampart. The mountains were plagued by trolls, ice dragons and strange, man-like apes, covered in white fur and brutish, but intelligent, as well as many other fell creatures who lived on the icy slopes or even in the depths below the jagged and cruel mountains. Caravans would gather in the town of Stowe until several hundred travellers were encamped there and then they would brave the dangers of the high pass together, for to travel in small numbers in the Archeret Mountains was to invite disaster. The people of Stowe themselves lived behind a high wooden wall and at night mounted a guard armed with long bows and steel-tipped spears, ever-vigilant for evil wanderers. While these people were devoted citizens of the Empire of Nara, they were different than those who hailed from the lands to the north and east. They were taller with fairer skin, though they still had the subtle features and fold-covered eyes of the Naran people. Their speech was heavily accented and they used many words and expressions that were unknown in the rest of Nara, doubtlessly learned from the caravans that passed by their village during the warmer months.

Stowe was many weeks travel from Marchit by horse and longer by caravan or sedan chair. Lydia knew that the only way to make it to the remote village in time for the meeting was by wyvern. She had never ridden on one of the winged steeds; their use was restricted to only the most wealthy and powerful people of Nara. Yet there was no other way to reach the village in time. She scribbled a note at the writing table, sealed it with red wax and pulled a cord that descended from the ceiling near the entry to her room. The cord was connected to a bell that rang in the small chamber at the base of the stairs, where several servants-for-hire squatted in wait.

Within moments a young boy knocked quietly at the door, and she gave him the note, addressed to a man who knew a man who was the brother of a wife of a servant of the chamberlain of Lord

Zhe. The man was one of the few agreed-upon intermediaries between Lydia and her master. She paid the boy a copper sovereign and sent him speeding on his way.

Having sent her message and confident that her request would be complied with, Lydia gathered the provisions she would need on this latest mission. Her mind raced through the possibilities and at one point she sat down and wrote a brief list of items. When she finished the hastily scrawled column, she suddenly laughed to herself. *I am actually excited,* she realised.

She found the goods she might need: rope, grapnels, spikes and a small handle-less hammer, slender cord, small bundles of powder that would flash when thrown to the ground, others that would produce a nausea-inducing stench and impenetrable green smoke, a small collection of other incendiaries, form-fitting black clothes, a small case of pastes and creams that could disguise the colour of her skin, a bundle of throwing knives, a long, thin dagger and her ruby-hilted sword. Long ago she had learned to wrap the ruby in gauze, so that the lineage of the fabulous weapon could not be guessed. She also took the tight-fitting girdle that allowed her to dress as a man, her Danithian disguise, a small whetstone and a purse of coins, which she added to the small pile on her bed.

When she had collected her requirements and checked them against her list, Lydia folded and bundled all neatly into a small black canvas rucksack. Finally she strapped the katana across her back where it wouldn't interfere with her stride and tucked the dagger into her belt. She looked around her room for a time and finding nothing else that required her attention descended the stairs after securing the door to her apartment and setting the traps she left there when she was away.

At the stair's base she bought a rice bun from a cafe and waited in the cool shade of the building's awning for the young boy to return from his errand. When he came running empty handed through the plaza and into the doorway she produced a second copper coin as a reward for speed and diligence. The boy bowed deeply as she left.

In the mid-morning sun the stone trolls were dozing in their iron cages, snoring obscenely and muttering in their foul language. Lydia avoided the cages, walking in a straight line between the two walls of bars. Though her first meeting with one of the creatures was many years before, she still had nightmares haunted by the sea troll and his horrible, licking tongue. The iron-bound gates had been opened for the day and Lydia passed through the phalanx of armoured soldiers standing in formation in the archway. She passed under the wall and out of the city for the first time in well over a year.

EIGHTEEN

At the base of the plateau, Lydia took a broad cobblestoned road that ran to the west, arrow-straight through endless grain fields. The route was busy with caravans, messengers, tradesmen, farmers, all travelling to the capital or to one of many outlying villages or cities that dotted the plains. In places travellers jostled and yelled in frustration with each other when the traffic slowed to a crawl. Lydia walked through the morning, never leaving the shadow of the city that loomed over her shoulder, and into the late afternoon. Eventually, the city began to shrink in the distance and traffic lessened as her fellow travellers went their own ways over the many roads that branched away from the thoroughfare.

As night descended over the plains Lydia came to a hamlet, a collection of wattle-and-daub thatched huts rising from the surrounding grain and rice fields, home to a small community of farmers. A half-dozen pigs roamed the street in a loose pack and a child was squatting beside the road urinating as Lydia strolled into the town. Young women carrying swords were unheard of in Naran society and a matron scurried from her house to collect the child as Lydia passed by.

The town's inn was a low, long building made of the same mud and stick construction as the rest of the village and topped by thatch that had greyed and was in need of replacement. When Lydia opened the weathered door she found it was sparsely filled by a collection of farmers and their wives, a scattering of travellers, a boisterously drunk blacksmith and a small group of soldiers who had stopped for the night. As Lydia entered the low doorway everyone in the great room turned to study her. A young woman from the west, taller than most of the men in the room, travelling on her own, dressed as a Naran woman and carrying a sword, was of great interest. They all watched as she found a seat at one of the rickety wooden tables in the dining room. Lydia took her katana from its sling and laid it across the table, so she could sit down without interference. This caused some chatter among the patrons which Lydia ignored as she waited for the innkeeper. She was used to veiled stares and the vague feeling of being out-of-place in the bustling city of Marchit, but here in the country the gathered eyes of the people bothered her more than she would have expected. *Like cattle staring,* she thought.

Soon the innkeeper, a short woman as broad as she was tall, rosy cheeked and bright-eyed, bustled to the table with a flagon of ale. She placed the drink before the strange traveller, took her order for the evening meal and left to prepare the food, and have her houseboy turn down one of her few private rooms for Lydia's use. The meal was brought by a wide-eyed, younger version of the innkeeper. As Lydia ate the conversation gradually returned to the inn as most of the other patrons lost interest in her. But more than once she found the eyes of the soldiers caressing her body, lewd smiles on their drunken faces. She could not believe that they found her attractive; it was obvious that Naran men found women of the west unrefined and thick-featured. Nonetheless, their eyes did not wander elsewhere. As she finished her meal and ordered another flagon of the excellent ale Lydia placed her hand upon her katana and gave a meaningful look to the men. They hooted with laughter and raised their mugs in mock salute to her breasts.

Lydia finished her ale, left a generous payment on the table and summoned the innkeeper, who bustled over and led her down a short, dark corridor with guest rooms along both sides until they reached the door to Lydia's room. It was a little smaller than the cell she had shared with Shandala at the school, but painted in sparkling white paint and immaculately clean. As Lydia dropped her pack onto the mattress the innkeeper hurried off and returned with a basin and pitcher of warm water, and then left Lydia to her toilet and rest. Lydia stripped off her clothes and washed the grit from her pale skin, then settled onto the lumpy mattress. She was pleasantly tired from the day's travels. Within moments she slipped into half-sleep.

Lydia sensed them before she heard their footsteps. The sensation was something real, palpable in the darkness; an electricity, the feeling of danger, nothing that could be touched or heard, but real nonetheless. Then she heard the sound of a body stumble into the wall outside her room; drunk, doubtless, and staggering. Though she had expected them, she had slept, knowing that she would need all the rest she could pinch during the following days.

Lydia went to bed in her clothes, and awoke from a dream about her father and a half-remembered birthday feast. Silently she rose from the sleeping mat and took the katana from the floor beside her, drawing the blade from its scabbard. She stood next to the door, pressed to the wall, and waited.

In a few moments a heavy blow drove the door inwards and one of the soldiers stumbled into the room. From the hallway one of his companions called out, "Let us play with your pretty little sword, princess!"

With a short slash, Lydia cut deeply into the man's neck as he staggered, half falling, into the room. He dropped his sword and fell motionless onto the floor. "One!" called Lydia, to the men outside.

Someone yelled, "She's killed the Sergeant. Let's burn the bitch out of there." A lit torch was taken from a sconce in the hallway and thrown into the room, landing upon the mattress, igniting thick linen sheets. Seeing that her pack was safely stored in the corner away from the fire, Lydia held her blade in front of her and stuck the end out of the door, using the mirror created by the polished steel to see if the soldiers were on both sides of the door, and if any were armed with a crossbow. She could see none, but that meant little.

An evilly grinning man, standing just on the other side of the wall, swatted at her sword and called out, "Peek-a-boo, sweetheart!" They were on both sides of the door and the smoke was growing thick in the tiny room. Lydia took her katana in both hands and thrust it through the wall beside the door with all her strength. The blade punched easily through the thin plaster and woven sticks underneath. When she withdrew it the dark blood from the man ran from the blade, staining the white wall. Lydia called out, "Two!"

Knowing that the men would now be cowering, if not fleeing, Lydia strode into the hallway, but ducked back into the doorway when she heard the twang of a crossbow. A poorly-aimed bolt streaked past, burying itself into the door at the end of the hall. Lydia left the doorway again in time to see the two remaining men flee into the darkness of the great room. Lydia threw caution to the wind and pursued them. In the gloom she spotted the men running to the front door, scrabbling to escape. They found the door locked and knowing they did not have time to break through the thick wood, the soldiers turned to face Lydia, raising their weapons.

Lydia, the trapped man is always a dangerous foe! Master Han had given that lecture time and again.

The man carrying the crossbow dropped the empty weapon and drew a katana from his belt. The other was carrying a short spear with a knife-like point, deadly as both a slashing and thrusting weapon. The men stood in an area that was clear of tables and chairs, and as Lydia stalked closer they spread to the edges of the clearing, trying to get onto her flanks where they could attack her from both sides simultaneously.

"Want to play with my little sword, boys?" she asked with a wry grin. Her dark eyes glowed in the dim light with a predatory gleam.

The man with the spear ran at her, thrusting straight for her stomach. Lydia spun easily from the blow and turned, her blade swinging in a wide arc, cutting deeply across the man's back. The katana bit through his thick cloth armour and into his spine before she wrenched it free. In the next moment the swordsman slashed at her middle in a two-handed swing, but with lightning speed Lydia recovered from the blow to the spearman and caught his blade in a parry, deflecting it and crouching as the man's swing over-extended and he stumbled past her. The swordsman tripped on the sprawled body of his companion, but did not fall. From her crouch she swept her foot out and across the man's ankles, sending him crashing backwards to the floor. His katana clattered from his grasp and slid out of reach. In a flash Lydia was atop the man, her knee driving into his chest, the point of her katana digging into his throat, raising a dark welling of blood.

"Three!" she snarled into the man's face. She turned the katana sideways across the man's throat and leaned forward. "Was that what you wanted?" She rose from his chest, walked to the man's sword and picked it up. Lydia tossed the sword to him, hilt first.

"Want to make it four?"

The man, blubbering in fear, instinctively grabbed the sword, but then dropped it, kicking it away from him as he scrabbled against the locked door.

"Please, my lady . . . please . . . I have a wife, children . . . !"

Lydia shook her head and walked to the man, standing over him, looking down into his eyes for a moment with a considering look. Tears streaked down the man's filthy face and from the rising stench she knew that he had fouled himself. His lips were quivering as his gibbered apologies mingled with supplications.

"Go get my pack. Now!" she commanded. The soldier scrambled past on hands and knees. She kicked him squarely as he passed. At a safe distance, he rose to his feet and ran down the smoke-filled hallway. When he did not reappear quickly, Lydia thought that he might have been overcome by the smoke, but just as she decided that she would have to crawl down the hallway and retrieve the pack herself, the man staggered back through the smoke, choking and gasping for breath. He collapsed at her feet and tried to fling his arms around her legs in supplication as she picked up the bag and slung it over her shoulder. She stepped away, and brought her knee up sharply under his chin. The man arched backwards and fell onto his back. His eyes fluttered as he struggled with consciousness. When Lydia stood over him his eyes cleared, and grew wide.

"Explain this to your wife and children, then." She deftly carved the Naran symbol for 'pig' on the man's forehead with the tip of her katana. She then wiped the blood from her blade on the man's tunic and kicked him savagely, so that his body was rolled to the side and then lay still.

Looking away from the senseless man, Lydia saw the innkeeper and her daughter clinging to each other, peering from across the smoky room. The innkeeper managed to gasp, "Please miss, let us pass. I must see to the fire . . . "

Lydia sheathed her sword. "It is nothing but a burning mattress, and it will pass soon. But you'll find another two of these in there," she kicked the unconscious man at her feet for emphasis, "And you'll need a mop. Now unlock this door." The innkeeper's daughter fled to the kitchen, drawing water from the small well while the innkeeper unlocked the front door with trembling hands. The man with "pig" on his forehead was lying motionless, and the spearman she had slashed across the back was feebly crawling under the nearest table. Lydia drew her blade once more, pressed it home between the knuckles of the man's spine, where it met his neck. The man slumped instantly, and his breath hissed from him. Lydia, then turned to the innkeeper and said simply, "He'll pay for the damage," as she left.

NINETEEN

When there was the faintest gleam of light on the horizon Lydia came to a small rest station in the road. There was a well, a small grove of fruiting trees and a shrine. It was an oasis among endless fields, one of many that had been established in every corner of the Empire. Lydia saw a carved post at the edge of the road. In the bright light of the full moon she could clearly read the inscription; "For the rest and welfare of the citizens of Nara, by the generosity of the Most Beloved Emperor." Drawing a bucket from the well she drank deeply and then leaned her pack against the post and sat with her back to the canvas.

Lydia closed her eyes but did not sleep. Her mind drifted back to the four men in the village, as it had repeatedly during her walk in the cool pre-dawn hours. She had enjoyed the fight. Not the killing, though there was a satisfaction in that as well, but the actual fight, the challenge of being outnumbered, the feeling of triumph as she narrowed the odds, and then the warm afterglow of the battle, knowing she had risked herself, defended her life, and prevailed. These feelings were what had been missing over the last year and she felt a small, contented smile on her lips as she waited in the growing light of the morning.

The feeling of adventure, she said to herself.

She did not have to wait for long. There was a sudden rush of wind raising a small cloud of dust from the road and in almost complete silence a wyvern appeared before her. The rider swung his leg over the saddle and dropped to the ground. He wore the armour of the Imperial Guard, a shiny steel breast plate, thick leather pants inset with steel plates over the calves and thighs, a black cape and a pointed steel helmet. A broadsword was slung across his back and in a long quiver fixed to the double-seated saddle he had just abandoned were a mass of short, thick-shafted throwing spears. As the man presented himself to Lydia the wyvern hopped awkwardly across the clearing to the well and snaked its long neck into the dark opening, noisily lapping at the water.

When the guardsman removed his helmet, he revealed that he was young, not much older than Lydia, and tall for a Naran. He bowed before her, and held his hand out to take her rucksack. He had a friendly, open face and lively, bright eyes.

"I am Lieutenant Masa, of His Most Glorious Majesty's Imperial Guard. I have been sent to carry you to the village of Stowe. We must leave, as it is many days from here even on the fastest wyvern."

Returning his bow, Lydia replied, "I am Damio."

When the wyvern drank its fill from the well it hopped back to the pair, looking like a great vulture while it eyed Lydia curiously with glowing red eyes. The young soldier stored Lydia's rucksack in a large saddle bag and offered her a hand in mounting the steed. She refused his help, putting her boot into the stirrup and throwing her leg over the beast's back.

"Like a veteran, I'd say," declared the soldier as he climbed into the front saddle, and settled himself.

"I've seen it done before," responded Lydia. He turned in his seat, grinned at her.

"Hold on, then!"

With a lunge the wyvern was in the air, its body rising and falling powerfully to the rhythm of powerfully beating wings. Instinctively she dug her legs into the scaled sides of the beast, which turned its head and glared Lydia with a slitted, glowing red eye.

Lieutenant Masa called over his shoulder, "Gently, please. She's sensitive, you know. She'll not let you fall."

"Sure . . . " responded Lydia, though she felt a looseness in her bowels as the road and rest area shrank in size to a thin ribbon and a small green patch in the growing light. The wyvern circled, gaining elevation with great beats of its wings. When they were bathed in the first rays of the morning sun that had not yet touched the dim world below, the beast set off to the west. The air at this height was crisp and the wind blew bits loose from Lydia's plaited hair. She soon became accustomed to the rhythmic rise and fall of flying, and dared to lean slightly over so that she could see the landscape passing below. Far behind was a dark smudge on the horizon, all that could be seen of the plateau and city of Marchit.

Lydia found herself absorbed in the endless passing patchwork of fields, so that she was surprised when the wyvern started circling downwards at midday. Sensing her question, Lieutenant Mara called out, "Break!" over his shoulder as he navigated towards a narrow river that crossed the road they had been following. From the endless pattern of fields Lydia saw a small grove of willow trees through which the river wandered. The wyvern slowed to a near stop in the air and plunged the last bit into a small clearing amid the trees, landing on its eagle's feet and turning red eyes to her passengers, as if seeking approval and recognition for such a smooth landing. Lieutenant Masa leapt to the ground and offered an upraised hand to Lydia. She ignored his offer and landed nimbly beside him.

The soldier took a loaf of dark bread and a small pot of dharam, a thick, nutritious paste, from the saddle bag. He tore a piece from the loaf and with his dagger spread a thick coating of dharam on the bread and offered it to Lydia. She took it with a dip of her head in gratitude. Lieutenant Masa prepared some of the bread and dharam for himself and the wyvern hopped to the river, where it could be heard lapping noisily.

The road was deserted for a distance in both directions, and other than the few peasants in the nearby rice paddies, the two travellers were alone. Where the cobblestone road crossed the river an elegant but sturdy wooden bridge had been built, now greyed with age. Overhead the willows swayed gently in the hot summer breeze.

Lieutenant Masa removed his helmet, stretched his shoulders and legs and then took a seat with his back to one the willows. Tearing off a chunk of the bread he respectfully watched Lydia as she ran through a series of drills that she had been taught at the school, developed to keep muscle and sinew strong and limber, as well as the sword arm firm. Her katana glittered in the bright sun and her thick plait swung from side to side as she thrust, swept, parried, recovered and thrust again in mock battle.

She practiced with a single-minded passion for quite some time and then promptly sheathed her sword and walked to the river where she scooped water in cupped hands and poured it over her head and shoulders. Having washed away the sweat and dust of practice, she walked to where Lieutenant Masa sat and took another piece of bread. She sat down across from the young soldier and returned his gaze.

The man swallowed his mouthful of bread, and then said, "It is unusual to see a woman carrying a katana in Nara," in his forthright manner.

"You should not ask questions of me, for I have no answers."

The man smirked slightly. "That was not a question . . . it was an observation."

"Yes, you are right. It is unusual to see a woman carrying a katana in Nara." She took another bite of bread and chewed, returning Masa's gaze with a cool distance. He laughed to himself, not dissuaded by her sarcasm.

"Well, you must be an unusual woman. Perhaps that is why you have a man's name." Lydia responded with a slight smile and a bow of her head, and Lieutenant Masa leaned his head back, closed his eyes and dozed for a short time.

Lydia liked the young man; he was direct, honest and friendly. She respected someone of his age who achieved officer's rank in the elite Imperial Guard, knowing that he must have greatly distinguished himself to earn such an honour. She would have enjoyed speaking with him, for she rarely spoke with anyone frankly, but she also remember Lord Zhe's warning that her mission, her role and her position must remain completely confidential. She knew that if she were to tell the young man too much or if the obviously intelligent soldier discovered the nature of her employment she would have to kill him. Lydia felt that she would greatly regret the man's death. As it was, she was still unsure how she would conceal her mission from him.

After taking a long drink the wyvern laid down next to the river, flattening its body amongst a patch of reeds so that only its long neck and reptilian head was visible, remaining as motionless as a tree-trunk. Lydia had just turned her gaze down the road when the head shot forward like an arrow and dove into the water, rising back again with an eel as long and thick as Lydia's leg in its mouth. The wyvern tossed the eel into the air playfully and caught it in a dagger-toothed maw, slicing the thick, muscular body into three sections with a single snap. The wyvern ate the remains in quick gulps and then hopped to where Lieutenant Masa lay. The miniature dragon settled itself like a great vulture and placed its head beside the man's lap. With his eyes still closed the Naran idly scratched around a deep pore in the thick-hided head that lead to the wyvern's ear. The creature licked its lips with a long, forked tongue and appeared to doze.

Lydia ran through her drills again and was just beginning to become anxious to continue her journey when the wyvern and Lieutenant Masa rose together. The Lieutenant asked if Lydia had rested enough, and when she nodded he carried out a quick inspection of the saddle's straps and fittings, tightening the girth slightly and pulling on the saddle horn to check its snugness.

By way of explanation, the soldier said, "She's very good at loosening her straps." The wyvern lowered itself, and he climbed into his saddle. Lydia pulled herself up behind him and in moments they were soaring high above the plains again, streaking to the west.

That night they slept in a barracks in a small city. Lydia had a room to herself and though she ate with the soldiers she felt no common bond with the men, and stayed at a distance from them. Her memory of the four men in the tavern was fresh and while these men wore a different uniform and were perfectly courteous to her she could not help wondering if she had slain three of their friends the night before.

They departed before dawn, and that day was a near duplicate of the first. Lydia felt as if she were becoming one with the motion of the wyvern, as if the rhythm of the wings was being adopted by her own body. That night they rested at another barracks, and when they took to the sky in the pre-dawn light on the following day, Lydia could see a line of dark, brooding mountains rise above the western horizon, just beginning to appear from the night's gloom. As they circled for height the first rays of sunlight reached the tops of the highest peaks, which briefly shone bright red.

During the day the plains and fields of Marchit gradually gave way to rolling hills dotted with cattle, sheep and goats, and rivers running through wooded valleys. The large villages and cities of the plains became small settlements, hamlets and single homesteads. The road abandoned its arrow-straight course and began to weave through the rougher terrain as it rose to the nearing mountains.

As the day waned they came under the shadow of the great ice-capped mountains that formed the frontier between Movenda and Nara. Lieutenant Masa pointed to a narrow gap between two large mountains that seemed no wider than the road below them, barely wide enough to allow a wagon passage. "The pass," he called out. The pass was high over the hills below them, and well into the maze of white-peaked mountains which stretched out to both horizons like a great wall.

"That is the Ice Gate, as it is called out here. To pass into Movenda one must travel through that narrow gap and face the dangers of the mountains. It is so high that not even Marra, my darling wyvern, can fly over." Hearing her name the bird-like dragonet turned her head and gazed at the soldier.

A river ran alongside the road that snaked out of the mountains, a ribbon of white in dark stone. The water left the road to the pass and tumbled over a great fall, higher than a strong archer could fire an arrow from a longbow, as the track reached the last sheer edge, a vast featureless cliff. At the bottom the river vanished in a cloud of mist from which it remerged, flanked by two of the many rolling hills. Having escaped from the high mountains the water foamed and tumbled over countless small shoals. From above the waterfall the road snaked down a thin path cut into the last stone wall, doubling back upon itself many times as it dropped to re-join the river at the base of the falls. Where the river and the road met once more, the town of Stowe had been built.

Stowe was built across both road and river, and each side of the high palisade that surrounded the town butted against sheer rock walls. There could be no entry into or out of the Empire of Nara through the mountains without passing through the town. Most of the settlement was built of river stones and roughly-dressed pine logs, and the windows of the many houses and supply stores were small, to keep out the bitter mountain cold.

Where the hills rose to meet the mountains they were clothed in pines, much taller than the highest masts Lydia could remember from her years at sea. From this dark forest, great trees had been hewn, drawn by the labour of many oxen and erected in a wall that completely surrounded the town. As they flew over Lydia could see the tiny shapes of men patrolling the parapets, peering often into the darkening forest and mountains.

This near to evening the people of Stowe were closing the two town gates, preparing their evening meals and lighting blazing watch fires on the towers that lined the walls. None thought to look skywards or they would have seen a wide-winged shape circle the town slowly before turning to the higher mountains, where it disappeared into the growing darkness.

The wyvern came to rest alongside the head of the great waterfall on a small shelf of stone that overlooked the town and the hills rolling off into the distance. There were no other travellers in sight, for the mountains' evil was especially active at night and travellers would stay in small fortified shelters along the path for fear of the wrath of the spiteful creatures of that high country.

Lydia and Lieutenant Masa climbed stiffly down from the wyvern's back, feeling the effects of a long day's flight in their sore muscles. In the near-darkness the soldier pulled Lydia's black rucksack from the saddlebag and handed it to her. She drew her katana from her back, shrugged into her pack and tucked the scabbard in her belt. The soldier watched in the gloom, silently, until he could resist no further.

"Damio, if that is your name, what are you doing up here, at night? Do you not know of the dangers of the mountains? Allow me to fly you to lower country for the night. We can stay in the forest and return at first light. I know not what plans you have, but could they not bend that much?"

The tone of her reply was cold steel. "I told you not to ask me any questions, Lieutenant Masa." Standing awkwardly for a moment, she felt that she had been too harsh with the dutiful young man, so she added, "What must be done must be done by me, alone."

"What terrible business could you have in this waste?"

"Something that does not concern you. Your questions imperil your life. You doubtlessly have been chosen for this duty because you can keep your own counsel, so I advise you to do so." Her voice was firm, but not unkind.

"Let me help you, Damio, or whatever your name is. I am one of the foremost swordsmen in the Imperial Guard, and a veteran of the war with the Sinjun Pirates, where I fought in five campaigns. I am not as young as I look, or as soft." The young man's earnestness almost disarmed Lydia, but she knew that she had to act alone.

"Tell me, Lieutenant Masa, are you married?"

"Yes, I am, and I have two children. But they all understand that my life belongs to the Emperor, and none of us are afraid for me to lose it in that service."

"Well, then, your Emperor has told you to bring me here, and leave me, is that not so?"

Gloomily, he nodded in assent.

"Then that is your duty. I am deeply honoured by your offer, and I am greatly indebted to you for your service over the last days. But I must travel the path from here alone." She reached out and took his arm in a surprisingly vice-like grip. She tried to make her voice sound like something other than a threat. "And if you value your wife and children, you *must forget* these last days. Do you understand?" Lieutenant Masa nodded silently, as he would to a commanding officer, and he turned to mount his steed. "Remember," Lydia called to him, "in seven days, after the fall of dark, I will meet you here, at the top of the cliff. Do not be seen!" Again the man nodded in agreement and he climbed onto the back of the wyvern.

As the beast hopped to the edge of the precipice, the soldier looked one last time at Lydia and called out in a hesitant voice, "At least tell me what your name is." But he found the rock shelf empty; the woman, really no more than a girl, he reminded himself, had vanished into the night.

Lydia was relying upon the reputation of the mountains for concealment. She knew that there was a fortified camp further up the track where several caravans travelling together for safety could gather within a high stone wall. The fortification was close, no more than a short walk, but higher than the flight of a wyvern could reach.

She planned to don the girdle and clothes of the Danithian youth. From the waterfall she would trek up the trail until she reached the camp, where there were certain to be merchants spending the night, for the trail was heavily used during the short alpine summer. She would beg entry to the gated compound and claim to have been taken from an earlier caravan by the white-furred Archeret Ape-Men, only to have escaped after a few days, and having made it back to the encampment after trekking through the surrounding mountains. She would explain her possession of the fine and obviously expensive katana by claiming that she had found it amongst the man-apes, the relic of some long-dead warrior, and used it to fight her way to freedom.

When her ploy was accepted, she would begin the next phase of her plan.

After watching Lieutenant Masa vanish below the edge of the high rock shelf from the darkness at the very edge of the mountain, Lydia re-emerged into the soft moonlight and carefully made sure that she was alone. She then quickly removed the clothes of a Naran woman, pulled on and tightened the girdle about her chest and dressed in her Danithian clothes. The shed clothes she placed in a small oilskin bag, which she buried in the soft soil under a large rock at the side of the river. Before returning the rock to its place, she took handfuls of the soft soil from underneath and smeared them across her face, into her hair and under her fingernails, and rubbed soil across the back of her neck and over her clothing so that she appeared to have been living roughly for some time. Lydia then returned the rock to the depression it had laid in, covering the small bag of her clothes, and removed the few traces that the place had been disturbed. With the remaining soil she dirtied her rucksack so that it matched her clothes and skin, and chaffed the black canvas in many places with a rough stone. Finally, to make the disguise complete she slung the pack onto her back and walked over to a small stand of wind and cold-stunted pines along the side of the road. The contorted trees grew close together, providing a windbreak for each other, and their thin, whippy branches grew into a nearly solid mass. Lydia leaned forward and ran through the trees. The rough branches cut into her flesh and ripped her clothes. When she emerged she was cut in a dozen places, bruised, and she had small pieces of bark and pine-needles in her hair, clothes and caked between her rucksack and her back. Lydia knew she looked like a fugitive who had fled headlong into the mountains, wild with fear. Satisfied, she started up the trail into the growing blackness of the Archeret Mountains, ignoring the chills that ran up her spine as she left the land of Nara behind.

The moon had set over the plains below before Lydia followed the narrow mountain trail into a small valley littered with great round boulders that lay on both sides of the river, some as small as a man curled into a ball and others as large as a house. All were nearly perfect spheres, polished smooth by some unknown force. The track widened and passed through the valley to a narrow crevice where it then continued to follow the river upwards. Beside the track on the opposite side of the boulder field was a large cavern or perhaps a deep hollow at the base of sheer cliffs. Around the outside of this shelter a high stone wall had been raised, and a small gate of stout timber brought up from the lands below guarded the entrance.

As Lydia warily passed among the boulders she began to hear the distant melody of foreign music echoing from the stone walls. Soon she came to a clearing in the forest of stone, devoid of all but one massive, irregular stone, and found that she was at the edge of the far side of the valley. Before her, the river's noise reverberated through the narrow crevice from which the road came, and beside the track the long wall stretched, only a stone's throw from the base of the sheer valley wall. Firelight from behind the wall danced far up the mountainside where it mixed with and finally vanished into the overpowering darkness of the mountains.

Lydia crept to a sheltered position behind the lone boulder and peered around the rock, hoping to see if the travellers had posted guards at the gates that might shoot an arrow into a lone figure in the dark. She put her hand on the rock as she leaned around its side. Despite the cool night air the stone was hot to the touch, and seemed to pulsate under her hand. She pulled away in sudden fright when the whole stone heaved and contorted, but was too slow to avoid the gigantic, stony hand that swept down and seized her. Before she could even shout for help Lydia was raised into the air and turned around. She felt a hot wind upon her face and realized it was the breath of some giant creature that was holding her before its face, studying her. *Too large to be a troll*, she thought. *What is it doing, sitting here watching the gate?* Her thoughts flowed steadily, despite the racing panic in her heart.

Before she could consider the answers, a voice as ancient, strong and coarse as the mountains rumbled from the darkness.

"Interesting. I did not see you there, little ant." Lydia started struggling against the stony grip that held her firmly, but without pain, and the voice said one more word, while two dark eyes glowed for a moment in the darkness.

"Sleep . . . "

Lydia fell limp in the giant hand and the creature carried her off into the mountains, never making a sound that could be heard by the men gathered inside the camp, just on the other side of the stone wall, a bowshot away.

TWENTY

Lydia awoke in a deep bed of dry moss on a low shelf of rock, peering up at the roof of a large cavern. Somewhere in the depths of the mountain, in the darkness behind her, a waterfall roared. A merrily babbling stream passed by the moss bed and disappeared from the edge of the cavern. Morning sunlight was streaming through the cave's mouth, and in the walls many small crystals glittered like stars.

Afraid that she would alert the creature that she was awake, Lydia lay still upon the moss, straining her ears for any sound that would betray its presence. When she heard nothing, she sat up and found her rucksack and sword next to her. She stood up, pulling on the rucksack and unsheathing the katana. After a low step in the natural stone, the cave opened onto a grassy shelf surrounded by empty space, like a balcony at the top of a tower. The stream that ran past her feet fell a short distance from the mouth of the cave into a small pool before finding its way out of the far side and slipping over the edge of the shelf.

By some magic the cave and the grassy shelf were warm, though surrounded on all sides by high, ice-capped mountain peaks. Lydia left the cave, lowered herself to the edge of the pool and noticed that snow and ice came right to the edge of the shelf.

"It is my home, and it is beautiful, is it not?" It was the voice that sent her to sleep, almost painfully deep and powerful, like the roar of an avalanche or a rockslide. Lydia fancied that the ground shook with the voice, and that she could feel the air from the creature's lungs on her skin, though she was unsure if this was just her terrified imagination.

Lydia turned to face what she was sure was certain death. Not five strides behind her, seated on the stone step at the edge of the cave was a man made of stone. Or perhaps he should not be called a man, for he was as tall as a small tree, and as wide as a large wagon.

While his shape was that of a man he also resembled a statute; roughly hewn from marble, but without the fine work completed, so that he was all rugged angles and stony protrusions, and covered in deep cracks and fissures. He was of the same grey-black colour as the mountains around him. His jaw looked to be a single jutting piece of stone, and his nose a fist-sized river rock. In deep wells within the massive head the thing's eyes glowed like rock heated to the point of melting. The creature's feet and calves were covered in thick green moss, growing like living boots.

"Welcome," it added when Lydia staggered backwards from the fearsome figure and came to a crouch beside the little pool.

"Why am I here?" Her voice was soft, weak.

"Because you are interesting to me. Because all of you humans are interesting to me, but, in particular, I find you most curious." The thing smiled, his face cracking and scraping like stone being torn asunder and then rubbed together. "I am the Mountains."

Lydia, still overwhelmed by fear, nonetheless began to become curious about the creature. Reason dictated that could easily crush her, pick her up and fling her from the shelf into the icy depths below, not to mention the way it put her to sleep last night with a mere word. If the thing wanted her dead, it would have dispatched her before.

"What do you mean, you are the Mountains?"

He laughed gently, a great rumbling sound. "Just that! As you are, so am I. You are you, and I am the Mountains. It is that simple. Do you not see?"

Though Lydia did not understand, she feared offending the creature by asking it to explain itself.

"Why are you interested in me?"

"Well, you are interesting, are you not?" The thing chuckled to itself again, and put an elbow upon its knee and its great stony chin its palm, looking Lydia over with its glowing eyes.

"How?" was all Lydia could manage to ask.

"Well, you are a woman, dressed as a man. While that is not so uncommon, you are also carrying a sword, and that makes you rather curious. But most of all, I caught you scurrying around outside the men's camp at night, when all others are afraid to venture forth. And for that matter, why is it that I could feel your touch upon my side, and see you when I looked at you in my hand, but I could not see you before, at a distance? I can see everything in these mountains, in all mountains, for I am they and they are me. I see without even looking. But not you. You, I can only see with these eyes that I fashion when I take on this form. So tell me, what is it that you are doing, scurrying around in the dark like that, and who are you?"

"I . . . .I am on a mission. For my master."

"Ho ho . . . .now that *is* interesting!" With a grating sound the creature rubbed its palms together in anticipation before placing them on its knees and leaning forward. "What sort of mission, and who is your master, and why did he choose you? Yes, yes, I have many other questions. Yes, yes, you are an interesting specimen indeed!"

"Sir . . . " Lydia grappled for the words. "Sir . . . I am bound to silence. To speak of these things is death, and it would dishonour me, which is worse than death!"

The creature flung back its head and laughed deeply. Lydia clasped hands to her head, afraid that the sound might burst her eardrums. The creature rose from his seat, for by this time Lydia had decided that the creature was a he, though she had no sure way of telling, and strode past Lydia to the edge of the precipice, where he flung his arms wide and raised his hands to the skies and his head to the morning sun. From behind the mountain they were perched upon a dark, thunderous storm cloud suddenly swarmed over the sky, blotting out the light. A lightning bolt streaked from roiling black clouds and engulfed the creature, which stood with arms still raised, bathed now in crackling energy. He lowered one arm and pointed the other to a distant mountainside. The lightning left his body, running up his arm and shooting from his finger, arcing to the distant rock wall. With a tremendous explosion, the side of the mountain disintegrated; snow, ice and rock all tumbled into the depths below. Without turning to face Lydia his voice boomed out, echoing from mountain to mountain, launching avalanches on all of the surrounding peaks and shattering ice-weakened rock. The force of the thing's voice drove Lydia backwards, and she sunk to her knees.

"Did I not tell you that I am the Mountains? What could be more terrible than my wrath?" Then, the creature lowered its hands, and the black storm clouds dissipated as quickly as they had appeared, and the creature turned to Lydia with a smile on its face and good humour in his voice.

"Now, come and have a seat, and tell me about yourself."

By the midday meal Lydia had reached her fight with the troll on the beach of that distant, fog-enshrouded island, and the death of Braide. The creature had been very curious about the karinga, and asked to see it. He was very disappointed when Lydia told him how it disappeared shortly before she had been taken from gallery of her father's caravel.

"Well, well. These things have a way of turning up again, you know. Most interesting, evil things are."

Lydia found the creature oddly companionable and had started to become comfortable telling him the secrets of her life. She had never spoken of many of the things she told him and as her tale unfurled, Lydia started to feel as if discussing her stormy past was lifting a weight that had hung from her. The creature sat silently for long spells and then would ask dozens of questions when some occurrence or person piqued its interest.

But by midday her voice was becoming raw and hunger gnawed at her, so Lydia asked if she might be allowed to have some of the loaf that she had put into her rucksack at the last barracks she had stayed at. The creature seemed genuinely embarrassed that he had not realised that Lydia was hungry or thirsty. She ate bread smeared with dharam and drank ice-cold, sweet water from the pool by which they sat. When finished, the creature urged Lydia to continue her tale.

Then she came to the deaths of her father, Moad, and Mrs Habden at the hands of Captain Dheree and his pirates. The creature's eyes glowed brightly and its stony brows knitted, though it did not interrupt her story. Lydia told of her rescue by the forces of Lord Zhe, her enrolment in the Great School, and despite her tremendous loyalty to her master, of the work that she did for the great man, even though to do so was a violation of her duties. With her tale finished she sat quietly, staring into the clear water of the pool as the creature considered her words.

After a long while he spoke again. "Yes, yes, I see now. Very, very interesting, Lydia. I did well to choose you. You do have something unique about you, something more than what Lord Azursus told you of. Your heart is different, almost as if it were not human at all! And while I must admit I have only heard of those who cannot be 'seen', as you call it, and never met such a person before, I have also met few of your type, as in humans, who are truly sincere, and they must be nearly as rare. And you are truly sincere, are you not?"

"What do you mean by 'sincere'?" asked Lydia, who was puzzled by the creature's odd comment.

"Well now, yours is a busy little race. A bit like ants or even bees you are, always cutting into stone and building with stone and running here and there. But there is something I do not understand about your busy little kind. While you build and destroy and race about, you, and I mean you as a species and not you personally Lydia, seem to never know where you are going and what you are doing. From my home here I have seen your kind build great cities hewn from my very flesh and then destroy them without ever truly knowing why they have done any of it in the first place."

"But I only do what I am told. How am I different?"

"Because you are. When you fought those men in the tavern why did you kill the three that you did? You did not have to, did you?"

"They were going to attack me, do things to me."

"But Lydia, from what you have told me, and I know that it is the truth, you were never in any danger from those men. You could have disarmed them, rendered them unconscious, and left them humiliated."

"Well, I guess wanted to see them punished for their . . . " she struggled for a moment to put a word to the concept she had in mind. "For their wrongness, I guess you could call it."

"And why did you leave the other one alive?"

She spoke suddenly, with a quiet vehemence. "I wanted him to tell others. Because I wanted him to warn others."

"Did you enjoy killing those three?"

Lydia shrugged after a moment's reflection.

"But you thrived on the idea of meting out Justice when you cut the last one, did you not?" She nodded at this.

The creature slapped his hands on his knees with a resounding noise. "Yes! Yes! You *are* interesting! How many times this day have you spoken of Justice in one way or another? I will answer for you: many, many times. Like most of your kind, you love the idea of Justice, fairness, a restoration of the balance of things after a wrong has been committed. But most of your kind is happy to let others mete Justice for them. From what I have seen, and I see far from up here, your type hides behind soldiers and officials and courts and royal decrees when Justice is called for. Perhaps this is a good way, for it avoids lawlessness, but then all of these are human institutions, and humans can and do fail. Therefore, your Justice, *human* Justice, fails. Not always, but often enough. And if something as important as Justice is not absolute, then it has failed. Do you understand?"

Lydia nodded her head, though she was unsure that she did. The creature studied her for a moment, and then continued.

"Now you; you are different. You see injustice and you act. Not through others, but with your own hand. You pay no heed to other's concepts of rightness or wrongness, and are content to pass judgement yourself, with no regard to the ideas of the rest of Humanity. That, Lydia, is not the way of most humans! The Justice that you win with your sword is human justice, and therefore it, like you, is prone to be misguided, but at least you seek to bring order in your own life before turning to others for help. You are sincere in your desire for Justice; you win it with your sword. Though you may follow the direction of another now, you may find that when you choose to do otherwise, when your quest takes you on another path, none will be able to stop you."

"But why does this make me unlike other humans?"

"Because other humans are destroyed by their anger at injustice. Because even if they act righteously other humans are destroyed even as they destroy others. They are destroyed by leading lives of violence, but where they fall to pieces you are made whole. What breaks their hearts makes yours beat more steadily."

After this Lydia and the creature sat for a long while, she contemplating the story of her life, the long and twisting route that had brought her to this high mountainside, and his strange and disturbing words. The creature was distant, absorbed in its own thoughts. Finally, Lydia turned to the huge figure beside her and asked, "What is to become of me?"

"How do you mean, Lydia?" He looked down at her with something like curiosity in his glowing eyes.

"I have told you what you wanted to know, so what are you going to do with me? I must complete my mission within six days,"

The creature laughed deeply. "Busy, busy little ants. Always so busy! Here is what I shall do with you, Lydia Estrella, daughter of Markus Estrella, Assassin of Nara. I am going to make you sit here upon the edge of this, the tallest mountain in the world, safe and sound within my house, and I shall make you watch a sunset from higher than any of your kind have ever been, or will go for many, many ages to come, and then I will carry you to the camp at the base of the cliff and put you back exactly where I found you. Does that suit you?" He chuckled, and rising from his seat, vanished into his cave. Lydia was again amazed at the lack of noise from the creature when he moved about.

He soon reappeared in the entrance of the cave and resumed his seat. In the creature's hand was a large piece of glistening black rock. He held it out for her to study.

"It is a stone that was made from living things long ago. One day your busy kind may find a way to harness its energy, for it has much. This may be the death of your type, or your rebirth into something new. But now, let me show you a little trick." He held the stone between cupped palms and pressed inwards with such force that the mountain they sat upon shook. As the rock shrunk under his tremendous force it began to glow white with heat, so intense that Lydia threw her hand up to shield her face. The creature hunched its shoulders for one last massive effort, and then held out a small, glittering object that had replaced the black stone. Without thinking, Lydia held out her hand and he placed the object in her outstretched palm. It was a diamond, as large as her thumbnail, and perfectly formed.

"Payment for your services, human," rumbled the creature's deep voice.

Coming from behind the mountain the last rays of the evening sun began to turn the sky into a vast wash of colours; yellows, oranges and even deep purples. But under it all was a sea of blood red, growing to dominate all the other colours until the entire sky was a sea of fire above their heads. Lydia held the stone he had given her in her outstretched palm and saw that it absorbed the colours of the heavens and glowed red in her palm. "Thank you," she said simply. "It is beautiful."

The creature replied, "Rebirth, Lydia. All life is rebirth; or it is death. Sometimes both. There is never one without the other, anyhow."

In the early hours of the morning he sat Lydia back in front of the gate and before she could say farewell to the strange creature with vast, godlike power, he was gone, vanished into the crisp mountain night.

As she walked slowly to the wooden gate, she realised that she had never told the creature that her surname was Estrella, or that her father's name was Markus.

TWENTY-ONE

The men of the caravans, men from many different lands, took the young Danithian into the compound, prepared a meal for him and grouped around as he haltingly told the tale of how he had fallen asleep when his caravan paused to take water at the river. He had awaken to find himself bound and being carried away by the white man-apes to a cave high in the mountains, where he found the katana he now carried in the severed skeletal hand of some long-dead warrior, cast aside in a large pile of human bones. At this detail, the men muttered amongst themselves in their many languages, for it was widely known that the man-apes of the Archeret Mountains craved human flesh beyond any morsel. The Danithian youth told how he had slain the creature guarding him with the sword and run from the cave into the broad daylight. The man-apes pursued him in great numbers, but he stumbled upon an icy slope and slid into a crevasse, far faster than the fell creatures could follow, and thus escaped. Finding himself bruised and cut at the bottom of the crevasse, but otherwise unhurt, he fled along a small stream, reckoning it would eventually join the river that ran alongside the track through the mountains.

One of the traders, a large man from Movenda, armed with a huge scimitar and covered in a fine lacework of battle scars and warlike tattoos, sat scowling throughout the story. The man wore a large white turban and a loose, heavy mail shirt that would have wearied a smaller man after a day's walk. When the young Danithian finished his tale the man spat into the fire with a fierce scowl and asked, "Could you lead us back to this cave of apes?"

Lydia had been fearing that the man had seen some flaw in her guise, and now she wondered if he were testing her. She appeared to think deeply for a moment and then shook her head.

"No, I could not. I can easily show you where the creek joined the river and the road, but the crevasse itself is long and had many other creeks joining it, and there are many ice slides along its length. I'm sorry, but I could not take you to the cave."

"It is a pity, Danithian, for we could return there, with those of the men here who are not afraid of a fight, and finish these foul monkeys for good. Long have I travelled the Great Road of Archeret, and many are the men I have lost to the evil creatures. I for one would like to be rid of them for once and all."

Lydia, relieved that the man seemed to believe her, responded, "I would gladly join you, sir, but I need to try to catch up with my caravan. They would have passed through some days before, and those I travel with will have given me up for dead already."

"Yes," the grave man nodded, "this is well. But at least now I know where to begin in my search, and I will one day find this cave, and destroy the evil that lives within." The squatting man rose from the fire and before he left told Lydia to rest, for the caravan would leave at first light, not long away now, and finish the journey by the end of the following day. "If you fall asleep again during the day, the apes will have you back as their guest for sure!" At this the man laughed and the others around the fire joined in. Lydia grinned herself and then found a space under one of the large oxen-pulled wagons and fell asleep, her head resting on her battered rucksack.

After a long, dusty day the caravans passed through the gates of Stowe. Once they were in the safety of the palisade the leaders left their underlings to unhitch and water the stock amongst the crowds of the town's central plaza while they reported to the Customs House.

Lydia, quickly forgotten during the pre-dawn bustle of breaking camp, had quietly followed in the vanguard of the caravan, finding a stick to lean upon so that she could walk in a manner more convincingly weary. Once inside the palisade she slipped away from the others and down one of the smaller but busy laneways of the town. She had been given a detailed plan of the town by Lieutenant Masa, which she committed quickly to memory before destroying, and so she easily located The Heavenly Cloud.

The inn was a large three storey stone and pine log building on a narrow laneway near the gate on the road to Marchit. Lydia stood upon the cobblestones in front of the iron-bound plank door and surveyed the building, pretending to squint at the carved sign that hung over the laneway, so as to not appear suspicious. The inn, which butted against adjoining buildings of the same height on either side, was dotted with only a few small windows, for the air this close to the mountains was frigid at night, and even during the day the winds were crisp. Some would allow her entry, others were too small. High above, the roof was thatched. There were no balconies or ledges on the face of the building, though the rough stone work of the facade would allow Lydia to quickly and quietly climb without the use of ropes or grapnels. But there was still the problem of the small windows, and knowing what room the meeting would be held in.

Lydia knocked heavily upon the door of The Heavenly Cloud. She had four days to finish and execute her plan.

The door was flung open by a slender girl, not much younger than Lydia. She bowed shyly to the weather-beaten young man who leaned upon a rough staff in the doorway. More of Lydia's plan fell into place, as if by magic.

Speaking in a husky, faltering voice and leaning heavily upon the stick, Lydia inquired, "Have you a room? I have had misfortune in the mountains, and must rest . . . " She started to sway gently, as if fighting a swoon. The girl leapt forward, taking Lydia by the arm and led her inside. Like most inns in Nara nearly the entire ground floor was one open room, dominated by a roaring fire in the centre, over which a spit turned with several pieces of meat roasting and dripping aromatic juice onto the coals below. There was the usual collection of battered tables and rickety three-legged stools and in the shadowy depths of the rear of the room Lydia saw large barrels of ale and smaller casks of wine, neatly stacked. The inn was only lightly sprinkled with patrons.

The girl from the door lifted Lydia's rucksack from her shoulders and helped her onto a low stool. "Sit, good sir, and I will bring you a strong ale. It will soon restore you." She hurried off to the back of the room, where one of the large ale casks had been tapped.

Without faltering in her disguise as a weary and wounded traveller, Lydia quickly studied the room more carefully. The other people in the room were a collection of men and a few women from all the corners of the globe. She knew that few if any of them would be from caravans, as merchants liked to stay close to their goods, maintaining a vigilant eye over their livelihoods. From the dress and snippets of conversation that she could hear they were a motley collection of monks, travellers, petty officials, soldiers and adventurers, many of whom had been forced to remain in the village while the imperial officials considered their applications for entry to the Empire of Nara. Without the artful use of graft and satisfactory grounds for entry a traveller could find themselves a guest of the town of Stowe for many months.

The girl returned quickly with a leather mug of dark ale, a half loaf of bread and a bowl of the thin, sweet yoghurt that the hill peoples of Nara relished. Lydia ate and drank with the deliberate slowness of a weary person who struggled with hunger and fatigue, but wished to savour every morsel of a feast. When she had eaten and finished the warm, hearty ale the girl returned in the company of a tall middle-aged Naran man. The man had a large scar across his cheek and a deep crease through his nose, memorial of a distant battle, and he walked with the erect poise of a soldier.

The girl put a protective hand on Lydia's slumped shoulder. "Father, this is the man who just arrived. I have fed him some small food and given him ale, but he looks poorly. Should I send for the healer?"

The girl's father crossed his arms over his leather apron and studied Lydia for a long moment. Finally, he shook his head and replied, "No, child, I am sure that if this worthy traveller was in need of a healer he would have requested one." Speaking now to Lydia, he continued. "Are you the one who was found outside the gates of the last camp of the pass this morning?" Lydia nodded, trying to appear both meek and weary. "Have you money to pay for lodging?" asked the innkeeper.

Lydia responded with a nod.

"What is your name, lad?"

"I am Damion, of Danith, sir. I have some money, and would beg cheap shelter, even in the stable for some nights so that I may regain my strength. I must try to find my caravan, which passed through Stowe some nights ago."

"Have you lodged an application for entry at the custom house, lad?" Lydia shook her head, looking surprised and confused.

"What is that, sir?"

"All who enter the Empire of Nara must lodge an application and be approved by the imperial officials. A few sovereigns might help, as well."

Looking desolate, Lydia hung her head. "I lost my travelling papers in the mountains. What can I do? Will they allow me to pass without papers?"

The innkeeper, who was also the owner of The Heavenly Cloud, shook his head gravely. "No lad, you will not be allowed to enter. And for you to enter without permission is a grave crime, punishable by death. You will have to wait here until you are strong enough to make the journey back through the Archeret to Movenda, where the border officials are more generous."

"But what of my caravan, sir? What will I do?" Fear crept into Lydia's voice, and the Innkeeper, a veteran of the Imperial Army and a man of resolve, frowned at the weakness in the young Danithian man's voice.

"As long as you can pay, you may stay here until some caravan who will have you along agrees to take you back over the pass. Perhaps if you act . . . " he thought for a moment, "like a man who had some experience with hardship, they will take you." His attempt at tact thinly disguised the man's contempt for the young traveller. Looking quickly from father to daughter Lydia saw that the father's disapproval was not mirrored in his child, who was looking from Lydia to her father and back again with growing concern, lest the innkeeper turn out the poor youth.

"Thank you, sir, thank you." A single tear ran down the Danithian man's cheek, and the innkeeper bowed curtly.

"Enjoy your stay, sir." He turned and left, leaving the girl standing in his wake. She took Lydia's flagon and returned quickly with a fresh draught of ale and a shy smile, and then turned her attentions to the inn's other patrons, who had begun calling for ale, and meat, and singing in small, merry groups.

The small bag of coins Lydia concealed in her black rucksack held, among more valuable currency, a large number of copper coins from the Realm of Movenda, each representing a tiny amount of money in Nara. Over the next days she spent them frugally, begrudging each one as if it was her last. Two days before the meeting was to occur, she ordered no food for the morning meal, asking only for a small cup of ale instead. The Innkeeper's daughter, truly a soft-hearted soul, noticed this and ran to her father, whom she found supervising the morning's labours in the stables behind the inn. She plead with him for sympathy and forbearance, asking only that the man let the boy from Danith work in some small way to pay for his lodgings, so that he might have some money for his return to his home country.

The innkeeper, with the deep bias of those who had spent much of their lives in the armed service of their land, still felt a mild dislike for the boy. The child, for he was really not more than an overgrown child in the Innkeeper's eyes, was too soft, too quick to cry, too quick to surrender himself to bad fortune. He was not surprised that his daughter was taken with the weakling; she had sympathy for everything lame, homeless and unable to fend for itself. He shook his head, remembering how she had taken in that three-legged dog, blind, toothless and ancient: how she had pined when it had perished. But if the man had one soft place in his heart it was for his daughter, and so he relented.

"He may stay for free for another week, but he must bring the wood, help with the supplies, and clean the crockery. You make sure that I get my fair deserts from the boy, you understand?" The girl nodded her head quickly, clasped her father's hand quickly, and then ran with her good news to the still-weak Danithian.

The young man was at first embarrassed, and tried to refuse, but when he saw that the girl was greatly upset at the prospect of her charity being rejected he accepted, promising enthusiastically to work twice as hard as he must so that he could prove that he was worthy of the girl's generosity. She then brought him a meal of yoghurt, flat bread and milk. When he had finished she showed the Danithian to the small room where the inn's crockery was washed.

Lydia was content as she washed the many dishes that were stacked in the room. Her plan was working better than she could have imagined.

On the last day before the meeting a man came to the inn from the mountains. He was large, heavily muscled but also graceful. While he would not have seen more than thirty years his face was battered and weathered. The traveller wore no uniform but his manner spoke of a man who had spent his life in service and combat. In his belt was a large scimitar and three long, curved knives. Also hung there was an iron ball the size of a man's fist, linked to a thin chain. Lydia had seen the meteor ball, as this weapon was called, used by masters and she knew that it was a formidable weapon.

He arrived in the morning, having ridden from the last encampment in the Archeret Mountains to The Heavenly Cloud on a large, sleek horse, as swift as the wind and as agile as a mountain goat. When he strode through the door during the midday meal a dozen conversations halted and the eyes of every person in the room followed the stranger as he crossed the room with the innkeeper's daughter trailing behind. The Movendan presented himself to her father, who stopped checking the contents of his ale kegs and immediately led the man upstairs. As they went the pair passed by the little cupboard where Lydia was just finishing the morning's dishes. Lydia saw that the pommel of the Movendan's scimitar was a steel ball, formed into a grinning skull with tiny rubies for eyes.

They returned after some time and sat at a table in the back corner of the room, far from the other patrons. Finding the innkeeper's daughter busy, the innkeeper and his warrior companion signalled for Lydia to bring two ales. She took two newly-washed flagons, filled them from the best keg of beer and placed the brimming mugs before the men. The innkeeper grabbed her arm and in a harsh voice ordered the boy to stand up straight.

"This is Damion. He's lost his caravan and he's serving me right now, until he can get back over the mountains. He's the only other person in my employ who tends to duties in the house, other than my daughter."

The newcomer ran a grim eye over the boy, and grunted, "He's not much of a man. Looks like a girl to me. Can he serve?"

"He'll do, sir, or I'll have him thrashed." The innkeeper shook Lydia's arm firmly. "Tell me boy, can you serve wine without spilling it on anyone?"

Lydia gave a meek nod.

"Good, because if you spill one drop I'll have you flogged and damned be my soft-hearted wench of a daughter. A few lashes would make your hide tougher anyhow. Now go finish those dishes, and then come and find me. We've got to clear a room for some guests."

"Yes, sir," Lydia responded quietly, and she hurried back to the washing room. She heard the Movendan warrior growl, "Pansy!" and then lower his voice further as he resumed his consultation with the innkeeper.

That afternoon, Lydia and the innkeeper cleared the furniture from the inn's largest residence, a well-appointed room on the first floor that faced the lane and was flooded with light from four small windows. When the room had been stripped of its furnishings they brought the inn's best table up from the dining room and placed four finely carved silk-cushioned chairs around the sides, ready for the meeting.

When Lydia finished with the night's chores, she found the innkeeper in the meeting room, polishing the table with an oiled cloth.

"Sir, do you have any more for me to do tonight?"

"No, if you've finished the dishes and filled the wood box in the kitchen then you are done. In the morning I want you to leave the dishes and take three casks of the wine from Harjii, the good stuff with the red stripe. Tie them in a sack and spend the morning with the wine sunk in the river to cool. Be back before the midday meal and make sure you are clean. And boy," he added with a fierce scowl on his face, "you better not dishonour this house tomorrow. The men will give you balls of wax to put into your ears so that you cannot hear what is said, so you'll have to keep your eyes open and make sure no one's glass goes empty. You hear?" Lydia nodded her head once gravely and then left the room as the innkeeper resumed polishing the table.

During the coldest, darkest part of the night, Lydia rose from her bedroll in the stable, dressed in her black clothes and hid her face behind a veil. With katana strapped to her back she climbed from the small, flea-ridden loft and crept silently to the back of the inn. Knowing that she would run the risk of being seen if she entered the backdoor Lydia quickly scaled the rough stone wall, pulling herself onto the thatched roof and running lightly for the front of the building. As she reached the roof's peak she disturbed an owl who had been peering down at her. In a silent explosion of grey feathers the bird took to the air, keeping a wary yellow eye on Lydia as it rose into the night. Not finding a trustworthy anchor for a line on the front of the inn, Lydia climbed down the front of the building using what hand and footholds she could find in the wall and slipped into one of the open windows of the meeting room.

The room was only dimly lit by weak moonlight filtering through the windows, but Lydia could clearly make out the long shape of the table and the smaller chairs around it. Ducking underneath the tabletop, she took a small bundle from within her tunic and unrolled it at her feet. She completed her task in a few short moments, making only the softest thudding noises, and then ran nimble fingers over her handiwork. *It will do*, she thought.

Astride the window sill and about to climb back to the roof, Lydia heard a heavy step in the hallway outside the room and a key slipping into the room's ornate lock. Silently, Lydia fell backwards, tumbling mid-air and landing on her hands and cushioned feet in the dark laneway. Light shone from of the windows overhead, and she hid quickly behind a line of empty beer kegs awaiting collection. Confident that her blackened body and face could not be seen, Lydia peered over. Staring out into the night with his large, scowling head jutting from the window was the warrior who had come the day before. Her heart skipped a beat and her hand silently darted to the throwing knife in her belt when his eyes passed over her, returned and seemed to be trying to pull her form from the blackness in which she hid. His glance rose when the large owl Lydia had disturbed landed silently on the eave of the building across the lane, watching the two inscrutable humans with large yellow eyes.

"Piss off," yelled the man at the owl. The bird ignored him, and with a grunt the warrior withdrew his head and closed the window. Lydia could see his shadow wandering from wall to wall, and the room went dark again. She remained silently enfolded in the shadows until the man had had enough time to return to his room, and then scaled the front wall of the building, crossed the slippery thatch roof and found her way quickly to courtyard at the rear of The Heavenly Cloud. Pausing briefly at the back door, ears alert for any noise from within, Lydia scanned the rear courtyard with night-sharp eyes. Finding nothing, she slipped back into the barn and her loft, where she removed her black clothes and cushioned slippers, placing them in her rucksack, and returned to her cold bed.

TWENTY-TWO

At first light Lydia arose, tightened her girdle and made her way into the darkened inn. She took three barrels of fine wine, a loaf of bread from last night's meal and a small pot of yoghurt and placed everything on a handcart with netting and rope, and a small bundle that she had carried with her from the loft. Then, chewing on a mouthful of bread, she made her way out of the gate of the back courtyard and down to the river that ran through the heart of Stowe. When she had secured the barrels in the netting, tethered them to a small tree and set them adrift in the river Lydia secretively rolled the bundle of her black clothes and the tools she knew she wouldn't need again into the dark, fast-running waters. Then she sat, back against a leaning tree, and turned her thoughts to the upcoming mission.

As the sun rose Lydia went through her plan again, making sure that she had not forgotten any contingency, that every possibility, however slight, had been tended to. She decided for the tenth time that she was ready. By the end of this day, four men would be dead, and she would have taken the next step towards the death of the Lord of Rimbu. She then lay back on the grassy bank and watched the clouds passing overhead, thinking of very little as the town awakened, and began its morning bustle.

When the sun was nearly overhead Lydia knew that the time had come, and that her first true test as an assassin was to commence. Everything in her life, from her endless practice with Braide to her fight in the tavern outside Marchit had been nothing more than a training ground for this moment. She rose, pulled the kegs of wine in from where they had settled on the river's bed and put them into the cart. On her return to The Heavenly Cloud she again mentally rehearsed her plan, this time with complete confidence. Lydia found herself excited, but more than any other emotion she felt a sense of pride for the job she had, in her mind, already completed. There just was no chance of failure.

After pushing the wobbling handcart to the backdoor of the inn Lydia handed the casks to the innkeeper's daughter, who laid her hand flat upon the side of each cask and nodded her head.

Lydia returned to the loft and made her final preparations. She took her rucksack and placed it in the low beams, wedged with the lacquered wood scabbard of her katana in a shadowy corner. She had thrown her knives, grapnels and every other piece of equipment that she would not need into the river that morning, and what she did need she secreted in a small pouch hung inside her girdle. If what else was concealed within her girdle was discovered, she would be found out and the pouch would not matter.

Lydia swept the dust from the beam with her hand, and from the pouch she drew a length of cord with flammable powder in the centre. She took a lantern stolen from the inn and lit first the wick then the cord from the lantern's flame. Then Lydia removed the chimney and wick from the lantern, leaving herself with a glass flask full of oil. Lydia placed the oil next to her pack with the unlit end of the cord in the liquid and stretched the fuse along the beam and ensured that nothing could found on casual inspection. The cord was magical; it cast no smoke, and would burn evenly, reaching the oil at the exact moment Lydia desired. She would know the moment by counting to herself, which she had practiced to the point where she could do a number of things, hold entire conversations or even fight without losing her place. Today, the number would be three thousand.

Crossing the courtyard, Lydia straightened her clothes, the grey and black Danithian garb she had purchased so long before in Marchit, and entered the back door of the inn. The innkeeper's daughter rushed over, handing Lydia a cask of wine wrapped in a cold, wet cloth.

"They've arrived, and they will be sitting down. Hurry!" With great urgency the girl pushed Lydia up the stairs. On the first floor two Naran soldiers wearing long mail shirts and pointed steel helmets were standing at attention on either side of the door, swords held bare. The innkeeper was waiting there too, holding a tray with four polished silver goblets and a matching pitcher.

"Here, you bloody pansy, take this and hurry up. I'll have you skinned if they are kept waiting." He handed the tray to Lydia and one of the soldiers stepped forward, sheathing his sword and running his hands over Lydia's body, squeezing her limbs and pressing the small of her back. Fortunately he kept his hands off her chest, and only gave a cursory pat to her groin, which was padded with a rag. Finding nothing, the soldier took two large balls of wax from his pocket and kneaded them until they were soft. He then pressed them into Lydia's ears so that the wax was driven deep inside, but the other edge of the ball stood out from the edge of her head. Lydia knew that if the men even suspected that she overheard their plans she would be put to a quick death. She had been relying upon this, knowing that the innkeeper would not risk the life of his daughter for the sake of one meeting, but that he would be happy to sacrifice the soft boy from Danith.

The door was opened and Lydia entered, carrying first the tray of goblets and then the cask of wine and a small folding stand from which she would pour the wine. While she set the stand up in the corner and settled the cask upon it the fierce man from the night before shut the door tightly and locked it with a key that he returned to his pocket. He tested the knob, finding that the lock had caught, turned and stood in front of the door, arms crossed, scowling at an unseen point over the heads of the men gathered around the table.

There were four of them, as the letter from Lord Zhe had foretold, all hunched over the table, discussing their plans in low voices. All were old, or well-into middle age, with long beards and intelligent eyes. Their clothes were made of the finest embroidered fabrics which showed no sign of travel or wear whatsoever. Through the balls of wax, Lydia could hear the cadence of their voices but could distinguish nothing else. She placed a cup before each man and carefully poured a draught. Ticking like clockwork, her mind counted to two thousand as she returned to her place in the corner of the room, beside the cask, the pitcher held rigidly before her. Her eyes flitted from cup to cup as the men drank and spoke. Twice she refilled cups, though the men did not notice her presence leaning over them.

They were all armed, but soft-looking, indulged nobles who only knew swordplay from lessons forced upon them as youths. Even their swords were garish and decorative. Yet Lydia knew that even a flabby hand could wield a weapon effectively, especially if driven by panic.

Two thousand seven hundred fifty. Two thousand seven hundred fifty-one. Two thousand seven hundred fifty-two. It was time.

Lydia refilled the silver pitcher from the cask and then meekly walked towards the table past the stoic warrior guarding the door. Two paces from the table she stumbled and the pitcher fell from her hand, splashing wine over the feet and legs of the two conspirators closest to her. She stooped over to pick up the pitcher but clumsily kicked it as she reached so that it skittered under the table. From behind she felt the looming presence of the huge warrior reaching for her, most likely with the intention of throwing the awkward foreign boy bodily from the room. Lydia ducked under the table as he grabbed for her and scrambled across the floor to where the pitcher rested against the far table leg. She reached up under the table's edge, shook her head so that the wax balls fell free and pulled off the thin strip of wood she had tacked into place the night before, freeing her bare katana from where it had been hidden under the tabletop. She then backed out from under the table, katana held high up under the tabletop where it could not be seen, and dragged the pitcher noisily across the floor with the other hand. Above her she heard the angry shouting of the two wine-splashed conspirators and the laughter of the other two, who had escaped the accident.

When she reached the edge of the table the great warrior's hands took her by the waist and started to pull her towards the door. With a quick flick of her wrist, she reversed her katana so that it pointed backwards; as the point flashed out from under the table the warrior dropped her waist and fumbled for his own sword. Lydia rose to her feet and fell backwards in a single motion, driving the blade behind her. From its low angle the tip of her blade lifted the edge of his mail shirt and bit into the big man's groin, driven deep by the momentum of her body. As she withdrew her sword Lydia heard him grunt explosively.

As soon as she pulled her sword from the man's gut, and before the others could fully realize what had just happened, Lydia slew the two men nearest her, each with a quick chop to the neck. She then turned just as the warrior, mortally wounded but with a berserker fire in his eyes drew the large iron ball and chain from his belt. Lydia, seeing the two remaining men huddle in the corner, swords drawn and held before them like narrow steel shields, knew that she would have to finish her duel with the warrior quickly before they gathered their courage and attacked her. The big warrior spun the meteor ball over his head, holding the chain in his other hand, even as blood poured upon the floor between his feet.

"Come boy, and join me in Hell!" The man loosed the iron ball, which, like the meteor it was named for, streaked towards her face. Had Lydia not known this weapon well she would have not had time to react to its lightning strike and it would have caved in her right temple with its impact. As it was, she barely weaved out of the way of the ball and as she did the man swept her feet from under her with a perfectly-timed kick. Lydia landed on her back, sword above her and only just had time to raise her blade in defence as the man swung the ball over his head and downwards with both hands. She held her sword out like a staff in both hands and rolled to the side. The ball passed over the blade in its path to her face, but the chain caught upon the blade, causing the ball to alter its course. Lydia felt the solid impact of the heavy iron sphere as it crashed into the floor less than a finger's width from her head. With the bleeding man leaning over her, Lydia lifted her legs, kicked him squarely in the chest and then jumped to her feet as the man staggered backwards, strength failing as his life spurted from his wound.

Lydia heard the two men shouting to the soldiers posted outside the door for help as they left their corner. They approached Lydia from either side, working their way slowly around the table even as the big warrior shook the stars from his vision, dropped the meteor ball's chain, and tried to draw his scimitar. But the big man's failing strength was starting to betray him, and the berserker light had left his eyes. Knowing the he posed the greatest risk, regardless of his wounds, Lydia drove the razor tip of her katana through the man's throat. He made a gurgling, croaking sound as blood began to spout from his wound and fill his mouth. The warrior stumbled backwards and then slumped against the door, staring incredulously at the young man that had just killed him as his vision grew dim and then went black.

The eldest of the men, the one that must be Cilliac, leapt to attack Lydia. As she recovered her blade from the blow that felled the warrior, she caught Cilliac's blade upon hers in a parry. The other man, the Movendan, swung his scimitar from behind her in a great arc, hoping to catch her between his blade and the katana she held at bay with her arm. Lydia dropped to the floor, allowing Cilliac's katana to push her downward, and the scimitar passed harmlessly over her head, creasing Cilliac's chest as it went. Lydia crouched lower, formed herself into a ball and rolled away from the two men. When she was clear she sprang to her feet and faced them again. The wounded man cursed as the two men turned towards Lydia, obviously planning to again attack as one.

From the door came a tremendous crash. Lydia knew that the warrior she had slain had insisted that he have all copies of the key to the room, but that the innkeeper would have more, despite the man's request. The innkeeper would have to run to his quarters to retrieve them. The soldiers outside were trying to break in, but the heavy body of the slumped warrior strengthened the door so that it resisted their armoured shoulders.

The remaining conspirators rushed Lydia. They attacked simultaneously, from opposite sides, so Lydia was forced to duck below one blade and parry the other. She chose to duck below Cilliac's blade, and as she did so his knee came up and crashed into her chin, sending her reeling back onto the lap of the dead warrior. For a split instant she saw a hundred shooting meteors, but her head cleared quickly. The men were closing to attack again. Lydia, still sprawled on the dead man's lap, flung herself up and sent the tip of her blade through the Movendan's belly. The man dropped his scimitar and grabbed the blade. As Lydia tried to withdraw the sword she severed his fingertips. But the blade stuck fast in the man's torso. Cilliac's blade was again coming for her. Lydia was forced to release her grip and roll away before his sword bit into her shoulder.

Two thousand nine hundred twenty three.

Cilliac stepped backwards and raised his katana in the classic over-the-head attack stance as Lydia sprung to her feet, hands empty. Seeing that his would-be assassin was unarmed the old man grinned. "Lord Zhe's assassins are slipping," he said mockingly just before he rushed at Lydia, blade streaking towards her head in a deadly arc. She stepped to the side, clear of his strike, so quickly that the man could not stop his downward blow, and struck the man with an upward palm to his face as the force of his own blow pulled him downwards. The man's nose collapsed and shards of bone drove into his brain, where they worked like tiny daggers. The old man's body spun to the side with the force of Lydia's punch and then fell to the floor. His dead eyes stared at the ceiling.

Two thousand nine hundred eight five.

Lydia placed her boot upon the dead Movendan's shoulder and pulled her blade from his chest, using the weight of own body to remove the sword. Behind her another crash shook the door, but it still held. She would slay the guards without compunction, for they would be traitors like their masters, but she did not want to kill the surly innkeeper or his simpering daughter. Blade still dripping, Lydia took Cilliac's hair in her grip and pulled him forward so that his brow nearly touched his knees. With a single clean stroke she severed his head.

Three thousand. Had she not known what to expect, she wouldn't have heard the distance shouts that came from the bowels of the inn, presumably from the rooms at the building's rear.

Lydia placed the head on the table, cut Cilliac's cloak from his shoulders and wrapped her grisly trophy. Tucking the heavy, wet bundle into her tunic she leapt from the window as she had the night before, into a crowd of fascinated bystanders gathered. They surged backwards as the blood-soaked figure plummeted into them, landing upon two feet and one hand like a cat, the other hand holding a red-soaked katana. Lydia sprang to her feet and raced back into the inn through the front door.

Inside the ground floor room the patrons who had been enjoying their midday meal were pressing to the back of the room. The thatched stable had just burst into flame and smoke was billowing from the hay lofts. Lydia pushed her way through the stunned people and was about to run out of the backdoor when someone grabbed her arm. Lydia raised her katana to strike, only to find her assailant staring at her with huge, terrified eyes.

"Why?" asked the innkeeper's daughter, "Why did you do this to us? Our guests, our barn? Who are you?"

Lydia paused for a moment, as if struggling for an answer, and then reached into her tunic, pulling out a blood-soaked pouch which hung by a thin leather thong. With a wrench she tore it free and placed it in the girl's hand, folding her fingers over the pouch.

"Because it is who I am," Lydia replied in her boy's voice. The girl gaped as Lydia pushed past the last of the patrons, and ran into the billowing smoke and spark showers of the burning barn. The magnificent steed that the Movendan warrior had arrived upon yesterday was tied in readiness for his departure. Flaming straw fell around her as Lydia found the horse. The beast rose upon its hind legs in terror as she came near. Dodging flailing hooves she cut the halter ropes binding the animal to the collapsing barn, grabbed the horse's mane and pulled herself up on his broad back.

The horse had been trained for war, but trapped within an inferno and having a strange person reeking of blood upon his back was too much. He desperately tried to kick the clinging human free, but when she struck him a stinging blow across the rump with the flat of her katana he came to his senses, allowing himself to be guided out of the barn and then into a leap that carried them both over the back fence to the alley beyond. The thatched roof of the barn collapsed with a roaring crash as the two, rider and steed, raced down the alley towards the gate leading to the Archeret Mountains.

Rushing to the aid of those who sought to quell the fierce fire at the rear of The Heavenly Cloud, the town's guards had left the gates unmanned. Lydia flew through the opening of the palisade and towards the peaks virtually unnoticed by any of the rushing people of Stowe.

Standing in the back courtyard, bathed in the fierce heat of the burning barn, the innkeeper's daughter opened the blood-soaked pouch. A single, perfect diamond fell out onto her palm and lay glowing red in the firelight.

"Who are you?" asked the girl to the image of the young Danithian she conjured in her mind's eye.

As she streaked through the tall pine forest towards the high pass Lydia passed the grey owl sitting high in the branches of a tree. The solemn bird was watching the road with large yellow eyes. It silently followed, lifting into the air on wide wings as the Movendan horse galloped past, driven by terror and the persistent smell of blood. Horse and rider, tailed distantly by the owl, hurtled towards the track that wound up the side of the cliff beside the waterfall, and then vanished into the mountains.

TWENTY-THREE

Lydia paused on the ledge where the mountain river tumbled into the great waterfall. Far below in the village of Stowe she could see a black pall of smoke in the afternoon sun, but from her perch she could also see that the villagers had halted the fire before it spread too far. She was relieved; while she had required something to draw the town's attention from the battle in The Heavenly Cloud and her escape, she had not wished to cause undue damage to innocents.

With the flat of her sword she gently slapped the flank of the magnificent steed that had effortlessly brought her to safety and that now stood beside her, sides heaving and lathered with sweat, reluctantly sending the horse back down the mountain to the town where it would be safe from fell mountain creatures. She watched as the horse trotted to the road that descended the rock face.

As the evening approached, Lydia knew that this stretch of road would be deserted by travellers. She turned from the expansive view of the valley below and found the rock hiding her Naran clothes. It had not been disturbed. Taking the oilskin sack from its hiding place, Lydia took off her Danithian disguise, her girdle and undergarments. During part of her flight she had ridden through the deep forest, away from the road, avoiding a long caravan that had just wound its way down from the high pass and was starting on the final stretch of road to Stowe. As a result, she was covered not only in the dried blood of her victims but patches of sticky pine sap, needles and the grime of travel. She unwrapped Cilliac's head from his cloak and placed the gory souvenir into the oilskin pouch that she had taken her clothes from, and then gathered all of the blood-stained garments. Tying them into a bundle with a rock the size of her head she threw them into a deep eddy at the edge of the river, where the swirling water turned back upon itself under a high ledge of rock. Then Lydia leapt into the water herself, diving into the same deep pool, and washed the day's soil from her skin with handfuls of fine, soft river silt. Tiny flecks of gold shimmered in the water as the current washed the sand from her, and she floated for a moment, enjoying the icy freshness of the mountain river on her bare skin before she waded back to shore and climbed into her Naran clothes.

The coming night promised to be cold and Lydia thought wistfully of a large fire by which she could lounge, laying back and watching the smoke vanish into the emerging stars. But to build a fire in this dangerous land would surely invite attention. Ignoring the growing chill Lydia found a fine-grained stone that fit nicely into her hand and sat on the water's edge, sharpening her sword meditatively. As she waited for night to fall, the euphoria of the day's victory faded and Lydia felt herself plunging into gloom. She could not fathom the cause for her lowness, but then unbidden, the fire-filled eyes of the innkeeper's daughter came back to Lydia, and she heard the question again, "Who are you?"

She had done her duty, magnificently at that, and had proven herself to her master. *Why should I care about the question of a half-witted innkeeper's daughter? Why do I feel so low, so unfulfilled? The conspirators are dead, Justice has prevailed. This is what I want.* The words, spoken silently to the murmuring river, provided no measure of comfort.

Not long after dusk there was a gust of wind as Lieutenant Masa and his wyvern appeared out of the night sky. Lydia rose from her reverie and wordlessly took the oilskin bundle that she had kept at her side and placed it in the winged beast's saddle bags. The wyvern snaked its head around and sniffed eagerly at the parcel; smelling blood, it eagerly licked its lips with a forked snake's tongue. Lydia scratched the wyvern's long jaw, saying quietly, "Not for you, dear." The intelligent beast snorted, allowed itself to be scratched for a moment longer and then hopped to the river's edge, where it peered into the dark water, hoping to catch a fish.

Lieutenant Masa must have noticed that Lydia was still damp, and seeing her shiver slightly he went to the twisted stand of pines and gathered fallen branches and needles, which he had soon built into a small but cheery fire. Lydia did not object. She knew that together, with his wyvern, they could defeat any mountain creature likely to be nearby. Squatting across the fire from Lydia and holding his palms out to the warmth, Lieutenant Masa spoke for the first time since his arrival.

"I am glad to see you well. Come, warm yourself by the fire." Lydia wordlessly joined him. "I see that there has been a fire in Stowe, and that the townsmen are searching for someone in the woods near the town." Lydia nodded silently. They both stared into the fire for a moment, hands and feet held to the warmth. She had nearly dried when there was a clatter and splash from further up the valley, the sound of a small rock fall rolling into the river.

She needed the warmth for the upcoming flight, but she had no desire to share of her adventures with the man. They no longer seemed like adventures to her. It was all more like slaughter.

Lydia rose from the fire and kicked the flaming embers into the river. "Come," she said, "Let's leave. I fear your fire may have brought us some company." The soldier called the wyvern, and after he quickly tightened the saddle straps they mounted and leapt from the high ledge, plunging into darkness until the wyvern spread her black wings and soared silently upwards into the night sky.

Perched in the top of a twisted pine alongside the river, the grey owl watched the pair vanish to the east with its yellow eyes, then took wing itself, flying silently to the south.

Three days later, the wyvern folded its wings and dropped onto a balcony, high above the central plaza of Marchit. For Lydia, it was the first time that she had entered that most sacred and forbidden place, the tower of the Emperor of Nara. She had requested that Masa provide her with a uniform and chest plate at the last barracks that they had stayed at, and she tied a black cloth across her face, so that to any who were watching she appeared as a tall, slender soldier with his face bound against dust.

She sprung from the back of the wyvern and retrieved the oil cloth bundle which was packed with salt to slow the decay of its grisly contents. She made a quick bow of salute to the earnest and helpful young soldier who had been her guide and companion during the last few days. With a return salute and a wave Lieutenant Masa guided his winged steed to the edge of the balcony and then they plunged into the air over the heads of the thousands of dignitaries and travellers gathered at the base of the tower, waiting for an audience with one of the lesser officials who held court from the lower levels.

A wide, tall archway led into the tower from the porch and on each side of the entry ten guards clad entirely in light but strong plate amour, wielding short halberds, stood rigidly. Lydia passed the erect soldiers and entered a large half-circle room edged with sweeping windows. The room itself was made of the same smooth, buttery yellow stone from which the Great School had been built, and in the centre was a table made of polished wood. The surface was inlaid with gold and gemstones in a fabulous pattern of swirls and eddies that vanished under great platters of food, succulent and exotic morsels from every corner of the empire, all prepared to perfection and presented with an artistic flair. Sitting at the head of the table upon a golden chair was Lord Zhe. He had just pulled the leg from a stuffed peacock and took a tentative bite of the rich meat as Lydia entered. She bowed in salute and then stood respectfully at the end of the table, awaiting her master's audience. In the dark corners of the room she saw the shadowy forms of men, guards, or perhaps advisors, watching her intently. She knew that an audience with her master would be formal and brief, for he could not be found to be involved with the tasks that she performed on his behalf, and that she would be watched closely for the entire time by the lord's bodyguards.

Finding the peacock flesh to his taste, Lord Zhe took another bite, and nodded towards the parcel that Lydia carried in her hand. "Come," he said around his mouthful of meat. "It is for me only to see. Bring it here and open it." Silently, Lydia bowed again and brought the oilskin parcel to him, loosened the string that held the bag and brushed the salt from the face of Cilliac. Lord Zhe gazed upon it for a moment, and then nodded. "Excellent. There is a small token of the Empire's gratitude for you on the table by the stairway. Your services will be required again." With a wave of the drumstick that he had been stripping Lord Zhe dismissed his assassin, directing her towards a stairwell partially hidden behind a silk tapestry. A black-robed figure stood by the opening with his hand resting upon a small, ornately carved table. As Lydia went to the stairwell, the man took a small box of plain black lacquered wood from the table and handed it to her.

After an eternity of spiralling downwards on the wide stairway that wound around the tower, frequently passing guards or rushing officials, and once a veiled figure who was carried up the stairs on an elegant sedan chair, Lydia emerged at the gates that led onto the plaza and found herself among a sea of people, both foreign and of Nara. After making her way through the throng Lydia walked swiftly down the tree-lined boulevard that led to the troll-manned gates and the little plaza over which her room looked. As she followed the boulevard out of the shadow of the tower a feeling of gloom weighed upon her, and she gained no pleasure from the warm breeze or the scent of the flowers in the trees overhead.

What did you expect from him? she asked herself. *You know that he cannot recognize you in public.* Still, Lord Zhe's dismissal seemed unnecessarily curt, and even a bit cruel.

Well before she reached her little plaza and high apartment, Lydia succumbed to hunger. She had not eaten since leaving the barracks that morning, when the sun was rising, and she felt a fierce gnawing in her belly. She found a small cafe in a shady nook, took a table at the base of a spreading linden tree, removing her katana from its and laying the weapon across the table. A serving maid appeared and placed a cup of cool ale before Lydia and after taking her order, vanished into the little cafe.

Even as she wrestled with doubts and questions she felt something warm and soft press against her leg. A cat had crept through the chairs and tables and was leaning against Lydia's boot, purring loudly. Lydia lifted the sleek grey body, slender and long but muscular, and gazed into its large yellow eyes. The cat met her gaze and purred more loudly. Lydia placed it upon her lap where it sat looking up at her, kneading gently.

The serving girl returned with a fresh mug of the thin ale and a bowl of rice and fried meat. She leaned over Lydia and tried to push the cat away, but Lydia held her arm. "No," she commanded, "it's good to have some company. Have you a bowl of water?" The girl wrinkled her nose at the indignity of serving an animal, but the veiled soldier with the blade and the sad eyes unsettled her, so she returned with a small cup of water. The cat leapt upon the table and greedily drank, it's long, slender grey tail waiving gently in appreciation. Finished, the cat licked its lips, washed its face and returned to Lydia's lap, intently gazing up at her with yellow eyes.

As the girl cleared the table and Lydia counted coins from her pouch for the meal, she asked the serving girl whom the cat belonged to. The girl replied that there were many living wild in the gutters and sewers of the area, and that they were diseased pests. "I will get rid of it for you, if you'll let me," she added.

Lydia rose from the table, and the cat, apparently sensing its peril, leapt to her shoulder, where it perched like a grey parrot, tail wrapped around her neck, glaring defiantly at the serving girl.

"No, I'll take care of him," Lydia replied. With the cat still perched on her shoulder Lydia left, and made her way along the crowded street to her home.

The apartment was as she had left it only a few days before, but the rooms seemed strange to Lydia, foreign. They had been her home for a year and she loved the view over the plaza, the warm summer breezes that wafted in from the balcony. She realised that she had not changed anything in the room since it had been given to her and that if her few belongings were to vanish no trace of her would be left in the place. The cat dropped to the floor and ran to the balcony where it peered through the stone columns of the balustrade, tail swishing as a flight of pigeons swept past.

Lydia summoned the servant boy from the ground floor and sent him with some copper coins to a fish monger who kept large carp alive in glass jars. "You can use a good feed," she told the cat, when the boy had gone. Then she took the black box from Lord Zhe, and sitting at the dressing table broke the wax seals and lifted the lid. Inside was a small sack of golden sovereigns, the richest coin of the realm, and a letter, also sealed with Lord Zhe's familiar blood-red wax.

To Lydia, Servant of Lord Zhe
From Lord Zhe, at his Most Glorious Imperial Majesty's
Palace, Marchit, the 12th day of the Month of The Pig,
Year 2139.

Lydia,

You have passed the final test, and are ready to take your place as my right hand, and the fist of Justice.

Rest until the week's end, then ride to the port of Wanddau, where the fast ship Gracious will take you to Rimbu. Bring me the head of the Lord of Rimbu.

Remember Lydia, he is not to be trusted. His tongue is silver, but his heart is rotted. Remember your father!

Lord Zhe

As before, the letter consumed itself in a flash when she had read it. Lydia collected the ashes and crumbled them into powder.

That is why he was so cold, she said to herself, thinking of Lord Zhe. *He distances himself so that I am free to strike at the source of rot without besmirching him.* With that thought, her heart grew lighter, and she found the cat on the porch, lifted him into her arms, and revelled in his rumbling purr.

There was a knock at the door and she opened it, taking a fillet of fresh carp wrapped in paper from the servant boy and giving him a copper coin. She turned to take the fish to the porch, where the slim grey cat had resumed basking in the sun, leisurely cleaning itself. Lydia dropped the fish in shock.

Where the cat had been moments before a giant python, as long as six men were tall and as thick as her torso, was slithering towards her, head raised high above the ground and gleaming yellow eyes locked upon hers. Lydia's sword was hanging from its hooks by the door, a few paces away. As she was about to lunge for it the snake struck, wrapping coil after heavy coil over her, pinning her arms to her sides. When the creature began to squeeze her, Lydia struggled for breath. It relaxed, slightly. When she exhaled the snake tightened its iron grip so that she could not inhale. The force of the snake was unlike anything she had ever encountered before. As it almost gently tightened itself about her she could feel the thing's muscles pulsing and caressing her through its cool skin. Red fog filled her vision before Lydia fell into blackness and knew no more.

TWENTY-FOUR

If anything, the Lord of Rimbu had grown fatter in the years since Lydia had last been in his presence. As she was carried into the room, unhooded for the first time in weeks, she twisted against soft but unbreakable silken bindings, desperate to free any part of her body that she could use to strike the hated man. But she had been bound fast while she was spirited away from Marchit in a shuttered carriage, to a small fishing hamlet on the southern coast of Nara. From there she was taken by a small, sleek cutter of Western design to the busy port of Rimbu, and since that time she had not been untied, even to attend to her toileting necessities. The indignity of it all added tremendously to the seething rage she felt for the fat man.

She had been treated decently, during her kidnapping, fed carefully by a detail of silent guards, allowed comfortable sleeping arrangements and given assistance by a lady-in-waiting when it was required, but she despite her constant vigilance, Lydia had not been able to escape. Apparently aware of the deadly skills of their charge, her guards took extraordinary precautions, knowing that not only would the young woman escape given the slightest opportunity, but that she would claim their lives as well. One of the men Lydia recognised. He had been at the assassin's school when she had first arrived and left shortly after, having completed his studies.

Regardless of the precautions of her captors, Lydia tested every binding and tried every trick she knew or could conceive of to escape, but with no success. And then she had been taken from the cutter, face covered with a hood and led like a dog to the presence of the bloated, corrupt, evil man that had caused the deaths of her father, Mrs Habden, and Moad, the stalwart friend and protector of her childhood. In blinding, all-consuming anger she redoubled in her efforts to escape as the fat man examined her in the stifling little cell she had been deposited in, but still she could not loosen her bindings.

There was another man in the poorly lit room, tall and given to lurking in the shadows, where he could not be seen. *I'll deal with you when I've bled the pig out,* she vowed to the concealed man.

Before the Lord of Rimbu was able to speak, Lydia choked out a vicious curse, and added, "I will kill you, you fat bastard, for what you did to my father. Nothing can stop me! I am going to tear your heart from your bloated chest . . . " Strong guards grabbed her shoulders from behind and pushed Lydia into a wooden chair across the table from the frowning Lord of Rimbu. They held her fast while she was bound to the seat with more silk rope. Still she struggled, and one of the guards had to place his boot upon the base of her seat to stop it from toppling. She had hoped to play her end of this meeting differently, to lull the man into a sense of complacency, but just seeing him drove her beyond control, and overwhelmed the restraint for which she had been so well trained.

"Lydia Estrella," began the Lord of Rimbu, "you are indeed your father's daughter. His heart would swell with pride to see your determination, but it would break in the next moment when he learned of your folly."

"I'll have your tongue before I take your heart, you bloated lizard," she spat. One of the guards held a gag out before her mouth, but the Lord of Rimbu waved the man away with a dismissive gesture.

"Lydia, did your father not tell you that we were old friends? Well, we were. Know that as a man, as an official of the Empire, I leave much to be desired, but in my friendship to your father I have never faltered." Her eyes burning with hatred, Lydia continued to struggle against her silken bindings, but remained silent. Lord Zhe had warned her of the dangerous silver tongue of the Lord of Rimbu. She tried to focus upon her rage and desperation on discovering a way to escape rather than on the lies of her most deadly enemy.

"I know that you blame me for the death my friend, your father, but it is not so."

"You lie, as you lied to him. You will pay, if not by my hand then by another's." Her voice was an animal's snarl, desperate and full of blind rage.

"Perhaps . . . " the man mused for a moment, "but then you will have your chance soon enough. But will you listen, consider, and then make a decision, Lydia?"

"What could you tell me that would convince me that you deserve to live?"

The man smiled sadly. "I can tell you that your father was killed by men hired at a distance by Lord Zhe, who had you taken from your life and brought to his school, where he could pervert your natural powers and bend you to his will. He who would pretend to be your father is the same man who destroyed Markus Estrella."

Spittle flying from her lips, Lydia flung herself forward in the chair, which toppled. Her face scraped along the baked clay floor of the room as she struggled in a frantic attempt at freedom. Unable to break the chair or loosen her bonds, she screamed "Liar!" in a blood-curdling shriek. As hot tears of frustration welled out of her eyes she saw the large man in the shadows come forward, and though she could not see the man's face his large black hands reached down, took hold of the chair she was bound to and lifted her upright. Lydia was about to sink her teeth into his hand when she realised that she was looking into the face of Azursus, the wizard from Sudeth. He kneeled before her, eyes level to hers, and face full of sincerity.

"Lydia, I travelled far from my palace in Sudeth when I received word from the Lord of Rimbu that you had been found, living in Marchit. From those around you, I have learned something of your story, though I have had to stay far from the powerful eyes and mind of Lord Zhe. But I cannot ask you to believe us, Lydia, neither of us can. I can only ask you to believe your eyes." Lydia, overwhelmed at the presence of the man she had met so many years before, who had first revealed her special nature to her, sat still, in shock.

Azursus rose, and to the guards commanded, "Bring her." Both he and the Lord of Rimbu left the room, leading Lydia, who was lifted in her chair and carried after them. They took her to the roof of a high tower, and when they had reached the top, they ordered the guards to wait in the room below. With a small gesture from Azursus, Lydia felt her chair lifted as unseen magical hands held her aloft. From the high tower the entire port of Rimbu stretched beneath her, a colourful patchwork of bamboo buildings and red, muddy pathways. A light breeze brought the scent of cinnamon wafting up from the docks.

"There, past the warehouses, in the harbour." Azursus held out his finger, pointing downwards at a large ship. The last time Lydia had seen that ship, archers in the rigging had sent a hail of arrows into her father's body. A warship, perhaps, or a pirate ship cunningly built to look like one. So cunningly built that it had fooled her father. It was Captain Dheree's vessel, or so like that craft as to be indistinguishable.

"It only proves that you are in league with them," spat Lydia, though her voice was less certain.

"Think, Lydia," responded Azursus sternly. "Did Lord Zhe tell you he had captured the pirate who ordered the deaths of those you love? Did he not tell you that they had been put to death, hung from the masts of their ship, which was burnt to the waterline, as is the custom in this land?"

Despite herself, she nodded.

"Then how is it that this ship is here?" Lydia stared silently at the hated ship, lost in a maelstrom of confusion, conflicting emotions and anger.

"Tell me, child," Azursus repeated, "how is it that the ship is here, in the port of Rimbu?"

A sudden understanding, like a sunbeam cutting through a thunderstorm, lodged in her head, driving away the clouds of confusion.

In a low but powerful voice, Lydia said, "Cut me free . . . "

The Lord of Rimbu, still wary, backed away, but Azursus lowered the chair, and drawing a short, curved knife reminiscence of the karinga from his belt quickly cut the ropes that held the assassin in check.

She rose from the chair and rubbed her wrists until the circulation returned to her hands. Azursus reached within his robe and brought out Lydia's katana, still naked, and handed the blade to her. "You'll need this . . . " he added simply.

The following morning between the dead of midnight and first light, at the time when men were in their deepest sleep and the night watch of an undisciplined ship had snuck away to the many dark and secret corners for an illicit snooze, a single figure slipped into the water alongside the Lord of Rimbu's warehouses and swam silently to one of the many large pirate vessels anchored in the harbour, a vessel that could easily pass for a frigate of the Naran Imperial Navy.

Lydia paused for a long moment, treading water just outside of the light cast upon the black water by three watch lanterns swinging lazily from the ship's rigging. A single man paced the deck, armed with a crossbow. She waited for the man to cross to the other side of the ship and then slipped underwater, holding her breath and swimming the rest of the way in the warm depths of the clear tropical water. When the ship loomed black above her head Lydia rose to the surface, startling a shark that was swimming slowly under the ship, sleeping even as it moved languidly. The large fish sped off as Lydia emerged from the shadow under the outwardly-jutting stern and silently swam for the netting hanging from the ship's side.

The watchman's head appeared again over the railing, but he did not see Lydia, for her face was black with a heavy, greasy paint. When he had moved along she quickly scaled the netting. Passing a porthole Lydia could hear the snoring of the crew within and was assaulted by the stench of dozens of unwashed bodies. Reaching the top of the netting Lydia hung off the side, drew her blade from the sling across her back and held the blade out behind her into the night, ready to strike when the watchman approached. She waited patiently for the man to appear, and when he was within reach her sword arced out, slashing him across the throat so that the pirate sunk to the deck, unable to call for help as he died. Lydia slipped onto the deck, bare feet making no sound as she crept around the dead man and gathered the night lanterns from their places in the rigging.

The ship was filthy, with piles of excrement in corners and streaks of filth down the sides. The weather-greyed and un-scrubbed main deck ran nearly the length of the ship, with only the great cabin at the rear rising up from the main deck and jutting over the water to the stern. As Lydia had swum across to the ship there had been no light in the stern gallery windows. Captain Dheree, if it was his ship and he was aboard, was asleep.

Three gaping hatches led to the lower decks of the ship. Lydia knew that the large hatch in the middle would lead into the ship's hold and the space beneath other two would be used as crew's quarters, the galley and store rooms. The main hatchway was closed under a heavy wooden cover lashed to the deck. The others were open. Lydia quickly checked that the other two hatch covers and lashings were nearby. She dropped a lantern into each of the openings, where they spilled their oil and immediately caught fire. Lydia quickly pulled the covers over and tied them shut, singeing her hands and forearms as spreading flames leapt from the lower decks. A great cacophony of shouts, screams and terrified wails erupted below as the spreading flames and billowing smoke found the crew. A thick black pall was pouring from the ship's seams and portholes as Lydia broke the last lantern against the door leading to the captain's quarters. When the door erupted into an impenetrable inferno, Lydia cut a short length of rope from the rigging and climbed the steep stair to the roof of the captain's cabin. Finding the aft rail sound, she quickly lashed the rope to the stout timber, took the other end of the rope in both hands and jumped out into the glowing night air. She reached the end of the rope and her body began to swing back towards the ship. Flying feet-first, Lydia burst through the centre window of the captain's cabin, landing on her feet and drawing her katana.

Dressed only in a shirt, Captain Dheree was standing before the flaming doorway, a heavy, double crossbow held in his hands and pointed at the centre of the inferno. Two women, both Rimbuan, faces heavily painted and otherwise unclad, clung to the man's legs, weeping in terror. He turned as the rear window exploded inwards and sent a bolt streaking into the night over Lydia's head, missing her as she crouched to the deck and took shelter behind the captain's chart table. He kicked at the women clutching his legs and waited for his assailant to emerge, crossbow ready.

Smoke was starting to thicken in the room and the heat grew. From below the deck came renewed screams as the crew discovered that their routes to escape had been sealed. The sound of a heavy axe striking wood could be heard, rhythmically thudding as the wielder tried to break through the ship's thick hull.

Lydia rolled from behind the desk and Captain Dheree, nearly blinded by smoke, fired his second bolt a moment too late. Nonetheless, the bolt buried itself deep in her thigh, striking bone. The assassin with the black face rose from the deck and took a step towards Captain Dheree, blood-stained blade held at the ready. The pirate threw the crossbow into her face and ran to where his cutlass was slung alongside his hammock.

The dockside harlots ran past Lydia and leaped from the shattered window, landing in the water below with a double splash. Lydia heard the screams of one of them. The shark from below the ship must have returned.

Lydia longed to toy with the captain, the man that had taken so much from her, but the room was engulfed in fire. Bright flame crawled under the door, up the walls, and flickered across the roof. She could feel her skin blistering, hair starting to singe. She also knew that the girl in the water below would have bled widely, and the scent of her life draining away would bring other sharks, eager to share in the feast. Lydia had to leave quickly.

The pirate threw the sheath of his cutlass aside and raced across the fiery wreck of his cabin, oily hair smoking, swinging his short, heavy sword with all of his strength. Lydia caught the blow with her own sword, but her wounded thigh gave way beneath her, and she fell to the deck, which burnt where her palm touched hot wood. The pirate, thinking that she had dropped her defence, swung his blade at her. Lydia raised her katana, deflecting the man's cutlass so that it passed harmlessly over her head. From her crouch, she reached out and grabbed the man's bare genitals and twisted them viciously. The man gasped and leaned forward in agony. Lydia, using his body as a support, pulled herself upwards and then when she was standing brought the hilt of her katana down on the back of his head and struck upwards with her uninjured knee at the same time, flattening his nose and breaking it in an explosion blood. He dropped his cutlass and clawed upwards for the girl's throat, eyes alight with berserk rage. He had just encircled her slender, muscular neck with his hands when her katana bit into his belly, driving through him and jutting out of his back. Still he grasped her throat, squeezing with all of his failing strength. Again the girl's sword punched into his body, this time angling up, under his ribs and finding his heart with its razor tip. Captain Dheree's lifeless hands dropped from Lydia's throat. She drove her blade into him another dozen times before her wet clothes began to smoulder.

With her own berserker strength, Lydia flung the man's body from the window. When it splashed into the black water an eruption of grey and silver fins greeted Captain Dheree, as the gathered sharks tore him into pieces. Lydia waited a moment and then dived as far away from the churning fish as she could, pushing off from the window sill. As soon as she plunged into the water she started swimming for shore, overwhelmed by fear of the circling terrors in the dark waters behind, even ignoring the searing agony of her wounded leg. As she reached the shallower water a great black shape rushed from the depths and rammed into her side, driving the breath from her chest. The shark circled, triangle fin impossibly tall as Lydia found her feet in the waist-deep water. She pulled the katana from her back while the huge grey fish passed, its eye rolling in blood lust while its vast maw sucked mouthfuls of Lydia's blood. With a heave it thrashed once and its great tail dug into the water, driving at Lydia with the force of a battering ram. She lowered her katana into the water, holding it before her with desperate determination. As the shark's maw opened and its rows of teeth jutted forward, ready to tear a chunk of flesh from Lydia's waist, the fish drove itself upon the blade, which sliced deeply into the shark's sensitive nose and ripped open one of its membrane-covered eyes. The shark heaved convulsively and then swam slowly away from Lydia, returning to the depths, where the blood seeping from the beast attracted its lesser brethren, who descended on the old patriarch, tearing him to pieces even as he struggled and gulped hungrily at the blood-rich water.

In the last stretch before she reached shore, Lydia's panic-stricken mind imagined that the great shark had returned for her and she leapt up the stairs that led up from the water, racing to get away from the blackness behind her. When she reached the top step Lydia sank to her knees, gasping for breath and fighting for consciousness even as the blood from the wound in her thigh ran down the stairs and into the dark ocean.

Behind her, the pirate ship was engulfed in flame. It would burn until midday, leaving only the timber below the waterline as a memorial. Captain Dheree, along with his pirates, was dead.

TWENTY-FIVE

When the barbed crossbow bolt had been removed and her wound treated by the Lord of Rimbu's personal healer, Lydia rested in an open, airy chamber within the bamboo palace. She spent the time between first light and the early evening passing in and out of feverish dreams, where she was haunted by the faces of those who had controlled her life, both living and dead. Then she would be floundering in the hot tropical water, the shark tearing her life from her body with horrible, gaping jaws, draped with ragged tatters of her own flesh. Just before she awoke Lydia was back in the village of Stowe with the innkeeper's daughter clinging to her arm, and trying to look into her soul with terrified eyes, the words "Who are you?" repeated on her lips, time and again.

When Lydia awoke she found Azursus sitting in a chair at her bedside, studying her face.

"You have grown beautiful, Lydia, like your mother." She said nothing, eyes fixed on the fading sky outside her chamber.

The man continued in his deep, dignified voice, "Did you see what you needed to see?"

The girl nodded, once.

"And you believe us?" Again she nodded.

"You may return with me, my child, to Sudeth. I must leave, as my royal duties have been too long neglected. From there you may regain your strength and then go northwards, to your home in Danith, where your aunt and uncle will surely welcome you into their home."

"No," responded Lydia quietly, "I am not going to run."

"I didn't think you would," replied Azursus, almost wistfully.

"I'm going to kill him."

"Yes, I thought as much. Well, you must rest now, and when you are recovered, these things can be discussed."

Over the next month Lydia was a constant source of worry for the Lord of Rimbu's healer. As soon as the wound in her thigh would start to improve Lydia would aggravate her injury by working too hard on the sparring ground, tearing the skin while locked in combat with the wrestling master of the Lord's guards, or pulling it open racing through the tropical rainforest bareback, firing practice arrows at elusive monkeys and birds while at full gallop. Though the angry purple bruise from the shark's impact faded, her thigh continued to hamper Lydia's progress.

In the end, the healer, nearly in tears, went to his master, and pleaded with the man to order the girl to rest. The lord had avoided Lydia, still remembering her lunging for him against her bonds like a rabid beast, spittle flying from her lips while she cried for his blood. In his youth, the Lord of Rimbu had been an adventurer of the world, fighting in many battles and matching wits with many foes, but he had never witnessed pure hatred of the strength that had burned in Lydia's large, dark eyes. And while he was convinced that Lydia had seen the truth of her father's death, a large part of him was still afraid of the girl, though she remained as a guest of his house. For the rest of his life he would always fear her.

The constant whining of the healer prevailed and one morning Lydia responded to a knock on her chamber door to find the large man standing in the doorway, without his usual entourage, looking somewhat nervous and embarrassed. She invited him in and he lowered his large body into the chair upon which Azursus had perched during her crisis, when she struggled for her life against Dheree's bolt. She sat upon her bed and faced the man that she had sworn to kill so many times.

"Lydia, I have come to speak to you. I feel that I must tell you now of the rest of the story of your father's death. I know that you spend day after day driving yourself, preparing for your assault on Lord Zhe, but I feel that to commit the act in righteousness, you must know the whole story."

The assassin nodded.

"As you know, your Father and I have been friends from the time that I was a lad. We served on the same trading fleets together, and as masters of our own craft we sailed frequently in each other's company, his ship and my ship alone across the oceans. I also knew your mother well, for she was always at his side, and many times I heard the story of how she had pulled him from the sea and saved him from certain death." He paused a moment, eyes seeing the distant past, the open waters and towering sails of his ship, his face once again bathed in salt spray. He cleared his throat, returning to the present, and continued.

"Yes, well, as time went by he followed his destiny and I followed mine, as we all must. His was to travel the seas, an honest trader and a loving father to you. And none have had a father with more love than you. My destiny was the way of the sword, adventure of the high seas, and it has led me to this throne, in this backwater of the Empire, where I rot amid my memories. But I wander off, like a silly old man."

"When news of your father's death arrived at Rimbu, some months after its occurrence, I was ravaged. I am no saint, but I have my principles and loyalty is one of them. Seeking revenge I placed a bounty on the head of the pirates who had taken your ship, but I was not to see that ship for many years to come. For you I had no hope, knowing that your father would not have let you fall into the hands of pirates." Lydia remembered the blow with which Moad had felled her. She wondered, *how close had I been to his knife on that day?*

"In hope of Justice, I doubled the reward, to a small king's ransom, and still nothing. So at last I lost hope, thinking that you had become one of so many casualties of the seas.

"But you will recall that when your father visited me upon his last voyage, I spoke to him of dangerous plots and unrest in the Empire. At the time I had only heard the rumours of these, tales of mysterious deaths, banishments and even assassinations. The Emperor has passed 150 this year, which is elderly even for a ruler, whom as you know live far longer than us mere mortals. So it is natural that there is unrest in those beneath the man; various nobles and officials trying to wrest power from their peers while the old man grows too weak to impose his order on his underlings. And always there is the question of who might replace the man, though Lord Zhe has always been the heir-apparent."

"Above all of this stood Lord Zhe. He was, and is, the hero of the Empire. The champion of so many wars, a valiant and fierce soldier, a persuasive and intelligent diplomat and a force for fairness and Justice in an Empire increasingly pulled down by corruption and lawlessness. Or so we all thought. As time went by, a pattern to the deaths and disappearances emerged, with those who opposed Lord

Zhe in even some small, insignificant way falling under the assassin's blade. While there is no proof against the man, the evidence against him is overwhelming. It is known that he is in control of the School of Assassins, and that he takes the finest into his service, using them to strike his opponents silently. Unable to oppose the heir to the throne publically, and terrified of his wraith should we move against him in secret, the lords of Nara have submitted to his rule, even before that of the Emperor himself."

"This brings us to you. Why would Lord Zhe, who commands an entire school of assassins, and thus has the choice of the most gifted in the land, go to such trouble to recruit and train you? As a foreigner, surely you must have realised that your effectiveness as an assassin was limited, at least in the land of Nara. After all, the assassin's greatest weapon is stealth, and it is difficult to be stealthy when you are so distinctive." Lydia, deep in thought, rose from the bed and walked stiffly to the window, her back to the Lord of Rimbu. He continued.

"When news of your disappearance reached Sudeth, Azursus mourned your passing as did I. He did not know of plans for you, though he feared them. He also sent out spies, hoping for news of your disappearance, but like me, he was unable to discover anything. It was if a mist dragon had taken you all and then vanished."

"But the Lord Zhe over-played his hand. Not a year ago, Lord Azursus' men captured an assassin, a man of Nara, who had been sent to slay the wizard. Some of what I have told you was discovered when he failed to ingest poison upon his capture and was left alive for the ministrations of Azursus' less gentle examiners. It is said that none may resist torture, if the torturer is clever enough to maintain life, and it must be true, for the man told of the plan to slay Lord Azursus. He had been sent from Nara, but did not know whom it was that he served, only that he had been sent. He did tell of a strange girl at Lord Zhe's school of assassins, a westerner. A girl of fierce passion and a master of the martial arts. The girl of whom he spoke was your age."

"But why did Lord Zhe move against Azursus?"

"We think that he must have worried that he might discover your identity as you began your work. Perhaps he is growing paranoid. But anyhow, Lord Azursus was quick to realise that there was a strong possibility that you had been taken, to be moulded into a pawn. He came to me upon the fastest ship at his disposal. I had known the man from my days as a seaman, but I was still amazed when the name Lord Azursus of Sudeth was called out at my gate."

"He then told me of your . . . gift. I knew that there was something special in you, something different to other mortals, but my powers are small, and unlike Lord Azursus I am no wizard, and cannot read the minds or hearts of others. Just as I suspected, he confirmed that there was a power in Lord Zhe and his kind that allowed him to seek out and destroy his enemies before they had even spoken of plans against them. He was of that special race which rules our world. Lord Azursus then explained your—gift to me, and I saw immediately what your value might be."

Lydia spoke without turning, her face clouded in concentration facing the rising sun. "What value is that? I am but an assassin."

"You, my dear, are no typical assassin. Of those, Lord Zhe has no need to search; he has a constant supply. You are, or could be, a most exceptional assassin."

"I know I am fast and determined, but I am not indestructible. Others may strike as effectively as I. What does Lord Zhe want with me?"

"Yes, true, there are many others, but while others may strike unseen at corrupt nobles, traitors or enemies of the most powerful, you can strike unseen at the powerful themselves, who can otherwise protect themselves with their inner sight. Others may be assassins, but you have been trained to be a killer of kings. And even emperors. You are a kingbreaker."

"But why would Lord Zhe wish to kill kings, or emperors? He will inherit the throne soon enough."

"Ambition has a way of overwhelming a man, my dear, and making him lose his sense of perspective. Those who live longest do so for a reason. Have you not heard that the First Lord of Talvon has lived for almost a thousand years?" When Lydia nodded, he continued. "Azursus tells me it is true, that there is a way that they may live that long. The spell of A Thousand Slaves for Eternity he calls it, but he will speak no more of it than that. Perhaps that is what Lord Zhe fears. That his father, a wizard of vast power, may cast this spell, and perpetuate his own life, making Lord Zhe wait for the throne, perhaps even longer than he might live."

Lydia, still facing the rising sun, shook her head. "No, it is not that. It is something bigger than a palace coup. Lord Zhe dreams of power beyond that which his father holds. He dreams of power over many realms. It is his insignia, pressed into the red wax of his letters. A talon holding the world in its grasp. He found me, raised me not only to kill his father, but to kill the rulers of the other lands. Movenda, Andaman, Sudeth, the Kingdoms of Sand, Gama, Danith, Morvia, even the dark lands in the southern seas that few have been to. Even Talvon. That was to be my service to him. I can see it now. Who could be better than one who had spent their entire life on the seas, travelling from one land to the next, at home where ever she wishes? Only one who could not be seen by those she would kill. It is me, in either case. The perfect assassin."

"Yes, Lydia, that is what we feared. As you can imagine, among the leaders of the world exist many alliances and enmities. One such friendship exists between the Kings of Sudeth and Movenda, some of the nearest and most tempting prizes among the many neighbours of Nara. We, Azursus and I, suspected that you had been taken to be used as a tool for total power by Lord Zhe. Lord Azursus sent to his master a message, telling him of our suspicions. The King of Sudeth then sent message to Movenda and a plan was created. Lord Azursus joined his mind to that of the Grand Vizier of Movenda, also a great sorcerer, and together they sent their spirits across the open seas until they found Captain Dheree, skulking not far from where you slew the troll. Upon his mind they cast a spell, making him yearn for the Port of Rimbu and also making him forget the bounty that I had placed upon him so long ago. When his stinking tub came into port, the first part of our plan had come together." The Lord of Rimbu paused for a moment and mopped his sweat-beaded brow with a handkerchief.

"For the rest of the plan we had to force Lord Zhe to reveal himself. We, meaning myself and the King of Movenda, would each send an emissary to a meeting with two discontent nobles from Nara, a meeting in which a plot against Lord Zhe was to be created, sponsored by the King of Movenda. It was felt that Lord Zhe, fearing the long sight of the King of Movenda and his Grand Vizier, would send his finest assassin to the meeting, and if that assassin was indeed you, we would know what happened to you on the seas between here and Jaru and by deduction, what you were to be used for. You, with your invisibility, would be the perfect choice for the job." At the mention of the meeting Lydia felt a deep knot forming in her stomach, and her hands grew claw-like on the balustrade.

More lives, this time innocent lives. These ones taken by her hand. That she had been in the service of Lord Zhe mattered little.

"So each of us sent a man to the meeting. I sent Cilliac, my advisor. A man I admit I disliked, but a valuable man that no one would suspect as being a sacrifice. He was to be the originator of the meeting, the leader of the coup."

"The meeting at Stowe . . . The Heavenly Cloud . . . "

"Yes. You were watched, by one with great powers, and our fears were confirmed. The deaths of our henchmen were warranted, for the knowledge of Lord Zhe's plans was worth more than a dozen advisors. Our spy received instructions before he left for the meeting: you were to be taken after you had met with Lord Zhe, or slain."

"A shape-shifter. You used a shape-shifter to follow me! The cat, the python . . . "

"Yes, and even before then, an owl, on top The Heavenly Cloud, watching also from the forest as you fled Stowe. He followed you to Marchit."

"But now Lord Zhe is aware of you, and he will have all of us slain."

"Yes, true. By now, he will know that you have failed, and he will have sent another in your place. The journey from Marchit to the coast by wyvern and then to here by fast boat would take a month at best, so we can expect a visit from Lord Zhe's servants at any time. Therefore, you will need for your leg to heal so that you may face the oncoming tide and hope to survive. You drive yourself, but you weaken yourself at the same time. In your heart you are ready to face your enemy, so rest, and wait. Let your body be ready as well, that you might be up to the task." Lydia nodded as she watched as a murder of crows flew past the window, calling to each other and warily studying the foreign woman with yellow eyes.

Several nights later, on the evening after Azursus' return to his duties in the Kingdom of Sudeth, a monsoonal storm hammered the bamboo palace and endless thunder shook the thick walls. In the streets and alleys of Rimbu small torrents turned blood red as the hard packed clay began to soften and then turned to fine sucking mud, only to be washed out to the sea in a great plume of silt.

Lydia lay eyes fixed on the ceiling, mind drifting away with the tattoo of the rain. At her side was her constant bed companion, the katana that had been given to her by the same man it would soon kill.

She had just slipped into a light unconsciousness, the assassin's version of sleep, when her eyes flashed open. Lydia was suddenly wide awake and alert, but for no reason that she could determine. Lydia had strung thin lines of woven spider's web across the floor, strong but invisible in the dark, and also across the balcony, so that anyone trying to enter would stumble and make a noise. She could be certain that no-one had entered the room, but still she was overcome with that strange prescience that she had developed in her time at the assassin's school. Something dangerous was near.

She took her katana in hand and was rising when she felt herself go numb. Lydia fell backwards onto the bed, eyes open and mind aware, but body held inert by some crushing force. From the darkness of the room a man emerged, entering the dim light coming from the open balcony as he pulled a black mask off his head. Master Nhil, the Emperor and Lord Zhe's chief assassin. Desperately Lydia tried to raise her hand, but she was completely paralysed. Only her eyes were free to follow the man as he pulled a table in front of her locked door and shut the screens across the arch that led to the balcony. He then sat on the foot of her bed, looking into her eyes with an unnatural calm.

"You may be the gifted student, Lydia, but I am the master. I have come for you. When you did not arrive at the port of Wanddau, the captain of *Gracious* sent word to Lord Zhe, and he sent me to enquire after you. And here I find you, at ease in the house of your master's enemy. How easily you fell, Lydia. You really are not as good as we thought you were."

A tropical spider, as wide as Lydia's hand and with a fleshy grey body, dropped from the ceiling on a single gossamer thread behind Nhil's head. Back legs pulled thread from bright red spinnerets while the front legs arched towards the Master's head, and dozens of bright yellow eyes glowed dully above large fangs that dripped poison.

Without turning, Master Nhil raised his arm and swung it behind him. As if by magic a short sword, no longer than his forearm, appeared in his hand and severed the thread from which the spider hung, dropping the heavy body to the floor. The man continued in his unperturbed voice, the blade disappearing into his sleeve again.

"I have come to take you back. His Lordship wishes a conference with you, and to see if you can be . . . retrained. We have sacrificed much, allowing foreign filth like yourself into our sacred school, and Lord Zhe feels that you should express your gratitude more fully." The master assassin rose from the bed and pulled a large pouch that was strapped to the small of his back around to his front, unlacing the bindings and taking several small lengths of rope and a gag out. He leaned across Lydia with the gag, for his spell of stillness would end soon and he could not risk her being overheard by the guards in the hallway. First he bound her wrists before her, then stuffed a wad of cloth into her mouth and bound it. For the instant that his eyes were focussed on the knot behind her head, a small grey furry arm shot out from under the bed and quick fingers untied the knot that bound Lydia's wrists. A small grey monkey raced across the room and climbed up the ornately carved screen that led to the balcony, chattering noisily when it had reached the top.

Master Nhil had not seen the monkey pull the thong from around Lydia's wrists, and he turned to look at the annoying creature for a moment, studying it with his distant, vacant gaze, before dismissing the creature as harmless and turning back to Lydia. As he returned his attention to her, she slashed at him with her sword, cutting into his arm as he fell back, puzzled. The distance she had between the katana and Nhil's arm was too small to build the force to strike mortally, but the razor-sharp blade bit deeply into the man's flesh.

Master Nhil reeled backwards, and then short swords appeared in both of his hands. Knowing that even though the spell was passing, she would still be too affected by the magic to successfully attack him again, Master Nhil confidently approached Lydia, blades rubbing against each other with a shrill noise. His eyes glowed with an evil light, the first emotion she had ever seen in the man. She raised her katana in defence, but found her arms weighted with lead, and the sword would not respond quickly enough. She braced herself for the bite of Nhil's blades.

He hissed as he raised his arms to strike, "Lord Zhe is your master, and you will go back to him, living or dead!"

With an explosion of orange, black and white, a tiger sprang upon the man, its body twice the assassin's size and each paw as wide as his face. The great cat flung itself upon the assassin, knocking him to the floor and standing upon his chest with its massive front paws. The master assassin struck out wildly with his short swords, slashing at the tiger's shoulders, but the big cat merely roared deafeningly, sunk its teeth into the man's flesh and tore Nhil's throat out with a single toss of its head.

The spell upon her broke with the death of the master assassin. Lydia scrambled as best she could to the head of her bed and away from the massive tiger, which now glared at her with glowing yellow eyes, and gave a short, coughing snarl. She lifted her katana in defence, but as she looked about her wildly for some way to escape the great cat's fur seemed to shrink into black skin, its face flattened and whiskers drew back into a face rapidly becoming human. Claws became fingernails and bent limbs straightened. Soon a man stood by the side of her bed, a tall, strongly built black man like those from the interior of Sudeth. A man strangely familiar to Lydia. He raised the back of one hand and licked it with his tongue, wiping it across his chin, smearing the blood of Master Nhil in a feline gesture as he introduced himself.

"Hello. I am Anthursus, son of Azursus. I have been sent to watch over you." The tall man sat upon the edge of Lydia's bed, watching her with his yellow eyes, and continuing to wash his chin with the back of his hand.

TWENTY-SIX

A month after the death of Master Nhil, Lydia slipped unseen from a nondescript trading dhow as it entered the crowded port of Jaru, swimming for shore in the darkness and making landfall on the Naran mainland unobserved. In the bustling port city she blended in with the throngs of foreign sailors, hearing Danithian voices for the first time in many years, as well as the tongues of a dozen different sea-faring lands. The sprawling stone city was a place one could easily vanish into, and the Danithian girl who had emerged from the ocean became a Naran boy. When he had gathered what he needed, the boy set off on the long walk towards the distant capital of Marchit. Three days out of the city, the boy became a tall, aristocratic woman who paid for a place on a fast carriage with gold sovereigns.

Two fortnights later the aristocratic woman stepped off the carriage at the last village before Marchit, thanked the coachmen, and took a room in a small inn. The puzzled innkeeper wondered what had gone wrong, for the tall woman vanished before dawn the following morning, leaving payment for the room on the pillow of her bed and departing even before the stable boy awoke.

No one paid any attention to the old woman who hobbled out of the same town that morning, on a slow journey to Marchit.

Autumn winds had turned the many trees that lined the great central boulevard of Marchit into masses of gold, yellow and red. Fallen leaves swirled around Lydia's feet as she shuffled towards the central plaza and Imperial Tower. She had carefully constructed the disguise she wore, that of an ancient woman, hands twisted and blotched, back stooped and moving with a dragging stride made possible only by a long staff, swathed in ribbons on which dozens of prayers had been written.

As when Lydia was a child, the Lord of Rimbu still delighted in the many small magics that a man otherwise not gifted in the dark arts could learn. Among these was a spell to make a person appear not as they are. The spell had come to the Lord of Rimbu from the Western Lands; it was embodied in a salve that was rubbed over the entire body. A jar of the salve would change a person's face, body, hands and even voice, but it was not without cost: when that person was transformed, their body would become that of the person they were aping. Thus, Lydia's shuffling walk and stoop were not mimicry; they were real.

As she crossed the plains in her slow, deliberate pace that morning Lydia found the city of Marchit transformed into a terrible mockery of itself. Once the festive and colourful capital of a prosperous Empire, rejoicing in the arts and music of its people, the city had become dour and bleak. War was looming on the horizon, a clash between Nara and the Kingdom of Movenda, a weaker nation, but nonetheless a formidable opponent. Everywhere along the road to the city banners in red shades were hung from pikes driven into the fertile plains, extolling the virtues of the Commander of the Imperial Armies, Lord Zhe, and his father, the Emperor. Besides the changing leaves, the red of the banners seemed to be the only colour in the once vibrant city.

Around the city was gathered a host, the collected armies of the five kingdoms that had been welded into one to form Nara. Their campfires stretched nearly to the horizon on the plains below the plateau of Marchit, making the city appear as if it were under siege. Even from outside the gates Lydia could see that the high tower where the Emperor perched over his lands was wreathed in a pall of wood and dung smoke from the fires. Adding to the feeling of oppression, the Imperial Guard had been ranging through the city, gathering young men and pressing them into the army, swelling their number for the oncoming fight, or into the Emperor's working gangs, who were swarming over the flat ground at the base of the ramp that led to the gates of Marchit, working on a vast project.

This was perhaps the biggest change of all: great cubes hewn of yellow stone were being quarried from a distant mine and brought to the ground before the city, where a massive monument was being raised. Already the first course of blocks had been laid upon the plains, a huge square with a hollow in the centre. The work was carried out by slaves, joined by those who were pressed into the Army but showed no promise with arms, peasants gathered from the corners of the Empire and a bewildering collection of draft animals ranging from asses and oxen to elephants and even a handful of the great, slow-moving *dradun*, crocodile-like lizards with long whip-tails, who stood as twice as tall as a man at their shoulder, and who could be tamed by the people of the Kingdom of Sands when newly hatched. Wyverns carrying knights of the empire and those who directed the project circled overhead, watching the long line of stone coming from the north, blocks fed day and night to the wooden hoists, rubble ramps and half-million hands who would place each carefully shaped yellow cube into place.

Despite the air of desolation and fear, the free citizens of Marchit were fierce patriots and on the day that Lydia crept into the capital, through the troll cages and past her old home, they were flocking to the central plaza, where it had been decreed that the Emperor would address the citizens of the city from his high balcony. Lydia hobbled along with the crowd, dismayed at the fatigue her supernaturally-aged body felt. Several times she had to sit and rest, struggling to regain her feet after each respite.

At the entrance to the great central plaza many legions of soldiers were standing in formation, surrounding the tower in a sea of black uniforms. They were the collected might of an Empire, summoned from their encampments upon the plains for a final address from the Emperor before their march to battle. Around the outside of the gathered army the citizens of Marchit and the surrounding plains pressed inwards, eager for a word of hope from their leader, for an explanation of the changes that had so suddenly robbed them of their happy lives, and their men-folk.

Lydia, crippled by her painful limbs and faltering strength, had nonetheless joined this throng; finding it impossible to approach the tower she stood with the citizens near the place where the tree-lined boulevard opened onto the plaza, leaning heavily on her staff. Her plan, devised alone for fear of discovery by Lord Zhe's ability to see into the minds of others, was to enter the city in her current guise, a person so decrepit as to be useless for the work on the plains, and therefore ignored by the Imperial Guard's press gangs. Once she was in the city she would take the jar of salve from her robes and anoint herself again with the magical cream, taking the face and body of a soldier of the Imperial Guard, a man she would find and study until she could guide the magic to create upon her body the perfect replica of the man, whom she would then dispose of, his body dropped into the sewers that ran beneath the city. Lydia knew that a general on the field, especially one as fanatically loved as Lord Zhe, must appear before his most loyal men, those of his personal guard, must keep them company on their journey to war and join them at their campfires at night. If he did not appear to be one of the soldiers they would grow to resent him during the long and difficult days ahead. On the road to battle, in her new guise, she would claim Lord Zhe's life with the katana hidden in her staff, wrapped with prayer clothes, a gift from the man himself.

It was a well-crafted plan. Many generals have fallen to the assassin's blade or poisoned draught upon the eve of battle, but as Lydia leaned heavily upon her staff, waiting for the Emperor she was idly thinking that she should have chosen a less worn body for her guise. She knew that Lord Zhe's men would be combing the city, looking for her, but still, she told herself, none would suspect an old woman, so near to the grave, as being an assassin of no more than twenty-one years.

Lydia's senses, dulled by age, failed to detect the men who gathered behind her and then started to work their way through the crowd, enclosing a net around her. A man dressed in black and with a shaven head bumped roughly into Lydia from behind, causing her to stumble to her knees and drop her staff. The man reached out and took Lydia gently by the arm, lifting her from the ground. He kneeled down for her staff, and when he straightened up Lydia found herself holding her withered hands out to Master Han, who smiled benevolently at Lydia.

"Now then, Mother, there is no need for a crutch. I have brought some of my young friends to help you to a more comfortable seat." Lydia struggled as she was seized, but her ancient body refused her the desperate strength she needed to escape. A man held each of her limbs while two more placed heavy iron shackles upon her hands and feet, and then joined these with a heavy chain. She was then lifted between two big men and dragged in the direction of the great tower, followed by Master Han, who carried her disguised sword. When the crowd around growled angrily as they watched an apparently harmless old woman being carried off, Master Han turned to them, and took an end of the painted ribbon wrapped around the staff in his hand, letting the staff drop so that the ribbon unfurled, revealing her katana bound between two sticks. He kicked the sticks away and took up the katana.

"Spies, spies everywhere. We must be vigilant, citizens!" He shook his head with mock shame and followed his men as they carried the feebly-struggling crone to her audience with those who awaited her in the Great Tower.

Lydia was taken through the waiting army and into the gates of the Emperor's citadel. Once through the high iron gates she was carried down a wide stair to a large cell, devoid of windows and having only one door, and then flung to the floor. The men who captured her stayed in the room, warily watching from a safe distance, waiting for the arrival of Master Han.

The cell was entirely of stone and reeked of blood, excrement and fear. Lydia's mind, so carefully trained against panic, ran through possible routes of escape, but as long as she was bound in the heavy iron chains and by the aged body she had assumed, she could find none. She therefore struggled to a seat, back against the wall, and waited for whatever her fate had in store.

Before long the iron door opened with a screech and Master Han entered, followed by an aged man dressed in a flowing robe of midnight blue and wearing a silver skull cap on his naked pate. The man stood over Lydia, and nodded in satisfaction. "It is as Lord Zhe predicted; she is disguised by the small magic of a dabbler. She's been trapped by her own foolish spell!" He cackled happily, sounding like an old hen.

Master Han joined the man, standing over Lydia and studying her with a scornful look. The man turned to Han. "What shall I do with her?"

"Lord Zhe wishes for her to be restored and brought before him."

"Very well, but she will regain her strength when the spell is broken."

"Yes. I do not think that Lord Zhe would have it any other way." Master Han turned, and ordered half of his guards to leave the room. They returned in a few moments, each carrying a crossbow for himself and one for a companion. Encircled by men pointing weapons at her chest, Lydia still struggled as Master Han and his companion tore her clothes from her, cutting them away from her shackles and leaving her withered body bare upon the cold stone. The man in the blue robe giggled, wrinkled his nose and said theatrically, "Disgusting," as he studied his subject.

He had a large black cauldron brought into the room, borne by two muscular slaves. The old man took a ladle from the cauldron and stirred the contents while muttering an incantation under his breath. When he dropped a pinch of spice mingled with the faeces of a sparrow into the water, it began to boil. Taking a ladleful of the steaming liquid, he poured it slowly over Lydia's bare stomach, where it caused her spotted and wrinkled flesh to bubble and blister, then wash away. The pain of her skin dissolving flooded Lydia's body and overwhelmed her mind. It was worse even than Han's mystic sword. Lydia flung herself away from the man, but she was pressed to the wall by the guards, and could not escape. He giggled again, and took another ladle of water and poured it over the first, washing more of the corroded skin away and revealing Lydia's actual flesh beneath. He took third ladle of the bubbling water and poured it over the aged skin next to the patch he had just cleared. Unable to stoically endure the pain, Lydia screamed. The men holding crossbows on her laughed, and the old wizard kept giggling. "Tsk tsk . . . little girls should not play with magic," he cooed.

The agony seemed to last for an eternity, and though Lydia was restored to her powerful, youthful body when it was ended, the pain of the cleansing left her weak and trembling, unable to resist when she was lifted and her shackles removed. She was then roughly dressed in a simple pair of black pants and the red shirt of a Naran woman, and the shackles were returned. As she was clothed, Master Han watched from across the room, saying only, "Master Zhe would not want to be insulted by your paleness. Yours is like the skin of maggots." The wizard who stood beside the master assassin chuckled and nodded his head.

When she was covered and her shackles replaced, Master Han squatted and took Lydia's face into his hands, forcing her to meet his eyes.

"You are the property of Lord Zhe, girl, and not free to wander where you chose. If you will not be a good cow, then you will be sacrificed. Soon, Lord Zhe will be telling his army that something terrible has occurred, that while his Father was preparing to address his beloved citizens an assassin struck him down, a woman sent from powers far away, hosted by traitors to the south and sponsored by the enemy of the Empire, the King of Movenda. Lord Zhe has found his father's ancient body pierced by the assassin's blade, and caught a foreigner trying to escape the tower. The assassin is to be punished by his own hand, her body to be flung from the high balcony and torn to pieces by the crowd. And the fools who view from afar, the kings of Movenda and Sudeth, will be none the wiser, for none of them can see that you are innocent. This is the price of invisibility, yes? So you see, my child, you will serve Lord Zhe, despite yourself." He rose from her side and beckoned to his guards. "Bring her. Two to carry her, two before and two after, with your weapons upon her. If you take your eyes off of her, I'll kill you myself before she has the chance."

Lydia was taken from the cell and carried up a spiralling stair to the chamber where she had met Lord Zhe after her mission to Stowe. The inlaid table was gone, leaving the room looking like a great, empty cavern. Lord Zhe was standing on the balcony, arms clasped behind him, gazing down over the massed army. He was dressed in the same black uniform as his men, with a metal chest piece and plates protecting his shoulders, thighs and calves. At his belt was the magic sword, with its steel pommel depicting an eagle's talon clasping the world, and leaning against the balustrade at his side was a thick, powerful war bow and a full quiver. He turned as they entered and summoned Master Han and Lydia to his side with a gesture. His gaze returned to the gathered army below. Master Han dismissed the other guards with a wave.

As they reached his side, Lord Zhe spoke. "It is beautiful, is it not? So much strength. So many lives. All mine to dispose of as I wish. They will follow me to avenge the death of the Emperor, and we will soon seize Movenda, taking what is mine by right of force. I will take from its people an army to conquer the world." He turned from the view of the thousands of soldiers amassed below, as if waking from a reverie, and with stunning force struck Lydia across the face with his fist.

"You are my *cattle* girl, no better than any of the rest of them." He waived a hand dismissively in the direction of his army. "You will do my bidding, alive or dead." He struck Lydia again with his fist. Her strength was beginning to return, so she spat in his face.

"No man owns me," she hissed in defiance.

Lord Zhe laughed delightedly and plunged his fist into her stomach. She doubled up, her breath forced from her body. Lord Zhe drove his knee under her chin, throwing her backwards across the floor. As Lydia slid across the polished stone she tasted her own blood. Lord Zhe turned to Master Han and took her katana from his hands, drawing the blade and studying the light that danced along the razor edge. He dropped the new lacquered wood scabbard the Lord of Rimbu had given her, engraved simply with the Naran symbol for "Justice" upon the ground, kicking it away. "Unlock her!" he commanded. For an instant, Han looked at his master in question, but he immediately remembered himself and took the keys from his pocket and released Lydia from her chains, then stepped away. She slowly rose to her feet, massaging her numb wrists. Master Han, aware of the girl's lightning speed, backed even further away, leaving her chains at her feet.

Lord Zhe disdainfully threw the sword to Lydia's feet and pointed at the door. "Master Han," he ordered, "wait outside." Han bowed and left the room, face blank.

Zhe watched him leave and then turned on Lydia. "I am the finest swordsman in the Empire, Lydia. This is the most powerful sword in the land. Do you really think you can defeat me?" He drew the katana he wore at his belt slowly, bathed in the glow of the green fire that danced upon its blade. Lydia knelt and took her own blade from the floor, keeping her eyes on Lord Zhe. Her head swam from the beating she had received, and her hands and legs prickled painfully as blood returned to them. But the cold steel of the hilt in her hand strengthened her resolve. As she rose Lydia grabbed the heavy chains and flung them at Zhe's head. With a stroke so fast as to be almost unseen, Lord Zhe slashed them from the air, his sword cutting effortlessly through the heavy iron links. They dropped to the floor at his feet. He raised his blade in preparation of her next assault, and smiled.

"Yes, that is it, Lydia, come and join your father. You know, I kept that woman, Habden, alive for years. She lived right here, in the city of Marchit, not more than a short walk from your school, a guest in my dungeon. I thought she might be useful to me. She only died this year. I had her strangled when you betrayed me. Her jailer tells me that her last words were of you."

Lydia, feeling herself slipping into uncontrollable rage, driven by the horror of Zhe's revelation, swept into the attack before the man could goad her into making a mistake. She slashed up from the floor, blade falling short into a feint, and ducked as his green katana swept over her head. She swept her leg out in an effort to kick the man's feet from under him, but he leapt easily above the attack, kicking her lightly under the chin while he was still in the air and sending her arcing backwards, sliding across the floor.

"You are a foolish girl to think you could defeat me in anything. Raise your sword to me, and I will cleave it through. Strike at me with foot or fist, and I will cut it off. I am immune to you, just like the rest of the petty fools." Lydia sprung to her feet and thrust in the fashion of a Danithian sparring blade. He easily stepped away from her attack, and caught her in the cheek with his fist, weighted with the hilt of his sword. Again Lydia fell backwards, this time her sword dropping from her hand and clattering across the floor.

"I would gladly spend all day teaching you humility with my fist, but you have one last duty to perform for me, and the crowds grow restive. Goodbye, Lydia!" He stood over the unarmed girl, raising his sword over his head, the green fire flooding the room and reflecting in his eyes. He paused for a moment, enjoying the look of hatred and frustration on his prey, and then swung downwards in a mighty blow aimed for the girl's head. She instinctively raised her hand in defence, face twisted in hatred and eyes glowing in the green light.

With no warning, the karinga appeared in her raised hand, and the once familiar surge of power and euphoric strength filled her, chasing the pain-spawned fog from her mind. Lydia caught Lord Zhe's weapon on the curved knife. The karinga sliced through Zhe's katana, severing the blade at the hilt. In an instant, the green light of the magic sword was extinguished, replaced with the angry red glow of the karinga. The broken blade dropped harmlessly across Lydia's chest, magical powers dispelled.

Lord Zhe backed away, staring dumbly at the hilt in his hands, eyes then darting to the glowing knife filling the room with its hungry red light. He reached behind his back and drew two long thin knives from hidden sheaths, and crouched to spring upon the girl again as she rose.

Lydia felt the power of the karinga flowing through her, like a drug, its heat running in her veins and filling her mind with cold determination. She rose to her feet, heart pounding triumphantly, thighs quivering with the pleasure of the blade's evil magic. Lord Zhe leapt, one knife slashing at her throat while his other blade plunged up to her gut. Lydia caught the wrist that held the higher blade with her open hand and twisted it downwards, while below the karinga caught the man's other knife upon it's curved back, driving it upwards towards Lord Zhe's own belt. For a moment they stood, entangled, staring into each other's eyes. Lord Zhe felt his muscles start to quiver as he tried to break the girl's grip on his wrist, but her strength was inhuman, and as he started to weaken the red flame of the karinga filled her eyes so that he was staring not into the large dark eyes of a girl, but two fiery pits. With a final effort, he tried to pull her feet from under her with his own foot, but she turned to the side, pivoting Zhe when he lifted his foot to strike and throwing him to the floor. Lord Zhe struck out from the floor with his knife, catching Lydia on the thigh, cutting deep but not enough to disable. She kicked him under the chin, a mockery of his punishment upon her, and when he fell backwards she leapt upon his chest, knees pinning his arms to the floor, the karinga, held in both hands, plunging into his chest, just above his right nipple, piercing his armour as if it were no more than foil.

It sucked at him, its red shine glowing hot, but Lydia drew the blade free. It came out with a wet noise, and spattered blood all over them both. She brought it down again, this time in the centre of his chest, and left it there, throbbing and glowing. She rolled off of the man, and sprang to her feet. Zhe clawed at the karinga, trying to pull it free, but when he grasped its hilt, his hand burst into flame, and he screeched.

Lydia watched as the karinga drew Zhe's life out. His rich skin went ashen, and his eyes grew wild. Somehow he managed to summon the strength to grip the karinga again. Both hands burst into fire this time, and the stench of scorched flesh filled the room.

Lydia kicked his hands away and drew the knife from Lord Zhe's chest. He looked up at her, eyes full of hate and mouth bubbling bright blood. She sank to her knees at his side, and began slicing into his neck, sawing with the glowing blade. Zhe kicked and clawed at her, flung himself like a speared fish and howled until his throat was slashed, but he could not stop Lydia's relentless cutting.

When Zhe's head came free from his neck, Lydia flung it aside, disdainfully. The grisly thing rolled to the balustrade, where Zhe's eyes turned back on his assassin, and saw, as their last living glimpse, the karinga turn into a puff of smoke in her hand, and vanish altogether.

Lydia ran to the balcony, recovered her katana, kicked the head of her former patron aside, and then took his bow and quiver. Without looking back, she crept stealthily to the chamber's door, where she knew that Master Han would be waiting. Lydia, still awash with the afterglow of the Karina's euphoria, slung the quiver over her shoulder and, having no belt or sash, stored her katana alongside the arrows, pulling one out and putting it to the bowstring when she was sure that the katana was secure. She then called out in a muffled voice that might have come from a wounded man, and stepped back. In an instant the door to the chamber burst open, and Master Han rushed through. Lydia's arrow sank deep into his throat. As he fell to the floor, Lydia's foot caught his temple, snapping his head about.

"You taught me more than swordplay, little man," she gloated, as he died at her feet.

The other guards saw their master fall and the headless, bloodless body of Lord Zhe beyond, and fled. Lydia ran out of the room and onto the stairway. She knew that to flee downwards would lead to certain death at the hands of the alerted guard, so she turned and sped upwards, putting a new arrow to her bowstring as she ran. Lord Zhe's chamber was more than three quarters to the flat top of the tower, but Lydia felt her leg, still recovering from the crossbow bolt fired by Captain Dheree and now newly injured by Lord Zhe, weaken under the punishing pace she kept. Below horns were blowing and the sound of men rushing up the curved stair echoed from the stone walls.

Lydia passed numerous doors as she ran, some bolted and others open. From one a crossbow bolt streaked, bouncing harmlessly from the wall after narrowly missing Lydia. She turned and fired an arrow into the face of the guard inside the room without slowing her pace.

At the top four of the elite Imperial Guard stood guard at the door to the Emperor's private chamber. As Lydia came around the last loop of the stair, her pursuers close behind, she dropped to her stomach on the stair. The men, alerted by the noise from below, fired their bolts at her. They passed harmlessly over her head. Dropping their crossbows, two drew swords and the others large, double-headed axes from their belts. Lydia slew two with arrows before she drew her katana from the quiver and dropped Lord Zhe's bow at her feet. A soldier with a katana ran down at the steps towards her; she easily ducked his slash, cutting his feet from under him and throwing his slumping body over her shoulder as he fell. The final man waited for her at the landing, axe gripped tightly in his hand. Lydia ducked a swinging blow as she left the stair, rolling under the blow and then striking out to the side with her katana, cutting the man across the back of his thighs, feeling her blade bite through his armour and flesh, coming to rest against bone. He collapsed and Lydia kicked his axe away from him. When he grabbed frantically at her feet she put the tip of her katana through his eye.

Lydia flung open the iron door to the Emperor's chamber and slammed it behind her. She drove home the heavy iron bolt just as a hail of arrows and bolts struck the door, fired from her pursuers on the stair. The room was large, a perfect circle, and lined with windows. Outside, the wyverns of the Imperial Guard circled, apparently unaware of the alarm below. In the room was a bed made of gold, hung with curtains embroidered with threads made of precious metals.

Beside the bed, spread across the floor, was an amazing model of the city and plateau of Marchit, and the plains around the capital. The re-creation depicted the town as it was, but at the foot of the plateau, where Lydia had seen the multitudes of slaves and beasts working that morning, a vast pyramid stood, reaching well above the top of the city's walls, over the tallest building within those walls, dwarfed only by the great tower that she stood atop. Surrounding the model was a bewildering series of runes in many different languages, all written in dried blood and encircling the miniature city.

Stretched across the city, arms outflung and one hand resting on the side of the great pyramid was the body of an ancient man, wizened and thin. A dagger protruded from his back, the pommel an ornate steel ball, etched with a likeness of the world, clasped in an eagle's talon. Lydia placed a hand upon his cheek. The Emperor was cold. Lord Zhe must have known she was coming for a long time before her arrival, for he had already struck his blow, and killed the father that had placed so much faith in him.

The centre of the room was a circular staircase made of jewel-encrusted gold, leading to the roof of the imperial tower. Lydia walked a circuit around the base of the stair, trying to see if anyone was awaiting her on the roof above. Behind her the iron door rang out with a crash; the guards were trying to break through.

Cautiously, Lydia climbed the stair. A distant storm was building over the plains, and thunder boomed in the distance. As Lydia's head rose above the staircase she ducked a sweeping blow from a sword.

She reached up, grabbing the man's wrist as it passed over her head, and pulled him down into the stair. His helmet fell and his bare head struck the metal of the staircase. She took the man's blade, and was going to run him through when she recognised the face of Lieutenant Masa. She threw his sword to the side and dragged his stunned body down the stairs to the miniature town, taking his hand in hers and placing it upon the cheek of the Emperor.

"See, he is cold. I have not done this." The man, clouded by the blow to his head and the sight of his dead Emperor, turned in a daze to Lydia, but she was already disappearing up the staircase to the roof.

Perched on the parapet, looking like a great crow, was Lieutenant Masa's wyvern. It had seen the attack, and had been waiting for Lydia. It snapped at her with its massive crocodile mouth, but stopped before springing onto the woman in brief confusion when she recognised Lydia's scent and the western girl's familiar face. From below, Lieutenant Masa called out "Marra, no!" and the wyvern hopped past the girl, snaking its long neck down the stairwell to see what had become of its master.

Wheeling overhead, a half-dozen other wyvern-mounted men saw Lydia emerge on the roof. As she slipped past the hunkered form of Lieutenant Masa's wyvern, she was struck a glancing blow across her back by the heavy bone club at the end of one of the swooping beasts' tail. Arrows clattered over the flat stone roof around her. She slashed at the tail of one of the creatures that narrowly missed her with its bony club as it swept past, causing the creature to roar in pain and circle away. The other five circled more warily. As she raised her sword in readiness a tail-club struck her from behind, crashing into her back and sending her sprawling. Determined to make a defiant last stand, Lydia rose, ran to where her weapon had fallen and lifted the sword once more.

I will not die a slave, she promised herself.

Behind her, Lieutenant Masa emerged from the stair unsteadily, his wyvern snaking her neck around him protectively, and eyeing Lydia with suspicion in its glowing red eyes. Masa's bare sword was in his hand. "Lydia, you must surrender," he yelled. "I will tell them that you did not kill the Emperor, but you must surrender!" She backed away from the man to the edge of the void that opened up behind her, holding her katana in one hand, and the black scabbard in the other.

"I'll be no man's dog, Masa, and I'll not be your slave either. Come and get me!"

"Surrender, and you will be treated justly," he replied, voice urgent.

Lydia raised her sword in defiance, just as the tail of one of the circling wyvern whipped out and swept her feet out from under her. Lydia fell into the void at her back, the top of the tower growing small as she plummeted. She could see Masa peer over the edge, watching her fall with despair on his face. She fell past Lord Zhe's balcony, passing the wide shelf with the grisly remains of her revenge in a flash that seemed to last an age. For an eternity she fell, looking backwards into the storm-darkened sky, afraid to turn and watch her fate rushing towards her.

From above the circling wyverns of the Imperial Guard a single shape appeared, dropping out of the storm clouds, streaking towards Lydia with the speed of an arrow. It was a falcon, wings tucked tightly against its body. The bird caught Lydia before she was midway down the tower. It grabbed her chest with its talons, looking intently into her face with bright yellow eyes. As she returned the bird's gaze it grew, brown feathers turning into black scales, and sharp hawk's face turning into the smiling reptilian head of a wyvern. Clasping Lydia in its talons, the wyvern spread black wings and soared just over the heads of the soldiers gathered at the base of the tower, who scattered in terror as the huge black shape swept down upon them. A few poorly-aimed arrows streaked by, but the beast and its passenger passed unscathed down the main boulevard and over the top of the great gates. In their cages the brutish trolls, sensing the excitement, roared and clashed fists against their chests.

The four remaining Imperial Guards circling the tower streaked after the fleeing pair, but they had been aloft since the morning meal and their steeds were growing tired. One turned back to their barracks to summon the rest of the riders before Lydia had passed over the city wall, but he found the building and the stables where the wyverns lived deserted. The mounted guard was a small, elite unit, and those who weren't guarding the Emperor were supervising the construction of the great pyramid.

The three remaining guards who pursued the fugitives lost sight of their quarry as the strange wyvern flew into the approaching thunderstorm, heading in the direction of the distant Archeret Mountains. The Imperial Guard's steeds, too fatigued to face the uncertain winds of a storm, refused to follow and circled at the edge of the storm, ignoring the shouts and spurs of their riders. Unable to force their mounts to enter the impenetrable darkness of the tempest, the riders returned to the city, where they gathered their fellows and streaked out across the land as soon as the tempest passed. Everywhere they searched, the riders spread word of the girl who had slain Lord Zhe, but they never caught her, or her mysterious steed.

As Lydia made her escape, Lord Azursus reclined on his balcony, ensconced in the treetops of his master's gardens. The dark shapes of apes moved about in the night-shrouded branches, and from time to time the wizard flung an apple to them, watching their antics with amusement as they fought over the prize.

At his side, upon a small round table, lay the karinga.

EPILOGUE

In the highest tower soaring over the city of Parnith, on the largest island of Talvon, there was a room with no windows and no doors, secured from the world by thick stone. The ghostly shapes of twenty-three men stood in a circle, facing each other over an open pit in the floor from which magical blue flames leapt. The men were of all ages, though most were ancient, older than humans could live, unaided by magic.

"She must die," said one spectre, dressed in the coat and flared trousers of Talvon, and more ancient than the rest.

"She has done nothing but defend herself," objected another, clad in the flowing robes of Sudeth. "My henchman knows her, has tested her as we all agreed, and has found that she is pure of heart."

"It does not matter," responded the first, "she must be killed. She may strike at us, where others cannot. She is too great a risk."

"If it were not for her, then we would be at war against that tyrant Zhe," responded the Sudethian.

"Yes, but now the Empire of Nara is split into five kingdoms again, each ruled by a mere mortal, without organisation, without proper rule. More and more lands fall in this way, while our numbers grow small. She stands against all that we have created in this world. She can strike at our very persons, hidden by our blindness, and that fool Zhe and his senile father allowed her to become a trained assassin, gave her the tools to complete her job. She must be killed!"

Around the room, twenty of the other rulers of the world, the most powerful of men, those gifted with the Sight, nodded their heads in agreement. Only two, the Kings of Sudeth and Movenda, kept still. Though they knew the decision of the council could bring even greater trouble than the civil war that threatened to tear Nara apart, they were bound by an ancient and sacred oath to obey the wishes of the council.

"Let it be done, then. She will die!" declared the First Lord of Talvon.

AVAILABLE FROM TICONDEROGA PUBLICATIONS

978-0-9586856-6-5   Troy BY Simon Brown
978-0-9586856-7-2   The Workers' Paradise EDS Farr & Evans
978-0-9586856-8-9   Fantastic Wonder Stories ED Russell B. Farr
978-0-9803531-0-5   Love in Vain BY Lewis Shiner
978-0-9803531-2-9   Belong ED Russell B. Farr
978-0-9803531-4-3   Ghost Seas BY Steven Utley
978-0-9803531-6-7   Magic Dirt: the best of Sean Williams
978-0-9803531-8-1   The Lady of Situations BY Stephen Dedman
978-0-9806288-2-1   Basic Black BY Terry Dowling
978-0-9806288-3-8   Make Believe BY Terry Dowling
978-0-9806288-4-5   Scary Kisses ED Liz Grzyb
978-0-9806288-6-9   Dead Sea Fruit BY Kaaron Warren
978-0-9806288-8-3   The Girl With No Hands BY Angela Slatter
978-0-9807813-1-1   Dead Red Heart ED Russell B. Farr
978-0-9807813-2-8   More Scary Kisses ED Liz Grzyb
978-0-9807813-4-2   Heliotrope BY Justina Robson
978-0-9807813-7-3   Matilda Told Such Dreadful Lies BY Lucy Sussex
978-1-921857-01-0   Bluegrass Symphony BY Lisa L. Hannett
978-1-921857-06-5   The Hall of Lost Footsteps BY Sara Douglass
978-1-921857-03-4   Damnation and Dames EDS Liz Grzyb & Amanda Pillar
978-1-921857-08-9   Bread and Circuses BY Felicity Dowker
978-1-921857-17-1   The 400-Million-Year Itch BY Steven Utley
978-1-921857-22-5   The Scarlet Rider BY Lucy Sussex
978-1-921857-24-9   Wild Chrome BY Greg Mellor
978-1-921857-27-0   Bloodstones ED Amanda Pillar
978-1-921857-30-0   Midnight and Moonshine BY Lisa L. Hannett & Angela Slatter
978-1-921857-65-2   Mage Heart BY Jane Routley
978-1-921857-66-9   Fire Angels BY Jane Routley
978-1-921857-67-6   Aramaya BY Jane Routley
978-1-921857-86-7   Magic Dirt: the best of Sean Williams (hc)
978-1-921857-35-5   Dreaming of Djinn ED Liz Grzyb
978-1-921857-38-6   Prickle Moon BY Juliet Marillier
978-1-921857-43-0   The Bride Price BY Cat Sparks
978-1-921857-46-1   The Year of Ancient Ghosts BY Kim Wilkins
978-1-921857-33-1   Invisible Kingdoms BY Steven Utley
978-1-921857-70-6   Havenstar BY Glenda Larke
978-1-921857-59-1   Everything is a Graveyard BY Jason Fischer
978-1-921857-63-8   The Assassin of Nara BY R.J. Ashby
978-1-921857-77-5   Death at the Blue Elephant BY Janeen Webb
978-1-921857-89-8   Kisses by Clockwork ED Liz Grzyb
978-1-925212-05-1   Angel Dust BY Ian McHugh

LIMITED HARDCOVER EDITIONS

978-0-9586856-9-6 Love in Vain BY Lewis Shiner
978-0-9803531-1-2 Belong ED Russell B. Farr
978-0-9803531-9-8 Basic Black BY Terry Dowling
978-0-9806288-0-7 Make Believe BY Terry Dowling
978-0-9806288-1-4 The Infernal BY Kim Wilkins
978-0-9806288-5-2 Dead Sea Fruit BY Kaaron Warren
978-0-9806288-7-6 The Girl With No Hands BY Angela Slatter
978-0-9807813-0-4 Dead Red Heart ED Russell B. Farr
978-0-9807813-3-5 Heliotrope BY Justina Robson
978-0-9807813-6-6 Matilda Told Such Dreadful Lies BY Lucy Sussex
978-1-921857-00-3 Bluegrass Symphony BY Lisa L. Hannett
978-1-921857-07-2 Bread and Circuses BY Felicity Dowker
978-1-921857-23-2 Wild Chrome BY Greg Mellor
978-1-921857-27-0 Midnight and Moonshine BY Lisa L. Hannett & Angela Slatter
978-1-921857-37-9 Prickle Moon BY Juliet Marillier
978-1-921857-41-6 The Bride Price BY Cat Sparks
978-1-921857-45-4 The Year of Ancient Ghosts BY Kim Wilkins
978-1-921857-58-4 Everything is a Graveyard BY Jason Fischer
978-1-921857-68-3 Havenstar BY Glenda Larke

EBOOKS

978-0-9803531-5-0 Ghost Seas BY Steven Utley
978-1-921857-93-5 The Girl With No Hands BY Angela Slatter
978-1-921857-99-7 Dead RED Heart ED Russell B. Farr
978-1-921857-94-2 More Scary Kisses ED Liz Grzyb
978-0-9807813-5-9 Heliotrope BY Justina Robson
978-1-921857-98-0 Year's Best Australian F&H EDS Grzyb & Helene
978-1-921857-36-2 Dreaming of Djinn ED Liz Grzyb
978-1-921857-40-9 Prickle Moon BY Juliet Marillier
978-1-921857-92-8 The Year of Ancient Ghosts BY Kim Wilkins
978-1-921857-28-7 Bloodstones ED Amanda Pillar

THE YEAR'S BEST AUSTRALIAN FANTASY & HORROR SERIES
EDITED BY LIZ GRZYB & TALIE HELENE

978-0-9807813-8-0 Year's Best Australian Fantasy & Horror 2010 (hc)
978-0-9807813-9-7 Year's Best Australian Fantasy & Horror 2010 (tpb)
978-0-921057-13-3 Year's Best Australian Fantasy & Horror 2011 (hc)
978-0-921057-14-0 Year's Best Australian Fantasy & Horror 2011 (tpb)
978-0-921057-48-5 Year's Best Australian Fantasy & Horror 2012 (hc)
978-0-921057-49-2 Year's Best Australian Fantasy & Horror 2012 (tpb)
978-0-921057-72-0 Year's Best Australian Fantasy & Horror 2012 (hc)
978-0-921057-73-7 Year's Best Australian Fantasy & Horror 2013 (tpb)

WWW.TICONDEROGAPUBLICATIONS.COM

THANK YOU

The publisher would sincerely like to thank:

Elizabeth Grzyb, Bob Ashby, Cat Sparks, Donna Maree Hanson,
Robert Hood, Pete Kempshall, Karen Brooks, Jeremy G. Byrne,
Kim Wilkins, Marianne de Pierres, Jonathan Strahan, Peter
McNamara, Ellen Datlow, Grant Stone, Sean Williams, Simon
Brown, Garth Nix, David Cake, Simon Oxwell, Grant Watson,
Sue Manning, Steven Utley, Lewis Shiner, Bill Congreve,
Janeen Webb, Jack Dann, Lucy Sussex, the Mt Lawley Mafia,
the Nedlands Yakuza, Shane Jiraiya Cummings, Angela Challis,
Kate Williams, Andrew Williams, Kathryn Linge, Al Chan, Alisa
and Tehani, Mel & Phil, Jennifer Sudbury, Paul Pryztula, Helen
Grzyb, Hayley Lane, Georgina Walpole, Rushelle Lister, Nerida
Fearnley-Gill, everyone we've missed . . .

. . . and you.

IN MEMORY OF
Eve Johnson (1945–2011)
Sara Douglass (1957–2011)
Steven Utley (1948–2013)

www.ingramcontent.com/pod-product-compliance
Lightning Source LLC
Chambersburg PA
CBHW020738250626
47155CB00003B/810